Christine Marion Fraser ... authors with world-wid ... many foreign languages ... she soon learned indep........ .... childhood years spent in the post-war Govan district of Glasgow. At the age of ten she contracted a rare illness which landed her in a wheelchair and virtually ended her formal education. From early years, Christine had been an avid storyteller, now she began a lone apprenticeship in writing, but it wasn't till 1978 that *Rhanna*, the first novel in the popular series, was published. She went on to write seven more volumes about island life and is also the author of the successful *King's* saga, the *Noble* books, three volumes of autobiography and three romantic novels.

Christine Marion Fraser lives with her husband in an old Scottish manse on the shores of the Kyles of Bute, Argyllshire.

Praise for Christine Marion Fraser

'Enchanting ... people so real and likeable that leaving them is a wrench at the end of the book. Begin reading Fraser now and you will wonder why you never did before' *Historical Novels Review*

'A charming tale from the best-selling Scottish author' *Newcastle Evening Chronicle*

'Warm and full of good humour ... The essence of village life is well-captured. The daily concerns of the women, in particular, are clearly evoked and with a great deal of fondness' *Metro*

'A lovely book and the author brings the people and the place of Kinvara alive' *Telegraph & Argus*

'A rollicking good read ... Fraser is Scottish publishing's best-kept secret' Jackie McGlone, *The Scotsman*

Also by Christine Marion Fraser

Fiction

Kinvara
Kinvara Wives
Kinvara Summer
Rhanna
Rhanna at War
Children of Rhanna
Return to Rhanna
Song of Rhanna
Storm Over Rhanna
Stranger on Rhanna
A Rhanna Mystery

King's Croft
King's Acre
King's Exile
King's Close
King's Farewell

Noble Beginnings
Noble Deeds
Noble Seed

Non-fiction

Blue Above the Chimneys
Roses Round the Door
Green Are My Mountains

KINVARA
AFFAIRS

Christine Marion Fraser

CORONET BOOKS
Hodder & Stoughton

copyright © 2001 by Christine Marion Fraser

First published in Great Britain in 2001 by Hodder & Stoughton
First published in paperback in 2002 by Hodder & Stoughton
A division of Hodder Headline

A Coronet Paperback

The right of Christine Marion Fraser to be identified as the
Author of the Work has been asserted by her in accordance with
the Copyright, Designs and Patents Act 1988.

2 4 6 8 10 9 7 5 3 1

A CIP catalogue record for this title is
available from the British Library

ISBN 0 340 76716 2

Typeset in Bembo by Palimpsest Book Production Limited,
Polmont, Stirlingshire
Printed and bound in Great Britain by
Mackays of Chatham plc, Chatham, Kent

Hodder & Stoughton
A division of Hodder Headline
338 Euston Road
London NW1 3BH

For Doreen and Ian,
with many thanks for all your
Highland hospitality

With thanks to Frank Gallagher (Big Fig), and Dougie Walker of Dunoon for helpful advice about the Territorial Army, also to Ken for his useful information regarding the Second World War.

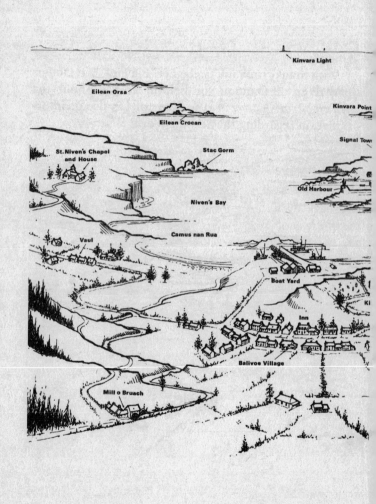

Kinvara Light

Eilean Orsa

Kinvara Point

Eilean Crocan

Signal Tower

Stac Gorm

St. Niven's Chapel
and House

Old Harbour

Niven's Bay

Camus nan Rua

Vaul

Boat Yard

Ki

Inn

Balivoe Village

Mill o Bruach

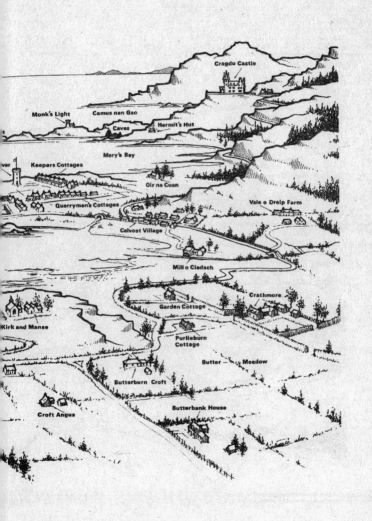

Cragdu Castle

Monk's Light   Camus nan Gao
                          Hermit's Hut
              Caves

Mary's Bay

Keepers Cottages

                    Oir na Cuan

        Quarrymen's Cottages   Vale o Dreip Farm

              Calvost Village

                    Mill o Cladach

                                   Crathmore

                    Garden Cottage

Kirk and Manse

                    Purlieburn
                    Cottage

                              Butter — Meadow

              Butterburn Croft

Croft Angus   Butterbank House

THE KINVARA PENINSULA

Spring 1936

Chapter One

The feeling of spring was in the air. Vaila could see signs of it all around her as she wandered through the woodlands of Crathmor House. The primroses were peeping shyly through the rich mossy earth; spears of wild hyacinths poked through coverings of last autumn's leaves; drifts of snowdrops stretched back as far as the eye could see; while the shiny dark green foliage of bluebells prodded boldly upwards, a promise of the longer days and warmer nights yet to come.

But none of that would be for a while yet. The mornings were still heavy with bitter frosts that turned everything white in the night, the hill peaks were sparkling against the blue of the sky, a recent fall of snow had buried some early lambs and the farmers had been kept busy digging them out and bringing them down to safer ground.

For two days the blizzard had raged, draping the fields and the hedgerows in great humping mounds of pearly white, blocking the roads in and out of Kinvara, snarling everything up, forcing Dougie the Post to sit in the Post Office and twiddle his thumbs, making Lizzie the Postmistress snap at him out of sheer frustration, causing everybody else to moan at one another because they couldn't lay their hands on newspapers of any kind and what else was there to do but retire to bed early and 'make bairns' if you were young and keen enough and didn't mind adding another to the family.

If you were past all that, or simply didn't fancy it, the only other choices were books for those who liked them, hobbies for those who had them, bed for those who had neither but who had to rise at dawn out of necessity or if they belongd to a breed conditioned to a lifetime of early habits.

The children of Kinvara had mixed feelings about their enforced absence from school. Many of them were the sons and daughters of crofters and farmers. It was their lot to rise from their beds at freezing first light to milk the cows, muck out the byres, groom and feed the horses. School or no, these tasks had to be carried out, but at least the hours spent in the classroom were a means of escape from enforced labour in the fields and all the discomforts that went with it.

A land covered in snow, however, meant a reprieve from the usual chores and for a precious few days the farm children were able to join in with the others as they whizzed down slopes on home-made sledges or simply played about in the dazzling white landscape.

But it didn't last, the salt-laden winds from the sea saw to that; the snow melted, the roads became passable again, Dougie the Post was able to resume his belated rounds, the school reopened, the bell tolled from the church tower, the feeling of being cut off from the outside world soon passed and life returned to normal.

The disappearance of the snow brought a renewed sense of freedom to everyone. Winter seemed to have shaken off its dark cloak at last; spring was in the air, the skies were opening up and expanding, each passing dawn brought fresh signs of life, new lambs were being born every day, and as Vaila made her way through the woods she experienced a great surging sense of euphoria.

She was fourteen now; her childhood lay behind her. In the last year she had blossomed from a shapeless girl into a young being with curves in all the right places. The bumps of puppy fat had smoothed out, her legs had grown longer, her waist more defined, the blemishes of adolescence were disappearing from her chin, her skin had grown smooth. Each day seemed to bring fresh changes to her appearance, subtle but there just the same, exciting her, making her feel more confident and sure of herself. Her stepmother, Hannah, told her she spent far too much time gazing at herself in the mirror but she simply couldn't help it. She found it fascinating to pose in front of the looking glass in the bedroom, to stare at herself from different angles, to arrange her hair in different ways and see how it affected the planes of her face.

Her nine-year-old half-sister, Essie, loved it when Vaila pranced around the bedroom, putting on airs and graces and pretending to be Lady MacKernon of Cragdu Castle. Essie would pose too, mincing around the room wrapped in her mother's best Sunday fur stole, her big blue eyes shining, her flaxen hair tumbling over her shoulders, laughter bubbling from her rosy lips when Hannah's step sounded on the stairs and she had to rush to her mother's room to put the stole back in the capacious naphthalene-scented bottom drawer of the dresser.

But Essie hadn't been there the day Vaila had viewed herself naked in the mirror, ridden with guilt as she did so, knowing how wrong it was to look at oneself like this, unclothed and unadorned, without vestments of any kind. Narcissism! She had heard Mrs Prudence Taylor-Young of Bougan Villa referring to the vain and preening young girls of Kinvara in such a fashion. But then, Mrs Taylor-Young with a hyphen was very old and must have forgotten what it was like to be young and growing up. She was also very upright and churchy and condemned anyone who dared to enter God's house with even a hint of rouge on their cheeks or a bosom too perky to be decent.

'Temptresses!' Prudence would snort. 'Ogling young men without a thought of the Lord on their minds, batting their eyes and using the church like a shop window for their displays of vanity.'

But Vaila soon forgot Prudence Taylor-Young in her fascination with the vision that presented itself to her in the mirror. Could this really be her? This tall, slender-limbed girl with breasts that had grown from little pimples into smooth rounded hills and a nipped-in waist that accentuated the curving contours of her hips.

Long legs, milky skin, a face that was flushed and disbelieving-looking as her eyes surveyed the final surprise. Hairs! Straggly bunches of them under her arms. More between her legs. Much more. Like a triangular piece of material cut from the black felt she had once used to make a witch's costume for Hallowe'en. No! Worse than that! More like a hunking great chunk of Dokie Joe's beard, yanked straight from his face and stuck onto the tender pale skin beneath her belly button.

Dokie Joe, who worked to Crathmor House, was very proud of his beard. It had taken him a good many months to grow it to the desired thickness and length. Now his wife, Mattie, complained of the time he spent in front of the looking glass, combing and trimming his 'great ugly mug' and telling her how lucky she was to have a man as handsome and desirable as he was.

Vaila had laughed along with everyone else at these exchanges between man and wife but she didn't laugh now at the idea of having a little beard of her own on such an incongruous part of her body. Was it there to keep bits of her insides warm, she wondered, and if so which bits and why appear now when those selfsame parts of her had been there all along with only the protection of her knickers to keep out the cold?

It surely couldn't be some form of decoration down there where no one could see it and no one would want to if they had any sense at all in their heads. It was all very mysterious and frustrating and the one time in her life she couldn't go to her father and ask for his advice.

She had known that 'something' was happening to her body, of course, especially the hairs, sprouting steadily away for the past year or so and giving her much food for thought. She had, however, refused to acknowledge their presence. At bedtime each night she undressed quickly and slithered hastily into her nightgown without baring any significant parts of her body to Essie's curious gaze. She no longer bathed

with her small sister in the big zinc tub in front of the
fire but did so alone and unobserved in the dimly lit
kitchen, covering herself briskly with soapsuds from
head to toe and getting the whole procedure over
with as quickly as possible while the rest of the
family occupied themselves in various other parts of
the house.

Essie had not taken kindly to the change in what
had once been a happy, carefree occasion, with sometimes even Breck, the family dog, getting into the tub
beside the sisters. The little girl had lamented long
and loudly over the passing of familiar rituals until
Hannah had taken her aside to explain that Vaila was
growing up and changing and needing more privacy
in her life.

Hannah however, had not explained to Vaila just
what changes she should expect and Vaila was left to
find them out for herself in the fullness of time. The
vision of herself naked in the mirror that memorable
day had brought many mixed emotions to bear on
her. Dismay and wonderment had set her stomach
churning. She had been sad yet happy at the same
time. Happy that her spots and her puppy fat were
fast disappearing, sad that the days of her childhood lay behind her. Although she had lost her own
mother while still an infant she had never felt deprived
because of it. Morna Jean Sommero would always live
on in her heart and hold some very special places in
her memory. Morna Jean and her father had known
a great love together and Vaila knew that she would
one day have a great love too, somewhere, sometime.
It was written for her, just as surely as it had been for
Robbie and Morna, in the stars, in the heavens, in the

universe. Even as a very young child she had known that and had been contented just to let the years carry her through to the destiny that one day awaited her.

Hannah, her stepmother, had been good to her. She had known happiness and love in No. 6 Keeper's Row. Hers had been a wonderful childhood. Free and unfettered she had roamed the hills and glens of Kinvara, learning about life and love and everlasting friendships.

Rebecca Bowman of the Mill O' Cladach was her greatest friend of all time, her earth sister, sharing all her trials and tribulations, her laughter and her tears. And it was to Rebecca she went after that day of seeing herself naked in the mirror, Rebecca she asked about the facts of life. At nearly sixteen Rebecca seemed to know it all and they had giggled together over hairy triangles, sprouting breasts, and all the other aspects of their changing bodies.

The adventure of growing up lay ahead for Vaila. As the days passed she became more sure of herself, less embarrassed about her blossoming figure, more conscious of the admiring glances thrown at her by the young and bold lads of Kinvara.

Life was good and sweet and exciting. She enjoyed her job at Crathmor House, she loved her employers, Captain Rory MacPherson and his good wife Emily, she adored their way of life and the many animals draped over the furniture in almost every room in the house, she got on well with the MacPherson children. None of them were affected or snobbish and they abhorred anyone who was.

Vaila was content with her life. It was rich and satisfying and wholesome. She was young and all the world was at her feet. The morning seemed made for her alone as she picked her way through the woodlands surrounding Crathmor House. The pink of the rising sun was touching the peaks of the hills; the waters of the Kinvara coastline were a shimmer of silver through the trees; frost-rimed leaves crackled under her feet; a red squirrel suddenly bounded out of the undergrowth in front of her to go scampering into the canopy of bare branches above, scolding her as it went, pausing to nibble at the nut it was holding in its tiny front paws.

She put her fingers to her lips and laughed. It was so good to be here in this early-morning hour that was all hers, feeling the frosty air stinging her cheeks, hearing the dry twigs snapping under her feet, glimpsing the beauty of the new day all around and above her.

She was alone for a few precious moments and she liked that. This was her time and no one else's. No need to talk, no reason to indulge in needless chatter, just herself and the woodland, alive with silent life and the promise of glories yet to be.

Chapter Two

Another movement caught Vaila's eye as she came into a clearing above Crathmor House. Down there on the bridle path near the river. Ponies. Two of them, weaving up through the silver birches as they entered the woods. Her heart gave a tiny jump. George Ian MacPherson, the eldest of the laird's sons, often came out riding at dawn. George was eighteen, impossibly handsome and charming, home on leave from military college, lighting up the old house with his laughter and fun.

But it wasn't George who came riding into the clearing in front of her. It was Mark Alexander Lockhart, a dark-haired boy of fifteen whose father was estate manager of Crathmor House. Sandy Lockhart had been with the MacPhersons for several years now and was an invaluable help to the laird in his management of not only the estate, but of the laird's pedigree breeds of Highland ponies and prize herds of Highland cattle.

Sandy's love of horses had passed on to his son who was now also employed by the laird as an all-rounder, helping with the general running of the place: the stalking, the cattle sales, the shoots, breaking in the ponies and much much more.

Mark's laughing brown eyes regarded Vaila with

some amusement as she stood there silently watching his approach. He was dressed in an old green jersey with holes in the elbows and corduroy breeches tucked into a pair of dung-spattered wellingtons. Vaila had never seen him attired in anything else but his working clothes, not even at village dances when all he did was exchange his wellingtons for a pair of battered-looking shoes and slick his unruly curls down with water.

He always smelled of hay and horses and never stood on ceremony with anyone, whether they be gentry or otherwise. 'If the king himself walked through the door Mark would just grin at him and go on supping his soup,' his mother would say despairingly whereupon he would lift her up in his strong young arms and not let her down again till she said she was glad to have a son like him who didn't put on airs and graces for anyone.

Everyone liked the young pony man the way he was, blithe of spirit, carefree and honest, always defying the rules and getting away with it, the envy of the more staid of his contemporaries who wished they could adopt his cavalier attitude to life and to hell with what anyone thought.

'I've brought you a pony,' he stated baldly as he came up to Vaila. 'I thought it was time I showed you how to handle one properly.'

'Oh, did you now,' she said with a lift of her head. 'Well, you can just think again, Mark Lockhart. I'm not dressed for riding anything, far less a pony. And I'd be late for work if I went with you. I simply don't have the time to go gadding about on horses at this time o' the morning.'

'Oh, yes, you do, you're early and you know it. I knew you'd be here gazing at the trees. You're always here in the woods when you leave the house for work. Come on, get up, you'll enjoy it once you get going.'

Her green eyes flashed. 'No, I won't. You'll only criticise everything I do. You think you're the only person in the world who knows anything about horses. I've only ever done it for fun and even then it wasn't so funny when I got off and could hardly walk for a week.'

Mark looked at her. Her tangle of black curls had escaped the little red beret that she wore and were ruffling merrily in the breeze, her nose was red, her skin whipped to roses in the bracing air of morning, her expression was one of defiance and determination, yet she couldn't keep down the corners of her mouth because of the way it was made, uptilted, generous, laughing.

He had loved this daughter of Rob Sutherland from the moment they had met. Four years ago now. He knew exactly when it was, where it was, how it was. They had been too young then to know anything about love, everyone had said that and had laughed when he once declared he wanted to marry her when he grew up. But he hadn't been too young, he felt exactly the same now as he had then. No, it wasn't the same; it had changed, he had changed, his feelings had grown stronger with the passing years, he was older, they were all growing up, even Vaila for all she sometimes spoke yearningly of her childhood days.

'I promise I won't criticise,' he said gruffly, 'don't be a spoilsport. It would only be for half an hour, it's all I can spare anyway, Dad doesn't know I'm here, I'm supposed to have started work by now.'

'Oh, all right then, anything to keep you happy.' Before he could make a move to help her she had mounted and was away before him, a wild little whoop escaping from her lips. 'Come on, pony man,' she threw over her shoulder. 'I thought you said you would show me how to do this.'

Laughing, he caught up with her and they rode together side by side through the woodland, the light of the sun gilding the trees as it climbed higher into the sky. When they reached open ground they urged their mounts into a trot then to a canter over the fields, faster and faster, Vaila's hair sculpting into black waves in the wind, her scarf streaming out behind her as she flew along.

'Hey!' Mark shouted. 'Don't go so fast! You'll fall off! Mind the ditch – and the fence.'

But his words were lost in the wind. She went racing on ahead of him and was back at the stables before him, dismounting, ready to face him with a triumphant shout when he finally came clattering over the cobbles towards her.

'Bugger you, Vaila Sutherland!' he cried as he jumped off his pony and stood looking down at her. 'That was a mad thing to do, scooting off like that! You made out a minute ago that you didn't like riding.'

His breath fanned her cheek, swift and cold, his brown eyes were alight in a mixture of anger and concern. She stared back at him, her face only inches from his, then she saw another expression creeping into his eyes and she stepped hastily back from him.

Two collie dogs came bounding into the yard to go straight to Mark and gaze adoringly up at him. Sandy Lockhart hove into view, George Ian MacPherson by his side, both men laughing and talking animatedly as they walked.

'Hey, Mark,' Sandy called as he espied his son. 'Where have you been? George here wanted his horse brought up to the house. I met him coming down to get it himself.'

'Sorry, Dad,' Mark imparted hastily. 'I was . . .'

For once he seemed lost for words but Vaila stepped into the breach. 'It was my fault, Sandy, I asked him if I could ride one of the ponies this morning and he thought it might be safer if he came along with me.'

'Ay, well, don't let it happen again.' Sandy glanced quizzically at his son's unusually red countenance. 'Not during working hours anyway.'

'It's all right,' George said as he shook his head, 'I needed the exercise anyway. I should have been up hours ago but decided to have a lie-in instead.'

George wasn't dressed for riding. He never was, preferring instead to wear an old jumper and jodphurs as opposed to more formal riding gear. Nevertheless, he looked extremely handsome with his ruffled fair hair shining in the sun and his blue eyes sparkling as they fell on Vaila.

'Glad to hear you're keeping your hand in, Vaila, we might do it again sometime, if you can spare me the time, that is.'

It was her turn to redden as he smiled disarmingly and took her hand to kiss it, a glint of mischief lighting his eyes.

'Come on, Mark,' Sandy's voice broke authoritatively into the proceedings. 'Take the ponies into their box and fetch George's horse. I hope you've got it ready for him.'

'Ay, Dad, just coming.'

The two men turned away but Mark hung back. 'Does he often do that?' he hissed at Vaila. 'Kiss you and slobber over you?'

'He wasn't slobbering. He's a gentleman, that's all, and he kissed my hand because I'm a lady.'

'Hmph, some lady, thundering over the fields like a heathen into hell. And what did he mean when he said he hoped you'd do it again sometime? Do what?'

'He took me out riding once or twice the last time he was home. He's a good teacher, attentive and patient. I learned a lot in just a short time.'

'Oh.' Mark's face grew dark. 'I didn't know about that. You didn't say anything.'

'Why should I? It was only for fun – and anyway, why should I have to tell you everything? You aren't my keeper.'

'I don't like you like this.' He sounded sullen.

'Like what?'

'All grown up and – and funny.'

She let out a shout of laughter. 'Funny! I'm speaking the way I always speak.'

'No you're not, you sound like a real little madam, and don't forget, you're only fourteen, you shouldn't really be mixing with a man double your age, even if he is gentry.'

'Double my age! George is only eighteen, and he isn't gentry, not the snobbish sort anyway. He's only a friend, I get on well with him, I get on well with all the MacPhersons. Besides all that, I'll be fifteen in June, soon I'll be able to do what I want and see who I want and there isn't a thing anybody can do about it.'

'Oh, we'll see about that,' he said tightly. 'The world is full o' charmers like George MacPherson ogling at girls like you who think the likes o' them are wonderful. You need looking after, Vaila Sutherland, and I'll always be around to see you don't get up to any mischief.'

He stood there in his old jersey and trousers, scowling fit to burst, and Vaila's heart softened. 'Don't change too much, Mark Lockhart. You're always so full of fun and laughter but now you're too serious and I feel I don't know you any more.'

Her words seemed to bring him to his senses. He straightened, his brow cleared, a smile flitted over his face. 'I'm sorry, Vaila, it's just, I was worried when you took off like that on your horse. It was all so good until then. I hope you enjoyed it and will maybe do it again some time.'

'Mark.' She put her head nearer his, their breaths mingled in the frosty air. 'Of course we'll do it again, I loved every minute, only things have changed now, haven't they? We're still just children to look at but inside we're different and nothing will ever be the same again.'

Her face was only inches from his. He glanced at her mouth, took a deep breath and stepped backwards. 'I know.' Sadness touched his eyes.

'Mark!' Sandy's voice rang impatiently across the yard. Mark turned and went quickly away, leaving

Vaila gazing after him with just a hint of tenderness and poignancy in her own eyes.

Then she too came to her senses and went rushing away to begin her day up at the big house.

Chapter Three

'Vaila! Just the young lady I wanted to see.' Captain Rory MacPherson, the laird of Crathmor, apprehended Vaila the minute she appeared in the back hallway of the house. 'I have a surprise for you.' He tapped the side of his nose with his finger and his eyes gleamed as he went on. 'Well, not exactly for you but for someone very near and dear to you. Young Andy has a birthday coming up tomorrow, I believe, and I think I have the very thing to make it a happy one for everybody.'

Vaila looked at the laird with real affection. Although he was gentry he had never put on airs and graces and was as much at home drinking tea in a humble crofthouse as he was dining with members of the upper crust, many of whom were lords and ladies and country gentlemen from near and far who came to shoot on the acres of grouse moor surrounding the Crathmor estate.

Captain Rory, as he was affectionately known, was, at fifty-four, a remarkably striking figure with his fresh complexion, well-groomed military moustache and little goatee beard. His abundance of silvery-blond hair was always swept dramatically to one side to hide the fact that he'd lost an ear in the war;

his bearing was upright and straight and totally commanding even if he erred a bit on the portly side.

People listened to Captain Rory whether they liked it or not. Some said he was an old rogue who gave out with one hand and took back with the other, but they didn't really mean it. He came among them as a friend who understood their day to day problems and helped out in any way he could – even if he sometimes went off the victor by a few pennies which he took by way of impressing the proper values upon his fellow men.

'Nothing good comes for nothing' was one of his own mottos and it didn't matter if beings like Shug Law of Balivoe called him a mean old sod behind his back and a hard taskmaster to boot. Captain Rory knew he was respected and liked and counted as a champion of the people and went boldly on his way, assured of his standing in the community.

Normally attired in clan kilt, lovat tweed jacket, and squashy tartan tammy, he had this morning forsaken all that in favour of a deerstalker hat, Inverness cape, checked knickerbockers, and riding boots, the reason being that he liked to go with Sandy and the other men to check his ponies on the hill and 'a kilt was a bit of an encumbrance on the broad back of a stallion'.

Despite the lack of his kilt he looked very grand indeed to Vaila's eyes and she smiled at him when he made his pronouncement regarding Andy's birthday surprise. He enjoyed a bit of drama, did Captain Rory, and it was a habit of his to keep the suspense going till the person to whom his words were directed just had to ask what it was he had in mind.

But Vaila was fly for his little games and she said not a word as he stood cocking an expectant eye at her while waiting for her to speak. When he saw that no questions were forthcoming his face fell slightly and with a giggle she unbent. 'All right, I give in. I'm dying to know what it is you have for Andy. I can't even make a guess because you sprung it on me so suddenly you haven't given me time to think properly.'

She was rewarded by a gleam of pure enjoyment in Captain Rory's eyes as he rubbed his hands together and grinned at her. 'Come round the front, Sandy should have brought her up by now, Sandy and Mark between them. Oh, wait till you see her, she looks good enough to eat, even though I do say so myself.'

Completely mystified by now, Vaila followed him out to the front hall. Before the door was reached, that of the sitting room opened and the laird's wife, Emily, came out, preceded by a dainty Siamese cat called Maggie who ran to the laird and proceeded to wind her purring body round his stout legs. Maggie had only been in the Crathmor household for six months, her arrival precipitated by the fact that the laird's old Siamese cat, Sheba, was now almost blind and infirm and unlikely to survive for very much longer.

The laird, heartbroken by this prospect, had bolstered himself up for the event by bringing Maggie into the fold, hoping that the younger cat's presence would keep Sheba ticking over for a while yet. Sheba had not, however, taken kindly to the new arrival and had shown just who was the boss by boxing the kitten's ears whenever she thought no one was looking and making her position of matriarch cat very clear indeed to the young upstart.

Because Sheba was by no means as helpless as she made out. She spent her pampered days lying on velvet cushions in the sitting room, howling her head off for attention and getting it too, for nothing was quite so startling as her ear-splitting yowls and her habit of displaying her yellowing fangs to any stranger who entered her abode. The Crathmor dogs, conditioned to years of Sheba's bullying, hardly gave her a second glance when she was in one of her moods but rather seemed to take great pleasure in her reduced state of mobility by teasing her and getting their own back in a variety of different ways.

For most of her adult life Sheba had gone everywhere with Captain Rory, terrorising the canine population of Kinvara as she went, her pussy face showing her scorn for anything that ran on four legs and smelled of dog. Whenever her lithe body hove into view the hounds scuttled for cover and this put Maggie at a great disadvantage when she began taking over as chief companion to the laird on his wanders.

The laird had taken a departure from the more exotic-sounding feline titles when he had bestowed on his new pet the homespun name of Maggie. And somehow it had suited her. She had soon proved to be the complete opposite of Sheba, both in nature and temperament. For one thing she adored dogs; she loved the Crathmor spaniels and wouldn't eat unless her dish was placed next to theirs. She fed with them, slept with them, played with them and walked with them. She was truly terribly upset when, on one of her early sojourns to the village, the first dog that she encountered ran trembling from her sight, memories of Sheba's sharp claws buried deep in its mind and scars of those encounters still showing on its rump.

Crestfallen and sad, Maggie was gradually realising that life for a Siamese cat was not going to be as easy as she had first expected. But she was learning not to rush things and was beginning to make some gratifying progress where other four-legged creatures were concerned. Meanwhile, the two-legged sort seemed always pleased to see her and when she had finished her rapturous greeting of her lord and master she turned her attentions on Vaila who duly fondled and petted her.

For once the laird was in no mood to spend time with his cats. He looked ready to burst with impatience as he stood there by the door. But before he could make a move of any sort there came a stampede on the stairs and his nine-year-old son, Ross Wallace, came bounding down, closely followed by his governess, Miss Dorothy Hosie, who was short and stout and sported a pince-nez perched on the end of her rather sharp nose.

Miss Hosie always wore a look of sufferance on her face. She had been with the MacPherson family for several years now and had 'somehow managed to knock some learning' into the heads of the three elder MacPherson children before the wider world had swallowed them up. Now only Ross Wallace remained under her wing and in her honest opinion he was the most unruly of all, as lively as a ferret, as wily as a weasel, clever and quick but 'quite unable to take anything of value into his brain since it was so filled to the brim with mischief there was no room for anything else'.

Ross Wallace longed for the day when he would be sent off to school and away from her ruling. This he told her quite openly to her face and now she had reached a stage of near-martyrdom, counting the days to her retirement and her freedom when all she wanted was a garden full of flowers and a life void of children of any race or creed.

'I want to see it too, Father! I want to see it too!' the little boy was shouting as he took a flying leap down the last three stairs and landed in a heap at his mother's feet.

'Come back this minute, you naughty boy!' cried Miss Hosie, making a mighty effort to retain her dignity in the heat of the moment. But her flight downwards had gained momentum on the way and she simply couldn't stop herself from falling into Emily's surprised arms, nor could she suppress the wail of anguish that erupted from her throat when she realised that she had made a fool of herself in front of everybody.

'There, there.' It was all Emily could find to say in the circumstances as she awkwardly patted Miss Hosie's plump shoulders in an attempt to offer comfort.

'That boy,' the governess choked, 'he'll be the death of me, I swear I don't know how I'm going to manage him for another day, let alone suffer him for another year. We were just starting on Chaucer when he took off as if all the hounds of hell were at his heels.'

The laird yanked his young son to his feet and made him apologise to his overwrought teacher, all the while thinking he might have taken flight too if he'd had to start his day wading through Chaucer – though the *Canterbury Tales* had been good – what he remembered of them.

'Well, that's that, then.' Captain Rory looked as if he had already forgotten the incident. 'Do as Miss Hosie tells you, Ross, though I'm sure she wouldn't mind you having a peep outside for five minutes since it's such an exciting day for everybody.'

The governess glowered at him through her pince-nez, Emily hid a smile, Ross Wallace positively beamed at his father and let out a little whoop of triumph. Impatiently the laird hustled Vaila to the door and open it with a flourish. 'Come on, everybody,' he shouted as if he was leading the charge of the Light Brigade. 'Outside this minute, you too, Miss Hosie, you are part of the family after all and must join in with whatever is going.'

Somewhat mollified, the governess followed everyone else through the airy glass vestibule, down the front steps and out of the impressive pillared stone portico that enclosed the main entrance. The sun had risen higher till now it flooded the countryside with its golden spring light; crowds of snowdrops and battalions of early daffodils danced merrily in the arrangements of big circular flower beds over by the older part of the house; the lawns stretched down to the streams and the woodlands; Dokie Joe and two of his under-gardeners were standing by the borders, leaning on their spades as they watched the master and his satellites emerging from the house.

'Ay, something big is happening there today,' Dokie Joe observed as he took off his cap and scratched his head. 'Though for the life o' me I can't see what it is.'

'I can only see a wee horse,' one of the other men commented drily. 'Surely nothing to get het up about in a place crawling wi' the beasts.'

But it wasn't a 'wee horse'. It was a dainty little brown and white Shetland pony complete with cart, splendid altogether in her red leather harness hung round with tiny jingle bells. Mark and his father stood one on either side of her as she waited patiently in her shafts blowing gently down her nose.

George was there too, grinning over at Vaila as he watched with everyone else to see her reaction. But she was too overwhelmed to say anything about the pony. All she could do was gaze at George and stutter, 'I thought you were going out riding, I thought you were all going about your business when I saw you down there at the stables.'

'I am,' George returned with a laugh, 'going riding that is, but first I had to come along with Sandy and Mark to be in on the fun. What do you think?' He ran his fingers through the pony's mane and looked at Vaila expectantly.

'She's for Andy, for his birthday.' The laird couldn't contain himself any longer. 'I know Breck is still sound of wind and limb but he's getting a mite long in the tooth to be pulling the boy around in that little cart of his. We've been keeping the pony under wraps so to speak, ready for the big day. I talked it over with Emily some time back and she agreed that it was a good idea. We'll be down at Keeper's Row first thing in the morning, complete with the Sheltie, ready to give Andy the surprise of his life.

We thought it best to let you know first, make sure you're there when we come along instead of making your way here as usual.'

Emily, who was fourteen years younger than her husband, was pink in the face with the pleasure of the moment. She was Captain Rory's 'bonny English rose', his pride and his joy and his prop through life, perfectly suited in her role as lady of the manor, fresh and unaffected and 'strong as a horse' in spite of her rather waif-like appearance. She had already borne four of his children, now another was on the way, moving the good folk of Kinvara to comment that he was 'a dirty bodach, just, and it was high time at his age to keep his tackle in his pocket out of harm's way'.

Emily, however, was not dismayed at the idea of having another child at forty. She liked having youngsters around; her older children were grown up and making their own way in life, Ross Wallace would soon be going off to school, so another baby would keep both her and the laird on their toes and help to keep them young.

At her husband's words, Emily looked at Vaila. 'I don't know what to say,' Vaila stuttered, 'except, thank you – Andy will love it, I'm sure of that.' She sounded dazed, aware of Mark's eyes on her, of George winking at her, of everybody else smiling and nodding and Ross Wallace dancing around, clamouring to get in the cart and go for a ride, of Miss Hosie fussing and telling him no, it was time for books and learning and hadn't enough time been wasted this morning as it was.

Vaila was glad when Maida Lockart, twin sister

of Mark, came running over the grass, long blonde hair flowing, cheeks pink from her exertions, eyes very blue as she came puffing up to smile at everyone in her disarming way. Maida was a girl with no particular interests, the complete opposite of her energetic brother who was always off on some quest or other. Maida just tagged along with anything that was going, helping her mother in the house after a fashion, playing with the horses, enjoying herself around the estate, agog to know what others were up to and asking endless questions in the process, wanting always to be somewhere with somebody without ever really being part of anything.

'What would you like to do with your life?' Vaila had asked once.

'Marry Joss Morgan when I'm older,' had come the instant reply.

'You'd better not let him see that,' Vaila had advised. 'Boys never like to be tied down.'

'Oh, I realise that, but I know I'm quite pretty and he's bound to notice me some day. Meanwhile I'll just wait for him and enjoy myself while I'm doing so. I don't want to work, not real work anyway. Mum says I don't have to because she likes my company in the house. Dad and Mark do enough for us all to be comfortable so it really has worked out quite well all round.'

This frivolous attitude of Maida's quite often irritated Vaila but somehow her friend's better points made up for everything. She was sunny and goodnatured; she loved children and they loved her; she adored animals and couldn't understand anybody who didn't. She could also be very funny when she liked. Along with her brother she was a perfect mimic and the pair of them could keep a company amused for hours with their nonsense.

This morning she was at her best sparkly self and Vaila was really quite glad of the diversion she created. She was dressed in a blue coat and a little matching tammy that brought out the colour of her eyes to perfection. Her blonde tresses had escaped their loosely tied bonds and were flowing round her shoulders in glistening cascades.

George eyed her with appreciation, Ross Wallace ran to her and clung to her hand, Miss Hosie tutted with annoyance and cast her eyes heavenwards, the pony nuzzled Maida's hand when it scented the tasty titbits she had brought along with her.

Vaila took the opportunity to make her way to Captain Rory's side. Standing on tiptoe she whispered into one hairy lug, 'I'll never know how to thank you for this. Andy's world will really open up now, he'll leave us all miles behind and won't call the king his cousin.'

So saying she grasped the laird's big hand in hers and pressed her lips against one warm hairy cheek. 'The pleasure is all mine, lass,' he beamed, gripping her hand till it hurt. 'And tomorrow it will be even more when Andy sees his new pony for the first time. I can't make up my mind whether I should tie a big ribbon on her head or hang happy birthday round her neck – or both – what do you think?'

They put their heads together and made their plans. The men led the pony back to her little box in the stableyard, Maida went also, Emily returned to the house, followed closely by Miss Hosie and her reluctant charge, Dokie Joe and the other gardeners resumed work on the flower beds, life at Crathmor went back to normal – but for the fact that Vaila hardly got any work done that day thinking about tomorrow and hoping that she wouldn't give anything of the big secret away when she at last went home to Keeper's Row that evening.

Chapter Four

Andy wakened early on his birthday morning. He lay for a minute, warm and comfortable in his bed, one lazy hand reaching out to touch Breck, the big speckled cross collie who had been his companion from infancy. Breck had come to him as a tiny pup many Christmases ago, thirteen in fact. They had both been babies then; now Breck was in his fourteenth year, still active and strong, but there was a whiteness in his muzzle, a dulling of his eyes, signs of deafness that couldn't be denied.

For most of his life he had pulled his young master along in the little cart Rob had made, loyally and obediently, opening up vistas for Andy that would otherwise have been lost to him. He had been born with cerebral palsy and had found mobility difficult in those early years. If it hadn't been for Breck he would have been confined to the house instead of becoming a well-kent sight in and around the local villages.

Now 'Breck and the boy' weren't such a regular part of the landscape as once they had been. Both the dog and his master had become older, and Andy had outgrown the cart. Nowadays he got around in a limited fashion on his own two feet with his dog at his side, a very different lad from what he had been, able to communicate as well as anybody, able to do many things that had once been denied to him because of his disability.

The old days were gone, never to return. They had been good years in spite of everything and Andy didn't regret them for one moment, but it was good, so good to be free of the fetters that had once bound him, thanks to his father's encouragement, his belief that one day his son would be as good, or better, than anybody else.

But as Andy lay there in his bed on his birthday morning his hold on Breck's ruff tightened and a tear gleamed in his eyes. He had just turned fourteen with all his life ahead of him, his dog was thirteen and was counted as old . . .

'It isn't fair, Breck,' he whispered. 'We came through it all together and should go through the rest o' it the same.'

The dog made a little noise deep in his throat. Andy bit his lip and rose abruptly from his bed to go to the window. It was barely six thirty. The world before him lay peaceful and still, bathed in that strange soft light that came before the sunrise, shadowed and secretive, the waters of Mary's Bay glossy and smooth, the sea beyond the breakwater rippling into darkness as it receded into the distance. And out there, the flashing of the Kinvara Light, that great octagon that spilled forth its comforting beams to the men who sailed the oceans of the world.

His father was head keeper of the light and had been for quite a few years now, leaving home for months at a time, living a strange near-solitary existence that would have driven other men crazy, having an affinity with the wind and the waves that some found hard to understand. Andy had been out there himself, going in the relief boat with his father and the other men, struck by an awe when first he had sighted the great stark tower and the bleak rocks it stood on.

He had spent three days and nights in that lonely place. It had been summer and the seas had been reasonably calm. He remembered the excitement in him as he trudged up the mural stairs to go in and out of the different levels, acquainting himself with the kitchen and living areas, the engine rooms and the lamp rooms where the timetables and logs were laid out.

And last but not least the great octagon itself, all of fifteen feet high, revolving slowly, its beams piercing the darkness, plundering the furthermost reaches of space and time and distance.

At least, that's how it seemed to him as he watched entranced, never wanting to take his eyes off it, mesmerised beyond measure by this close-up view of something he had hitherto only ever seen from a distance.

He had thought never to be able to sleep with all the excitement of such an adventure but he had, lulled by the waves frothing over the reefs, the muttering of the seabirds resting below. He would also never forget the savoury smells wafting up from the kitchen when he awoke, nor the feeling of camaraderie as he sat round the table with the men, delving into great piles of ham and eggs and drinking mugs of strong hot tea.

At low tide they had gone out to the rocks to fish. The sun had beat down, the gulls had screamed overhead, his father and Big Jock Morgan between them had shown him how to bait his line properly. At first he caught nothing, then the fish had started rising, one after the other, ensuring there was enough for tea that night with some left over for the next day. Afterwards he had sat with his father in the gloaming, smelling the scent of the thrift growing in the rock crevices, watching the sun dipping down into the sea, a great fiery ball that looked like a huge squashed orange the nearer it got to the edge of the ocean.

Then the afterglow, ethereal bands of light and colour that glistened and gleamed all around in echoes of brightness till the night fell in tones of velvety blue and green.

The silence of the dark spaces had enclosed Andy and his father as they sat there, not speaking, just looking and listening and enjoying.

'I understand now, Father,' Andy had said at last. 'Why you have to go away. Why you must have all this to yourself every now and then.'

'It isn't always like this, Andy,' Rob had said quietly.

'No, the bigness and the greatness must be even more. Wild and free and challenging. I'm glad I came. I used to look over here and wonder what it was like, now I can picture you going about, tending the lamps, looking from the windows to us over yonder – watching you.'

Andy laughed now over those early simplistic views of his. He had never witnessed the storms nor the thundering waves that could lift rocks weighing as much as fifteen tons from their foundations. He had seen it at its quietest and couldn't imagine it at its worst, especially during the equinoxes when the weather was at its most frightening.

Rob had experienced it all and had described to his son what it felt like to be surrounded by lashing seas and screaming winds: the sense of being cut off, the feelings of isolation, the comparative warmth and safety inside the lighthouse which had stood the test of time for nearly one hundred years. When he came home on leave Rob said it was like coming into another world and for a few days, until he settled, he was full of excitement and expectancy and went around visiting friends and family and reacquainting himself with all the old haunts he had known since his boyhood.

Andy was quietly pleased that his father was home this time for his birthday and the thought spurred him into action. Going over to the dresser he poured water from the pitcher into the basin and gave himself an extra good splashing. It was cold. Spluttering and gasping he dried himself briskly with a big rough towel till soon the blood was coursing through his veins and he was tingling all over. He gazed at himself in the mirror. The brown eyes that looked back at him were luminous and filled with life. He had always been thin but now he saw a change in himself. His arms, though still wiry, were becoming more muscular, his chest was growing deeper – and were those just a few hairs sprouting out from the smoothness of his skin? He grinned to himself in satisfaction and was so lost in his own personal assessment he jumped when a rap sounded on the door.

'Andy!' It was Vaila's voice. 'What are you doing in there? Hannah wants you down for breakfast.

Right now. This minute. Give Breck out to me and I'll smuggle him downstairs, you know you aren't supposed to have him in your room.'

'Coming, Vaila.' He opened the door a peep and ushered the dog into his sister's keeping, then he rushed into his clothes, glad that he no longer had to wear the callipers that had featured so much in his earlier life. His limbs obeyed the signals from his brain much quicker than of old; his legs, though still knobbly and thin, were much stronger than they had been and he could walk without his knees rubbing together. He was able to get to Calvost village without collapsing on the pavement as he had done when he had first attempted it. But it wasn't enough! He cursed the fact that he still had to rely on other people to get him further afield and longed to be able to visit Willie Whiskers, the blacksmith, under his own steam.

He finished tying his shoes and glanced at the window. It was going to be a lovely day. The sun's rays were pouring down from behind a puffball cloud, glinting on the water, shining on the slates of Quarrymen's Cottages. Sounds of activity reached him from below. Pots and pans rattling, cupboard doors banging, Rob's deep voice, his mother's light one, Essie's giggle, Vaila's laughter, Breck's bark, muffled to a suitable level because he knew better than to make too much noise in the morning.

He could also smell bacon sizzling. That meant a special breakfast – because it was his birthday. A surge of excitement went through him and opening the door he went quickly downstairs.

It *was* a special breakfast. Two double-yoked eggs, sunny side up, rashers of crisp bacon, sausages so fat their skins had burst, black pudding and tattie scones, layers of crumbly golden toast, straight from the fork that Vaila was holding to the fire while Essie stood by with the butter. Andy's mouth watered as the heaped plate was set before him and he got ready with his knife and fork.

In his corner Breck's mouth was watering also, but he knew he had to wait for the scraps. At least that was what he thought, until Hannah put him outside with a bowl containing fragments of black pudding and charred sausages that had stuck to the pan and though quite palatable were unfit to be served at table.

Breck didn't stop to wonder at this unexpected treat. He did not, however, forget his manners, pausing long enough to give Hannah a cursory wag of his tail in gratitude before burying his nose deep in his bowl. 'I can't stand the way he sits drooling in that corner watching every mouthful we eat,' Hannah said by way of explanation. 'Far better to get him out o' the way so that the rest o' us can enjoy our food in peace.'

Her voice was disapproving but it was only a cover-up. She had become soft where Breck was concerned; he had been part of life at No. 6 of the Row for a long time and while she still grumbled about the dirt he brought in on his paws and still referred to him as 'the brute' it was only out of sheer habit.

In the beginning she hadn't wanted him, now she didn't like to think of a house without him. He was a comfort to her in the long dark nights when Rob was away, his value as a guard dog was paramount, he was loyal and brave, intelligent and quickwitted. He also had a wonderful sense of humour and enjoyed the mock-seriousness of the games that she and he played, particularly when she chased him all round the house with her broom and he ended up peeping at her round the kitchen door to see if she had called truce or not.

Hannah had mellowed over the years. She no longer worried nearly so much about small domestic crises but was inclined to take life as it came. Her faith in her husband's feeling towards her had deepened. Once she had doubted if he had felt very much for her at all, knowing how dearly he had loved Vaila's mother, Morna Jean Sommero. But he seemed to have buried all that in the past and was much more relaxed in his attitude towards his wife. Theirs would never be a passionate relationship, but for Hannah it was good and satisfying and she hoped he felt the same. He seemed to have settled down and was no longer tormented by that first great love of his – except occasionally she had seen him gazing down towards Oir na Cuan, that little white house on the edge of the ocean where he had once known such profound love with Morna Jean.

Oir na Cuan was empty now, the Lockharts having vacated it some years ago for a bigger house on the laird's estate. The tiny cottage had since been let to holidaymakers and other casual tenants just passing through.

It had never really been a home since Morna Jean had lived in it and there were some who said it was haunted. Lights had been seen in the windows, noises heard in the rooms, Effie Maxwell, the district nurse, claimed to have sighted a shadowy figure flitting past an upstairs window but then she had always been full of imagination and silly fancies and no one believed any of her stories for a minute.

Life went on, nothing stayed the same. Hannah's days were full and busy and she had no time left to mope or speculate. The house, the children, the little baker's ship in Calvost village that she ran with the help of Janet Morgan, her next-door neighbour, all helped to keep her on her toes.

Her contentment and confidence showed in her appearance. She was rounder than she had been; gone were the lines of disenchantment from her face. It was sweeter, more attractive, her brown eyes held a sparkle in them, her mouth was inclined to smile more and she didn't take herself nearly as seriously as she had. Oh, it was true, there were times when her spirits plummeted, usually when Rob went back to lighthouse duty and she was left once more on her own. But she had learned to snap out of her moods. She had the children to turn to for company and comfort – especially Essie, the child of her heart, the beautiful little daughter she had dreaded bringing into the world after her disappointment over Andy.

But Andy was no longer a disappointment, he was the little man of the house when his father was away, the strength she needed when she was low, the learner, the writer, the philosopher, the boy whose poems and stories had already been published in journals and magazines and him just thirteen years old.

But he wasn't thirteen any more. He was fourteen. Time was flying by, her family were growing up. Vaila was almost a young lady and one day she would leave the nest. Andy would stay, though, Essie too – she couldn't bear to think of her life without Essie, she was only nine and she was a mother's girl, ay, Essie would definitely be around for a long long while yet . . .

The breakfast things were rattling, Vaila was clearing away. Hannah snapped out of her reverie – it was time for Andy to open his presents. Occasions of merit always called for the same proceedings in the Sutherland household, be it birthdays or Christmas. Breakfast had to be got over with first so that everyone could enjoy the ritual. Andy's face was glowing as he opened his parcels, small but appropriate things his family had bought or made, secretively and enjoyably when he wasn't around.

Rob gave him a carpentry set, knowing that his son's love of working with wood matched his own. 'You can help me out in the shed now, Andy,' Rob nodded. 'How about us both making a rocking horse for Emily MacPherson's new baby? It will be quite an undertaking but if we work hard enough we could have it ready for Christmas, even allowing for my times away. Emily's a good sort, she's always sending Vaila home with titbits for the table. It could be our way of repaying her for her kindnesses.'

Andy's heart quickened. He felt grown up suddenly. He would be a man out there in the shed with his father, a domain that Rob had cherished as his own – until now.

'Can I have a rocking horse too?' Essie gazed at her father with her big blue eyes, eyes that were languid and dreamy and utterly irresistible to all who looked into them. There was something not quite 'there' about Essie. She lived in the world yet was never wholly a part of it, preferring instead to inhabit her own small realm of fantasy and make-believe. She was always dressing up and pretending to be somebody else, she loved reading books of fairytales and for days afterwards would act like one of the characters. 'I'm Snow White today,' she would announce seriously to her mother. 'I want to wear my white frock so that I can look like her and later I'm going over to The Dunny to see Wee Fay because she's just like one of the dwarves in my book.'

'You'd better not tell her that,' Hannah would reply with an indulgent smile.

'Oh, no, I won't, I just want to look at her and Little John and imagine what they would look like marching along with shovels over their shoulders.'

'I hope you don't meet the wicked witch on your travels,' Hannah laughed as she played along.

'No,' Essie would declare solemnly. 'I'm changing the story to suit myself. The wicked witch won't get me because I'll get her first and then I'll meet my Prince Charming and be happy ever after.'

No wickedness or opposition existed in Essie's world. People were bowled over by her childish innocence and beauty and were always giving her things. At an earlier time in her life she had gone through a spell of rebellion and naughtiness in a bid to break away from her mother's apron strings and show her independence. All that was done with now she was older and had proved a point. She had reverted to her true self: she was sunny-natured and pliant, slow to rouse, quick to forgive, affectionate and utterly true to those she loved and who she knew loved her.

She was also very good at wheedling and it was no surprise to her when Rob smiled at her request and said, 'We'll see, first things first, who knows what Santa will bring when the time comes. But don't you go telling either the laird or Emily about the rocking horse for the baby, it's to be a surprise and the wicked witch *will* get you if you dare to breathe one word.'

'I won't, Daddy,' the little girl promised placidly and turned her attention once more to the scrutiny of her brother's birthday cards. Andy's long fingers were probing each parcel all over again, jotters, pens, books, a pair of handknitted socks from Kangaroo Kathy, whose habit of wearing her lapbag wherever she went had earned her the nickname.

Andy's brow furrowed. Something was missing. Aunt Mirren always sent him a parcel and a card on his birthday, making sure it was delivered well on time for 'opening day'. She was good at things like that, never forgetting any of them when a special occasion arose. This morning there was nothing and a sense of disappointment beset him. It wasn't the presents, it was the thought. He liked Aunt Mirren though she wasn't really his aunt. She had visited them at Keeper's Row several times in recent years and they had all become fond of her.

He glanced at the clock and wondered why Vaila hadn't left for work. She was usually out of the house by half past seven at the latest – and it was well past that now.

A movement outside the window caught his eye. Vaila looked up quickly, something in her face he couldn't quite define, an elation, an excitement. Essie had sensed it too. She stood up, her eyes went to

the window, she made to run forward but Vaila
restrained her and held out her hand to her brother.
'Come on, Andy,' she bade him through a bubble
of laughter. 'Now your birthday is really about to
begin. Close your eyes till I tell you to open them.
No questions, no cheating, no peeping. Just do as I
tell you and trust me.'

Utterly mystified, Andy screwed his eyes shut and
allowed his sister to lead him outside while Essie
giggled her way along at his back and his parents
wondered to each other what all the fuss was about.

Chapter Five

Word had got around. Dokie Joe's tongue had been busy. Curious as to the reasons for yesterday's little gathering in Crathmor's driveway he had wheedled the truth out of Shug Law who worked in the stables of that establishment.

Shug had hummed and hawed and said he had promised not to give the big secret away but a few swigs of the hard stuff from Dokie Joe's flask had soon eroded his loyalty. In no time at all he was pouring everything into his friend's willing ears and that gentleman had not been slow to spread the news.

It came about, therefore, that the laird met with quite a reception committee when he arrived at Keeper's Row the following morning, driving his big black Humber motor car, Emily and George occupying the passenger seats, Mark and Maida bringing up the rear with the pony while Ross Wallace sat triumphantly in the cart, holding on to the red leather reins and waving to all and sundry as if he were royalty.

'My, my, it certainly is quite an occasion,' observed Big Bette MacGill as she stood at her door watching the approach of the little procession, massive arms folded across her great dumpling of a belly, her double chins creasing into trebles as she lowered her head to peer over her specs.

'Ay, ay.' Bette's husband, Mungo, came to the door to add his piece, his large bald head shining as he stepped into full daylight. 'Captain Rory never did do things by halves, he aye liked an audience and no doubt word o' his good deeds will be all over Kinvara before this day is halfway through.'

'I wish I had a pony.' Babs MacGill, a hefty, if smoother, replica of her mother, elbowed her way through the small gap between the parent MacGills to make her presence immediately known. 'It would save you having to take me everywhere in the trap, Da, *and* I'd get to my work on time. Prudence Taylor-Young with a hyphen gets mad at me even if I'm a minute late and makes me do the brasses twice in one week for spite.'

'Ach, a pony would never hold you up.' This came from Tom who was forever pulling his sister's leg about her weight. 'It would collapse in the road from sheer exhaustion and might snuff it altogether like old Sorry did on the pier a few years back. Shug Law always did say it was the weight of Ma's new bed that killed his horse and you're a mite heavier than any bed could be.'

'I'll thank you, my lad, to leave my bed out o' it,' Bette hooted indignantly. 'Shug Law aye did speak a load o' nonsense and had to blame somebody for the state his poor old nag was in when she went and died on him.'

'And don't you dare make out I'm fat,' Babs cried hotly. 'I'm just pleasantly plump. Cousin Maudie

46

says it's the way I'm made and nothing will ever change me.'

'Bet something could.' Tom pursued the subject relentlessly. 'If you got a bike it might help to skinny you down a bit.'

'Ay, and you could catch the lads a bit easier on a bike.' Joe, the eldest of the MacGill boys, added fuel to the flames. 'They wouldn't be able to run away from you the same and maybe would like you better once you stopped squashing them up against walls the way you do now.'

'The lads *do* like me.' Babs, almost in tears, was getting ready to stamp her feet. 'They're all after me at the dances and the ceilidhs. The last time I was at one Carrots Law told me he hated thin girls and enjoyed dancing with me because he had something to hold on to.'

Babs halted at that juncture, remembering her rendezvous with Carrots in a shed after the dance, how he had told her he loved her mammoth breasts, her big bum and, later on, her 'squishy bits' which he had explored for several heart-stopping minutes before she had knocked the breath out of him by sitting on top of him and 'jiggering him like a sow in heat'.

She hadn't seen so much of Carrots after that and the truth of Joe's words hit home like a knife. But before any of them could say another word Mungo silenced them all with a few heavily sarcastic ones of his own.

'If that's the case, Babs, why aren't you married by now? Come to that, why aren't any o' you married – even Joe for all he's twenty-four? You'll have to let go of the apron strings some time, your mother and me aren't getting any younger and could be doing wi' some daughters-in-law to get you lot off our hands. Babs is nineteen and young yet but you two lads should be ashamed o' yourselves still being single at your age.'

Joe, who had never known any success with girls, wriggled and looked embarrassed, as did Tom who liked girls but was so afraid of them he didn't know how to go about winning any over for himself. The boys had moved and lived in the shadow of their monumental mother all their lives. She had always ruled the roost, first at No 1. Keeper's Row, now at nearby Gable Cottage. Her family were well and truly under her thumb and only felt safe when she was there to motivate their actions.

Tom was more of a rebel than his brother and vowed one day to leave home and make a life for himself. But that was for the future. At the moment it was easier for both boys to hide behind their mother's skirts and cover up their own inadequacies by tormenting their sister about her lack of conquests. Babs was strong, she could take it, nothing would ever really get old Babsy down as long as there was always enough food on the table and a place to lay down her head at night.

Tom spied Maida coming along with the pony. Now there was a girl who was worthy of some attention. Maida would never get fat or bossy, she was as pretty as a picture, nice-natured, a bit unsure of herself like him but that in itself was a good point because bold girls scared the *shat* out of him. Far better one who did as she was told. At fifteen Maida was too young to get serious over anybody but it would do no harm to ask her out some time – if he could pluck up the courage. Talk had it that she wore her heart on her sleeve for Joss Morgan but he had been seen with Rebecca Bowman of the Mill O' Cladach so Maida was wasting her time there. Tom gazed long and hard at the girl who had attracted his interest and decided it was now or never to give it a try . . .

The laird was thoroughly enjoying the attention he was getting as he drove past the row of houses. George smiled to himself as his father slowed the Humber to a crawl. The old rogue was certainly making the most of his moment of glory. He had a weakness for the centre stage, a love of the spotlight. This flamboyant nature of his found its echo in his eldest son. Being in the limelight was second nature to George, who adored being seen in a crowd. He was popular and sought after wherever he went and was used to getting his own way. Because they were two of kind, George and his father didn't always see eye to eye; they disagreed, they argued, they sulked, but they also laughed a lot together and their spells of harmony were more frequent now that George was away from home so often.

Emily was the staying force whose level-headedness kept them all together. She was fair, honest, kind, and she could have had anybody to be her husband but she had chosen Captain Rory MacPherson of Crathmor and had never rued the day.

'I'm glad you married the old goat,' MacPherson the Younger regularly told his mother.

'Oh, and why is that, George?' she never failed to parry.

'Because you wouldn't have had the honour of having me as your eldest son and think what a loss that would have been to everybody – including the old goat.'

George smiled at his mother in the seat beside him and put his hand over hers.

'Your father is enjoying himself this morning,' she whispered softly.

'He's gloating, Mother, simply gloating, there's no other word for it, you of all people should know that. I thought all this was supposed to be secret, now it looks as if half of Kinvara is out in force and the other half is bound to show up at any moment.'

'It *was* a secret, George,' she hissed back reprovingly. 'It's hardly your father's fault it somehow got out. People see things, they put two and two together, in a way we're under the microscope and it's no use trying to hide. *You* of all people should know that, having been brought up with it all your life.'

'You always stick up for him, don't you?' George said ruefully.

'Of course I do, he's my husband and I love him, it's as simple as that.'

'I hope I find a love like that some day.'

Gently she squeezed his fingers. 'I'm sure you will, George. You're handsome and charming and irresistible, but you're also very aware of your own importance and rather selfish to boot. Give and take is what it's all about and I hope you find that out before you're very much older.'

'Wise old thing.' He grinned, unperturbed by her words.

'Not so old.' She smoothed her skirts round her knees and patted her stomach. 'This didn't come from the fairies, you know, it takes youth and vigour to get pregnant at my age.'

'Wise young thing,' he laughed, 'and here was me thinking the old man was past it. It will seem strange, having a baby about the place again. I had thought Master Ross Wallace would be the last of the line and quite enough for anybody to bear.'

'Tell that to Miss Hosie, I'm sure she'll love you for it. Meanwhile let's just enjoy the moment and hope young Andy Sutherland will enjoy his too when he finally sees his very own pony for the first time.'

Andy did enjoy his moment, though at first he was far too astounded to take in very much of anything. When the laird drove up to the door of No 6. of the Row in his sleek black Humber motor car it was surprise enough for all of the Sutherlands. When he was followed by Mark and Maida leading the pony and a cheer went up from the onlookers no one quite knew what was going to happen next. Then the laird stepped out of the car and went straight up to Andy to shake his hand and wish him a happy birthday before indicating the Sheltie with a dramatic sweep of his hat. 'For you, lad, to get you around better. Breck isn't as able as he was so perhaps this will help to make up for it.'

Silence followed his statement. Everybody smiled, everybody nodded. Dolly and Shug Law, who had been down at the pier with their cart collecting coal from the puffers, arrived on the scene. 'Ach, my, would you look at that now,' Dolly said with tears in her eyes. 'Our dear good laird is at it again, making his people happy, giving to the sick and the poor. Always dreaming up ways to make our lives easier. God bless him, the dear darling man that he is.'

The laird had been Dolly's hero ever since he had presented her with a horse on the demise of her own broken-down mare known as Sorry. But there had been strings attached to the offering. Shug had been coerced into paying for the new horse by the sweat of his brow. For the first time in his life he had undertaken work on a regular basis and had been employed as a stableman at Crathmor ever since. Not that this in any way met with Shug's approval. Not a day went by but he grumbled about his bad back and the unfairness of life in general.

'A darling man!' he snorted at Dolly's rapturous musings. 'A mean old sod more like! It's all for show, mark my words, he'll soon have Rob's lad working his fingers to the bone to pay for that fancy wee pony, bad legs or no.'

'A patron of the people.' Dolly, purporting not to hear, took a drag at her clay pipe and gave a cackle, an action that exposed three broken brown teeth in an otherwise empty aperture.

'Hmph.' Shug was not impressed. 'If you go on like that you'll be having him the patron saint of Kinvara and nobody ever knowing the truth of the matter in generations to come.'

'Och, no.' Dolly's grimy fingers wormed their way into the battered brim of her ancient felt hat to give her head a good scratch. 'He'd have to be a Catholic for that to happen and he'd also have to be dead, nobody ever became a patron saint while they were still alive and our dear Captain Rory has many good years in him yet – God willing,' she added with a seraphic air that did not fool Shug in the least, neither of them having been to church in their lives except to clean the steps and polish the organ as Dolly sometimes did to atone for her lack of attendance.

Chapter Six

The laird had presented the pony in style with a big pink ribbon tied in a bow between her ears and a placard round her neck bearing a suitable birthday greeting. When Andy at last went to look at her he was lost for words as he had never been in his life before, even during his difficult speech days. He was shy suddenly, he wished only to be alone with his family. Why was everybody here? Why were they looking at him as if they could eat him? Like vultures at a feast.

The pony nuzzled his hand. He was overcome with the welter of emotions running through his veins. Tears pricked his lids. He couldn't find the words to even say thank you to the man who had made all his dreams come true. Such freedom lay before him now, wide and empty spaces, places he could go alone to just think and dream . . .

'What are you going to call her?'

Janet Morgan was there by Andy's side, a blonde young woman of thirty-three who had been friend and neighbour to the Sutherlands for as long as Andy could remember.

'Bonny,' he replied without really knowing why. 'I think I'll call her Bonny.'

'Bonny.' Janet gazed at him but she didn't see him, her blue-grey eyes dreamy and faraway as she repeated the name. It was like an echo from the past for her as she thought about little Bonny Barr who had come to her from the nearby Fountainwell Orphanage only to be returned to her natural mother after a few months. So many years ago now but Janet had never forgotten the beautiful handicapped child who had been so desperate for a home and a mother to love. Janet had wept bitter tears after Bonny's departure and over the years she had wished with all her heart that the girl would come back to visit. She would be about fourteen by now, the same age as Andy.

'Why did you choose that name, Andy?' she asked quietly. 'Do you remember Bonny Barr who came here to stay for a while with me and Jock? She was very little, just four years old. You and she played in your cart with Breck pulling you through the streets of Calvost? Do you remember anything about her at all?'

Andy shook his head. 'I don't think so – the name just came to me . . .' His hand went out to play absently with one of Essie's golden ringlets. 'At least, I think I do some things, she had fair hair, like Essie's, and blue eyes, and she was always asking me out to play just to get a ride in my cart.'

'You do remember,' Janet said softly. 'And I think it's a wonderful name to call your pony. She is a bonny wee thing and I wish you all the happiness in the world when you go out with her.'

'Can we go too?' Some of the young lads from Quarry Cottages had arrived in force and were look-ing over Bonny with lively interest, tugging at her reins, tussling her mane, running their grubby fingers over her back, tangling them into her flowing tail, unnerving her as she stood there.

'Get back!' Big Jock Morgan, Janet's husband, sometimes known as Morgan the Magnificent because of his marvellous physique and bearing, strode in among the troublemakers to quickly disperse them with a few well-chosen words. They all respected the big man who was deputy headkeeper of the Kinvara Light. His very appearance was something to be envied and admired and he always stood out in a crowd with his blond beard flowing over his sark and a ringlet of hair tied into a black band at his nape.

But even more they respected Rob Sutherland and stood by silently when he left the laird's side to come quickly over to his son to help him into the cart, Ross Wallace having jumped down to make room for the rightful owner.

'Come on, Andy,' Rob directed, his dark eyes flashing, 'You know what to do, you've watched me often enough. Just take up the reins and the pony will do the rest.'

'Can't you come with me, Father?' Andy sounded nervous. All eyes were on him, waiting to see how he would cope with this latest venture in his life.

'I'm a bit too big for that, it's only a little cart,' Rob laughed. 'But don't worry, I'll guide the pony along if you like, she's a sedate wee thing so there shouldn't be anything to worry about.'

Andy didn't fancy the idea of this one bit. It would make him look like a cissy in front of everybody, especially the boys from Quarry Cottages who, hands dug deep in their pockets, were watching his discomfiture with some amusement.

Andy hesitated, overwhelmed and unsure of himself. His balance might let him down, it was all right in the normal way of things but now he felt shaky and insecure. Bonny might be a small pony but here in the cart he was still a long way from the ground – at least it seemed that way to him as he sat there, feeling as if he were about to topple off his seat at any moment.

'He's afraid,' one of the boys dared to pipe up.

'Cowardy custard. Cowardy custard,' chanted another.

'Ay, it was all right when it was just the dog,' sneered the biggest lad. 'The pony's too big for him – even though it's so tiny you could pick it up and birl it round wi' one hand.'

'I'll pick you up and birl *you* round with one hand!' Hannah, who had been having a chat with Emily, came over to glare at the upstarts who backed away as one, not liking the fighting look in Hannah's eyes.

Satisfied that she had made her point she turned to Andy. 'It's all right, son, don't mind them, we're here, no harm will come to you, just take the pony a little way down the road. It's now or never and just think of the difference she'll make in your life once you get used to her.'

'Ay, that's right, Hannah, it's time this lot went about their business. School goes in at nine and none o' them look as if they've even washed their faces yet.' Big Bette, her voluminous apron billowing in the breeze, thundered across to the group to add her contribution. Lifting one hefty hand she cuffed the nearest boy on the ear and he ran off yelping. The rest followed suit, not daring to linger one second longer in the intimidating presence of the fearsome Mrs MacGill.

'There, that's sorted them out.' Bette dusted her hands together, smoothed down her apron, and looked mighty pleased with herself. 'They've no right to be here anyway, and I'll tell their mothers so when I see them. Idle good for nothings, all o' them.'

Andy, visibly relaxed by now, took a deep breath and settled himself more comfortably in his seat. But before he could make another move Essie scrambled up beside him, then Breck, placing himself at his young master's side with a most haughty expression on his face.

'That's a boy,' the laird approved jovially, 'it's your turn now so just sit back and enjoy it.'

'I'm getting a horse too,' cried Essie, quite carried away with excitement. 'Daddy's making me one for Christmas.'

Rob threw her a warning look. She blushed and immediately subsided. Andy took up the reins. Bonny began to move away. Everybody cheered. The cart wheels rumbled on the stony track. Bonny's hooves clattered. Andy's eyes glowed. The winds from the sea caressed his face, ruffled his dark hair, the open road lay before him, the world unfolded. He wanted to go on and on and never stop.

'Freedom!' Beside himself with euphoria he shouted the word to the skies.

'Freedom!' came Essie's echoing cry. 'Free for all time and forever, Andy!'

Not to be outdone, Breck lifted his nose heavenwards and barked. It was a new experience for him, to be riding along in style like this instead of having to bear the weight of a burden at his back. His tongue hung out, he took in everything as he went jolting along, The expression on his face was one of complete enjoyment mingled with canine superiority. There was not one dog in the neighbourhood as proud as he was in those novel moments of riding alongside his master in his new pony and trap that sunny, bracing, special March morning.

'Ay, he'll be all right now.' Captain Rory, quite carried away, took off his hat and whirled it over his head as he watched Andy's triumphal parade. 'By God, it's been worth it, just to see him trotting about, there'll be no stopping him from now on.'

A feeling of déjà vu seized Hannah as she stood there with everyone else. There was a dreamlike quality about the whole episode. Hadn't all of this happened before? In another time, far off and almost forgotten? A memory buried deep in the mists of long ago but coming back to her bit by bit as if it was just yesterday. The little cart Rob had made for his son, the neighbours gathered to watch, Andy coming out of the house, supported on either side by his father and his Granma Harriet.

Hannah's hand went to her mouth as the memories came flooding back. Her doubts that her son would ever be able to do anything for himself, let alone go off on a silly handmade cart pulled by a dog in harness. It had been embarrassing, it had been ridiculous – but it had worked. Andy's horizons had opened and expanded. 'Breck and the boy' had gone everywhere together. Wherever they went people had welcomed them and showed them hospitality and kindness. They had looked out for Andy, protected him from trouble, and they were still doing it, showing their affection for him, caring for him, even Big Bette for all her bossy and overpowering ways and her interference in other folk's affairs.

As for Rob, his faith in his son had never waned, he had always believed in Andy, right from the time the boy was a helpless, hopeless babe with nothing on his side except his father's unwavering love.

A lump came to Hannah's throat. She slipped her hand into that of her husband. He took it and squeezed it and smiled down at her and she knew he was thinking the same thoughts as herself, reliving the uncertainties of the old days but glad that everything seemed to be falling into place now.

'I wonder how we can ever thank Captain Rory,' Rob said with a glance over at the laird who was extolling the virtues of the Humber to Mungo who desired a motor car for himself but was never likely to get one in his position as 'humble barber to a balding population'.

The laird didn't listen. Mungo was always bemoaning his lot though he looked 'stout and rich and fit enough to burst' and was certainly not lacking in nourishment.

'Oh, we'll dream up something,' was Hannah's reply to her husband. 'You've already thought o' the rocking horse, he'll get a kick out o' that and will most likely have a go on it himself long before the new baby grows big enough to use it.'

*   *   *

Andy was coming back, windblown and red-cheeked, well pleased with himself, delighted with the pony, hardly able to wait for it to stop, tripping himself up in his haste to get over to Captain Rory and throw his arms round that gentleman's portly frame. It was only then that Andy's pent-up feelings got the better of him. To his eternal shame he burst into tears and buried his face deeper into the folds of the laird's hairy neck.

'Let it go, lad, let it go,' Captain Rory soothed, patting the boy's thin shoulders and swallowing a tear that had risen in his own throat. 'This is just the beginning of a new life for you, new doors will open all the time, just see if they don't.'

The neighbours had dispersed to school and work by now and only a few remained, most noticeably young Tom MacGill who was too taken up with Maida to bother about anything else. Emily was standing at the edge of the dunes admiring the view, Vaila was chatting to George, watched grimly by Mark, Joss Morgan had just come up from the shore where he'd been gathering seaweed for the Henderson sisters, sorry to have missed the presentation ceremony. Maida immediately switched her attention from Tom to the newcomer, only too eager to regale him with all that had taken place in his absence.

Crimson-faced and embarrassed, Andy loosened his grip on the laird's person, expecting to see a few interested spectators at least, but everyone was too taken up with their own affairs to be bothered any more with his.

His mother was hurrying Essie into the house to give her face a quick wash before school, the rest of the stragglers were scurrying about their business, Mungo was waiting with his trap to take Babs along to Bougan Villa before Prudence Taylor-Young raised the roof altogether about his daughter's bad timekeeping.

'Can you give Essie a lift too?' Rob was shouting. 'She's going to be late for school if she walks there.'

Before Mungo could answer, Andy had climbed back into his little cart and had taken up the reins once more. 'I'll take her, Father,' he said, unable to keep a note of pure triumph from his voice. 'If anybody can get her there on time, Bonny can.'

The independence had started in earnest. Rob gazed at his son, shook his head, and smiled. Essie came out of the house to be bundled in beside her brother. Hannah was too careful of Andy's pride in his abilities to voice any concerns she might have been feeling regarding her daughter's safety on the journey to school.

'It's all right, Mother.' Andy as usual, knew what Hannah was thinking. 'I'll take care o' her, I've got the feel of my new pony already, you can trust me.'

'Ay, away you go.' Hannah spoke brusquely in an attempt to hide the many emotions the morning's happenings had invoked in her. 'But don't forget to come back. Remember Bonny's legs aren't all that big, she'll run out o' steam some time and will also need time to adjust to her new surroundings.'

'I'll make a space for her in the byre,' Rob promised. 'It will have to do until I can fix her a place of her own.'

Andy lifted the reins and spanked away with his

sister. Rob and Hannah stood gazing after them. 'They're growing up, Rob,' she said with a sigh, 'Andy's world is getting bigger, all the lads are after Vaila and her not fifteen till June.'

'They'll be with us a while yet,' Rob replied. 'Andy's got a long way to go before he's ready to leave home, and Vaila's got her head screwed on, she won't jump at the first lad she meets.'

'I know.' Hannah glanced at him rather strangely. 'She said something once about never marrying until she finds the great love o' her life. She was just a wee lass then, but somehow I think she meant it, as if it's been imprinted into her mind since the beginning.'

'She's a romantic,' Rob answered lightly. 'She'll change as she goes along. At the moment she's too young to be realistic.'

'Yours was a great love, Rob,' Hannah murmured. 'The one you shared with Morna Jean. I've never ever tried to fool myself about that.'

He shifted uncomfortably, hoping that she wasn't going to start raking up the past again. 'That was a long time ago, Hannah, what I had with Morna was special and unforgettable, but what I have with you is also special. We've come through a lot together, we've shared the good and the bad times and grown in maturity over the years. God willing, we'll grow old together and no regrets about what might have been.'

'I wasn't criticising you, Rob, just telling you what I know without malice of any sort.'

'Hannah, are you coming?' Janet was at her door, ready for the walk down to the little baker's shop in Calvost known as The Bread Oven.

'Oh.' Hannah's hand flew to her mouth, she began fumbling with the ties of her apron and rushed into the house to get her coat. In minutes she and Janet were hurrying down the track, leaving Rob to make his way to the back of the house to begin clearing a space in the byre for Bonny.

Chapter Seven

It was dinner time the following day. Rob was at the sink washing his hands when he looked up and saw the figure of a woman walking up the track towards the house. His heart missed a beat. That outline, the way the woman held herself, reminded him so much of someone else who had moved so gracefully through the days of her life. Time stood still for a moment. He was whisked back through the years to another existence, another era, sometimes unreal, sometimes misty, yet always there at the back of his mind.

He had tried to forget Morna Jean. He had immersed himself in his job and in his family. Knowing how unfair he had been to Hannah in worshipping the ghosts of the past he had set out to prove to her that she was the woman in his life now. And it had worked. His affection for her had grown into something more over the years. He did love Hannah now, not in the wild and passionate way he had loved Morna, he would never feel that way about anyone again, but there was something comforting being married to Hannah. It was like being in quieter waters, safe from the storms of life.

The old Hannah hadn't been in the least bit

comforting. She had been unsure and jealous, lacking in confidence, martyr to a host of doubts and uncertainties about her marriage, afraid all the time about many things but most of all about his feelings for her.

All that was over. Sensing the changes in him she too had changed for the better, her responses to him were warmer and more impulsive, she was able to see the funny side of life and could laugh more at herself.

She was still the same Hannah in many respects; nobody could ever completely change their spots. She could be dour and gruff and critical and could throw her weight about with the best of them. Quite often the old moody Hannah emerged in periods of stress and difficulty. She was reticent where strangers were concerned and took her time getting to know people outwith the family circle with the result that they often took her to be off-handed and mean. But on the whole she was better than she had been and the home was a much more settled place because of it.

Busy as she was with the running of the house and the shop she had very few leisure hours to herself but always made a point of taking a day off now and then to spend it with her family. This was just such a day. She and Rob had gone with Andy in the morning to allow him to show off his new pony to Johnny Lonely, the hermit who lived in a hut under the cliffs in Mary's Bay.

Johnny had also changed in the last few years. He wasn't nearly as reclusive as he had once been. He got out and about more and had begun mixing with his fellow men, albeit cautiously and rather self-consciously, the result of having spent so many years in his own company. He was less suspicious than of yore and his neighbours had begun to relax a little when he was in the vicinity, not nearly as worried as they had been about his snooping and prying into their affairs.

He had also cleaned himself up a good deal and was seen to be really quite a handsome and cultured man underneath all the hair and the grime.

'Not old, in his prime still,' Mattie MacPhee decided. 'And I hear tell he's quite a learned man for all his strange ways. Talk has it he's got books and music in that smelly hut o' his, I've heard it myself, drifting out into the bay, classical stuff and screeching women singing opera, the likes o' which I myself have never listened to but which sounded quite nice in the open air like that.'

There was of course much speculation as to how this metamorphosis in Johnny had come about. Some said it had all to do with the Bowmans, that Johnny had known Miriam Bowman in his past and had gotten some old festering sore out of his system in a confrontation with her. Others muttered darkly that it was more Rebecca Bowman who was at the core of it all. Hadn't she been seen, visiting Johnny in that dreadful hovel he called home? The pair of them as close as close could be with their heads together as they talked and laughed and seemed not to notice or care if anyone saw them.

'It was all right when she was just a wee lass,' Jessie MacDonald opined meaningfully. 'Now she's growing up fast with a shape on her that belongs to a woman. 'Tis a wonder to me that Joshua Bowman allows his daughter anywhere near Johnny Lonely, never mind lets her visit him in that lonely place down in the bay.'

Rebecca let the gossips think as they would of her. She was Rebecca and she didn't give a hoot about small talk. She loved Johnny Lonely, who was more a father to her than the self-righteous Joshua could ever be, and vowed she would go on trusting in Johnny and caring about him in her own fierce and passionately loyal way as long as there was breath in her body.

Andy Sutherland also loved Johnny and had done from an early age. Johnny had taught the young and insecure Andy so much. About life and about nature and all the wonders of creation that existed around and above him. He had also awakened the boy's interest in the great mysteries of the universe and much of what Andy wrote now came from those first inspiring teachings.

Johnny seemed to be waiting for Andy as he came along on Bonny, Rob holding on to her reins to steady her as she picked her dainty way down over the dunes to the beach, Breck trotting gamely alongside, nosing into the rock pools and the nooks and crannies, barking at the gulls but making no attempt to chase them as he had done in his callow youth.

'I heard all about it,' was Johnny's greeting as the trio of people came nearer. 'I'm glad for you, lad, right glad, she's a bonny stout wee beast. The laird and myself have not always seen eye to eye but he has a good heart in him as I myself have just found out to my benefit.'

Johnny was very excited and garrulous that morning, more so than anyone had ever seen him before.

The reasons for this would come later, but first he had presents to give Andy for his birthday. A leather-bound volume of Robert Burns verses, old, fusty, but well looked after and intact; a carved figurine of a mermaid made from a piece of bleached driftwood; a bottle filled with tiny pebbles and bits of coloured glass gleaned from sea and shore; a huge conch shell in which the sea roared when applied to the ear which Andy did immediately, delighted with gifts of such simplicity but of rare intrinsic value.

Hannah had brought tea and pancakes and they all sat on a wooden bench outside Johnny's hut to partake of the repast, Hannah rather guiltily accepting the praise for the pancakes which had been made by her sister-in-law, Maudie, with just a little help from Hannah herself. Still, Hannah excused herself, she had supplied the flour, the sugar, and the lemon juice, *and* she had mixed the batter till her wrists ached.

'More bubbles, you must let the air in, Hannah,' Maudie had kept directing till Hannah could have seen her and her batter far enough. Small wonder therefore that she said not one word about Maudie when the last pancake had disappeared with just a morsel each to Breck and Bonny from Andy's share of the little feast.

'They're just as good as Aunt Maudie's.' Andy's face did not change its expression as he spoke the words but the sidelong glance he slid his mother said it all, making that lady jump to her feet and exclaim, 'Lunch! I've got nothing ready *and* I've got the whole house to clean. You two can come along later when you're ready.'

Andy and Rob had spent a few minutes more in

Johnny's company. Time passed pleasantly while the slanted rays of the sun spilled golden pools of light into the water and the seals called to one another down on the rocks in the bay. The men and the boy sat silently, soaking in the peace of the place, till a lone holiday-maker appeared round the rocks, making Johnny beat a hasty retreat into his hut and the others to make their way home, smiling a little at the hermit's antics. There was nothing Johnny loathed more than a 'nosy tourist' since they saw him and his way of life as either a marvel to be wondered at 'in this day and age' or a sideshow to goggle at as if he was 'an alien being straight from the planet of Mars'.

Hannah was rushing round the house with her broom when Andy and Rob arrived, one to go upstairs to his room with his new treasures, the other to go to the sink to wash his hands. That was when Rob saw the woman coming towards the house, carrying travel bags and looking exhausted the further she advanced, tendrils of fair hair escaping her hat as the brisk breezes from the sea caught and harried her.

'Mirren,' he murmured, knowing now that it had been she all along, not some wraith-like creature appearing to him as a reminder of the past but a human being whole and real and very much of the everyday world.

He raised his voice. 'Hannah! Mirren's here! Coming up to the door at any moment. I'll just go out and help her with her bags.'

'Mirren!' Hannah turned an aghast face. 'But how could it be her? She's in Shetland – and I'm in my pinny! Oh, how could she do this? Not let us know she was coming? The bed in the boxroom isn't aired and hasn't been for ages. I've got no food in the house and Big Bette will be shut for lunch . . .'

But she was speaking to thin air. Rob had disappeared outside. Hannah gave vent to a few curses then scuttled to shovel up the little pile of dirt she had gathered on the hearthrug. Breck got in the way of the broom, and in her anxiety she lifted it up like a lancet and began chasing him all round the kitchen till he took refuge in one of the cupboards.

This was the sight that met Mirren's eyes as she came into the kitchen, Breck peeping round the door of the broom closet, Hannah brandishing her brush at him and vowing all sorts of vengeance into his swivelling lugs, streaks of dust on her face, her brown hair hanging in rather attractive loops about her face.

'Just like home,' Mirren laughed. 'I do that with my collies. It's supposed to be serious but they think it's a game and love it, even when I'm bawling my head off at them.'

Hannah could never picture Mirren bawling her head off at anything or anybody. She always appeared to be cool, calm, and collected and never seemed to let anything ruffle her feathers. But there was often a hint of steel in her blue eyes, an occasional flash of fire that took away their coolness. No one could ever take advantage of Mirren and get away with it and she was held in high regard by all who knew her.

'I'm sorry you caught me like this,' Hannah apologised as she hastened to tuck her hair back into place, her hand going self-consciously up to her face as if to hide the flush of embarrassment on her cheekbones.

'Hannah, it's only me.' Mirren laid her handbag on the draining board and went over to kiss her sister-in-law. 'Don't get so het up. It isn't your fault I'm here so unexpectedly. I wanted to bring Andy his birthday things and thought it would be a good idea to surprise you all. I promise I won't get in the way. Don't worry if the bed isn't aired or if the cupboard is bare. I've brought enough food to last for a month and you know I'll muck in and help out with anything that needs doing.'

Hannah released a lungful of air and went to the stove to swing the kettle over the fire. 'I did panic when Rob said it was you coming to our door but I'll be fine when I've made us all a nice cup o' tea. Sit down, Mirren, you look done in, get your breath back and don't talk for five minutes till I recover mine.'

Mirren laughed. Hannah had a way of expressing herself that could be very droll at times. There had been a time when the sisters-in-law hadn't liked each other very much. After the death of Morna, Mirren had wanted to take Vaila to Shetland and bring her up as her own. At that point Hannah had intervened, insisting that the child be raised in Kinvara where she belonged. Relations between the two women had been strained for a while but common sense had prevailed in the end and now the pair got on very well together and enjoyed each other's company whenever they met.

Rob had come in with the bags. Dumping them down he went over to Mirren to kiss her on the cheek and ask her how she had got here.

'Courtesy of Willie Whiskers,' she answered promptly. 'He was at Achnasheen station collecting stuff from the train but only brought me as far as the smiddy. From what I gathered he had dallied too long at a wayside inn and was anxious to get back to Maisie before she bashed his head in with one of his own hammers.'

Her face was animated as she spoke. Rob was struck anew by her likeness to Morna, for although she was as fair as Morna had been dark there were certain little mannerisms that marked them down very firmly as sisters. The way she inclined her head, her expression when she was listening, the curve of her mouth, her gestures, a hundred small things that made him want to look at her in fascination yet not look at all for then it would all came flooding back, the heartache, the longing, the remembering.

Mirren in her turn was thinking how much she liked Rob Sutherland now that time had changed their circumstances. Once she had blamed him for taking Morna away from her, the little sister she had brought up single-handed when their parents had died in a boating accident. Morna had been her life, her reason for keeping on the family farm in Shetland and working all the hours God sent.

She had been devastated when Morna had left to carve a niche for herself in Kinvara where she had met and fallen head over heels in love with Rob Sutherland. That had been the beginning and the end for Morna. She had lived and died for this man and had probably drawn her last breath with his name on her lips.

Mirren looked at him. At thirty-nine a more attractive man would be hard to find, rugged and dark, hard-muscled and strong, eyes that saw everything, a smile that could melt an iceberg, a strength in him that came deep from the recesses of his inner self, passionate, steadfast, a man whose heart could rule his head to the point of obsession – as it had done with his beloved Morna Jean.

Andy had heard the voices in the kitchen and came clattering downstairs to go straight to his aunt and throw his arms around her. In the talk and exchanges that followed Hannah relaxed and forgot her earlier worries. Mirren had brought not only gifts for Andy but eggs and ham, butter and cheese, a whole chicken ready roasted, a bottle of best malt whisky, a gingerbread cake and some tiny iced fairy cakes for the children to enjoy.

'No wonder you had so many bags,' Rob told her with a laugh. 'I'm amazed you got everything here intact, the way Willie Whiskers drives that cart of his. Like a bat through hell as Maisie calls it when he's in a hurry to get to the Ballivoe Inn.'

Essie and Vaila were delighted to see Mirren when they came home from school and work. She brought with her a freshness, a breath of Shetland air, a sense of the great dramatic skies and vast spaces that they all knew and loved, having spent summer holidays at Burravoe House on a spit of land beyond Bridge of Walls.

Vaila and her half-brother, Aidan, who lived with his grandparents at Vale O' Dreip, the big rambling farmhouse on the slopes of Blanket Hill, had visited their mother's grave for the very first time in Shetland four years ago. Solemnly they had stood there in that secluded windswept spot, Aidan with his hands clasped behind his back, Vaila's in the same position as softly she read out the words on the stone.

'Morna Jean Sommero. Nineteen O two to nineteen twenty six. Beloved wife of Finlay Sutherland, sister of Mirren, mother of Vaila and Aidan. Sleep till the morning breaks and the dawn lights the day with its silvery beams.'

And at the bottom of the moss covered stone: Goodnight, Morna, from Robbie. An addition that Rob had insisted on after he had viewed the stone and had seen no mention of his name to tell of the part he had played in the young woman's life.

The hands of Vaila and Aidan had entwined in those reverent moments and they had wept their childish tears of sorrow for a mother who had been taken from them in the flower of her youth. Neither of them had ever forgotten that day. They had always been close as brother and sister, having lived in the same house till Morna's death, but somehow those cherished moments in that little graveyard, overlooking the places their mother had wandered in her childhood, had bound them together even more. Vaila loved it when she went to Shetland to see Mirren or when Mirren came to visit at No. 6 of the Row and that night she went to the little boxroom at the end of the hall to curl into bed beside her aunt and listen to the tales of the Shetland upbringing that Mirren and Morna had known together when they were young and all the world was at their feet.

Chapter Eight

It was very pleasant having Mirren in the house. She was a good help to Hannah and didn't mind menial tasks like peeling the potatoes, dusting and cleaning. She was also a very good cook and often had dinner ready when Hannah came home tired out after 'a day in The Bread Oven', an expression that had become a bit of a joke in the family since she was often flushed and warm from her hours spent labouring over a hot stove.

Harriet Campbell, Hannah's mother, had thought it would be a good idea to have an oven installed in the shop so that bread and cakes could be baked there and then on the premises. It had soon proved to be a runaway success. The wonderful aromas wafting from the shop tempted folk inside to sample the mouthwatering array of home baking for themselves. Lady MacKernon of Cragdu Castle was a regular customer since she liked to hand-pick pies and pastries for her dinner guests.

So too was Emily MacPherson. Captain Rory liked nothing better than a flaky sausage roll packed with his flask when out on his wanders with his dogs and his cat. Steak and kidney pie was a regular feature on the Crathmor menu and had actually superseded more exotic dishes like roast pheasant and duck.

Even haughty beings like Miss Dorothy Hosie had succumbed to the temptations of The Bread Oven. Not that she would ever admit to this of course and would never have condescended to go to the shop herself. Instead, with the lure of a few coppers, she had persuaded young Joan MacNulty, the kitchen maid, to do this for her, the goods being smuggled in via the back stairs of Crathmor and on up to Miss Hosie's quarters where she could enjoy her little feasts in private.

The success of the baker's shop lay with Harriet Campbell and Maudie Sutherland. Harriet was adept at the decorative side of the business; she could produce all sorts of effects with her swirls and sworls of icing and her embellishments were very much in demand on christening, birthday and Christmas cakes.

But it was Maudie who was 'the main man at the helm', as the seafaring Charlie Campbell liked to put it. Maudie, whose 'flair wi' the flour' was legendary, could turn out anything from a humble meat pie to a feast fit for a king. Her elevated position as queen bee of The Bread Oven had quickly become established. Lesser mortals like Hannah and Janet, who, by their own admission, were just there as slave labourers, did all the fetching and carrying and buying in of supplies. Nevertheless the place wouldn't have survived without them and they went home at the end of each day weary but satisfied in the knowledge that they had done their bit to ensure the survival of the business.

Maudie however, already the mother of two lively children, seven and eight respectively, now had 'another one in the oven' as Maudie herself laughingly put it, with the result that she had been forced to take some time off. This meant more work than ever for the remaining staff of the shop. Hannah was exhausted each night and only too ready to put her feet up while Mirren cooked the dinner.

Mirren, whose efficiency had often been the bane of her sister-in-law's life in the old days, had learned to overcome her bossy tendencies to a certain degree. It was all right on her farm in Shetland where she had to be continually on top of the men under her rule, but here in Kinvara it was different: she was relaxed, she was on holiday. Hannah would never have stood for anything else other than a certain amount of respect from visitors in her own home. Mirren recognised that fact only too well and made herself amenable to everyone, not least Hannah who was really enjoying her sister-in-law's visit, to the point of wishing that she could stay longer than the week she had set for herself.

Rob was glad of this fact. He'd had enough of warring women in his time. In the beginning he hadn't seen eye to eye with his mother-in-law, Harriet; Mirren and he had fought over Morna and later for Vaila; Hannah had once upon a time been more than difficult to live with. Now everyone seemed to have settled down and matured in their outlook.

Despite occasional disagreements he got on well with the forceful Harriet. Hannah was altogether a different person; where Mirren had once been a square peg in a round hole she was now fitting in, she was less prickly than she had been, she seemed more contented – yet he sensed something about her this holiday that didn't quite fit in with this image.

He couldn't put his finger on it but it was there just the same, a sparkle in her blue eyes, a zest that made it impossible for her to sit still for long, a suppressed excitement that made him look at her once or twice as if he was expecting her to say something that seemed always to be on the tip of her tongue.

'Mirren's got something on her mind.' In bed one night Hannah confirmed what he had started putting down to his imagination. 'She's like a cat on a hot tin roof. I keep expecting her to burst at any minute, she spilled tea all over my clean kitchen floor yesterday and made a cup mark on the sideboard this morning. Mind you, she wiped it up before it did any damage and as it was she who cleaned the floors I shouldn't really complain. I just wonder what's got into her, that's all. In every other respect she's a treat to have in the house and I'm taking an afternoon off tomorrow so that we can all go up to Vale O' Dreip together to see Rita – Annie MacDuff said she'll stand in for me and I must say I could be doing with some time off.'

'I'll come too,' Rob said promptly. 'It's been a while since I've been to see my mother and I know Vaila loves to see Aidan whenever she can. She's got a day off tomorrow too so we'll make it a family affair – and just think, Andy can go under his own steam this time. What a triumph that will be for him, to prove to my father once again that nothing in this world can stop him and that he can get around with the best o' them.'

*   *   *

At sixty-one, Ramsay Sutherland was a fine handsome figure of a man with flashing ice-blue eyes, deep auburn hair and a nature as fiery as his colouring. Ramsay had always liked to get his own way and had managed to achieve this to a certain extent throughout his life. But he had made one mistake too many when he had fathered little Euan Blair in an ungodly union with the then Catrina Simpson, whose marriage to Colin Blair had been instigated more through necessity than love. When Colin had died some years ago in a tragic accident at sea Catrina, in her despair, had simply upped and left Kinvara, leaving Rita to bring up her son and Ramsay to be reminded of the part he had played in the affair every waking day of his life.

Ramsay was an upstanding member of the community, a fanatical devotee of the Free Church, a man whose reputation as a law-abiding citizen had gone untarnished in the eyes of those who came to him for advice and help.

No one knew about the deadly black mark in his copy book, with the exception of Catrina's sister, Connie, and Rita, whose feelings for her husband had died a long time ago and who only went along with the farce of his respectability for the sake of her children. The intricacies of the relationships that the boy's being had created within the family didn't bear thinking about and Rita had always watched and waited and wondered where it would all lead in the end.

But she had brought the lad up well, despite the fact that there was always an unease in her that someday someone would look at him and see how much he resembled his true father. At almost ten he was a replica of Ramsay in every way, from his bold blue eyes to his thatch of bright hair, the arrogant way he conducted himself, his assurance and confidence in company. Smart and clever and quick, he liked to shine in everything he did and was inclined to swagger and boast to his young contemporaries. This was not always to his advantage and it was no unusual occurrence for him to come home from school with a black eye and his clothes in tatters.

Secretly Ramsay admired the boy's fighting spirit, for while there was often a clash of personalities between them there also existed a strange understanding as to what made the other tick. Ramsay had never wanted Euan in his house; he was afraid all the time of the inevitable questions that had arisen when Catrina had left her son at Vale O' Dreip. She had never come back for him. No one, not even her sisters or her grandmother, heard from her except at Christmas and even then it was just a card with often a different franking mark, making it seem that she never stayed in the same place for long.

She sent Euan little gifts on his birthday but he appeared to have forgotten her as much as she had him and Ramsay cursed her for this every waking day of his life. The only way to bear such a cross was to try and bring the boy up to his way of thinking and introduce him to the teachings of the Free Church. So Euan went faithfully to that establishment with the man he simply called Uncle Ramsay. He bowed his red head in prayer and was chaste and good and obedient from the minute he went inside to the minute he came out again. Then he reverted to the

Euan everyone knew and dreaded for his cheek and incorrigibility.

There was however a better side to the little boy. He was kind and generous to a fault. If he took with one hand he gave back double with the other. He was affectionate and responsive to those he knew and loved and his devotion to Rita was so intense she was sometimes moved to laugh and tell him. 'God help the lass you fall in love with. You'll smother her to death with those strong young arms o' yours and never let her come up for air.'

Euan had several loves in his life. He adored Aidan who had also been brought up at Vale O' Dreip after his mother's death; he worshipped Maudie and was as much at home in her house as he was in his own; Rob was another of his favourites as were his children but it was Essie he clung to most. They were both of a like age; she was the perfect foil for him with her dreamy ways and her ability to make him feel ten feet tall when she listened to his chatter and his bragging and seldom contradicted him in anything he suggested by way of adventure. He also enjoyed listening to the tales Essie told about the wicked witches and the princesses who existed in her make-believe world and many were the enjoyable hours they spent laughing and talking together. In his room at the farm he kept a store of home-made costumes and props so that they could both dress up whenever Essie came to visit.

He loved it when the Sutherlands from Keeper's Row called on those at Vale O' Dreip and when he saw a little procession of them coming up the farm track preceded by Andy and Essie in the new cart he let out a yell and went running to meet them to fuss over Bonny and ask a million questions before they even got as far as the yard outside the house.

Hearing the voices, Aidan, a dark-haired delicate-looking boy of twelve, came out of the house to welcome his sister, speaking rather breathlessly as he had just recovered from one of the asthma attacks that had plagued him since his mother's death. Aidan had always been the apple of his grampa Ramsay's eye, a child who had never given anyone any trouble from the day he was born and who was pleasant and kind to everyone around him. His health was a constant source of worry to both Rita and Ramsay, the latter's concern mingling with a disappointment that the boy might never grow up to make a good farmer. But Ramsay also recognised that Aidan mightn't make a go of farming anyway, for although he loved animals he had never shown any inclination to work with them, preferring instead to nurture his interest in his fellow men and immerse himself in books, the depth and likes of which Ramsay might have associated with scholars double Aidan's age.

If it hadn't been for his health, Ramsay would have sent his grandson away to recieve further education. He was immensely proud of Aidan's abilities to hold intelligent conversations with adults from all walks of life, impressing them so much with his knowledge they were often moved to ask which branch of the family he had got his brains from, a question that was sure to make Ramsay scowl and retaliate with a few smart answers of his own concerning the 'high bred Sutherlands from away back'.

Never mind that those selfsame Sutherlands had known neither riches nor wealth, but had been good and decent hardworking folk who made their living from the land in much poorer and harder circumstances than he would ever know in his present-day role as gentleman farmer who rode about his acres on a horse bossing his men about and hardly ever getting his hands soiled. Ramsay thought he knew all there was to know about Aidan. What he didn't know was that the boy often went to the little Catholic church in Vaul to slip into one of the pews and listen as Father Kelvin MacNeil read the sermon. At other times he simply went there to light a candle and soak in the atmosphere of the place, preferring it to the Free Kirk to which he only went on sufferance and out of a desire to keep the peace. Aidan doted on Father MacNeil and everything he stood for, but even more he idolised Joss Morgan who had been his hero for as long as he could remember. Going to the church that Joss attended was one way of getting near him and Aidan cherished this little secret part of his life more than anyone would ever know.

George Ian MacPherson, who had brought a message to Ramsay from his father, was in the kitchen drinking tea when the visitors arrived. Rita went immediately to refill the pot as everybody piled in and the big farmhouse kitchen suddenly seemed to shrink in proportion as the seats were taken. Ramsay, quick to notice how George's attention had become diverted at the appearance of Vaila, requested that Andy go outside with him to show him the Sheltie. Over the years Ramsay had grudgingly come to respect and admire his eldest grandson for his endeavours to rise above his disabilities. There now existed between them an odd kind of comradeship. In his own inimitable way Andy had helped his grandfather to erase some of his prejudices against imperfections in the human species and had made him see that even those with physical handicaps could contribute a great deal to society.

Ramsay was therefore not as uneasy in Andy's company as he had been and so the boy and the man arose to go out to the yard together to look over Bonny, leaving the way clear for Breck to slip into the warmth of the kitchen behind Ramsay's back. Ramsay did not like animals in the house and only tolerated the laird's Siamese cat, Maggie, because it would not have been in his interests to offend such a valuable friend as Captain Rory.

George had been quick to offer his seat by the fire to Vaila but she opted instead to sit with the rest of the womenfolk on the couch opposite, thus giving him the opportunity to eye her and make her blush every time she glanced up and saw his gaze upon her. She thought for a moment about Mark, how he would have scowled at the young MacPherson if he had been here to witness such attentions. But Mark wasn't here and Vaila set out to enjoy the little game that had sprung up between her and this handsome, cocky, charming young man of the élite.

It would do no harm to torment him a bit for a game was all it was to her, though that didn't mean to say she didn't experience a tiny flutter in her breast when she saw him glancing rather pointedly at her mouth – as if he would like to eat bits of her in one gulp before coming back for the rest. She put her hand up to stifle the giggles that had arisen in her throat. George raised his brows as she let out a muffled squeak and hastily she stuffed a piece of scone into her mouth and turned her attention to Mirren who was keeping the company amused with her talk of Shetland and all that went on there.

Ramsay came back in with Andy, Breck slithered behind the couch and went to sleep; Rita got up to make more tea; Ramsay glowered a bit at Vaila who was having a fit of the giggles; Essie and Euan went upstairs to play charades. Rob fell into a conversation with George about the merits of Highland cattle and no one was prepared for the sudden intrusion of Finlay into the scene, his face red, his pale blue eyes round and excited as he burst through the door and cried, 'Quick, someone, quick! Maudie's gone into labour! She thinks the bairn might pop out at any minute! I don't know what to do! She's pacing about like a bull in a cowshed and I'm frightened in case she has it on the carpet!'

'Do as you've done twice before, get the nurse!' roared Ramsay, irritated as he often was by this youngest son of his who was so useless in times of crisis. The womenfolk had risen to their feet, Hannah quickly opting to stay with the children, the rest making for the door and George's trap after he had obligingly offered to lend his services.

Ramsay and Rob between them took hold of Finlay's shoulders and ushered him outside to the shed where the Vale o' Dreip's family trap was kept. In minutes both the trap and the horses were ready and in a very short space of time the Sutherland brothers and their father were thundering down the stony farm track to Purlieburn Cottage wherein lived

Effie Maxwell, the district nurse. There was no need for three strong men to make such an errand of mercy, one would have been enough, but in those fraught moments all of them felt the need for action of some sort and a brisk jaunt into the village of Calvost was as good a way of getting it as any.

Chapter Nine

Finlay had been right about Maudie. She *was* pacing about in a demented fashion, not like a bull in a cowshed as he had described but very much like one extremely large pregnant young woman in distress, treading the floorboards of her kitchen and calling out forcibly for God to give her a quick deliverance from her pain while her two children, on the start of their Easter holidays from school, stood by watching with their thumbs in their mouths.

'It's coming!' Maudie gasped as soon the new arrivals came tumbling over the doorstep. 'My waters burst a good whiley back, like a river in spate they were and Finlay just standing by as if he was about to be drowned in them at any minute. Oh, Mammy, Daddy! I canny bear it any longer! Somebody make me a cup o' tea or I'll be dead in two minutes flat wi' thirst.'

Mirren and Rita took over then, taking one arm each of Maudie's and bundling her up to the bedroom while Vaila went to put on the kettle and George stood by looking as if he didn't know quite what to do next.

'Talk to the children,' she cried rather desperately, her black curls falling over her brow as she made a dive for the tea caddy, not an easy item to find in the chaos of Maudie's kitchen.

'What will I say to them?' he asked somewhat dazedly, not quite so sure of himself now that he found himself in a house where the drama of birth was about to take place.

'Surely you must know that,' she returned rather snappishly, her own hands shaking a bit as she poured water into the teapot. 'You had wee brothers and sisters of your own, these are no different and they won't bite.'

'I don't know about that. I've had some previous experience with Maudie Sutherland's children; one kicked me on the shins once for no good reason while the other stood by laughing and looking as if he would like to do the same.'

'Oh.' Exasperated, Vaila ran the children over to the couch, stuffed some biscuits into their hands, and told them, 'Wait there and be good till I tell you to move.'

But seven-year-old Kyle was having none of that. 'I want to pee!' he yelled at the top of his voice.

'And I want to see my mother!' yelled Morven at the top of hers. 'I want to see the baby being born from her tummy and smack it to make it cry when it comes out!'

'Sit!' George at last came into his own. 'Put your biscuits down, fold your arms, and don't dare move one muscle or you'll have me to reckon with. That is an order from a higher authority and must be obeyed.'

The children sat. They laid their half-eaten biscuits on a cluttered table, meekly folded their arms and stared goggle-eyed at George as if he was the big bad ogre personified.

Vaila gazed at him with new respect. 'Was that how you treated your own brothers and sisters?'

He choked on a bubble of laughter. 'No, that was how they treated me – and it worked, every time. Once they even tied me up and left me in the attic for one whole afternoon. I let them do it, of course, it gave them a sense of power from which they've never recovered. Now they go strutting about, bossing Father around and threatening to tie him up if he ever gets out of hand.'

They collapsed together in a giggling heap and that was how Mirren found them when she came downstairs in a quest for Maudie's tea and a basin of hot water.

'Just coming, Aunt Mirren,' Vaila said breathlessly and a trifle guiltily. Mirren went back upstairs. Vaila looked at George. 'Will you take it up or will I?'

'Oh, you,' he said quickly. 'A higher authority I may be but only here in the kitchen with these two warriors. I've got no desire to butt in on a woman's domain and Maudie knows you better than me anyway.'

'You boil the hot water, then,' she directed and left him rolling up his sleeves while she bore the tray of tea upstairs, gulping down her nerves as she went along the passageway wondering what she would find when she at last opened the door of the birthing room from whence the most alarming sounds were issuing.

The bed was laid over with old sheets and news-papers and on it Maudie lay, screaming her head off and calling every so often for help from her mammy and daddy, both of whom were back home in a tenement close in Partick, unaware of the small drama taking place within River House on the Vale O' Dreip estate.

Maudie, her plump, good-natured face twisted in pain, suddenly stopped screaming and shot up on her pillows. 'Mammy, Daddy,' she whimpered. 'It's damt well stuck! Oh, wait till I get Finlay for this! I'll cut the balls off him and feed them to the pigs, that I will! Take it away, someone, please take it away and I promise I'll be good for the rest o' my life and never ever swear again.'

As soon as Vaila opened the door with the tea both Rita and Mirren turned enquiring faces. 'Is Effie here yet?' Rita asked, panting a bit from all her efforts.

'There's still no sign of her.' Vaila tried not to look at her Aunt Maudie in the bed but her eyes were drawn there like a magnet. All she could see however was a mound of sheets with Maudie's legs sticking out at the bottom. 'Tea, anyone?' she asked in a small voice but nobody heard her. Rita was looking at Mirren. 'Have you done this before?'

'Only with cows and sheep.'

'Me too.'

They each took a deep breath and turned once more to the bed. Vaila stood there with the tray, not knowing what to do next till Mirren cried, 'Get the hot water, Vaila, and bring some towels from the cupboard. Go, quick, and don't take all day coming back!'

Vaila went, almost falling downstairs in her haste. George was there in the kitchen, enveloped in a cloud of steam, and the children were still on the couch, both having fallen fast asleep with their hands folded firmly over their middles.

'Towels, quick!' Vaila cried.

'Where?'

'In the cupboard.'

'What cupboard?'

'Oh, I don't know, probably the one over the hot-water tank, though knowing Aunt Maudie they could be anywhere.'

They searched, bumping into one another in their haste, George finally unearthing two threadbare apologies for towels, one with the logo *I Belong To Glasgow* written on it in bright purple lettering.

'Right, upstairs with them this minute,' Vaila said firmly.

'I'm not going up there on my own,' George protested, his handsome face reddening at the very idea.

'We'll go together, then' Vaila decided. 'You take the hot water, I'll take the towels.'

'I'm still not going in. The warriors might wake up at any minute and wreck the place with no one there to keep an eye on them.'

'I thought you were coming out to be an officer in the army. You won't get very far being frightened at the sight of a tiny wee baby being born.'

'It might be tiny but its mother isn't. One swipe from her could knock anybody flying and from the noise she's making I wouldn't like to be the one to get in her way.'

They had reached the bedroom door by now. Vaila opened it a peep and went cautiously in, then George's hand came through the aperture, forcing her to take the basin and the jug of water before he went bolting away down the stairs two at a time.

The moment of birth had arrived for Maudie's baby. Nobody noticed as Vaila stood there in fascinated wonder, the towels and the water forgotten, watching the tiny wet head appearing, then the shoulders slithering out, aided by Mirren and Rita and Maudie pushing till her face resembled a balloon that was near to bursting.

'Oh, Mammy, Daddy,' she cried in a last tremendous breath before the baby was out, squirming, bawling, kicking, a bundle of vitality that needed no help from anyone to get its lungs to inflate.

'It's a girl.' Rita wrapped the baby in the logo-emblazoned towel and handed it over to its mother who took it, the tears of pride and relief pouring down her face.

'Tea, quick,' Rita gasped. With hands that were now steady, Vaila poured a cup. Rita grabbed it. But she didn't give it to the new mother; instead she applied it to her own lips and drank it down in two noisy gulps. 'I needed that,' she said as thankfully she sank into the nearest chair to the accompaniment of tension-releasing laughter from the other assistant midwives in the room.

Vaila went downstairs in a daze. Morven and Kyle were awake, sitting on the couch as if they were stuck to it and gazing at George as if awaiting further instructions. 'Stay there,' he ordered authoritatively,

'I'm taking Vaila outside for a few minutes to get some air. When I come back I want to see every finger and toe in the same place as now. If you move one muscle I'll know all about it and will have to take further disciplinary action.'

The children went rigid in their endeavours to retain their immobility. George's lips twitched. Turning away he put his hand under Vaila's arm and hurried her outside to the little knoll under the apple tree where he wrapped his arms around her and stroked her hair. 'There, there,' he said soothingly. 'It must have been terrible for you up there. I'm sorry I wasn't plucky enough to come in with you but knew I wouldn't really be welcomed at such a private event.'

Vaila lifted her head and looked him in the eye. 'It wasn't terrible, it was wonderful. I've seen calves and lambs being born of course but never ever a real live human baby. For months now I've watched Aunt Maudie growing bigger yet somehow the lump in her belly didn't strike me as being a real live human being until I saw it being born.'

'I might have known you'd say that.' George's voice was low and seductive. 'You're quite a girl, Vaila Sutherland, and I'm glad I was here to share the experience with you.'

'Only some of it,' She hid her smiles against the lapel of his jacket. 'Don't forget, you chickened out at the last minute and made me go into that room on my own. It had nothing to do with feeling unwelcome. You were just downright scared and you know it.'

'I've already admitted that.' His face was very close to hers. She could feel his breath fanning her cheek.

Before she could move away he lowered his head and touched her lips with his. 'Promise me you'll come out with me sometime,' he murmured. 'You're young yet but another few months should soon solve that. Till then I'll be waiting . . .'

All at once a tornado seemed to hit them and Mark was suddenly there, pulling George off Vaila and punching him on the nose with such force he was sent flying onto the grass to lie there shaken and disorientated.

'Stay away from her. Just stay away,' Mark was shouting furiously. 'Dare to go near her again and I'll kill you, even though you are the laird's son.'

Vaila rounded on him. 'How dare you do that to him? Who do you think you are, bossing people about and interfering in my life? Don't you know you're making a fool of yourself as well as jeopardising your job at Crathmor? Oh, what's the use, you're a fool, Mark Lockhart, and I'll never speak to you again after this!'

She ran to help George to his feet. He was wiping blood from his nose and shaking his head in an effort to clear it. Leaning on her arm he allowed her to help him to the bench under the apple tree where he hunched his shoulders and placed his head between his knees.

Vaila was aware of voices. Finlay had at long last come back with Effie and they were going into the house. She looked at George. 'Come inside and I'll get you a brandy. You look as if you could be doing with it.'

'No, I'll be fine in a minute. I don't want anyone seeing me like this and I'll be off soon anyway. You go on, I think Mark might have something to say to me and won't want anyone around to hear what it is.'

Vaila hesitated, wondering if it would be safe to leave the two young men alone together. But Mark, who had retreated a few yards, appeared to have calmed down as rapidly as he had flared up and with a last angry glance at him and an anxious one at George she ran back to the house.

As soon as she had disappeared George, still wiping the blood from his nose with a large spotted hanky, got up and went over to Mark. 'Normally I wouldn't have let anyone get away with that but this time I'm going to make an exception because of two things. One, you're a damned good pony man and I wouldn't like you to lose your job because of what happened. For another, you and I have always been friends and I wouldn't like that to change just because I made a pass at Vaila. She'll be free to choose whom she wants to spend her time with when she's grown up a bit more. For now, you have some growing up to do yourself and will need to learn not go flying off the handle at the least provocation. Agreed?'

Mark, decidedly shamefaced by now, stuck out his hand and said gruffly. 'Agreed, and I'm sorry I punched you on the nose, but that doesn't mean to say I won't do it again if I have to, only next time I'll make sure you see me coming before I let fly.'

George gave a wry grin. 'If there is a next time I'll be glad to take you on. I can't and won't promise not to touch Vaila again. She's a very beautiful girl. Every time I come back to Kinvara I see a difference in her but she has a bit of maturing to do yet and I mean to be around to enjoy seeing that happening.'

'That makes two of us,' Mark returned grimly. 'You're in a different class from Vaila, you're used to getting your own way and are only amusing yourself with her till you find someone of your own ilk. She's a bright girl and will soon get wise to you.'

'I'll take my chances on that.' George had had enough of Mark's verbal fencing and began to move away. He had made his peace in a very chivalrous fashion but wasn't prepared to argue the point any further. The two parted amicably enough but it was an uneasy truce and both of them knew it.

Chapter Ten

Effie had gone upstairs as soon as she had arrived at River House. From the baby she had removed the towel that proclaimed its allegiance to Glasgow and had proceeded to cut the birth cord and tie it in a neat knot. She then turned her attention on Maudie and ended her administrations by dressing the new mother in a fresh cotton nightgown and pink bedjacket to await her visitors.

The baby was placed on Maudie's billowing bosoms and that lady lay beaming on her pillows, posing for all she was worth, all enmity against her husband forgotten now that the trauma of giving birth was over.

Downstairs, without George's commanding influence, the children had reverted back to their normal boisterous selves and were running about the kitchen, whooping and yelling and demanding to see their new sister. Morven was still determined to give it a smacking to make it cry, a procedure she deemed necessary to its survival after she had heard her elders discussing one 'poor wee thing' who had arrived purple at birth and needed to be thoroughly slapped as well as turned upside-down in order to get its life forces to function.

As soon as Effie made an appearance in the kitchen,

Finlay put Kyle on his shoulders, took Morven's hand and marched with them up the stairs to view the latest addition to the family, much to the relief of everyone in the room, not least Effie who declared herself to be 'whacked' after all the labours and excitements of her working day.

Now the nurse sat, a cup of tea in her hand, the family's large ginger tom on her lap, her fifteen-year-old mongrel dog, Runt, sound asleep at her feet, congratulating Rita and Mirren on the fine job they had done in her absence, albeit in a rather offhand manner since she didn't take kindly to playing second fiddle to anyone who was 'not in the profession'.

She then went on to wax lyrical about the part Mark Lockhart had played in getting them all up to River House safely, a wheel having parted company with Ramsay's trap on the way back up the farm track.

'Mark was passing on his way to the smiddy with some ponies,' Effie went on to explain. 'In no time at all he had organised Willie Whiskers and a new wheel was brought up and fixed on. Oh, he's a good lad is Mark. He came with us the rest o' the way just to make sure we got here safely and I won't forget his kindness to me when he saw how upset I was. He's young, I know, to be carrying a hip flask around with him but he's out in all weathers in that job o' his and I was glad o' the wee drop he held to my lips in order to revive me.'

Pausing just long enough to drain her cup of its contents she went on, 'I'll never forget the bumping I got when that trap broke down. 'Tis a wonder to me every bone in my body remained intact and I know my bladder will never be the same again for I just about wet my breeks when the accident happened. Ramsay, of course, was most unsympathetic and was only worried in case his damt axle was broken as well. If he hadn't been driving so fast none o' it would have happened and I would have been here in time to deliver Maudie o' her bairn.'

She gave a disdainful sniff at this point. 'As it was he made us later still by insisting that he and Rob be dropped off at Vale O' Dreip on the way up here. Out o' harm's way as he put it though in my opinion he was just plain scared to be in the same house as a woman giving birth and wanted Rob to keep him company till it was all over. The nurse before me told me how he used to take himself off when his own bairns were being born and never reappeared till he was certain it was safe to do so and the messy bits cleared up.'

At this point she turned suddenly to gaze questioningly at Vaila, her large pointed nose positively twitching with curiosity when she shot out, 'And what was all that about with young George MacPherson? I saw you out there as I was coming in. Your arms around him and Mark standing by watching. Surely you're no' into seducing the lads at your age and making them fight one another for your attentions.'

Effie's reputation for nosiness was second to none. She revelled in juicy gossip and chitter chatter of all kinds and Dr Alistair MacAlistair of Butterbank House had always been hard put to instil in her a sense of the propriety that was needed in a job such as hers. Effie, however, went on her way regardless, cheerfully probing, poking, needling, revelling in the confidences that some were rash enough to disclose, believing that promises were meant to be broken and that secrets existed only to be revealed.

'She has nothing in her life but that pig and that dog o' hers,' Donald of Balivoe had always sourly maintained, while Gabby Cochrane of Clockwork Cottage believed it was the lack of a man in her life that made Effie the 'prying old witch' that she was.

But Effie stoutly refuted all such slights on her character and said if she'd been married she would never have reached her present age of forty-two in sane and sound health. She was quite happy, she declared, living with her adored animals for company and her croft to keep her occupied. A husband would just have cluttered up her house and driven her crazy with his wants and demands.

Her buoyant nature and relish for life did indeed uphold this statement. Despite her loose tongue she was well liked in the community and was a reliable source of information for those cronies of hers who were just as eager as she was to make their neighbours' affairs their own. There were times however when Effie's tongue was just a mite too sharp for her own good and that day in Maudie Sutherland's kitchen was one of them.

After the incident with George and Mark, Vaila was in no mood for interrogation of any sort and her face reddened at Effie's words. Before anyone knew what was happening she had flown into one of her hot tempers. Green eyes flashing she told the nurse to mind her own business, pointing out that what she did with her life had nothing at all to do with anyone else and that it was high time Effie, instead of delivering

children, had one of her own before it was too late –
if any man had the courage to go near her.

'As for that nose of yours,' she ended furiously,
'you know where you can put it! It's long enough
and big enough and would be as well up there out o'
harm's way instead of out here sniffing around like
a bloodhound in heat!'

With that she threw out of the house, leaving
behind an electrified silence, though on Mirren's part
it was tempered by a memory of Morna saying something similar to Ramsay many years ago when he had
gone to Oir na Cuan to meddle in matters that did
not concern him.

'Well!' Effie found her tongue, her large mobile
mouth trembling as if on the verge of tears. 'Who
would have thought it of Vaila? And her just a
child who should be showing nothing but respect
for her elders. Looking as if butter wouldn't melt
in her mouth when all the time she's sizing up good
people like myself and thinking terrible things about
them. It just goes to show what is going on in her
mind regarding matters that are personal and private
to a body like myself. Oh, I've never been so insulted
in all my born days. Never! And I'll take care no' to
go near that particular Sutherland for many's a long
day to come. I'm sorry for you, Rita, I really am,
having a grandchild like that in the family, running
wild wi' boys and going mad wi' rage just because she
was asked a simple question that was only innocently
intended.'

During this discourse Rita had arisen and was over
at the window, her hanky stuffed to her mouth, the
tears running down her face. But they weren't of

sorrow or of shame. She had loved every minute of Vaila's impassioned words to the nurse who had, on countless occasions, been the source of much irritation to Rita on her sojourns to Vale O' Dreip, both to pry into the affairs of that household and to dispense the sort of gossip that would have been best kept to herself.

Rita wished, oh how she wished, that she'd had the courage to speak out as Vaila had done just now and it was all she could do to hide the tears of her merriment in the folds of her hanky and choke back the bubbles of laughter rising into her throat.

Over by the fire, Effie was somewhat gratified by what she took to be a show of regret on Rita's part. The nurse removed the cat from her lap and slid her foot from under Runt's head. She got up, she went over to Rita to commiserate with her on her misfortunes. If it hadn't been for a timely interruption from Mirren, declaring that she smelled burning, Rita would have disgraced herself in front of the nurse for evermore.

As it was, Effie was fully occupied for the next few minutes. A glowing cinder had erupted from the fire to land directly on Runt's back and the smell of singeing hair filled the room. Effie shrieked and ran to wet a towel she found under the sink, this time emblazoned in crimson with the words, *Scotland Forever. Who's like us? Damned few and they're a' deid.*

Vaila went running away from River House, fuming with rage, mad at herself for having let go as she had but glad that she had put Effie in her place. It had been too much to bear after all that taken place between herself and the two boys. As if that hadn't been bad enough! Mark hitting George, threatening him, dancing around him like one demented. Oh, wait till she got the young pony man to herself! She would give him a piece of her mind all right! He had no right to interfere in her life. Once upon a time, not so long ago in fact, she had liked Mark; they had got on well together and had laughed and played in easy-going harmony. Now he had changed into a creature she didn't know at all and didn't want to know if he went on behaving like a madman.

Poor George. She could still see his face when Mark had flown at him like a bat out of hell! And he'd been so kind to her too. His arms around her, his words of sympathy, his lips so close. She shivered at the memory. It was all too much. She wasn't ready for that sort of thing yet – except – just a little while longer with him would have been nice . . .

She pulled herself up. Why was she thinking these things? Maybe Effie was right about her after all. It would be very easy to get a bad name in a place like Kinvara. She *did* enjoy the company of boys. Despite herself a small thrill went through her at the idea of them fighting over her. But *seducing* them! That was taking it a bit far. She wasn't even very sure of what the word meant though knew it had something to do with being a temptress. The sort of expression Mrs Prudence Taylor-Young would use if she'd been witness to the incident.

Vaila went on her thoughtful way, the fire fading from her cheeks as her temper gradually abated in the clear cold air of the March day. She began to remember all the good things Effie had said about Mark. How he had come to the rescue when Ramsay's trap had broken down, his consideration towards the nurse, his help in getting them up to River House all in one piece.

'Oh!' Vaila put her hands up to her face as she recalled her own angry words to Mark. In just a short space of time she seemed to have upset quite a few people and now she didn't know what to do by way of appeasement. She wasn't going to apologise to Effie, not yet anyway, and she certainly wasn't ready to go running to Mark with her tail between her legs. She tried to imagine what Rebecca would have done in like circumstances but knew the answer to that almost at once. Rebecca would have allowed both offenders to stew in their own juice for a while. The miller's daughter did not forgive and forget so easily and was quite relentless in her dealings with anyone who had wronged her. Stalemate could exist indefinitely where Rebecca was concerned and it was only a very few favoured individuals who had ever heard utterances of apologies from her lips.

Vaila sighed. There seemed no ready solution to her problems. The tall chimneys of Vale O' Dreip hove into view. With emotions running high she pushed open the gate and went on into the yard, pausing for a few moments at the door before squaring her shoulders and going resolutely inside to be immediately met with a barrage of questions which she was able to answer to everyone's satisfaction.

'It was wonderful to see a real live human baby being born,' Vaila enthused.

'You saw it?' Hannah asked wonderingly, 'You were there?'

'Just at the end, when it was coming out,' Vaila answered with perfect candour. 'I went to get towels and George helped with the hot water but he wouldn't come into the room with me to see it being born.'

'I should think not,' Ramsay stated firmly. 'The birthing room is a woman's domain and certainly no place for a young gentleman like George MacPherson. Where is he by the way? I thought he would have brought you down in his trap with Rita. It's well past teatime and she should be here by now to make it.'

Hannah looked at him rather contemptuously and was about to make some derogatory remark regarding his lack of domestic capabilities when a warning glance from Rob stayed her tongue. Hannah had never known an easy-going relationship with her father-in-law. It was only in recent years that she had started coming to Vale O' Dreip on a regular basis and then it was only to visit Rita and allow the children to meet up with one another.

Vaila likewise did not always see eye to eye with the grandfather who had rejected her as being 'a bastard of unknown origin' before he had discovered that she was Rob's child and therefore a true blood Sutherland after all.

Now that young lady looked the master of the house straight in the eye as she told him, 'George isn't coming down, he left River House in a bit o' a hurry. Uncle Finlay will bring both Granma Rita and Aunt Mirren back in his own good time.'

'Hmph! I don't like your tone, my girl,' Ramsay snorted. 'And what's all this about George leaving in a hurry? He seemed keen enough to be in on the action the last time I saw him. I hope you and he didn't have words. I saw the way you were making eyes at him when you were sitting here in my kitchen earlier and just hope you haven't upset him in any way.'

'I didn't make eyes at him.' Vaila defended herself hotly, her temper rising to the surface once more. 'He was making them at me as fine you know. Just because he's a MacPherson doesn't mean to say he can't behave like any other man given half a chance.'

'That's right.' Hannah got up and put her arm protectively round her stepdaughter's shoulders. 'Master George likes the girls from all I hear and besides, men don't make eyes at girls, they ogle them, it's a plain fact, as I myself have noticed whenever they are in the company of attractive young women.'

Ramsay felt uneasy. He found himself at a disadvantage. On one hand there was his granddaughter with the spirit of Morna Jean Sommero flashing out of her eyes, on the other was his daughter-in-law whom he had once ignored as a being not worthy of his attention. He had rejected both of them in different ways and now it seemed they were paying him back.

Vaila was young yet, he could handle her, she was blood kin after all and was affectionate and loving despite her fiery nature. Hannah was a different kettle of fish altogether. That thinly disguised hostility in her eyes, the way she had of watching him, as if she knew more than she let on about his past, about the mistakes that tormented and worried him to this day.

He was never easy with Hannah in the house; she even more than Rita had the ability to make him squirm and wonder what was going on in her mind. He knew she put up with him only on sufferance and felt that she was just waiting for a chance to get her own back on him for the way he had treated her. Revenge. It was a dirty word. She had asked more questions than anyone when Euan had been dumped on his doorstep and he had caught her once or twice staring at the boy in a puzzled fashion. To this day she wondered aloud what had prompted Catrina to take such a drastic step.

'Her own son,' she would say, gazing at Ramsay as she spoke, 'Running off and leaving him like that, here at Vale O' Dreip, and her with a family o' her own to look after him right here in Kinvara.'

Ramsay somehow always managed to bluster his way out of the hot seat but he hated his daughter-in-law for her doggedness. Like a cat with a rat, never letting go, holding on grimly by the throat, slowly choking the life out of him . . .

Ramsay shifted uncomfortably at Hannah's words. Was she getting at him? Again? This time using a different approach? One that he didn't care to enlarge on since it seemed to be directed at him personally.

Rob saw his father's face and stood up. 'Come on, you lot, it's time we were going. Vaila, go upstairs and get Essie, she can ride home with Andy in the cart and Finlay will no doubt give Mirren a run back in time for her tea.'

A relieved look flitted over Ramsay's countenance as everyone made for the door. But the triumphant one that Hannah threw at him soon wiped the smile from his face. He stood on the step watching the visitors making their way down the track, and not even the comforting touch of Aidan's hand in his could take away the doubts festering in his mind.

Chapter Eleven

The talk that night in No 6. Keeper's Row was all about Maudie and her new baby and moved from there to a humorous account from Rob regarding the breakdown of his father's trap and Effie's certainty that she would have 'died altogether' but for Mark Lockhart's timely intervention.

Vaila kept fairly quiet at this point, not wishing to mention Mark's name in case George might be linked with it and everyone started to ask too many questions that might involve her.

She was glad therefore when her Granma Harriet arrived with her husband Charlie Campbell of Butterburn Croft, both of them bearing belated gifts for Andy's birthday, Harriet's voice booming out as she explained they hadn't been able to manage on the exact date because Charlie hadn't quite finished the beautiful model he had made of a sailing ship which he now proudly handed over to his delighted step-grandson.

The arrival of the visitors gave Vaila the breathing space she needed. No one could get a word in edgewise when Harriet was on the scene. She sat herself down, accepted a cup of tea and was quiet for two minutes as the day's happenings at River House were related all over again, during which time Rob and Charlie took the opportunity to slip outside to the shed where the first stages of the rocking horse for Emily's baby were in progress.

Hannah had no sooner finished speaking than her mother, a strong attractive dark-haired woman of 'sixty and a bit', leapt into the momentary lull with a tasty titbit of local news. 'You'll never guess,' she began, tossing off her scarf and her hat as the heat from the fire began to make her sweat, 'I was speaking to Mattie MacPhee in The Bread Oven this afternoon who was speaking to Maisie Whiskers in the butcher's this morning and it was only because Maisie was in Big Bette's shop first thing that she heard the news before anybody.'

'Heard what, Mother?' Hannah asked anxiously, bemused as she frequently was by her mother's rapid and often confusing accounts of village gossip.

'About Jessie MacDonald, of course,' Harriet returned, looking at her daughter as if she wasn't quite all there.

'I can't read your mind, Mother – not that I would want to – it would be far too muddled,' Hannah said with more than a touch of her own particular brand of sarcasm. 'Slow-witted I may be but at least I know what I'm talking about when I do talk. What is it about Jessie MacDonald that you're so anxious for us to hear you can't even get the words to come out properly?'

Harriet threw her daughter a pained look before continuing in a somewhat slower vein, as if she was spelling out the words rather than speaking them. 'Jessie has played her final trump card, that's what.

For years now, ever since I married Charlie, she's fumed and fretted about not having a man o' her own and blamed me for stealing Charlie from under her nose. Well, now she's got one, at last she's hooked a pair o' trousers, worn and threadbare they may be but it's what's inside them that interests Jessie, no' to mention what's lining the pockets. If she's lucky she might get some mileage out o' them yet, but it's no' so much the money as the status. Jessie aye wanted the status that only a wedding ring can give her and now she'll go around with her nose in the air and think she's the only body in the whole o' Kinvara to get herself wedded to a man o' some standing.'

Hannah gave up then. With a flippant little flourish of her hand she signalled for Vaila to take over where she had left off while Andy and Mirren smiled to one another and Essie climbed onto her grandmother's lap to play with the stag horn buttons of her Aran cardigan.

'Granma,' Vaila began carefully. 'We still don't know who this man is that you're talking about, except that he wears worn trousers with money in the pockets.'

'Gabby Cochrane of course!' Harriet exploded. 'Surely that goes without saying. Jessie's been after him for years, ever since thon time she looked after him when he was ill in bed after his heart attack. Oh, she must be laughing up her sleeve right now and poor Gabby must be wondering if he's done the right thing accepting her after years of avoiding her. He was quite happy being a widower and a canny one at that. He was aye careful wi' the pennies and must have put by a tidy little nest egg with nothing else to spend his money on but his keep.'

'Well, now we know,' Hannah said a trifle sulkily. 'At least Jessie was never successful in getting Charlie to the altar after he made it plain he preferred you to her.'

'Of course he preferred me. He would never have wed that particular MacDonald. The resentments are still simmering away in her head about the wrongs the Campbells did to her clan way back in the dark ages. Charlie was lucky to escape her clutches as he did. He got a prize when he got me and hardly a day passes but he tells me so.'

The menfolk had come back and Charlie went off with his prize, much to Hannah's relief since there were occasions when her mother's overbearing manner was hard to deal with.

After that, comparative peace reigned in the kitchen till Mirren, who had been fidgeting a good deal since Harriet's departure, suddenly jumped to her feet and said breathlessly, 'Oh, what's the use. I can't keep this to myself any longer, and since it's been a day of surprises I might as well spring one as well. I'm getting married, to a Shetland fisherman called Erik Magnusson. We've known one another for a number of years now but recently we became even better friends and decided on a wedding ring. So how's that for a bombshell to end the day?'

'Married?' Rob gazed at her in amazement. She had always shown resistance whenever he had broached that particular subject and had repeatedly maintained that she had never met anyone she liked well enough to share her life with. Self-sufficient, self-contained, cool and collected, that was Mirren, always claiming that the farm and the animals were enough for her and implying that she had no need for anything else to make her happy. Now, it seemed she had at last given in to her most basic feminine instincts. Mirren would no longer be Mirren alone but Mirren with a man, one who was going to give her the companionship and warmth that Rob had always felt she needed. Yet he was momentarily thrown off balance by her announcement. He and she had started off in opposition to one another but all that had gradually changed till now they shared thoughts and feelings that only they could understand, bound as they were by a common bond, the undying love and devotion they had known for Morna Jean, the intimate memories they shared whenever they met and spoke with one another. Mirren being married wouldn't alter that. But even as Rob tried to convince himself he knew that nothing would ever be quite the same again. Mirren was going to have a man of her own now, never again would she turn to him for the solace that his strength and companionship had provided . . .

He remained immobile in his seat, unable to go to her with his congratulations, while everyone else exclaimed and fussed over her and vied with one another to see who could talk the loudest.

'Can we come to the wedding?' Essie asked, her big blue eyes dreamy and faraway as she pictured a white bride in all her finery marching up the aisle.

'Will it be in Shetland?' Vaila added, enthralled at the idea of returning to that green and blue paradise over the sea.

'Can I wear my kilt?' cried Andy, whose pride in his heritage knew no bounds. Whenever he could he donned his clan tartan and a wedding was as good a chance as any to rig himself out in all his splendour.

'Of course you can all come and yes it's to be in Shetland.' Mirren laughed, pushing her hair back from her sparkling face as she spoke. 'One of the reasons for me coming here was to invite you across. I want Essie to be a flower girl, Vaila my bridesmaid. It's to be in the summer so I haven't got all that much time to prepare for it. That's why I can't stay here any longer than a week though I wish it was more the way it's flying in.'

The children gave whoops of joy and spoke excitedly among themselves, Hannah began to flap when she heard how soon the event was to be and declared that she had nothing in her wardrobe but rags and decided that they had all better make a journey to Inverness to do some shopping in the not too distant future.

Mirren looked at Rob, something in her eyes that seemed to beg for his approval, his understanding. He got up. He went to her and folded her to the hard wall of his chest, his mouth brushed her cheek. 'I'm so happy for you, Mirren, it's what I've always wanted, to see you settled with someone who will take care of you and love you.'

The fragrance of her hair infiltrated his senses, her skin was soft against his lips, a lump came to his throat and he drew back from her abruptly.

'And you, Rob,' she murmured. 'I'd like you to give me away if you will. As you did my sister to Finlay, so long ago now and yet so very very near.

Do you think you could bear to go through all that a second time?'

He swallowed. He gazed at her for a long long moment and then he nodded, 'Ay, I'll do that for you, Mirren. If you'd asked anyone else I would never have forgiven you. Right now, you'll have to excuse me. I promised Charlie I'd go down to the harbour to see him for a minute on some project he's working on.'

He strode across the room, wrenched open the door and went outside. But he didn't go down to the harbour. Instead his steps took him through the gathering twilight to the dunes above Mary's Bay and from there to the sheep track leading down to the white sands of the gently curving beach. He could have found his way blindfolded to Oir na Cuan, that little white house standing still and quiet at the edge of the ocean, its windows blank and empty where once the panes had been filled with lamplight and sunlight and dancing flickers of moon-silvered reflections from the sea.

The sturdy stone wall surrounding the house was broken in places where the sheep and the elements had invaded, the tiny garden, once full of roses and pinks and little blue hyacinths, was overgrown with weeds and nettles and all manner of thorns. Yet still the daffodils struggled through the tangle, the snowdrops poked above tufts of grass, the path, its edges ill defined, was yet clearly visible. Here, long ago, his feet had trodden, taking him eagerly to that sturdy wood door now hung with cobwebs and rose runners trailing down from the gutters.

The summer visitors had long departed; the house hadn't been let for several seasons. It was neglected and abandoned and rumour had it that the laird was thinking of removing the roof in order to avoid paying taxes. Rob had never been back to see it since Morna's death and now he stood, feeling the sadness and the emptiness all around him yet some separate part of him floating away to relive the warmth and the life that had once existed in this spot. The echoes of long ago came to him, that well-loved laughter, ringing inside his head, never letting go. He knew he shouldn't have come but somehow that last request of Mirren's had brought memories flooding back that he didn't care to recall.

As he turned away, the cold wind from the waves pulled at him – like a hand tugging at his clothing, wanting him to stay, trying to keep him in a time warp from which he needed all his strength to break free . . .

Johnny Lonely had lit one of his beacons above the great soaring cliffs of the Point. The orange glow against the darkening sky served only to enhance the loneliness of the bay, the bleakness of his mood.

Something compelled him to look back and he fancied he saw a face at one of the windows, a blob of grey-white in the blackness, a spectre of his imagination, coming back to haunt him, letting him know that his place after all was up there in Keeper's Row in the land of the living.

Chapter Twelve

Vaila had gone out at her father's back but her steps led her to a different place, a big sturdy grey building set among the fields of the laird's estate, predictably named The Paddocks, lamplit and welcoming and warm too when Grace Lockhart opened the door and ushered Vaila inside.

Sandy Lockhart was sitting by a roaring fire with his stockinged feet on the range, smoking his pipe and reading his paper by the light of a huge lantern hanging from the ceiling. Maida was very prettily perched on a stool by the piano, her fingers fluttering daintily over the keys but failing to produce more than a few listenable notes.

'It's just to pass the time,' she told her friend as she came forward into the room. 'I would love to be able to play properly but somehow never took in very much of what I was taught by my music teacher.'

'Money for old rope,' Sandy intervened sourly. 'Maida was never meant to play a mouth organ, never mind a piano, but that teacher o' hers kept saying the girl had it in her to learn if only she would try.'

'Trouble is, I never did try.' Maida sighed, tossing her fair tresses off her face and smiling beguilingly at her father.

'Will you have a cup o' tea, Vaila?' Grace Lockhart asked, throwing a look of despair at her daughter who merely turned her back and began rummaging among the books on the shelf.

'No, thanks, Grace,' Vaila said quickly. 'I only came to hand this book about ponies back to Mark. Is he at home at all?'

'Oh,' Maida swung round. 'That's the book I've been searching for. Really, I wish Mark would tell me when he lends things out to people. Give it here to me, Vaila, and I'll put it back on the shelf where it belongs, then come up to my room for a few minutes. I want to show you the dress I got for the village dance next week. I know everybody will be there and I want to look my best. Perhaps you could come here to our house and we could titivate one another.'

'No, sorry, Maida, but I won't be going. Hannah is taking us to Inverness to get some new things. Aunt Mirren is getting married in the summer and everyone is in a spin, including Aunt Mirren who says she'll never have everything ready on time.'

'Oh.' Maida looked disappointed. 'You never come anywhere with me these days, Vaila. Always you're busy somewhere else and I just keep getting left behind. I haven't seen anything of Joss either and I'm beginning to think he's got something else on the go. He and that Rebecca Bowman seem as thick as thieves though I can't think why anyone would want to be in the company of such a bossy person.'

'Summer's coming,' Vaila said quickly, hating it when Maida was in one of her complaining moods. 'We'll go on picnics together, all of us, the way we did when we were younger.'

'That would be good.' Maida brightened immediately. 'Only thing is, all of you are working now and it won't be so easy for us to get together as we used to.'

'That problem could be quite easily solved.' Sandy glanced pointedly at his daughter.

'Oh, but it's better that I should be at home for Mother's sake,' Maida said sweetly. 'I'm good company for her and a help to her around the house. Isn't that so?' she ended in an appeal to Grace for confirmation.

'Ay, that's so, though sometimes I think it would be better if you were employed somewhere, Maida, you get so bored in the house and ought to get out more.'

'I'm not bored. Besides, I do get out, I'm always with the ponies in the paddocks, helping to groom and feed them.'

'Mark went out,' Grace explained as she saw Vaila's discomfiture at being in the midst of one of the frequent family arguments regarding Maida's idle nature. 'But he should be back soon if you care to wait for him.'

'No, it's all right, I'll see him another time.' Vaila said her goodbyes and made for the lobby, escorted by Grace as far as the door. 'Ach, Vaila,' she sighed, her sweet face hovering between smiles and regret. 'It's a pity you and Mark argued. He thinks the world o' you and would never deliberately hurt a hair o' your head.'

'He told you!' Vaila gasped. 'He shouldn't have done that because we never, at least . . .'

Grace laid a hand on her arm. 'He didn't have to, I know my son, he's like an open book where you're concerned. That's why he went out, he often does that at night, to be by himself, somewhere out on the moors where he can get peace to think and dream. I'll tell him you were here. It will comfort him to know you cared enough to want to see him.'

'Not to apologise,' Vaila flashed back. 'It's he who needs to do that. Oh, I'm sorry, I didn't mean to shout, I've done enough o' that for one day and don't worry about Mark and me. We've always been good friends and it will come out right in the end – only he doesn't own me, nobody does. I've told him that often enough and maybe someday it will get through to him.'

She went off into the night and went straight upstairs when she got home, going to the little box-room at the end of the corridor as she had done every night of Mirren's stay. Wrapping herself in a blanket she cuddled into her aunt and they talked together about the forthcoming wedding then went on to giggle over the day's happenings at River House.

'I should never have said the things I did to Effie.' Vaila held her breath as she remembered the scene. 'At the time I just couldn't help myself but it was a terrible remark I made about her nose. Every time I think about it I just freeze inside and know I'll have to make amends with her before very long.'

'It brings to mind a remarkable picture,' Mirren agreed. 'Just as it did many moons ago when your mother made a like comment to your Grampa Ramsay. One that put him very thoroughly in his place and made him respect Morna for evermore.'

'Really?' Vaila was totally entranced by this revelation. 'What did she say, oh, please tell me what she said! I won't be able to bear it if you don't.'

Mirren related the incident almost word for word, so vivid had it remained in her mind over the years. When she was finished the woman and the girl clutched one another and tried to smother their mirth into the pillows.

'Definitely like mother like daughter,' Mirren said when she could at last get air.

'I'm glad. I would hate to be a mouse and never stick up for myself in this life. Only thing is,' Vaila sounded pensive at this juncture, 'I'm worried about Granma Rita and what she must think o' me. Did she say anything to you about it?'

Mirren drew a deep breath. 'She couldn't – until afterwards. She almost died laughing over by the window and might have done too if a cinder hadn't fallen out of the fire on top of Runt. Effie had to go to his rescue with a wet towel, which gave Rita the chance to recover. I'm supposed not to tell you any of this in case you should get the wrong ideas about your elders, so keep it under your hat and don't breathe a word to anyone.'

'I won't, Aunt Mirren,' Vaila mumbled, too tired by now to get up and go to her own bed, asleep in minutes after all the excitements of that notable day.

The time soon came for Mirren to go home. The day before she left she and Rob went walking, taking the lonely road that led over the moors in order to escape the watchful eyes of the neighbours. It was a fresh cold afternoon in early April; the rustic grey-brown of the heather stretched away for miles, the brackish waters of the peat bogs reflected the slaty blue of the low-bellied clouds. A shower of rain on the bare horizon was sweeping over the distant hills like a hazy dark curtain, blotting out a glimmer of gold that had been there just minutes before.

It was a bleak empty landscape at this time of the year but if one looked close enough there were new signs of life everywhere: tender fresh heather shoots were springing up from the winter-black earth; the bog myrtle was sprouting its pale green buds; the rowan trees for all they were stunted and twisted were showing just a hint of new growth; water hens were dabbling busily among the sedges in the lochans; a buzzard soared majestically in the heavens while hares bobbed in the bushes and one lone deer peeped warily out from a rock spur some distance away.

It did not seem wrong for Mirren's hand to be held firmly in Rob's as they went along, snuggled close together to keep warm, an easy silence existing between them till she broke it by saying, 'Are you really glad for me, Rob? To be getting married, I mean? I know it came as a bit of a shock to you but you always did say I would make a good wife for someone.'

'Of course I'm happy for you.' His hand gripped hers tighter. 'It did come as a bit o' a shock but that's only because I was used to the idea of you being on your own, never giving anything o' yourself away, Mirren of the controlled and self-contained nature, an island unto yourself where no man dare land for fear of rebuff.'

She gave a short and mirthless laugh. 'You have a very poetical if direct way of expressing yourself, but you're right. I suppose I was waiting, looking for some super man who I knew in my heart didn't really exist. I think it was after seeing you and Morna together. How much you meant to one another, how deeply you loved and were so perfectly matched. I kept waiting for that to happen to me but now I know I was waiting in vain. A love like that rarely happens in anyone's lifetime and as the years went on I began to realise that I could easily end up alone and lonely if I went on believing in a dream.'

'You sound a bit like Vaila. She dreams of that too. The perfect love, the great hero of her romantic notions to come and sweep her off her feet. She's young yet and I can only hope she'll outgrow her ideals, for while it seemed that Morna and I had a matchless union we also brought a great burden of unhappiness to bear on one another. It is said that all our troubles end when we fall in love but in truth they are only just beginning. Being in love was a torment for me and my darling Morna and to this day it still is. I can't deny I'll ever forget her, the flame for her burns in me still and I know now it always will, no matter where I go, whatever I do. But thank God there are different kinds of love in this life. I've been lucky, I've been surrounded by every sort, and I hope so will you, Mirren, for you deserve to be happy.'

'Oh, Rob.' She clung to his hand, so warm and strong and reassuring. 'I wish, oh, how I wish . . .'

'Mirren.' He was looking at her urgently. 'You do love this man, don't you?'

'I'm thirty-eight, Rob. The farm is getting a bit much for me to run single-handed.'

'Is that your only reason for marrying him? Don't you love him, Mirren?'

'As much as I'll ever love any man. Erik is good and kind and trustworthy. He understands how I feel and it's enough for him. We'll be fine with one another, and at least I won't have to be alone any more during the long nights of winter when every other person in the world seems to have somebody but me.'

Rob put his arms round her and kissed her, a kiss that was warm on her lips and seemed to tingle through every hungry space in her body. Then he took her hand again as they turned and made for home. The rain shower had passed over, the sky was growing brighter, and over yonder above the misty green of the faraway hills, the golden light was back again, sweet and precious and beckoning.

THE KINVARA PENINSULA

Summer 1936

Chapter Thirteen

Hannah got the surprise of her life one morning in May when she opened the door to see Lord MacKernon of Cragdu Castle standing on her doorstep. It wasn't so unusual for Captain Rory MacPherson to drop into any house in the village that he fancied, being as much at home drinking tea or supping soup in a humble but and ben as he was enjoying a dram at his own fireside.

The MacKernon, as he was known, was a different matter entirely. The very position of his ancient clan seat, perched as it was on a cliff top, seemed to elevate him and his kin to another plane in the universe, one that might have been in heaven itself so infrequently was his lordship seen in and around the villages. His business interests in America and England took him away a lot and often he could be gone for months at a time, leaving his house and his lands in the hands of his staff and his managers.

He was certainly no stranger to the community at large, the summer fêtes and festive parties that he held in and around the Cragdu estate being among the most popular events in the local social calendar. All who had sampled The MacKernon's hospitality were loud in their praises of his generosity and many a deprived Kinvara family had reason to be grateful to him for the winter fuel he provided for their fires and for the food he put on their tables.

Dolores, his Boston-born wife, better known as Roley to her family, wasn't quite as elusive as her husband and thought it great fun to make little trips to the local shops and participate in some of the events of village life, occasionally accompanied by her elder son, Max Gilbert MacKernon, and his wife, Catherine, who had once taught in the Balivoe school.

Hannah was therefore understandably flustered to see the master of Cragdu standing there outside her house, his thin aristocratic face wearing an expression of benevolence when he saw how much his appearance had startled her. She looked around quickly, wondering perhaps if he had made a mistake coming to her door, her glance taking in the gleaming motor car in front of her. It was an ostentatious sight, The MacKernon's Bentley, parked outside No 6. of the Row, two large but elegant deerhounds sprawled in the back seat, the sleek lines of both the car and the dogs looking incongruously out of place next to the crumbling remains of an old farm cart that had been there for years and was used as a plaything by the Row's children.

Hannah knew that quite a few curtains must be twitching by now. Hastily she dried her hands on her apron and was about to extend one to the visitor when Breck did an unforgivable thing. With a very deliberate look on his face he went over to the car, lifted his leg, and generously sprayed the chrome hubcap of the wheel before going to the rear of the vehicle to gaze defiantly up at the two hairy deerhound faces that were gazing down at him.

'It's all right.' The MacKernon held up his hand to ward off Hannah's embarrassed apologies. 'My own dogs do it, they wouldn't be dogs if they didn't, but luckily they usually aim at other people's vehicles, otherwise those belonging to Cragdu would be reduced to rusting heaps by now.'

With a crimson face Hannah bade the visitor enter, wondering to herself as she did so how she was going to cope with a gentleman of his standing. He did not however beat about the bush, coming to the point of his visit almost as soon as he was seated.

'It's really Andy I've come to see,' he explained as he settled himself more comfortably and placed his hat on his lap. 'I have a proposition I would like to put to him and wonder if you would be so good as to fetch him for me.'

Only too glad to give herself a breathing space, Hannah went out to the lobby. Normally she would have bawled at her son from the foot of the stairs but on this occasion she thought it would be better to go up and get him.

Andy was at his desk in his room, so absorbed in what he was doing he hadn't been aware of anything that existed outside his writing domain. He was therefore just as excited as his mother when he heard about the gentleman who awaited him downstairs.

'He's in the kitchen.' Hannah's hand flew to her mouth. 'Oh, I didn't even ask him into the parlour, I was so flabbergasted at the sight o' him. What must he be thinking? Breck's hairs everywhere. The breakfast things not properly cleared from the table. That stain on the rug where Essie spilled tea. Books and papers scattered on the window ledge . . .'

'Mother, what does he want?' Andy broke in anxiously.

'I don't know. He just asked for you as soon as he came in. Something about a proposition he wanted to make.'

There followed a rapid exchange of unanswerable questions between mother and son before the boy squared his shoulders, took a deep breath, and went stoically downstairs as if he was about to face a lion in its den and was girding his loins for the confrontation.

The MacKernon looked oddly at ease as he sat there in a big scuffed moquette armchair by the window, Breck's head on his knee, his glasses on the end of his nose as he scanned the pages of last week's newspaper, not at all disturbed by the homeliness of his surroundings nor by the fact that he shared his seat with one of Essie's grinning rag dolls.

'Ah, Andy.' At the boy's entrance he put down the newspaper and leaned forward. 'Sit down, I'm not going to eat you, just to tell you about a little idea that's been in my mind for some time now.'

Andy sat. Breck went immediately over to his young master and lay at his feet while Hannah busied herself making tea and surreptitiously scraped one or two mouldy patches from some pancakes that had been lying too long in the pantry, all she had in the house by way of titbits.

The Clan Chief was telling Andy that he had heard

all about Captain Rory's kind gift to him on his birthday and went on to say, 'I saw the pony myself, before MacPherson gave her to you, and a handsome little beast she is too. But you'll grow out of her in a couple of years and will need something bigger and stronger to pull you along. If you came to work for me at Cragdu you could earn some money to buy another when the need arises. My library is in a dreadful state, everything needs sorting and cataloguing. I know how interested you are in books and all the reading you could ever want is there on my shelves. It would take up a year of your time at the least and afterwards you can be free to do as you like – if you wanted to that is. There would always be something at Cragdu to keep you busy but we can discuss that later.'

Hannah smiled to herself when she heard all this. The people of Kinvara were continually amused by the competition for supremacy in the popularity stakes that prevailed between Captain Rory and The MacKernon. Rivalry had always existed between the two houses, mostly regarding land rights and ownership, and she couldn't help wondering if this was just another ploy of The MacKernon's to get even with the laird.

He sounded genuine however and the glow on Andy's face was rewarding enough for anybody, whatever the reasons behind the offer. There came a lull as tea was laid on the table and the pancakes, which Hannah had heated in the oven and spread lavishly with butter and jam, were offered.

The Clan Chief sat back as he drank his tea and ate the pancakes with relish. 'I must say, Mrs Sutherland,' he commented when at last he was wiping his sticky fingers on his handkerchief and mopping the jam from his luxuriant black moustache. 'You certainly know how to cook. These were delicious and even more palatable warmed up like that – which reminds me: my wife sent me with a message. She's a great fan of The Bread Oven as you know and wondered if you would be good enough to lay aside two of your large apple pies which she'll collect personally later today.'

'The Bread Oven!' Hannah's hand flew to her mouth. 'I nearly forgot, I should have been there half an hour ago. Oh, I'm sorry, your lordship, of course I'll do as you ask and will see to it myself the minute I get there.'

The Clan Chief stood up. He made mannerly apologies to Hannah for keeping her from her work then laid his hand on Andy's shoulder. 'No need to give me your answer right away, young man. Take a trot up to Cragdu when you've had a chance to think about it. If I'm not there, my wife will see to you, failing that, John Taylor-Young, my secretary, is always in his office for a chat and a bit of advice.'

He took his leave. The Bentley sprang into life and purred gently away. Hannah allowed a few minutes to elapse before going out to watch as the car receded into the distance. The curious face of Janet's cousin, Kathy MacColl of Vaul, appeared in the aperture of Janet's door. ''Tis yourself, Hannah,' she observed as if surprised by the other woman's presence, her fingers rummaging in the lapbag that was an essential part of her apparel and had earned her the nickname of Kangaroo Kathy. 'I was after seeing a motor car at your door and couldny help noticing that it was none other than the Clan Chief himself. Mind you, I wasny really watching to see who it was, for I know myself how annoying nosy neighbours can be. But I have to say I saw just the same and was really impressed by the sight o' that big shiny motor car sitting outside your house. When I was living in the islands my Uncle Tam told me it had all to do with my peripheral vision. Seemingly it was born before me and was a legend in the family. As soon as I could speak I was able to relate to everyone my first impressions of my very own birth though I'm thinking it's as well I don't remember much of what went on beforehand as even I am prone to bouts o' squeamishness.'

Kathy took her knitting out of her lapbag, propped herself against the door post, and went on rather breathlessly, 'It was a great tale at ceilidhs and the like. My Uncle Tam, bless him, used to say it would be a marvellous moneyspinner on the stage but that was before he ran away with Morag who was his second cousin on his mother's side. A sad, sad day that was for the family because we all liked Uncle Tam even though he used to do terrible things under his sporran when he was drunk and incapable.'

Hannah was continually bemused and occasionally terrified by the little Hebridean woman's whimsical mode of speech and was never so glad when Janet appeared just in time to check her cousin's fanciful flights of imagination. However Janet in her own way was just as curious as Kathy and couldn't help asking a few probing questions of her own regarding the visitor.

'Ay, it was The MacKernon right enough,' Hannah stated laconically. 'Come to see Andy on a business matter.'

Cousin Kathy and Janet both stared and Hannah relented enough to give away most of the details of The MacKernon's visit, ending, 'Oh, remind me, Janet, I've to put two large apple tarts aside for her ladyship by special request of the Clan Chief himself. She's coming to the shop later to collect them personally.'

'Och, she is a nice soul just, and so natural with it,' Cousin Kathy stated as her fingers busily flew. 'I myself had a visit from her once when she came to see how I was getting on with an Aran jersey I was knitting for her husband's birthday. She sat there in my kitchen, as ordinary as you like, supping tea and eating sugary doughnuts for all she was worth. "Call me Roley, everybody does," she gushed wi' those big teeth o' hers – put ten on a safety pin and leave at back of work, knit two together start o' next row. Boston-born she may be but there's nothing snobbish about her at all and I myself would like it fine if she and me could have another good chinwag some time real soon.'

Dazedly Hannah wondered if Roley had ever recovered from the first and was glad when Janet went to put on her coat and said she would meet Hannah at the door in five minutes so that they could make their belated way to The Bread Oven.

Andy was sitting at the table when Hannah went in, his chin in his hands as he gazed unseeingly out of the window.

'What do you think, Andy?' Hannah asked quietly.

'Would you like to go to Cragdu to work for The MacKernon?'

'It's a new door, Mother, straight into Cragdu Castle,' he said wonderingly, his face slightly pale with excitement. 'Captain Rory told me they would open up for me and thanks to him I can get anywhere now under my own steam – even to Cragdu. It sounds grand, the library, cataloguing the books, my first real job. I'll be able to help with my keep and buy you and Father lots o' nice things when Christmas comes around.'

Tears sprang to Hannah's eyes. 'I'll write to Rob this very night,' she promised, 'and tell him all about it. In fact, we'll all write, Essie too though she hates putting pen to paper except to make up fairy stories.'

Andy pictured his father, out there in the light-house, opening up his mail, rejoicing in the fact that his son was going to work for The MacKernon, making his way in the world like any other boy of his age.

Janet put her head round the door. 'Come on, Hannah, Cousin Kathy wants to walk along with us and says we ought to get going before the rain starts.'

Hannah groaned but went to put on her jacket, bracing herself for the journey to the baker's shop with Kathy in tow, no doubt chattering all the way and finding it in her to relate more mind-boggling tales about the Hebrides, of which she seemed to possess a bottomless fount.

Chapter Fourteen

Andy wasn't the only one for whom new doors were opening. Big changes were about to happen in the life of Johnny Lonely, the hermit who lived rough in Mary's Bay under the lowering cliffs of Cragdu. For weeks now Johnny had been awaiting a summons that would lead his footsteps to Crathmor House and when he returned to his hut one sunny morning in early June it was to find a note from the laird pinned to his door.

Carefully he set down his creel of lobsters and with hands that trembled slightly he scanned the short message then stood for a few moments to gather his thoughts together. The sea was blue that day, stretching back to an azure sky that was hazed with heat. The little islands beyond the bay were like pale ghostly ships that seemed to melt into an almost non-existent skyline. A stranger looking at them wouldn't have known they were islands at all but just a continuation of the pearly vapour hovering over the water to merge with the mists above.

Johnny gazed at the well-known and well-loved scene without really seeing it. The bubbling song of a curlew came to him from the rock pools down below, mingling with the piping notes of the oyster catchers and the strange haunting cry of the lapwings swooping and dipping as they made their way to the nesting fields.

Johnny knew it all so well. For more years than he cared to remember this had been his home, shared with the creatures of land and sea, a love-hate relationship when the winter winds roared and four thin draughty walls were his only protection against the elements. It was a strange and lonely life that he led. In the beginning, when it was unfamiliar and new to him, he had been afraid and uneasy for most of the time, but as the years passed he had grown used to the solitude and hadn't wanted very much to do with the world that existed outside his own small sphere.

In recent years all that had begun to change; the ghosts of his past had to some extent been laid to rest and gradually he was clawing his way back to the social niceties that everyone else took for granted. He was mixing more with his neighbours, facing life again, starting to enjoy meeting people but only those that he really liked and trusted. He had always avoided idle chit-chat and gossip and was careful to keep himself apart from instigators of trouble. But on the whole he was liking his fellow men better, he was ready for a change, he felt it in his bones. He didn't want to be known as Johnny Lonely any longer, the 'recluse who lived in squalor and poverty' as some of his more uncharitable critics had labelled him.

He glanced once more at the note before going into his hut to get down on his knees and rummage among the assortment of odds and ends that he had collected in his long association with nature's bounty. At last he found what he was looking for, a large cardboard box, battered and dented but still reasonably intact, lying beneath a pile of wooden spars he had gathered to make shelves.

Slowly he opened it. The faint odour of napthalene filtered out to him, still lingering after all this time. The first object he saw was the photograph of a little girl, sitting on a swing, bright-eyed and smiling, her youth and vigour held suspended in that one moment before the shutter clicked.

'Katie,' he whispered huskily, his fingers trembling once more as he plucked the picture out of the box to hold it reverently to his heart. The box was full of mementoes from his past: letters, postcards, photos, a tiny teddy bear that had been Katie's, a red ribbon she had worn in her hair . . .

With a sob he pushed it all aside, unable to bear these poignant reminders of the small daughter he had loved with such devotion and lost in such tragic circumstances. The items he wanted were there, lying at the bottom of the box: a white shirt; a tweed jacket; trousers; shoes; underwear; a tartan tie.

The shirt was yellow with age; the shoes had lost their shine; the rest of the garments were crumpled and creased but all were considerably better than his present shabby attire. He removed his wellingtons, he undressed. He washed himself from top to bottom with carbolic soap dipped into a bucket of cold water, then dried himself and donned the fresh clothing, though 'fresh' might be rather a hopeful description for items that had lain undisturbed for so long.

At last he looked at himself in the cracked mirror propped on top of a cupboard made of driftwood. He combed both his hair and his recently clipped beard and smiled wryly at his reflection. Not such a bad sight for one who lived rough as he did. 'Johnny, my lad,' he mouthed, 'you're coming out. After this day nothing will ever be the same again and the world had better watch out for you.'

He went outside and put two large lobsters in a bucket of sea water. In normal circumstances he never secured his hut but it was summer, a few spare holidaymakers might be lurking, and so he jammed his door with a stout piece of wood and went off with the lobsters, taking a short cut to Crathmor House and the future that he hoped awaited him.

Rebecca was down on her knees praying, her clasped hands to her lips as her father uttered words she had heard so many times in her young life they had become meaningless to her. She opened one eye a peep and glanced outside. The June sunshine was beating hotly through the windows of the mill house kitchen and the sounds of the seashore filtered into the room: the waves beating gently to the shore; the gulls calling as they glided on the thermals; the crooning of the eider ducks in the bay; a corncrake rasping its way through the meadows, monotonously and steadily, ruining Joshua's concentration, unsettling and irritating him. She could tell that by the way a muscle in his jaw was working, the knitting of his bushy black brows, the way his eyes narrowed when he opened them to gaze round at his family, as if to make sure their attention wasn't lapsing, no matter the distractions.

The eyelids of Nathan and Caleb were twitching but yet remained closed, Miriam looked as if she was asleep right there on her knees, so still was her demeanour, so lifeless her pale, drawn, resigned features.

Satisfied, Joshua resumed his droning monologue regarding virtuous living and chaste thoughts, sounding as if he didn't believe very much in what he was saying either but was so used to a lifetime of uttering sanctimonious words they had become second nature to him. His black beard bristled, his lips became lightly flecked with spit, a fly on his collar was enjoying a spot of blood left over from the razor he had scraped across his face that morning to keep his sideburns in trim.

Miriam watched her husband through half-closed lids. She wished, oh how she wished that he would keel over right there and then and never get up again. She tried to imagine him lying there, helpless and still, silent at last – the Lord forgive her, it was a terrible thought, but there was no way she could stop the godless visions pouring into her mind.

Any feelings she might have had for him had shrivelled and died long ago, all that was left now was heart-numbing loathing and a desire to see him suffering as he had made his family suffer for more years than she cared to remember. Yet once she had loved him and would have done anything for him. She had even left her husband and her home in the

Borders to be by this man's side, taking her little daughter with her on a road that had only led to heartbreak and despair. Katie had died trying to find her real father again, a lonely death in a roadside ditch, cold, afraid, lonely.

Unable to forgive herself Miriam had left Joshua only to meet up with him again years later when he had bewitched her all over again. With Rebecca on the way she had entered into a bigamous marriage, too naive to realise that all he had wanted was her hard-won savings and a cloak of respectability so that he could carry on cheating his way into the hearts and minds of other vulnerable women.

She had gone with him from pillar to post, from one part of the country to another, always running away from something or someone till eventually she had persuaded him to return to her native Scotland to begin a new life in the old Cladach mill. Little had she known that coming to Kinvara would bring her back to the man known locally as Johnny Lonely, the husband she had deserted all those years ago in a small Border town where he had been a respected and much-loved head teacher in a school for boys.

In a confrontation with Joshua, Johnny had revealed the facts about the preacher's past life and had told Miriam the truth about her sham marriage to Joshua. Since that day Johnny had seldom let Joshua out of his sight and was constantly on hand to make sure that he behaved himself and didn't escape again, if only for his family's sake.

And that was the reason Miriam stayed too, for the children. She hadn't been much of a mother to

them but she was all they had and they had a few
years of growing up to do yet – especially Nathan.
Miriam shifted one stiff hip, closed her eyes, and gave
herself up to a state of mind-numbing blankness that
almost amounted to self-hypnosis.

Nathan felt his weak bladder filling up and prayed
to God not for purity of spirit but for the strength
to hold in his water till his father had finished
speaking. He wriggled and tightened his buttocks,
wishing he had the courage to just get up and run
to the sanctuary of the latrine where he often went
to sit and gaze at the world through a split in
the door.

It was amazing what could be seen through
that small crack. It was like a telescope, making
everything seem bigger and brighter, yet looking
in from the outside it was difficult to discern
anything in the cramped dark enclosure. Perhaps
human beings were like that, gazing out on their
surroundings from the slits of their eyes yet unable
to see inside one another. But the eyes were the
mirror of the soul. Johnny Lonely had told him
that, and he knew his father's soul must be as
black and empty as his eyes for although his mouth
spoke words of goodness and light his spirit didn't
hear them.

Nathan remembered the last time Joshua had hit
him with that hated leather belt he wore round his
middle. It had been when everyone else was out of the
house. No one knew about these hidings his father
gave him to 'keep him on his toes' and he was too

terrified to tell anyone, not even Rebecca who had always tried to shield him from harm. Nathan vowed that one day he would run away from the mill and the misery that had been his under his father's rule. He would be fourteen soon, small for his age and not very strong, but he would find the strength to do something with his life. He had always wanted to be an engine driver and some day he would; Rebecca had told him he could do anything if he really wanted it badly enough.

Caleb was thinking about girls, especially that Maida Lockhart with her seeming fragility yet that air of sexual hunger about her that made him sweat every time he thought about her. He had kissed her once or twice and that last time in the Crathmor paddocks he had managed to feel one of her breasts before she had pushed him away with an odd little secretive smile on her face. The size of that breast had surprised him and just went to show that some things were not as they seemed from the outside. These fluffy frocks she wore certainly covered a lot. That breast had been big and firm and just asking for it, the way the nipple had hardened under his thumb. Caleb licked his lips and tightened his thighs and wanted to run to the latrine but for a very different reason from that of his brother.

Maida of course thought herself to be in love with Joss Morgan but Joss certainly didn't love her. He and Rebecca were always mooning about with one another and one day there could be trouble if Joshua found out. Joss was a Catholic and Joshua didn't hold with any religious teachings other than his own. Maida didn't seem to be bothered with religion of any sort, she didn't seem to be interested in anything very much – except – Caleb's heart quickened. He would get her. One day she would give it to him on a plate and smile when he came back for second helpings. He was sixteen now and could do what he liked. If it wasn't for Maida he would get out of this place but hadn't yet decided where he could go if he did.

The old man was still droning on. God, was there never an end to it? Where did he get it all from? Some deep dark snake pit within his black soul? Or was it just something that spouted out unbidden like skitters from a cow? Caleb sniggered into his hands and purported not to see the dark look thrown at him by his father.

Rebecca eased one cramped knee and allowed her thoughts to wander. In her mind she was no longer in the mill house kitchen but was somewhere else – in the arms of Joss Morgan, the woodland still and peaceful around them as they lay with arms entwined on the mossy earth, the blackbirds trilling from the leafy canopies above. She and Joss could talk for ages or just be quiet together; she knew him better than any other human being on the earth, even more than Johnny Lonely or Vaila Sutherland. They were kindred spirits, sharing so much of one another's thoughts and feelings, afraid sometimes of the spiritual bonds that tied them so closely. They argued certainly, fiercely and hotly, but always they came back together, more committed than before, drawing ever closer with each heartbeat, every kiss and touch. They weren't lovers yet, but she knew one day they would be. Childhood was gone from them now and they were ready for love. It took them all their time to contain their rising passions – those kisses, warm on her lips – those feelings, mounting inside her till there was an ache in her belly every time she remembered his hands on her thighs . . . her breasts tingled at the thought, she moved restlessly . . .

With a start she came back to earth. Joshua was glaring at her, asking her to repeat what he had been saying. She stared defiantly back at him. 'I'm sorry, Father,' she said loudly and boldly, 'I wasn't listening, my knees are in a cramp, I can't concentrate.'

'Mine too.' Caleb followed her example and stared steadily at his father.

'And mine,' Nathan added in a burst of desperation.

'Go to your room, Rebecca,' Joshua ordered angrily. 'Pray for your soul – and don't come out again till you have fully repented.'

Rebecca was glad to escape to her bare little room with its rough walls and sparse furnishings. But she didn't pray for her soul. Instead she went to her window, opened the sash and simply climbed outside. Her room was at the back of the house and it was on the level so there wasn't much of a drop. She had done this many times before and would do it many times again. The hot sunshine beat down on her, skylarks were singing up above, poppies and cornflowers waved in the meadows. She took a deep thankful breath and went off into the freedom of the glorious summer's day, knowing exactly where she was going and the shortest way to get there.

Chapter Fifteen

The laird was delighted with the lobsters Johnny had brought. 'Emily loves a good fresh lobster,' he said enthusiastically, standing there in his knickerbockers in his oak-panelled hall with the bucket in his hand, peering into the watery depths as if he would like to consume the contents right there and then. 'She can't get enough to eat these days and grows bigger by the minute.'

Johnny was looking awkward as he stood there gazing abstractedly at the stags' heads which adorned the walls, running his finger inside his collar and repeatedly swallowing his Adam's apple.

'Come away in, Johnny.' Captain Rory saw the hermit's discomfiture and steered him towards the sitting room where he invited him to sit down on a big comfortable sofa.

'You'll have a drink?' The laird was already over at the trolley, filling two large glasses with whisky, one of which he pushed into Johnny's hand. 'Bottoms up,' he cried heartily, 'Nothing like a drop o' the amber liquid to settle the stomach. Have some of that cake to soak it up though I myself prefer to take it neat and unhindered.'

The minute Johnny settled himself, the laird's Siamese

cat, Maggie, now very definitely a spoiled and cosseted feline since Sheba's much-mourned passing some weeks ago, jumped up on his lap to share daintily in his cake, her purrs filling his ears as he tried to balance both his glass and his cake in one hand in order to pay her the attention she was demanding with the other.

Captain Rory sat himself down and gazed at the hermit with affection. 'Now then, Johnny, you know why you're here. I want you to knock some sense into my youngest son. I wish you to take him for morning lessons leaving Miss Hosie to do her bit in the afternoon. I told you all this a while ago but I've been busy with one thing and another and also wanted to give you enough time to get used to the idea. Are you game, Johnny? Do you feel up to Ross Wallace? He's a good lad really but needs a bit o' discipline to keep him in order, nothing too drastic, just a man's touch. Miss Hosie has been finding it hard going trying to make him pay attention and I thought about you and how suited you might be for the job.'

Johnny took a good draught of his whisky and coughed. 'If you don't mind me asking, Captain MacPherson, how did you find out I was a teacher? I've been wondering this ever since you visited me a few weeks back. No one knows except . . .'

The laird put his hand on Johnny's shoulder, 'Ask no questions, Johnny, just say a little bird told me. It's all for the best, it's time you made some changes in your life, a house goes with the job, nothing fancy, a small cottage down by the woods, all the winter fuel you'll ever need and as much privacy as you want. You'll like it once you get used to it, no one will harass you, peace and quiet a'plenty and only the deer and the ponies for company.'

He paused for a moment and remembered his meeting with Miriam Bowman down on the shore. A strange, sad, lost-looking woman with haunted eyes and a hopeless expression. He and she had got talking and after a while she had opened up to him and it had all come pouring out, her true relationship with Johnny, the sham of her married life to Joshua, the tragedy of Katie's death, the shame and guilt she felt about leaving the good life she had known with Johnny for the unhappy one she had led with Joshua.

'I wish I could make it up to Johnny,' she had sobbed pitifully. 'He was a brilliant head teacher in a boys' school but I took all that away from him when I left him so heedlessly. When I think of the existence he's led since, shutting himself away from everyone, alone and lonely, pining for Katie, nothing much in a life that could have been so fulfilled if it hadn't been for me.'

There was very little that Captain Rory could do to help Miriam but from that day he had vowed to do something for Johnny. Now here the man was, refined and clever-looking under all the hair, a spark in his eyes that told of the life forces within, something about him that suggested strength and forbearance, nothing humble in his demeanour, pride and dignity in every line.

'I've asked Miss Hosie to come down and be introduced to you.' The laird sounded apologetic about this but had no chance to enlarge on the subject. As if on cue a light tap sounded on the door and Miss

Dorothy Hosie entered, flushed and slightly nervous-looking, her grey hair neatly coiffed, really quite attractive in a sparkling white blouse and generously cut skirt that successfully concealed her dumpiness.

Johnny stood up; a shower of cake crumbs and one very indignant cat descended on the carpet. He whipped off his hat, which he had forgotten to remove at the door, the governess was introduced to him, he held out his hand, briefly she laid her own in his callused palm then pointedly moved away from him.

How could the laird do this to her? She had been led to believe that a properly trained and respectable tutor was coming to relieve her of some of her duties after she had complained that she could no longer cope with the unruly Ross Wallace single-handed.

Now here was this dreadful man, smelling of fish and carbolic soap, a hermit and a scrounger, living like an animal in that smelly hut of his, tinkering about in his broken-down boat, scouring the wastes for his doubtful living.

'Sit down, sit down, Miss Hosie,' the laird invited affably. 'I was just telling Johnny here about my son and how hard it's been for you trying to keep him in order. Johnny is more than willing to join forces with you and help out in any way he can.'

Miss Hosie positively bristled at this. It made her sound incompetent in the extreme, a person unable to exert any sort of authority over one child, and no mention of the fact that the said child was nothing but a total upstart without manners of any kind, the fault of which certainly did not lie with her.

'I did not find it hard to keep your son in order, Captain MacPherson,' she intoned stiffly. 'I merely said he was difficult to handle and not at all easy to pin down when it came to drumming some learning into his ears.'

'Same difference,' the laird said flippantly, enjoying the sight of Miss Hosie's floundering and determined to prolong it. Johnny was worth ten of her and serve her right if she had her nose put out of joint. She had been getting on everyone's nerves lately with her whining and moaning and dropping hints about leaving them all in the lurch if she had to stand much more of Ross Wallace.

'I can assure you, Miss Hosie, Johnny has all the necessary teaching qualifications and I'm sure you and he can work out a suitable routine for my son.' Captain Rory was growing restless. It was a fine day and he wanted to be off to the hills to look over his ponies, but first he needed a cup of tea and some sustenance so he breathed a sigh of relief when Vaila came in with a laden tray and laid it on the table.

'Good girl, just what I needed.' He smiled at her approvingly and asked how Andy was enjoying his job at Cragdu Castle. 'Good, good,' he nodded when she had given him a glowing report. 'Mind you, MacKernon was aye grippy with the pennies. I hope he's giving your brother his due as far as wages go. It would take Samson and Goliath between them to get that library of his sorted out. A shameful way to treat good books and Andy deserves all he gets by way o' perks and sillar.'

Emily came in with her youngest son to partake of tea with everyone else. Ross Wallace was on his best behaviour. He had always been fascinated by Johnny and was so delighted at the idea of having him for a tutor he found it in him to be gracious and charming to his governess, offering her sandwiches and cake in his nicest manner and making her feel so much at ease she actually laughed when he made a little joke.

The atmosphere became lighter. Johnny ate and drank but made himself scarce as soon as he was finished. He was ill at ease when he was in company for any length of time and was glad when the laird suggested that they ought to go and view the tiny cottage that was to become the hermit's home.

'It's a start, man,' Captain Rory said kindly, glancing round the cosy little kitchen/living room with its well-worn but comfortable armchairs and deep sills that the previous tenant had filled with treasures from the woodland. 'And it's yours for as long as you want. Your time with my son will be for a year at least. After that there will be plenty of openings for a man of learning such as yourself. Good tutors are hard to come by and I'll make sure you'll always find a place. Meanwhile, I'm off. I'll see you in the morning, bright and early, and make sure you come armed, you'll need all the ammunition you can get to deal with Ross Wallace.'

He went away chuckling, leaving Johnny to acquaint himself with his new home: a reasonably sized bedroom smelling of fresh air with white muslin curtains at the window and a big fluffy counterpane on the bed; another tiny room with a single iron bedstead on which reposed a scruffy brown teddy bear wearing a large yellow ribbon round its neck. Who had left it there? he wondered. A little girl? So excited at the idea of going to a new home she had gone off leaving it behind? A boy? Setting off to school and a new life? Considering himself too old and too big to be bothered with teddy bears any longer?

Johnny went out of the room. He opened and closed cupboard doors and explored the overgrown garden with its wee hoosie situated behind some lavender bushes outside the back door. He stood for a long moment, gazing at the woods and the fields surrounding the house and the purpled hills way off in the distance. Then he went back into the house to the room with the iron bedstead where he sat down and touched the head of the teddy bear with his big rough gnarled fingers.

And Johnny Lonely bowed his head and cried that day, the teddy bear held tightly to his heaving chest as all his pent-up years of misery and loneliness came flooding out from a heart that had been sore and heavy for so long it had almost forgotten how to let go of the emotions that had held it in deepest bondage.

Chapter Sixteen

The Henderson sisters of Croft Angus weren't at all surprised to find Rebecca standing on their doorstep asking for Joss. They had come to like the miller's daughter very much indeed and now a state of near-conspiracy existed between them regarding Rebecca's relationship with the boy they thought of so highly.

Their dislike of Joshua Bowman was intense. He snubbed them whenever their paths happened to cross and looked at them as if they were creatures that had just crawled out from under a stone. Secretly they rather enjoyed the feeling of getting back at him by encouraging his daughter to get together with Joss as much as possible, both of them mesmerised by the idea of such young and romantic love blossoming on their own doorstep so to speak.

Rebecca in her turn was fascinated by the two who were known locally as The Henderson Hens because of their passion for keeping all kinds of poultry. In their striped butcher's aprons and big clumpy boots, their thickly lensed glasses and deep booming voices, they were certainly no ordinary individuals and were the topic of much curious speculation in the community at large. The more they tried to remain in the background the more their neighbours sought to peel away the veil of mystery that surrounded them. But in all their years of living in Kinvara nobody had discovered very much about them, much to the chagrin of beings like Effie Maxwell and Mattie MacPhee who were famed for their questing noses and their ability to hold on to 'a body's personal affairs like cats to rats' till something just had to give.

Rebecca did not pry and poke or ask too many questions, which were more reasons for the sisters to like her so much. They appreciated it when she came to visit and often invited her in over their doorstep, as they did now, leading her into their quaintly furnished kitchen with its twin rocking chairs, blue checked curtains and heavy ornamentation, much gleaming brasswear, little cross-stitch samplers made and proudly displayed by Wilma, 'the arty one', and big bowls of fruit and vegetables, nurtured and harvested by Rona, 'the practical one'.

'Sit down, dear,' invited Wilma beamingly, her horsey teeth flashing out as she spoke, 'Joss ought to be in soon and then we'll all have a nice cup of tea together.'

'Yes, sit down, dear,' echoed Rona. 'The darling boy works so hard and is always thirsty when he finishes. I've made some nice little scones and jam tartlets specially for him, he always has *such* an appetite with being in the fresh air all day and of course we just adore any excuse to spoil him.'

Rebecca talked easily with the sisters and soon had them laughing with her snippets of village news and colourful accounts of country life brought to the mill by local farmers.

The sisters were thoroughly entertained, for while

their own lives were anything but an open book they revelled in hearing about those of other people and when Joss at last came in they were wiping their eyes on their aprons at Rebecca's very apt descriptions of some of the more notorious local characters.

Joss reddened slightly at sight of Rebecca. He was hot and dirty and smelly, certainly in no fit state to sit at anyone's table nor indulge in frivolous chit-chat in the presence of Rebecca, so neat and clean in her severe grey dress and white cotton pinafore, her mass of dark hair caught up and held in a tortoiseshell clasp at the nape of her neck, a gleam of mischief shining in her eyes when she glanced up and held his gaze.

'Come in, come in, dear boy,' Rona cried heartily. 'Tea is all ready and waiting to be poured. Don't be shy, we won't keep you, just long enough to sample some of my little jam tartlets which I know are your favourites.'

'I'll have to wash my hands first,' he said quickly and seized the bucket from under the sink to go rushing outside to the well to fill it. He brought the brimming bucket to the surface and placing it on the grass he stripped off his shirt, cupped his hands, and splashed water all over himself, paying special attention to those areas of his anatomy which needed it most.

He wished he and Rebecca could just go off and spend the afternoon together but at this time of the year his services were much in demand in farms throughout the vicinity and he only had an hour or so before going off to the next one.

Still, one hour was better than none and he went back into the house to be fêted and fussed over by the sisters before he and Rebecca were able to take themselves off into the sunshine of the glorious June day. As soon as they were out of sight of the house he took her hand and they walked along in silence, their steps taking them into the heart of the countryside where only the birds held sway and an occasional rabbit popped its head out from the thickets. No one to see them, no one to disturb the spell of enchantment brought to them by the nectar of wild flowers growing in the hedgerows, the ripple of tall grasses swaying in the soft breezes, the scents of the cornfields glowing golden and ripe under the summer sky.

'Are we going to the river?' Rebecca asked, laying her head on his shoulder and holding his hand tighter. For answer he kissed the top of her head and walked briskly on, only slowing down when the gleam of tumbling water appeared through the trees. But they carried on for a little longer till they reached a deep dark pool known as the Giant's Bathtub, fresh and foaming and beckoning, a favourite place for fishermen when the salmon were leaping in the autumn but now quiet and deserted.

'I'm going in for a swim.' He said just that and quickly began to strip off. In a very short time his clothes lay in a heap where he had dropped them and he stood before her naked, a tall fair boy of sixteen, well built and strong, his muscles hard from the manual labour that had been his lot since schooldays.

'Are you coming?' His blue eyes held her dark ones, she hesitated only briefly before she too rushed out of her clothes, resisting the impulse to cross her arms over her naked breasts for then it would look like false modesty and Rebecca had never been a girl to hide behind self-deception of any sort, except when she was younger and told lies to cover up the stark realities of the nomadic existence she had led under her father's rule.

In her childhood she had been a somewhat plain young person, thin and serious with a maturity in her expression that had made her seem old beyond her years. Time had changed all that; at seventeen she was a tall willowy beauty with great dark eyes and a head of thick blue-black hair that was the envy of her peers. No longer did she wear the spectacles that her father had ordered she should from as far back as she could remember. She had discovered that she simply didn't need them and knew he had only made that ruling to stop her from indulging in so-called sinful vanity.

Joss had never seen her without her clothes, those drab shapeless garments she wore almost like a uniform and which so successfully hid the contours of her body. Now his expression became still and quiet at sight of her full creamy breasts, her small waist, the long graceful legs that were folded ever so slightly over those other feminine parts that he didn't dare look at too obviously. The last thing she took off was her tortoiseshell clasp. Her curtain of raven hair fell over her white shoulders, he shifted slightly, the hot sun beat down on them, wordlessly he took her hand, together they plunged into the pool, screaming as their warm bodies hit the cold umber waters of the Giant's Bathtub.

Gasping and choking they swam over to each other, they held one another and kissed, they splashed and laughed and indulged in love-play under the water, their naked limbs entwining, their bodies meeting and merging and breaking away, tantalising one another in a game that had no rules but for those made by themselves, with their eyes, their hands, the stirring passion smouldering within them.

'Hallo there!' A voice was hailing them from the bank, though at first they didn't recognise it as such but thought it was just a continuation of the echoes of their own voices, all around them, bouncing from the rocks, carrying over the water. Then Joss glanced up and saw a figure, etched against the blue sky, an oddly familiar figure, bent slightly forward as he shouted and tried to attract their attention.

'Father MacNeil.' Joss sounded incredulous 'What's he doing here? Oh, the mercy o' the Lord be upon us and give us deliverance from our sins. Father MacNeil of all people, catching us out like this.'

'Joss, stop that, you sound like my father,' Rebecca scolded but she followed Joss's example just the same as he scrambled up the rocks to the bank, his hands folded over his belly in an attempt to hide his state of nudity.

'It's all right.' The priest politely averted his eyes as Rebecca rushed over to her little pile of clothing. 'Don't bother dressing for me, I was just coming in myself. This is one of my favourite places when it's hot. I don't often get the chance but when I do I like to go skinny-dipping in this part of the river.'

'You do?' Joss stared at the priest, fair and tall and boyish-looking at thirty-seven, a man who could still surprise everyone with his unconventional views on life and broad outlook on religion. Young and old of whatever denomination thought the world of Father Kelvin MacNeil and Joss thought the world of him now because he showed no shock at finding two young people swimming in the river as naked and unadorned as nature had made them.

'Yes I do, and I haven't come all this way just to go back again with my tail between my legs. Keep cavey for me, I promise I won't be long. I've got some sandwiches in my bag we can share later so just you sit here where you can't see me and yell if anyone appears.'

Without more ado he went off to strip under cover of the bushes and then he was in, yelling as loudly as anyone with the shock and the pleasure of freezing water on burning skin while Joss and Rebecca kept guard till he reappeared, fully clothed, tingling and fresh-looking, going to the saddle bag of his bike to retrieve his packet of sandwiches and hand them companionably round.

'At least it makes a change from chapel.' He winked at them and they all burst out laughing in appreciation, Rebecca louder than anyone, a wonder in her that she had once rejected this man because he was Catholic and therefore a being to be avoided because he did not conform to her father's strict beliefs.

Once the sandwiches were finished he got up. 'It's been fun, but not a word to anyone. I'll keep quiet about you if you do the same for me. Agreed?'

'Agreed.' They shook hands, they grinned at one another. Then a serious expression flitted over his face, taking away the laughter. 'I'm not going to preach because you get enough of that in chapel, Joss, but I'll just say this: be careful, you two. I can see how much you care for one another but don't get too carried away, you're both very young and I wouldn't like to see either of you getting hurt. Remember your responsibilities to your families as well as to yourselves.' A smile lit his face once more. 'That's it, nothing too drastic, just a little word of advice from someone who has seen the havoc that can be wreaked in people's lives by even one act of thoughtlessness.'

And then he was off, riding leisurely away on his bike, back straight, hair drying to fairness in the sun, one last wave that made him wobble for a few yards before he disappeared from sight round a bend.

'You know what would have happened if he hadn't come along?' Joss said quietly.

'Yes, I know, but the time has come for us, Joss, in spite of what Father MacNeil just said.' Her eyes were very dark and mysterious as she uttered the words. 'But not here, not now. I'll meet you in Mary's Bay at nine o'clock tomorrow night, be there sharp and don't let anyone see you.'

His own eyes had become very blue and intense as she spoke. 'All right, nine o'clock, I'll be there . . .' He gave a sudden yelp. 'I'll have to go, I only gave myself an hour and it's well past that now, come on.'

They took hands and flew, the magic of the day over but an excitement building in them at the idea of tomorrow – and the unknown.

The afternoon was almost over when Rebecca climbed back in through her bedroom window where she paused to regain her breath for a few minutes before tidying herself and quickly drying her hair. A footfall sounded outside her door and Caleb came into the

room, demanding to know where she'd been. '*He's*
on the warpath,' Caleb went on in some annoyance.
'He wanted to give you another lecture and sent me
to fetch you half an hour ago. I managed to cover up
for you somehow but only just. Where have you been
and who have you been with?'

'As if you need to ask.' Rebecca was over by her
dressing table, snatching up a brush from its worn
surface to pull it briskly through her tangle of black
hair. 'Don't get so het up, you know I'd do the same
for you if I had to. There's always Maida to consider.
I know how much you like her and want to go to her
and you could too if you put your mind to it.'

'I know why you're so keen for me and Maida to
get together,' he said sulkily. 'It's Joss Morgan, you
want him all to yourself, and Maida gets on your
nerves with her mooching about after him. That's it,
isn't it?'

'Of course that's it.' Rebecca had never pulled any
punches with this particular brother and she made no
concessions now. 'She's only wasting her time with
Joss and you know it. Maida's weak, she wants what
she can't have, she's just a pest to Joss and a thorn in
my side. You're besotted by her, she'll come round to
you in the end but don't go rushing at her like a bull
in a china shop. I know you, all brawn and no finesse.
Maida's the sort who likes to be wooed and it would
do no harm to see her now and then. Father doesn't
have eyes in the back of his head for all he looks like
a gorgon. You could easily slip out now and then and
he would never be the wiser.'

Caleb drew in his horns. For all his brash and bold
ways it hadn't occurred to him to do as his sister

suggested. He had been so long under his father's thumb it seemed strange to even think of breaking away but the idea grew on him as he stood there staring at this amazing sister of his with her flashing eyes and stubborn chin and that aura of strength she always carried with her.

'Your pinny's got mud on it,' he said abruptly to hide his feelings. 'And it's all crumpled. You must have been having a fine old time to yourself for that to happen. You're supposed to be in here grovelling about on your knees in repentance, not gadding about outside like a little heathen.'

'Oh, bother.' She twisted round to look at the large dirty mark on her sparkling white pinafore. 'So it has, be a dear and get me a fresh one from the washing line – and don't let *him* see you. I've had enough explaining to do for one day.'

Sister and brother gazed at one another in understanding before he turned and went from the room with a thoughtful expression on his face.

Chapter Seventeen

It was a night made for young lovers. The great white disc of the full moon rode high in the heavens, lining the clouds with silver, casting its dazzling beams over the rippling reaches of the Atlantic Ocean and spilling them into the calm waters of Mary's Bay. So bright was the light it cast its moon shadows over the land. Rebecca and Joss were plainly silhouetted as they went flitting along, cannily and cautiously, now here, now gone, as they endeavoured to stay hidden among the dunes and the marram grasses and finally the great bastions of rock rising sheer out of the sands lower down in the bay.

'Someone's bound to spot us,' Joss whispered in Rebecca's ear. 'That moon's like a bloody great torch shining down on us, putting us in the spotlight for the whole world to see.'

'Don't be silly, there's no one out here at this time of night, and stop swearing, it makes you sound common, you don't do it in front of Wilma and Rona so why should you do it in front of me?'

'You sound prudish, I hate it when you're prudish. And why did you bring me out here anyway? Never telling me where we were going? Everything secret and hidden, like a couple of children going off on some silly adventure.'

'It isn't a silly adventure – it's – oh, why are boys so unromantic? I thought you wanted to come with me, yesterday you were all for it and now you're acting like a baby.'

'I *am* all for it, and I'm not acting like a baby. I just don't want anybody to see us, that's all, more for your sake than mine. You know what folks are like hereabouts, all ears and flapping tongues, you can't pass wind in a place like Kinvara without somebody somewhere hearing it.'

'You *are* unromantic, and dirty. How can you talk like that in front of me, Joss Morgan? I really thought I liked you but now I'm not so sure. I suppose there is another side to you I know nothing about and wouldn't want to know if truth be told.'

'You're no angel yourself, Rebecca. I've heard you swearing too, really vicious stuff when you don't get your own way and blast everything and everyone to damnation.'

They disentangled fingers and stood glaring at one another, breath coming fast, nostrils dilated, throwing daggers with their eyes, till they released their tensions in laughter, kissed to make up, and joined hands once more. 'No one will see us, Joss,' she said softly, 'I want that even less than you for then I would have to answer to my father and everything would be spoiled. I've got something really wonderful to show you so stop arguing and let's get going before it's too late.'

*   *   *

No one did see them – except for Johnny Lonely, who saw everything that went on in Mary's Bay and could tell many a tale about the people and events that had taken place there at some time or another. Johnny also knew where the two young people were going. At first it had only been Rebecca; now there was Joss as well, and Johnny hoped that neither of them would ever be hurt by all this. Where would it lead? How would it end? That bugger Bowman would have something to say if he found out his daughter was in cahoots with a Catholic.

Love. It was such an unreasoning emotion, especially at Rebecca's age, all-powerful, all-consuming. He'd felt like that once, long ago, far far away, in another life, in another time. Now there was no one alive who owned a place in his heart – except for Rebecca. She was like a daughter to him and he would always be here to help her if need be, only he wouldn't be so available to her now that he was about to make a new life for himself.

She had always come to him, here in Mary's Bay, with her worries and her problems and together they had talked them through. Now it wouldn't be so convenient for her to visit him and he could only hope that she would still come to see him at Woodbank Cottage.

He'd had no chance to tell her that he was moving. No one knew yet, except for the Crathmor folk – and that old bat Miss Dorothy Hosie.

She didn't mix much in the community but he knew she had a spicy tongue in her head and would no doubt use it to spread the gospel. It didn't matter; in a very short space of time his change of direction would be common knowledge and the heads would nod, the speculation would begin, blown out of all proportion, twisted round, embroidered, till soon they would have him living like a lord at Crathmor House ruling the roost with a rod of iron. Johnny smiled to himself and set off back to his hut to begin the task of sifting through his possessions, some to keep aside, the rest to put into a pile for burning. Nothing of the life he had known in this solitary place would ever be seen by curious eyes. Every scrap would be destroyed; only his few precious keepsakes would remain to tell of the life he had known before fate had robbed him of all that had once been good and worthwhile.

The moonlight poured in through the windows of Oir na Cuan like a great brilliant lantern, shining on the faces of Joss and Rebecca as they stood gazing at one another in the silent kitchen of the house. 'This is where I come when I want to be alone,' Rebecca explained, her voice catching with excitement at her audacity in being the instigator of this rendezvous with Joss, just the two of them, here in Oir na Cuan, alone with one another as they had never truly been before.

'Come on.' She took his hand and led him upstairs to a tiny bedroom with a camped ceiling and items of furniture arranged against the walls. 'I've been getting it ready for ages. I wasn't able to bring anything very much from home, we've got so little it would be difficult to take even a duster without it being noticed. But it was all here anyway, I just freshened it up a bit.'

'Suppose somebody comes?' Joss glanced nervously

towards the window. 'If we got in so easily any-body could.'

'No one will come,' she said with assurance. 'People think it's haunted and though they might come and look they won't dare venture inside. They've glimpsed my face at the window, they've heard noises. Effie Maxwell came snooping once but never came back. She told everybody of course, trust Effie to spread the word. I was careful never to let anyone see me properly so stop worrying and come over here.'

She led him across to the bed and they sat on its edge, an awkward little silence springing up between them. 'Joss.' She tickled his ear with her mouth. 'We can just talk if you like. We needn't do anything else till we become used to being alone like this.'

'It's just – it feels funny,' he said uncomfortably. 'Sort of forced somehow. It was different when we were outside, the wide spaces all around, fooling about, being natural – not like this – planned – in someone else's house, all secretive and furtive and sneaky.'

'I thought you'd be pleased.' She sounded distant suddenly. 'I looked forward to this. At first it was just me, coming here to escape my father, not wanting to share it with anybody, enjoying the feeling of being by myself for a change. But all along I had you in my mind and the more I thought about bringing you here the more I wanted it to happen.'

She got up and went to the door. 'I see now I was wrong, you're all tensed up and strange and I won't bring you back ever again.'

With that she flounced away downstairs but he was behind her, spinning her round, taking her into his arms, holding her and kissing her, leading her into the kitchen where he threw some cushions on the floor and pulled her down beside him. 'It's all right, Rebecca,' he said huskily, 'I am glad we came, more than anything else I want to be somewhere alone with you and this is as good a place as any . . .'

His body was hard and warm against hers. They undressed each other, swiftly and silently, their naked limbs entwined, their lips met and merged, they were carried away on a tide of youthful passions and longings that made them too eager to please one another, too anxious to be good at something that was new and strange to them.

It was the first time for them both; the uncontrolled passions erupted out of them, inexpert seekings and plunderings, burning kisses and murmured nothings, strivings to express feelings that couldn't be expressed in the heat and in the longing. In the end he went whirling away before her and she endured the pain of his eager thrustings without protest, content just to be here, in the arms of Joss Morgan, the boy she loved with such devotion it was almost an honour to please him like this.

'We're just beginners, it will get better,' she told him when afterwards they lay locked in their young lovers' embrace. 'We must tell one another what we like and what we don't and in the end we'll be so good nobody in the whole wide world can teach us anything about our bodies and how they work to please us.'

He smiled, lazily and sleepily. 'You're quite a philosopher, Rebecca Bowman. Sometimes you leave me far behind with your views on life. I'm only a humble farm lad, remember, mucking out the chicken houses and the pig pens and smelling of both at the end o' each day.'

'You're far more than that to me, Joss Morgan,' she said seriously. 'I'm only a miller's daughter, lugging sacks of corn about, listening to the mill wheel grinding and my father bawling out orders, but that's only a small part of me, the rest is inside and that's the part that matters. What you do isn't always what you are, what others see is often what you are not.'

'Too complicated.' Joss laughed. 'But I think I know some of what you mean. People see me as just a farm labourer when all the time that's not really what I want to be. I do it because I have to though mostly I'm thinking of other things. The real me wants to travel the world. I want to do something exciting with my life, and that's why I've decided to join the Territorial Army as soon as I'm old enough. Captain Rory and The MacKernon have somehow buried their differences and are starting up a unit, here in Kinvara, someday quite soon.'

'You won't be a real soldier, will you?' Rebecca sounded anxious. 'The country isn't at war or anything so there's no need for you to go away and fight. I couldn't bear it if you left me here on my own.'

'Och, don't be silly.' He drew her in closer and kissed her tenderly. 'Of course I'm not leaving you, except maybe to summer camps and even then I won't be far away. The MacKernon is planning to open up a part o' his land as training grounds and Captain Rory will take us once a week in the village hall to show us some o' the things he learned in the war. It's only for fun so stop worrying, we'll still be able to meet as often as we do now, and if I ever get to see some o' the world I'll take you with me and we'll never ever be parted.'

'I don't like it, Joss,' she said bleakly. 'It's as if you're growing away from me already – when our life together is only just starting.'

'We'll always be together, Rebecca. You know how I feel about you and I wouldn't be able to bear it either if we couldn't see one another. It's just somewhere to go to pass the time but I promise I'll never be far away from you.' He drew her head down and cradled her to his heart. 'Stop fretting and just lie here beside me. I have to rise early and will need to go soon. Mam likes me to get my beauty sleep. If I go home too late she'll know I've been tom-catting.'

'Tom-catting! Is that what you call it!'

'It's only what the other lads say,' he returned gruffly. 'I can't come out with all that fancy stuff.'

'Making love, Joss,' she said firmly.

'Oh, all right then, making love. Now be quiet for a wee while and don't talk. It's been quite a night and I need a few minutes to get my breath back.'

The hush of the ocean outside the window lulled and soothed them, bringing normality to bear in the aftermath of their wild searchings for love and fulfilment. Their awareness of one another was like a bright torch burning between them, heightened as it was by the precious hours spent together in the house known as Oir na Cuan, that small abode sitting so quiet and so peaceful at the edge of the ocean, guarding its secrets from the rest of the world.

* * *

It was as Johnny Lonely had foretold: word about his teaching post and his move to Woodbank Cottage had leaked out. The villagers gathered and gossiped, favourite meeting posts were well attended, the doctor's surgery in Butterbank House being one of the most comfortable spots with its aura of conviviality, its worn but welcoming seats, the air about it that nothing there would ever change even supposing the earth itself were to be knocked out of orbit.

True, there was always the smell of carbolic and antiseptic to contend with, the moans and groans of those with aches and pains; others sneezing enough germs to infect the whole planet; Effie bustling about with her medicine trolley knocking people on the shins, but all in all it was better than a draughty shop doorway or a few swift exchanges in a rainy street.

'I aye knew there was something different about Johnny,' Jessie MacDonald began sagely. 'He has that clever look about him under all the hair and the grime and we all know about the books and the music he kept in that broken-down hut o' his.'

'Ay, different right enough,' Mattie MacPhee said drily. 'You would have to be daft altogether never to have noticed that. He had the books and the learning but who would have thought he would end up at Crathmor teaching Captain Rory's son? With a house into the bargain. It just goes to show that anything is possible in this world, even for hopeless creatures like Johnny Lonely.'

'His real name is Johnny Armstrong.' Effie came out of a tiny side room to add her piece, sounding very knowledgeable as she did so. 'I heard Emily MacPherson referring to him as such when I was over at the big house checking up on her pregnancy. Don't ask me anything more, I had to pretend no' to be listening to her ladyship's conversation but there you are now, our very own hermit suddenly has a job, a house and a real name to his name.'

'I always knew he was some sort o' teacher,' Hannah put in with a faint air of superiority. 'He was aye so good with Andy, helping with his reading and writing, such a patient way with him. I tackled him about it once but he just muttered some nonsense and ran from the house as fast as he could go.'

'I still think it all has something to do with that Miriam Bowman.' Mattie looked thoughtful at this point. 'I mind when she first came here and Johnny went all queer whenever her name was mentioned. He was spying on the mill house too, I myself saw him down on the shore watching the place but he scuttled away as soon as he saw me watching him.'

'Ach, he will be fine at Crathmor,' Dolly Law said solicitously. 'Captain Rory, the good kind man that he is, will personally take Johnny under his wing and see that he comes to no harm.'

'He'll still have his work cut out for him – the soul.' Jessie nodded. 'I hear tell young Ross Wallace is a real handful and there's that dragon, Miss Hosie, to contend with as well, a real spinster if ever there was one and peculiar in the fact that she's never made any attempt to find herself a man. Poor Johnny will need the patience o' Job to cope with the likes o' her.'

Jessie spoke with more than a touch of benevolence; her feelings towards her fellow humans being much mellower these days. She and Gabby were to be married in the autumn, an arrangement that had

Gabby sometimes petrified, sometimes resigned, mostly philosophical in that he had known Jessie a good many years and had found her to be a hard-working woman who kept his house clean and his belly filled. Most importantly, she understood his need for privacy and left him alone to get on with his own pursuits without any noticeable interference. It would also be good to have someone to talk to in the evenings as well as a woman's touch in the home and a warm bed at night instead of a cold empty space at his side.

Mattie, who for years had teased 'the MacDonald woman' about her unmarried state, had received the news of the forthcoming marriage with a sense of disappointment. A married Jessie wouldn't be nearly as much fun as a husband-seeking one but that didn't mean to say Mattie was going to let go so easily. Being Mattie she always found something to say to ruffle the other woman's feathers and revelled in the fact that Jessie had a fatal knack of leaving herself wide open to comments of an unwelcome nature.

'Ay, well, we certainly canny say the same for you, Jessie,' Mattie began innocuously enough, 'reticent Miss Hosie might be about men but you just about burst a blood vessel chasing first Charlie then Gabby. 'Tis a wonder to me you have any strength left to prepare yourself for your own wedding. Gabby will be lucky if you have any left for your first night in the marriage bed though on the other hand you might just eat him altogether wi' that hunger you have on you for anything in trousers.'

It was as well that Dolly Law chose that opportune moment to light up her clay pipe. The flabbergasted expression on Jessie's face was priceless. She turned purple, then white, she opened and closed her mouth and might have exploded altogether with her pent-up indignation had not Dolly released an extra-large mouthful of smoke into the atmosphere, making everyone cough and splutter and yell at her to 'put the damt thing out.'

'I came here to be cured, no' to be choked to death wi' fumes,' Kangaroo Kathy protested vehemently, the sprained thumb she had recently suffered making her extremely irritable since it had restricted her knitting activities to a bare minimum.

'Out, Dolly, out!' Long John Jeannie, the doctor's wife, so named because she was forever 'mending the arse' of her husband's combinations, appeared in the waiting room with drawn brows and pursed lips.

'I'm no' going anywhere,' Dolly stated defiantly. 'I have as much right to be here as anyone else. I'm needing a cough bottle for my chest and I'm no' leaving these premises till I get it.'

'I meant your pipe, Dolly,' Jeannie said grimly. 'Put it out this minute or you *will* be shown the door toot sweet. I don't know how many times I've told you, no smoking no drinking inside these walls.'

'The doctor smokes a pipe,' Dolly argued. 'And I've never taken a drink in this house.'

'I've seen you, Dolly,' Jeannie returned calmly, 'Swigging beer out a bottle and having the cheek to ask that it be filled with cough mixture when it was empty. No wonder you have a bad chest and most likely a stomach ulcer too from years o' knocking back the hard stuff.'

'That's for the good doctor to diagnose,' Dolly said snootily as she knocked out the contents of her pipe into the depths of a sorry-looking aspidistra reposing in a dark corner.

'Dolly!' Jeannie looked as if she would like to kill this rebellious 'outlaw' woman there and then. 'That is a living plant in case you don't know! I myself gave it to the doctor many years ago on his birthday and I'll thank you not to defile another thing on these premises or it's out you go, both you and your pipe!'

'A living plant.' Dolly looked as if she was quite capable of spitting into the large bowl containing the aspidistra. 'I've seen better-looking rags hanging on a dead tree. It likely enjoyed that bit o' baccy and will feel the better for it in a day or two. As for giving it to the doctor on his birthday, that must have been a hundred years ago! It looks worse than any fossil I've ever seen, alive or dead, and if you had any decency in you, Jeannie, you would give the poor thing a proper burial and be done with it.'

With that she jammed her ancient felt hat down over her lugs, stuck her unlit pipe between her few remaining teeth and marched out of the room, only to turn at the door with a parting shot. 'If I catch pneumonia it will be your fault, Jeannie, and if I do I'll tell the doctor why. It is a sad day indeed when a sick woman like myself is denied proper medical treatment, and all because I dared to take pity on a shitty aspidistra that was on its last legs anyway!'

She went off cackling, Jeannie's bosom swelled to maximum proportions as she drew in an enormous lungful of air and emitted a strange gurgling sound.

'Pills, anyone?' Effie was coming round with her trolley, a row of feet was hastily tucked in, the surgery door opened, a patient came out, the doctor's voice shouted, 'Next!', a measure of order came into being, but not before Dolly's grinning countenance appeared at a window, blowing smoke all over the panes and making faces at Jeannie's rear as she disappeared into the private depths of the house.

A SHETLAND WEDDING

Summer 1936

Chapter Eighteen

Shetland in summer was a palette of vast cloud-patterned skies and a verdure so varied it seemed impossible that so many colours could be woven into the one landscape. Wildflowers of every hue grew in fragrant abundance in the meadows: pinks flourished in rock crannies on the shore; buttercups made a golden blaze on the machair; wild thyme carpeted the clifftops.

The sounds of Shetland were just as spectacular as the sights with larksong filling the air from morning to night and the seabirds making a terrible din on the nesting ledges of the cliffs that rose sheer out of the sea. Terns swooped and dived; gannets plummeted into the waves; puffins bustled with beaks full of eels; gulls screeched and fought with one another for the best sites to rear their young.

The wedding party from Kinvara arrived *en masse*, swamping the accommodation set out for them in Burravoe House and two of the renovated shepherds' cottages that Mirren normally reserved for summer visitors. It had been a long journey from Kinvara; everyone was tired and wanted only to eat and sleep on that first night. They retired early and arose late, refreshed and eager to enjoy the adventure ahead,

Maudie in particular being very volatile and excited as she sat at the breakfast table, helping herself to a great mound of bacon and eggs followed by crunchy toast piled high with butter and marmalade.

'It's a fair treat to get away from the bairns for a while,' she enthused, somehow managing to get the words to come out between a packed mouthful of food. 'It was that nice o' Aunt Bette and Rita to offer to look after them. I know they're in good hands and won't cause any trouble, even wee Isla for all she's just a few months old and teething into the bargain. Morven and Kyle are well-behaved bairns as a rule – except when they get worked up and fight one another like cat and dog. It's that terrible red-haired temper Morven has on her, she chases Kyle like a fiend, in and out o' the house, up and down the stairs, yelling blue murder at the top o' her voice, making me drop what I'm doing and rush to separate them before she has the chance to kill him altogether. Oh, ay, many's the warmed backside the wee bitch has had from me but bairns will be bairns and where would we all be without them?'

Her toast finished, Maudie reached out for a large buttered bannock and crammed half of it into her mouth before going on, 'Oh, I feel as if I've got wings! I can't remember when I last had a holiday. It must have been on my honeymoon to Mull though even then it wasny much o' a rest with me feeling obliged to help Finlay's cousin in the kitchen all day and him chasing me round the bedroom all night.'

Finlay flushed slightly at this but made no answer, simply because he had learned it was no use trying to stop his wife when she was in full flow.

'You'll have to help out here too, Maudie,' Hannah pointed out. 'We all will, Mirren will have her hands full trying to cope with us and getting herself ready for her wedding.'

'Och, I know all that, Hannah.' Maudie looked reproachfully at her sister-in-law. 'As if I was the sort o' body to just sit back and do nothing – as my Aunt Bette would very well tell you,' she added with a dimpled grin. 'I'll be doing a lot o' the cooking in case you didn't know and in many ways will just be swapping one stove for another.' She smiled beguilingly at Hannah. 'Even so, it is nice to know you'll be on hand to help with the fetching and carrying. In fact, you'll all be doing that, just as Babs and the boys did when I stayed wi' Aunt Bette in Keeper's Row and became the head o' the kitchen.'

'At least it will make a change from The Bread Oven,' Janet laughed.

'Ay, one set o' pie dishes for another,' Harriet said wryly. 'It's a good job I brought my apron with me.'

'Och, we'll all muck in,' Charlie said easily. 'Don't forget, I was chief cook and bottle washer in my own house till you insisted on taking over, Harriet. I might just be a man but I can turn out a nice cheesy omelette with the best o' them. It was always one o' my specialities and might be on the menu tomorrow if I can fight my way in to the stove.'

'Aren't you lot finished yet?' Mirren popped her head round the door. 'It's a beautiful day outside and I'd like some help with the plucking. We'll need lots of chickens for the big day and I thought me and my little helpers could sit at a table in the sun and get to work.'

'Out, bairns,' Harriet ordered in her forceful way.

'Ay, all hands on deck,' Charlie said with a grin.

'I can't pluck chickens,' Maida said, looking pointedly at her nails as she spoke. 'I don't want to get my hands ruined.'

'And my fingers aren't strong enough,' Essie said with a melting smile at her granma. 'They're too little to be pulling feathers. I'd rather try on the frock Wee Fay made me.'

'You've tried it on dozens o' times. If you can pull wool through a bobbin you can pull feathers.' For once Harriet did not allow herself to be swayed by the little girl's charms. 'And it's high time you did some work, Maida, you weren't invited here to sit around looking like a mannequin so outside with everyone else if you know what's good for you.'

Vaila hid a smile at the disgusted expression on her friend's face. Maida had come to Shetland on the strength of Joss coming too, but Joss had opted out at the last minute as had Rebecca, each of them knowing that Maida would have spoiled it for them with her possessive attitude towards Joss.

'I wanted to come,' Rebecca had told Vaila. 'And it was truly kind of Mirren to ask, but Joss doesn't want to encourage Maida's clinging and I don't want to go without him. Besides, it's a Protestant wedding, and you know what my father's like about any faith other than his own.'

Vaila hadn't pursued that particular subject. She knew things were more serious now between Joss and Rebecca. They could hardly bear to be apart for any length of time; when they were she hardly spoke about him, when they were together they both tried very hard not to show their feelings. Vaila realised that something big had happened between them and she was mad at her friend for not sharing her secrets, no matter how much she was persuaded.

'If I ever fall in love I'd let you in on it,' Vaila once said.

'I *have* let you in on it,' Rebecca returned steadily. 'You know how I feel about Joss and how he feels about me.'

'Not *all* of it,' Vaila had persisted. 'It's changed, it used to be just fooling around and laughing, now it's something more and I wish you would tell me.'

'Don't be silly,' Rebecca had said sharply. 'You're too young yet to know anything of that sort so stop asking.'

'I'm not too young, you're only a couple o' years older than me and we used to share everything. Earth sisters, that's what you said.'

'You'll always be my earth sister.' Rebecca had sounded very patient and elderly at this point. 'But it was different when we were just children. I'm more grown-up now and I suppose my outlook on life has developed. Don't worry, it will happen to you as well and then we can share everything again like we used to.'

'It must be a great love that you have for Joss,' Vaila had sighed romantically. 'That's the kind I want some day and I'll never marry till I get it.'

'You have Mark, he's nice and he thinks the world of you.'

'I know he's nice, George MacPherson is also nice, but I don't feel anything but friendship towards either o' them.'

'That's what I mean. Although your body is developing you've still got the mind of a child and you had better just content yourself being one till you are able to grow in maturity of thought and spirit.'

Rebecca could be very infuriating and superior when she liked and Vaila had flounced away before her temper got the better of her. Even so, she wished her friend was here in Shetland with her. They could have had such fun, all of them together in this marvellous place, picnicking, swimming, walking and talking.

But despite Rebecca's absence Vaila did have a wonderful time in Shetland. It wasn't all work and preparations for the wedding. George had gone back to military college some weeks ago and without his presence Mark was his old self, full of fun and mischief, doing unexpected and ridiculous things. They all went for picnics to the little bays and coves near Burravoe House, Mark gathering Vaila into his arms to run with her into the sea, Essie, Andy and Aidan splashing together and having a great time, Maida daintily gathering shells to add to her collection, looking like a nymph of the waves as she wandered along the shoreline in her floaty dress and getting herself noticed by a young fisherlad in the process.

After that she wasn't so keen to tag along with Mark and Vaila and made excuses to stay behind. The younger children also found other interests to occupy them, giving Mark the chance to go off with Vaila to places further afield.

He was buoyant and happy and transferred his

mood to her; they talked as they had in the old days and giggled over silly things, never tiring of each other's company and wishing the holiday would last for more than just a few days. Mad moods would seize him suddenly and one day he took her hand and made her run with him to the edge of a cliff, only to stop short at the very last moment to spread out his arms as if he were about to fly away. She laughed and spread her arms too and went waltzing with him over the machair, both of them singing as they danced along, collapsing against one another with laughter when they spied an old shepherd watching them and scratching his head as if trying to decide if they were really as crazy as they seemed or were just typical of the tourists who came each summer to the island.

'Ay, we are daft – both of us!' Mark yelled before grabbing her hand to flee away with her, his face alive with mischief and fun as he laughed and kissed her and sped her on and on till they fell exhausted to the ground where they lay panting and gazing up at the great expanse of sky above.

'I wish we could stay like this forever, Vaila, just you and me and all this, never to go away again.'

'If we don't go away we can't come back,' she said lightly, 'and it isn't always like this, Mark, warm and wonderful and welcoming. Shetland can be really freezing in the winter. Aunt Mirren had her roof blown off two years ago and sometimes it's so cold she has to wear two pairs of drawers as well as a couple of vests.'

'You know what I mean.' He propped himself on one elbow and gazed down at her, his black curls ruffling in the breeze, his eyes very dark and intent.

'I don't have to explain. Back home in Kinvara you're always too busy to spare time for me, and if you're with someone it's always someone else. That George MacPherson, for instance, fawning over you, gaping at you as if he owned you. I've never forgiven him for that day up at River House and I'm glad I belted him the way I did.'

'And I've never forgiven you for doing it!' she blazed back. 'You had no right to hit him. He was only being kind and trying to calm me down after I saw Maudie's baby being born.'

'A fine excuse – and I had every right. I told you I'd watch out for you and I meant every word I said.'

'Watch out for me, ay, but that doesn't mean to say you have to go snooping around spying on me. I told you before, Mark Lockhart, I will not have it, and the sooner you get that into your head the better!'

They lay back, seething with rage, saying nothing for fully five minutes before she relented and said softly, 'Mark, we really will have to stop this. Every time we're alone we seem to end up fighting. It's maybe better when we're with the others, we're just one o' the crowd then and can't get on one another's nerves as we're doing now.'

'You don't get on my nerves, at least you do when you stick up for George MacPherson with all his fancy talk and posh manners. Why can't you see it my way for a change? I've known you longer than him and have more rights than he does.'

She looked at his passionate young face, all the laughter gone from it, sober and serious, something that might have been a tear glistening on his long lashes. 'It's too soon for us, Mark,' she murmured softly. 'We need time – I need time. Go back to the way we were. It was good then and it could be good now. I'm only just starting to get used to growing up and you must be the same.'

'All right.' Abruptly he stood up and held out his hand. 'I'll wait, I'll go back, I suppose you're right, we are too young, I won't say anything serious to you for at least another week – and then I'll ask you to marry me.'

They both burst out laughing, joined hands, and were away again, running over the flower-strewn machair, waving to the people they met along the way, never stopping till they reached the road and the track leading to Burravoe House and all the bustle of the wedding preparations that lay within.

Chapter Nineteen

The wedding took place in the same little church that had been the setting for Finlay's marriage to Morna many years ago. A lot of things had changed since that day: Morna was dead, Finlay was now married to Maudie, Vaila and Aidan were almost grown-up, everyone was older if not necessarily wiser. Life went on and yet it seemed to have stood still for Rob as he waited with Mirren outside the church.

The measure of time seemed as nothing to him at that moment. Was it not just yesterday that he had stood on this same spot with Morna on his arm? Waiting to give her away to another man, everything in him rebelling at the idea, his heart almost bursting with the pain and the sadness of knowing that he could no longer call her his own. Not that she had ever really been his, never to properly have and hold as he would if he had been free to marry her.

His heart was brimming over as the hurt and the longing came flooding back. He moved restlessly; Mirren felt his tension and gave his arm a little shake. 'I know how you feel, Rob,' she whispered. 'It's all coming back to me too. I can see her yet, so pale and so lovely . . .'

She bit her lip and for her sake he took a hold of

himself. 'You look lovely too, Mirren, and part o' my feeling is for you also. I've come to know you well since Morna died, we've shared a lot of our thoughts and our memories. I imagined it would go on like that, you alone, me able to come to you when I needed to talk about the things we both understand. I never thought the day would come when I would be giving you away to someone else. I was being selfish thinking that way. I have my life to lead, you have yours and I'm glad you've found someone to share it with you.'

'I'll always be here for you, Rob,' she said rather shakily. 'Oh, why am I crying already, I mustn't go into church blubbing like a baby and looking terrible.'

'Here.' He whipped out a clean handkerchief and gently wiped away her tears. 'I think I love you just a little bit today, Rob Sutherland,' she said softly.

'And I you,' he returned with a rueful smile. 'Weddings. They do that to people. Make them say things they normally wouldn't.'

The organ had struck up, the strains of the 'Wedding March' floated out, Rob took a deep breath and led Mirren up the steps, followed by Vaila in her white bridesmaid's dress and Essie in her pink one, a perfect little flower girl with her golden hair braided through with rosebuds and an angelic expression on her flawless features.

The church was packed out with family and friends. Mirren was a well-liked and respected member of the community and it seemed as if the whole of the parish was there to see her being married. The Kinvara menfolk made a striking contribution to the scene in their various modes of clan dress: Big Jock Morgan in his Black Watch kilt; Charlie bearing the Campbell colours; Finlay, Rob and Aidan in their Sutherland tartan; Andy almost bursting with pride in his. The womenfolk too looked eyecatching in their big hats and their finery. But it was on Mirren, fair of face and figure in her creamy satin dress, that all eyes were turned. Vaila held her train, Essie half giggled as she walked beside her sister trying to keep in step.

Erik Magnusson was tall and spare with a nut-brown face and deeply set piercing grey eyes. He was softly spoken and shy and hadn't had much to say for himself in the last hectic day or two. Harriet had already wondered aloud if he was really the right sort of man for Mirren but his voice was steady and sincere when he took the wedding vows and his eyes when they looked into hers were those of a man very much in love.

And in the hours after the ceremony everyone changed their opinion of him as gradually his shell of shyness cracked and his true nature began to show. The men shook hands with him and welcomed him into the family, the womenfolk kissed him and liked the way he courteously held doors open for them and made sure they were comfortable.

The tables groaned at the wedding feast as not only chickens had been prepared but ducks and turkeys as well, while a whole suckling pig was roasting over the fire in the huge farmhouse kitchen. Legs of lamb and shanks of beef lay ready for carving on the sideboard, great mounds of fluffy home-grown potatoes sat steaming on the hotplate, together with every kind of vegetable. Maudie had surpassed herself in the last few days. The sweet trolley was packed with trifles and jellies, pink and white meringues, fruit tarts and soufflés, but pride of place went to an enormous four-tiered wedding cake with all the trimmings, though this last had been made in The Bread Oven and transported with every loving care over the sea to Burravoe House.

'Oh, it fair brings back memories o' my own cake,' Maudie sighed dreamily to Hannah as she stood in the kitchen lovingly eyeing her beautifully decorated creation. 'Aunt Bette made it for me – at least I aye suspected Wee Fay had a hand in it too though never would I hurt Auntie's feelings by telling her that.'

'I can't remember much o' mine,' Hannah admitted. 'All I could think about was Rob, how handsome he was and how lucky I was to be marrying him.'

Maudie gazed thoughtfully at her sister-in-law who was looking very sparkly-eyed and attractive in the wide-brimmed hat and green two-piece suit she had purchased in Inverness some weeks ago. 'Ay, he is a handsome man, is Rob, and I know half the women in Kinvara have been after him at one time or another, but he is lucky to have you, Hannah. It was a grand thing you did when you forgave him for Morna Jean and took Vaila into your home to raise her as your own daughter.'

'Oh, Maudie, do you really think so?' Hannah had drunk a fair number of drams at this stage and was looking decidedly misty-eyed.

'Of course I do,' Maudie maintained stoutly. 'There's no' many women would have behaved as you did and I for one raise my glass to you.'

The glasses chinked, Maudie took a deep draught of whisky, straightened her hat, threw her arm round her sister-in-law's shoulders and together they staggered unsteadily back to the dining room where Erik was vying with Charlie Campbell to see who could tell the best story of the sea, the pair of them making everyone laugh with their ridiculous accounts of mermaids and kelpies and warty old witches rising cackling from the waves to carry some unsuspecting sailor down to the depths in their horny clutches.

It was soon time to cut the cake, presided over proudly by Maudie, looking as if she would like to grab the knife and do the job herself so anxious was she to see the blade positioned exactly between the sections bearing the pink iced rosebuds.

The dance in the barn later, for locals and guests alike, was an event to be remembered by everyone. Erik, who was an excellent fiddler, simply could not resist joining the trio of musicians who had set themselves up in a corner. As the guests danced and sang the night away, moods became mellower, inhibitions were thrown to the winds. Hannah relaxed in Rob's arms and couldn't remember when she had enjoyed herself more; Maida, who had caught the bride's bouquet, floated dreamily round the hall with her young fisherlad and wondered what Joss was doing; Harriet and Charlie made a handsome pair and flirted like young lovers; Janet and Jock held close to each other and just enjoyed the music; Mark and Vaila were caught up in the romance and the mood of the moment and stayed quiet and close to one another; Mirren at last got Erik to herself and didn't part with him again till it was time for them to leave for the lone little house on the other side of the bay where they were spending the night before sailing off on honeymoon the next day.

'Take care o' her man,' Rob said gruffly as he gripped the big fisherman's hand.

'Have no fear, Rob.' Erik nodded. 'She'll be safe with me, I'll never let anything happen to her.'

Mirren's cheek was warm and smooth when Rob kissed it. 'Be good,' he murmured huskily, 'and be in touch when you get home to let us know how you are.'

'Not too good, Rob, I'm a married woman now, remember.' She tried to inject humour into the words but her voice caught on a tear and she turned quickly away to join her new husband.

Before going home, Vaila and Aidan made a return visit to their mother's grave to lay flowers on the mossy earth and pause for a while to speak silently to her with their hearts. 'She's here, Aidan,' Vaila told her young brother. 'Here beside us. I felt her all the time in the church when Aunt Mirren was being married. It's so strange, last time I was only two years old and I was a flower girl at her wedding to Uncle Finlay. You weren't even born yet so can't really be expected to know anything about that day. I don't remember anything much about it either – except the smell of flowers. Maybe it's just in my imagination, maybe it isn't.'

'She was born and raised here.' Aidan sounded as

if he was seeking answers too. 'I suppose it's only natural for us to feel her all around us.'

'I know.' Vaila touched his shoulder. 'You and me, Aidan, we were hers, her children, it's good to know that, isn't it?'

'Ay, it's good to know it, Vaila.'

They joined hands and walked out of the little kirkyard that gazed out to the sea and the sky and the places Morna had wandered as a child with all her life before her.

Rob went to the graveside too and saw that the children had been there before him. He added a single red rose to the spray of carnations already there and stood for a while, just enjoying the peace of the place, hearing the sigh of empty spaces all around him, seeing the cloud shadows floating over the earth. 'We all miss you, my love,' he said softly. 'Even Hannah, who speaks of you often and the fine times you shared when she used to visit you at Oir na Cuan. You were in church when Mirren got married, I could sense you there and I know you are happy for her. Goodnight, sweet darling, never leave my side as I never leave yours.'

Hannah was waiting for him at the foot of the brae. He went to her and took her hand. 'Thanks, Hannah,' he said quietly. 'You're a good woman to bear with me as you do.'

'Far better for it to be out in the open, Rob, instead of hidden and silent and hurting.'

'Ay, but there aren't many women who would understand that. You have a big heart in you, Hannah, and I want you to know how much I love you for it.' He put his arm round her and they went off together, back to Burravoe House to pack and get ready to leave the dreams and the memories and the happiness they had shared in the green and gold idyll that was Shetland in summer.

A SMALL INTERLUDE
KINVARA

Christmas/New Year
1936

Chapter Twenty

Essie got her rocking horse for Christmas. When she awoke on Christmas morning and went rushing away down to the kitchen it was there in a corner of the room, a magnificent creation altogether, painted white with blue lifelike eyes, a blond mane and tail, and a red leather harness hung with tiny silver bells. The rest of the family crowded round as the little girl went over to just stare and stare at it, her eyes big and bright and filled with wonder.

'Is it really and truly mine?' she asked in awe. 'To keep for all time and forever?'

'Ay, it's yours all right,' Rob laughed. 'Andy and I worked our fingers to the bone getting it ready for the big day so you'd better keep it for all time and forever or we'll have something to say about it.'

'Oh!' The child clasped her hands together in a theatrical gesture. 'It's the most beautiful horse in the whole wide world and I'm going to call him Prince Charming. He'll carry me everywhere, to fabled lands far away and maybe even to the moon if I make enough magic for him.'

She turned to her father and her brother and hugged them each in turn, thanking them for the gift in her sweet and loving fashion, making them feel that all their efforts had been worthwhile when they saw the sparkle in those great blue eyes of hers and the dimpled smile on her bewitching little face.

'I'm going to be an actress when I grow up,' she declared solemnly. 'I'll say things to make people laugh and cry and I'll wear the most beautiful dresses that ever were made. You'll all come and see me and be proud o' me and I'll still have Prince Charming in my dressing room 'cos he'll be my good luck charm wherever I go.'

'An actress, eh?' Rob played along. 'Well, you'll make a good one, Essie, living as you do in your own wee world o' make-believe.'

'I know,' Essie agreed with a nod of her golden head. 'And Euan will be coming along with me when the time comes. We play-act all the time at Vale O' Dreip and have a grand time wrapping ourselves up in old curtains and pretending to be Roman Emperors.'

'Come on.' Rob lifted her onto the red leather saddle of Prince Charming and she sat, not moving or saying anything, just stroking the blond mane and gazing shyly at her family. 'I want him up in my room,' she said gently. 'I can only spin my magic when I'm alone and no one else is looking.'

'As long as you don't rock him in the middle o' the night when I'm asleep,' Vaila said with feeling. 'I know you, Essie, I've heard you before, reading these fairy stories of yours, muttering and mumbling by the light of a candle.'

'I will only ride him when I'm alone,' the child said with more than a touch of the dignity that had been growing in her lately. 'Ordinary mortals don't understand celestial beings like myself and it's better that I don't mix with any o' you too much in case you ruin my concentration.'

They all burst out laughing at this, including Essie herself. 'If you're going upstairs you'd better get dressed,' Hannah told her daughter as she rattled pans on the stove and poured boiling water into the teapot, bringing them all back to the more practical aspects of life. 'You'll catch your death in that flimsy nightdress. Put on a nice warm frock and don't be rocking yourself on that horse all morning, because the breakfast will be ready soon and we're all anxious to open our parcels.'

Prince Charming was borne away by Rob and Vaila between them, Andy following along at their heels, Breck sneaking away too in spite of the delicious fragrance of sizzling bacon filling the kitchen. He knew he would get his share later; it was one of those special mornings that called for special breakfasts and Hannah was too busy to even think of chasing him with her broom which was safely tucked in a corner out of harm's way.

The year of 1936 drew to a quiet close for the people of Kinvara. For most it had been an uneventful twelve months but for some it had been exciting. Two weddings had taken place, three funerals, and two christenings, one being that of Isla Munro Sutherland of River House, the other Fiona Joy MacPherson, Emily's tiny new baby.

Local happenings were the life blood of the remote

communities that dotted the Kinvara Peninsula. Individual events were the things that mattered, neighbours, family, friends were the most immediate concerns for all those who had to live and work and play together, whether in discord or harmony or just plain indifference. The last was a rare attitude for a people who had 'noses on them like ferrets' and positively revelled in knowing all there was to know about their neighbours.

But despite the insular nature of rural life world news was digested avidly via day-old newspapers. Everyone knew there had been some trouble with Fascists in London's East End and even though there were some who didn't know or care what that meant they read it anyway and felt safe from the unrest of city life. Other items were more interesting, especially those concerning the royal family. Edward VIII had announced his abdication from the throne to marry an American divorcée called Wallis Simpson which meant his brother, the Duke of York, was bound to become king.

Not that anything of that nature mattered greatly to the people of Kinvara. The royals were nearly always referred to as being of England, as if the rest of the British Isles didn't exist. It was far more worrying to read about the warnings from Winston Churchill regarding Germany's threat of rearmament but comforting to know that the pacifists were totally against the views of the old political renegade though Jessie MacDonald called that 'ostriching', as she'd always had a soft spot for Churchill.

Kinvara as a whole drew the blankets of the old year over their heads and looked forward to the new with an optimism that came from deep within. As Donald of Balivoe maintained, 'Resilience has been bred in us. God help anybody who doesny know how to howk a tattie from the land for they shall be damned.'

When Dokie Joe had questioned the sense of this statement Donald had looked at him with pity and had said scathingly, 'It's the roots, man, the roots,' before stalking away with his nose in the air and an assurance in his stance that made Dokie Joe scratch his head in puzzlement and decide to look up his book on Scottish myths and folklore to see if he had perhaps missed something along the way.

'Don't you know anything?' his wife Mattie had questioned when he had come home to hunt through a motley collection of books on a shelf. 'Sons o' the soil was what Donald meant! Anybody wi' any brains would know that without asking. It's that beard o' yours, Dokie, it's taking the strength away from your head. If you grow it any longer it will be touching the floor, though that might no' be a bad thing since I could aye use it for a sweeping brush when my old one wears out.'

'My beard stays,' Dokie Joe said loftily, lovingly stroking the long black whiskers that were his pride and joy. 'And if you were half as proud o' me as Maisie Whiskers is of Willie you would be washing my beard for me and combing it out as well.'

'More like hanging it on the line to drip dry!' Mattie hooted merrily. 'With yourself on the peg to go with it! As for Maisie being proud o' Willie's fungus, that is just a rumour. She told me herself it takes up more space in the bed than she does and swears she'll hack the whole damt thing off if she ever gets the chance.'

Dokie Joe did not deign to answer this. He went to the mirror, he took a comb and carefully pulled it through his whiskers. There and then he made a New Year resolution, that never never would he chop off his beard for anyone, even supposing he had to end up throwing it round his neck like a scarf for everyone to see and admire.

A shamefaced and repentant Mattie made a resolution as well. She had been too hard on her husband, criticising him as she had. His was a lovely beard, almost as thick and luxuriant as his brother Willie's and twice as eye-catching. Going to Dokie Joe she told him this. They kissed and made up and she didn't mind one bit when the hairs on his face tickled her chin and it was also nice later in bed when he snuggled up to her all cosy and warm and tickled other bits of her as well!

The year of 1936 closed and gave way to another. Resolutions of every sort were made, kept for a while, and broken. It was all in the game, the game of life, full of hope and faith and high expectations for a bright and happy future.

KINVARA

Summer 1938

Chapter Twenty-one

The last two years had been excellent ones for Johnny Armstrong, the title by which he had come to be known. No longer could anyone refer to him as a hermit leading a solitary existence with a name to match. Johnny's world had opened and expanded, he had earned a place in the community and walked freely among his fellow men with his head held high. He was respected and liked wherever he went. People no longer spoke about him in whispers or looked at him askance as they had done of old.

He had smartened up his appearance a good deal. Gone were his scruffy clothes and hair that 'you could go for a walk in' according to previous fatuous remarks. Everything about him was tidier and more pleasing; women told one another they could 'fair go for him' whenever they gazed upon his full sensuous mouth, aesthetic features, and lean agile body.

'Strange,' Effie mused, 'I aye took him to be an older body wi' thon great tufts o' beard covering his face, but seeing him now I reckon he must be a man still in his prime and a handsome one at that. In all my born days as a woman I've never come across any man I could warm to, now I have this funny wee thrill at the pit o' my stomach whenever

Johnny gazes at me wi' those spooky dark eyes o' his.'

'I felt it too,' Maisie Whiskers admitted. 'I was in the smiddy all by myself one day when Johnny came to see about the laird's horse. "The stable lad is sick," he said in a funny steamy sort o' voice. "So I will just ride the stallion back to Crathmor myself, Maisie. There is nothing like a good ride to get the circulation moving, as I'm sure a chancy woman like yourself will agree." With that he doffed his hat, gave me an odd suggestive sort o' look, and went galloping away at top speed.'

'He never said the words!' Mattie snorted derisively, sounding like a horse herself in the heat of the moment. 'You're just making it up to be upsides down wi' Effie. As for a steamy voice, he was likely terrified to be alone wi' you and little wonder he went galloping away as if the de'il himself was at his heels.'

'Ay, you're right there, Mattie.' Jessie nodded, for once agreeing with her adversary in order to keep the fanciful Maisie in her place. 'It is terrible just, to be spreading such rumours about a decent law-abiding citizen like Johnny. Besides, a ride on a horse does nothing for the circulation, as I myself found out years ago when I was foolish enough to get on the back o' one.'

'No, you will be a lot better off sticking to Gabby,' Mattie said with malicious enjoyment. 'You don't have to put a saddle on him to get him ready and can savour the thrills and spills in the comfort o' your own bed when the mood takes you.'

'You get worse every day, Mattie MacPhee,' Jessie returned heavily. 'At least I still have the thrills and spills, which is more than I can say for you now that you're getting on in years and will likely be past doing anything with anybody that has two legs and wears trousers.'

'Ach, there is no reason for any o' you to get so het up.' Dolly pushed a plug of tobacco into her pipe with a nicotine-stained finger. 'Johnny has no need for anybody else when he's got that governess to keep him amused. I heard tell he and she are having a fine old time to themselves up at Crathmor. The new nanny has big ears on her, she hears them laughing and talking in Miss Hosie's room. Sometimes Johnny brings his gramophone along and there they go, jigging and hooting around, dancing and swaying and God knows what else, getting up to mischief no doubt and her such a snooty besom the rest o' the time.'

'Surely you're no' suggesting there is some kind o' liaison between them, Dolly?' Effie said in shock. 'Johnny would never dream o' looking the road that woman is on. She treated him like a floor cloth when first he went to Crathmor to teach the laird's son! If any man has his pride it's Johnny and I for one will no' believe a word o' such rumours till I have seen the truth o' them for myself.'

'It's true,' Dolly said loftily. 'Law by name, law by nature, that's me. I myself saw them when I delivered washing to the big house, lurking in a doorway, holding hands like a couple o' bairns and looking as if they would like to do more.'

'He was taking a skelf out of her finger!' Effie hooted scathingly. 'Or trying to. In the end I had to go there and do the job myself. She told me she got it on the ragged edge o' the front door and Johnny came to her rescue when he saw the state she was in.'

Dolly put her nose in the air and sniffed. 'Some folks will believe anything, especially vulnerable women like yourself who has no real experience o' the world. The man is flesh and blood, the woman is too, though even I have a hard job believing that.'

'No real experience!' Effie exploded. 'I will remind you, Dolly Law, as the district nurse I am a woman who has seen everything, including people like Miss Hosie, whose blood froze in her veins long ago and likely petrified everything else that is of an organic nature!'

'Ach, don't blind us wi' your science, Effie, truth is stranger than fiction.' Mattie rubbed salt into the wound with fiendish glee. 'Miss Hosie will likely be smouldering wi' passion and lust and will have a willing slave in Johnny. Don't forget, he has been starved of love all these years and will be only too ready to leap into bed wi' somebody, even if it is a spinster woman wi' no blood in her veins.'

'I am a spinster woman, Mattie.' Effie's voice was trembling by now. 'Which doesn't mean to say I am not a flesh and blood human person. I am warm, I am sensitive, I do not have a wedding ring on my finger but that in no way suggests I am some sort o' alien creature without feelings.'

'It was you who said she was petrified!' Mattie was growing tired of the subject. 'She can be a fly on a dung heap for all I care! And talking o' dung, I need some for my tatties. Big Bette has it in sacks and is selling it dirt cheap to get rid o' it.'

'Dung! In the grocer's shop?' Jessie cried, aghast.

'Ay, in amongst the cakes and the puddings to make them grow better,' was Mattie's parting shot as she went about her business, leaving everyone else to go about theirs after five more pleasurable minutes of not-so-neighbourly chit-chat.

The talk about Johnny and Miss Hosie, if not exactly accurate, did hold a grain of truth. After a decidedly icy start the governess had gradually warmed to Johnny and had come to realise just what an asset he was in the difficult task of knocking some sense into Ross Wallace's head.

Johnny had taught the boy wisely and well. Over and above academic lessons he had shown the laird's son how to appreciate the wonders of nature; the man and the boy were often to be seen wandering the woods or the seashore, collecting specimens of interest, taking them home for identification, making notes and dates in a large album which Ross Wallace had proudly if prosaically entitled *My Very Own Nature Diary* with his name at the bottom.

So enamoured was the boy of his tutor he had begged his father not to send him away to school till he was at least twelve and Captain Rory was quite happy to comply with these wishes. In common with everyone else he was delighted with the changes in the boy. He had calmed down, he was more mannerly and considerate, he was eager to learn and absorbed knowledge like a sponge, his toleration of his governess had greatly improved. Above all he was happy and had, in Captain Rory's opinion, turned into a decent human being instead of the wild and woolly child he had once been.

Miss Hosie's gratitude for this metamorphosis showed itself in odd little ways. She had begun by inviting Johnny to have afternoon tea with her in the privacy of her own sitting room, the tarts and the cakes being transported fresh from The Bread Oven via the kitchen maid for a bribe of just threepence.

At first Johnny had been wary of these unexpected invitations. What was the old bat up to now, he wondered? She who had once rejected and scorned him was now extending the hand of friendship, in her own room too, cut off from the rest of the house by a back stair and a heavy baize-covered door. In his imaginings Johnny saw her as a fat little spider, waiting in her web to snare him and inject him with her venom till he became a helpless hopeless creature without powers of any kind.

But he went just the same, if only from a sense of curiosity, and had been astonished to find her a most affable and pleasant hostess, one who apologised for her previous uncivil behaviour towards him, going on to hope he could find it in him to forgive the rancours of the past and accept their future together as colleagues and friends. The afternoon had passed in a most agreeable fashion. He had felt at ease in her company; their talk was on a similar level, her accounts of earlier travels abroad holding his attention to such a degree he had been sorry when the hands of the clock told him it was time to go.

After that their little meetings became regular features, sometimes moving to the evenings when they had some marvellous talks together seated at a roaring fire, toasting scones and marshmallows, listening to classical music on the gramophone he brought from Woodbank Cottage. He began to spruce himself up even more, buying a suit and a new hat from his wages, going to Mungo's barber's shop to have his hair and beard trimmed.

When the good weather came he and Miss Hosie went walking, meandering arm in arm through Crathmor's woods and gardens, confiding in one another. She told him about her strict upbringing as a daughter of the manse, he eventually enlightened her about his past life: his post as head teacher of a boys' school, the troubles that had followed, the loss of his wife to another man, the death of his daughter, his wanders and his travels, without hope or happiness of any sort.

'Oh, you poor man,' she had cried, her face reddening at the recollection of her earlier treatment of him. 'I'm so sorry. I wish I had known. Oh, it's been too bad of me! And you such a clever man. I must try never to take people at face value in future. Such a sad, sad tale. Did you never see your wife again? Did you ever find out what happened to her?'

But Johnny had drawn the line then, shocked at himself for having revealed so much, swearing her to silence on the matter, withdrawing into himself at the very idea of his carefully guarded secrets being broadcast to all and sundry.

'Of course I won't breathe a word to anyone,' she had declared stoutly. 'As if I would. I value our friendship too much to bandy our confidences about. Please don't worry, Johnny, I might be an old bat but

I am not blind and I do know what people are like in a place like this.'

She had screeched with laughter then and Johnny had laughed too, relieved that he hadn't given everything away about his life for then it would have affected the Bowman children and that was the last thing he wanted. As it was he didn't see nearly so much of Rebecca these days. His house wasn't as convenient for her as Mary's Bay had been, and he was worried that his hold on Joshua had slipped to some degree for there had been talk about him reverting back to his old ways, getting too big for his boots, brow-beating his family, throwing his weight around in the community.

Johnny vowed to renew his vigil on Joshua as soon as he could. Meanwhile life at Crathmor was happy and busy; the summer holidays would soon be here and with them would come the family. He had been invited to join with them in a reunion dinner; Miss Hosie would be there too. The thought of that comforted Johnny greatly, for try as he might he could never completely rid himself of the shyness that had become inherent in him. It was second nature for him just to remain in the background at social gatherings, listening and watching, taking it all in and enjoying the quirks of human nature in the process.

Chapter Twenty-two

From school, college, and university, the family duly arrived to spend a holiday at Crathmor with their parents. The old house became alive again as voices chattered through the rooms and footsteps rang in the hall.

George had passed out of military college some eighteen months ago and was now a second lieutenant with The Argyll and Sutherland Highlanders. Vaila's heart missed a beat when he came striding through the door an hour or two earlier than his siblings, handsome and glowing in his tartan trews, khaki jacket, Glengarry bonnet, and Sam Browne shoulder belt. When he saw her in the hall with a tea tray in her hands he went striding over to lift her up and swing her round, laughing at the expression on her face when he set her down with everything intact, including the teacups.

'George MacPherson!' she gasped. 'You shouldn't do mad things like that! I could have dropped everything! When are you going to settle down and behave like a grown man?'

'I am behaving like one, and you didn't drop anything, not even the scones.' He stood back to gaze at her and his eyes twinkled. 'Mmm, I must say you look splendid, well worth coming back for. I hope you haven't been pining for me. On the other hand I hope you have, since it would be nice to think you go to bed every night and cry your eyes out, wishing only for the day of my return.'

'I'm far too tired at night to cry for anybody, George, not even you.' She smiled at him teasingly, finding it hard to resist the appeal in his blue eyes.

'Not even for dear old Mark? Is he still eating his heart out for you? Or has he seen sense at long last and decided that I should have you all to myself?'

The opening of the sitting-room door put an end to further conversation. Emily came out. Rushing over to her eldest son she threw her arms round him and cried, 'You look wonderful. As handsome as ever and twice as cocksure. But what are you doing standing out here? Your father's been waiting. You may bring the tea in, Vaila – that is if it isn't cold by now.'

Vaila reddened and went hurrying in with the tray, feeling that she had been put very thoroughly in her place. George winked at her as she set out the tea things and handed round plates before departing the scene, still smarting a little from Emily's gently sarcastic remarks. She had been right, of course. George was a top-drawer MacPherson of Crathmor while she was just Vaila Sutherland of Keeper's Row, a servant who ought to know better than to be hobnobbing with the gentry.

She would tell George that too, as soon as ever she could. Meanwhile she went to the kitchen and vented her spleen on young Joan MacNulty who was sitting with her elbows on the table reading an ancient penny dreadful and stuffing a large piece of walnut cake into her mouth behind the cook's back.

'*He's* home, isn't he?' Joan said slyly. 'That's why you're all red in the face and looking as if you would like to kill somebody. Oh, I know all about it, you're down here, he's up there, supping tea and acting the part. It was all right when he was younger, the mistress didn't mind then. Now she'll be expecting him to behave himself and find someone o' his own standing to get serious about.'

'Shut up!' Vaila said viciously. 'You know nothing, Joan MacNulty, except what you feed into that fat face of yours! You would do well to remember *your* place is at the sink washing dishes. If you don't get on with it this minute I'll tell Mrs Grundy you've been slacking again and see how you like the back o' her hand across that big bum o' yours!'

'What's that? Did I hear my name?' A large fierce-looking woman with a red face appeared suddenly out of the pantry, making Joan scuttle about her business and Vaila go about hers, vowing to herself that it was high time she put a stop to George's flirting no matter how much he tried to woo and flatter her – and the sooner she told him that the better.

George just grinned in his indolent way when she tried to talk to him. 'Mother didn't mean anything. She loves you as much as I do and sees you as part of the family. She was exhausted that day I arrived, getting everything ready for us coming, arranging things, seeing to the baby.'

He put his hands on Vaila's shoulders and made

her look at him. 'Fiona's a handful, eighteen months old and already tearing around like an express train, biting people if she doesn't get her own way, kicking the ponies before they can kick her. I warned Mother but it was too late by then. Now we have a female version of Ross Wallace on our hands, terrifying everyone in sight, cutting her teeth on bullets, sharpening them on nails.'

Vaila's mouth twitched but she wasn't going to allow herself to yield. 'That's as may be, George, but I still think you ought to leave me alone. I am not for you, I have no money, I have no position. Pride is my only asset and that I mean to keep at all costs.'

'Vaila, Vaila,' he chided softly. 'We are not that sort of people. You ought to know that by now. You've grown up with me and my family. The old goat thinks the world of you, the young goat thinks the world of you, so cheer up and stop looking like a younger version of Mrs Grundy who has scared the wits out of me ever since I was knee-high to a grasshopper.'

'She's only been here two years – and you were anything but a grasshopper then.' Vaila felt herself softening but went on steadily. 'Find yourself a nice rich girl, one who's more suited to your requirements. I'm quite happy as I am and have no wish to climb up any ladders in case I fall down again.'

'I don't want a nice girl, Vaila. Nice girls are boring and dull as I've discovered to my cost. I have no money either but one day I'll inherit Crathmor and then I'll be in a position to keep you in the manner you deserve if you ever decide I'm good enough for you.'

'I'm not deciding anything, George. I'm only seventeen, I want to see a bit o' life yet, I want to do things I've never done before, I want to enjoy my freedom for a while.'

'I'll give you some freedom,' He grinned at her and put his thumb under her chin. 'We're all going riding tomorrow morning, Angus, the girls and I. Helga Rose asked me to ask you to come. We'll take a picnic and have a great time. Do say yes, Vaila, everybody else will be paired off and you wouldn't want me to be all on my lonesome, would you now?'

Vaila giggled despite herself. 'Och, all right, just this once, but only if I can manage to get off my duties for an hour or two.'

'It's all arranged, Mother's permission, she thinks you need some air to buck you up.' He moved closer and touched her mouth with his. A tingle of pleasure went through her, and she found herself very much looking forward to a ride in the countryside with George and the girls.

It was great fun for Vaila to be in Helga Rose's large airy bedroom, trying on the riding habit that the eldest daughter of the house had said she could borrow. Helga Rose was a sunny good-natured girl with her mother's English rose complexion and her father's droll sense of humour. She was also built on the generous side. She and Vaila giggled together as the owner of the riding habit, a row of pins sticking out of her mouth, made alterations to the jacket and arranged a few hasty tucks in the jodhpurs.

'There isn't time to sew anything in place,' she

informed Vaila, 'so you'll just have to be careful when you're on your horse. I daren't put any pins in your bum. Think how that would be if you took a tumble and roused the whole neighbourhood with your yells.'

Maggie came into the room, all purrs and waving tail and sure of a welcome. She was immediately picked up by Helga Rose who snuggled the cat to her face and looked ecstatic. 'Mmm, she feels so soft. Sheba would never let me do this, she was always too ready with her claws and her teeth and only ever let Father handle her. Oh, it's so good to be home. I'd forgotten how restful Crathmor can be, I'll be going on to university to study medicine after the summer so mean to make the most of my holiday . . .'

A tornado entered the room at that point, namely tiny little Fiona Joy, stampeding away from her nanny in hot pursuit of the cat, stretching out her waving hands to the animal who jumped down in terror at sight of the toddling warrior and took refuge under the bed.

'Come here this minute you wee besom!' Nanny Armour came puffing into the room, cap askew, face scarlet, as she bent to pluck the child up to her heaving bosom.

'No! Me get Maggie!' came the defiant screech, 'You go away! Go away! I don't want you!'

'I'm sorry about this,' the girl apologised as her charge wriggled and scratched as good as any cat and attempted to wrest her captor's ear from her head. 'I've never known any child like this in all my days as a nanny! If she doesn't settle down soon I'll – I'll pack my bags and leave and won't care if I never see the wee menace again.'

'One down, a dozen to go,' Helga Rose said wryly as the nanny staggered from the room with the screaming Fiona Joy. 'And what was that I said about Crathmor being peaceful? I think we'll have to lock my little sister in the dungeon and throw away the key. Ten years should see an improvement – or better make that twelve to be on the safe side!'

The horses were ready and waiting in the yard behind the house. George eyed Vaila with approval when she made an appearance and told her how good she looked in a riding habit. Her face broke into smiles. She wondered what he would have said if he'd known she was held together by pins. The next instant the smile froze on her face when she spied Mark astride one of the horses. 'Did you know about this?' she questioned George.

'Sophie wanted him to come,' George said offhandedly. 'She's always had a soft spot for Mark and has in fact been seeing quite a bit of him since my sister brought her here for a holiday.'

Vaila didn't wait to hear more. Guiding her horse over to Mark she hissed furiously, 'Just what are you doing here, Mark Lockhart?'

'I could ask you the same thing.'

'George wanted me.'

'Sophie wanted me.'

'That's that, then.' Her mouth tightened. She felt oddly deflated. 'I didn't know or I wouldn't have come. I haven't forgotten what you did to George up at River House.'

'It won't happen again,' Mark said through equally tight lips. 'I'll never make a fool o' myself like that again – not over any lass, and that's all I have to say on the matter.'

There was something different about Mark that day. Gone were his untidy clothes, his mud-spattered wellingtons, his careless appearance, and in their place was an extremely well-cut riding habit, complete with long boots and leather crop. His curly dark hair had been cut, his face was shiny and clean in the morning light. There was no trace of dust or horse dung anywhere and he looked every inch a young gentleman as he sat there astride his gleaming chestnut mount.

'You never bothered to dress yourself like that for me,' she said shortly, annoyed to feel her face flushing. 'It goes to show what the gentry can do to people.'

'So I see,' he said meaningfully, eyeing her smart outfit which to all intents and purposes seemed to fit perfectly over every winsome curve. She clicked her tongue, tossed her head, and turned away from him to rejoin the others, back straight and proud despite the fact that one of the pins in her jacket was scratching her arm.

'Where's Maida?' George's younger brother, Angus Neil, was gazing around him in puzzlement. 'She said she would meet us here at nine and it's well past that now.'

'We'll wait five minutes then we'll get going,' George decided. 'She knows where we'll be and can always catch us up.'

A few minutes later they were on their way without Maida, the horses' hooves clattering on the cobbles of the yard, the excitement of the moment making Vaila forget her annoyances and just give herself up to enjoyment. They rode into the open countryside; the wind was on her face, the scents of the summer fields were in her nostrils, she felt glowing and alive and gave a little shout of pure joy when George came alongside and threw her a dazzling grin. He was looking his best, young, dashing, handsome, handling his horse with great panache, spurring it to gallop faster, inciting her to do the same till soon they were both in front of the others.

Only then did they ease their steeds to a trot to gaze at one another, conveying their unspoken thoughts with their eyes till he guided himself close to her and reached over to kiss her warmly on the lips. She kissed him back, engulfed in timeless moments of romance, of summer sun and heady perfumes, feeling a dizzy excitement growing in her as his kiss became longer, more passionate.

There was also something else, the notion that Mark might see her like this and perhaps be just a little bit angry. She didn't want him and George to fight over her again – Mark was going his way, she was going hers – except – some little wicked contrary bit of her wanted Mark to come along. He wouldn't be able to say anything, not with Sophie there, not when she and he were supposed to have some sort of relationship blossoming between them . . .

The moment was over. George withdrew, red-faced and dazed-looking. 'We've got to get together, Vaila,' he told her unsteadily. 'I'm only here for a short time, we have to make the most of it while we can.'

Vaila sighed and wished boys could be content with just romantic love. They wanted to get serious too quickly, making everything complicated and impossible.

Mark came riding up, a thunderous look on his face, and she knew he had witnessed the little interlude between her and George and hadn't liked it one bit. She looked at him coolly. 'You'd better go back for Sophie, you're her partner after all and mustn't neglect your duties.'

He glared at her, he glared at George, his fists balled, without a word he turned his horse's head and cantered back to Sophie Marie with anything but a gentlemanly expression on his countenance.

Chapter Twenty-three

Joss was working in the Crathmor stables, having promised to stand in for Mark who had gone off for the morning with the MacPhersons.

Mark had grinned at the look on his friend's face. 'Don't worry, Maida won't be around, she's coming with us so you'll be perfectly safe here by yourself. Angus has taken a shine to her and wants her to keep him company on the picnic.'

Joss had looked uncomfortable at Mark's words. It was as if Maida was an ogre, one to be avoided at all costs, when all the time she was just a pretty young girl who was full of fads and fancies and harmless dreams.

'I don't have anything against Maida,' Joss had said awkwardly, 'It's just, me and Rebecca . . .'

'I know,' Mark nodded understandingly. 'I feel the same about Vaila, only she doesn't feel the same about me. I've seen how much Maida pesters you but she doesn't really mean it. She's got a notion into her head, that's all, she'll grow out o' it once she sees you don't feel the same way about her. We're alike, Maida and me, we've fallen for people who don't return our feelings.'

They had left it at that. Joss went along to Crathmor

on the appointed day and was really enjoying working with the ponies, feeding them and grooming them and generally seeing to their well-being. So engrossed was he in his task he didn't notice Maida coming in till she was standing on the other side of the pony he was brushing, smiling at him, her big blue eyes gazing at him quizzically, as if waiting for a pleasurable response to her unexpected arrival.

'Maida!' he cried, not so much pleased as shocked by her sudden appearance. 'What are you doing here? I thought—'

'I knew you'd be surprised,' she broke in, taking his reaction as a sign of welcome. 'I was supposed to go with the others but I saw you coming down here earlier and decided I'd rather be with you instead.'

'You saw me?' Joss stuttered, remembering how careful he'd been coming here, making sure no one was about yet feeling safe anyway. Mark had said he and the others were gathering in the yard behind the big house; the horses had been made ready early and brought up from the stables.

'Yes, Joss, I saw you.' Maida leaned over the pony's back and took Joss's hand. 'I was late and took a short cut through the endrigs. You were coming along by the lane and I knew you were making for the stables . . .' She pouted a little. 'I can't think why Mark didn't mention you coming here. Otherwise I would have told Angus I couldn't manage to go to the picnic.'

'Mark asked me to stand in for him at the last minute,' Joss lied quickly. 'I thought at first I couldn't come and only did it as a favour.'

Maida's hand tightened on his. 'You do know I'd

rather be with you than anyone else, don't you, Joss?'

'Ay, I know that, Maida, but I have work to do and can't stand here gossiping.'

'Oh, Joss.' She came to him and slipped her arms round his neck. She was extremely attractive that day, dressed as she was in a long frilly skirt and pale blue blouse that set off her eyes, her hair a tumble of gold about her shoulders, the swell of her breasts enticingly displayed. He realised she must have gone back to the house to change and the thought of that further enhanced his discomfiture.

'Come on, Maida.' He tried to wriggle away from her but she pulled him in closer.

'Don't you think I'm pretty, Joss?' she asked, the tip of her tongue showing between her white teeth. 'Don't you love me just a little bit?'

'You're like a sister to me, Maida.' He tried to sound matter-of-fact but was finding it difficult to keep himself cool and detached. It was warm in the stables, he felt the sweat breaking on his brow.

'You don't really mean that, Joss,' she whispered. 'How can I be like a sister to you when I know you want to kiss me and touch me? Brothers don't do that, at least, mine doesn't.'

Her mouth was coming closer to his, she was pressing her breasts against his chest. They were firm yet soft, surprisingly big. He could smell her perfume, see the pulse beating in her neck. The pressure of her hands was becoming more urgent and he allowed himself to melt against her, to take what she was offering.

Her lips found his, she moulded herself to him, the

mound of her soft little belly rubbed against his, her hands slipped down, she started to undo his trouser buttons, a pulse in his groin began beating, he gave a little groan as a burning need invaded his loins. It would be easy, so easy just to go along with her. What harm could it do? No one would ever know. Rebecca needn't find out. Once. Just this once . . .

With a howl of rage he pushed Maida away and did up his buttons. 'Get out, Maida! Just get out and don't come back!'

Her lip trembled. 'How can you say that, Joss? You know how much I care for you and want you. It's always been like that, just you, only you. Caleb Bowman and Tom MacGill have been after me for ages but I only flirted with them a little bit. I never gave them any real encouragement because I wanted to save myself for you.'

She put her face in her hands and began softly to cry. 'It's *her*, isn't it?' she sobbed. 'Rebecca Bowman. Why do you love her so much? What do you see in her? She isn't your type. She's aloof and snobbish. She doesn't even come from around here. She seems to think she's better than everyone else yet you go after her as if she were the most beautiful and interesting girl in the world. She's strange and horrible and I can't think why anybody would want to love her.'

Maida's impassioned words found their echo in Joss's own questioning. He had often wondered about Rebecca's deep attraction for him. She was strange, she was different, he and she were like chalk and cheese, she could be aloof when she wanted to be, she was often rude to people she didn't trust, she could be cold and unfriendly yet from the beginning he had felt drawn to her like a magnet. How could he tell people about the loyalty that burned within her like an undying flame? Her deep devotion to those she loved. Her intelligence. Her quicksilver mind. Her wit. Most of all, how could he ever explain the deep and passionate love he had for Rebecca? Theirs was the language of hearts and minds and souls. He couldn't imagine his life without her. He had occasionally tried to visualise what it would be like with someone else, out of curiosity, out of lust sometimes when faced with busty bouncy ready girls at village gatherings.

He could have let himself go with Maida but was thankful that he hadn't and his voice was even when he said, 'Rebecca *is* my type and to me she's the most beautiful and interesting girl in the world. Go and live your life, Maida, get yourself another lad. With your looks you could have anybody.'

'I don't want anybody else, I want you, Joss, and – and if I can't have you neither will she. I could always tell her father about you two, he hates Catholics and would soon put a stop to your clandestine meetings.'

'Do that and I'll never speak to you again. I mean to marry Rebecca when I'm older and have saved enough money. To hell with her father and what he thinks! Och, please don't cry, you know how I hate it when I see girls crying. You and I can still be friends – but not in the way you want.'

Maida tossed her golden ringlets. 'I can make you love me, Joss. You've always taken me for granted but some day that could change. You wait. Just you wait!'

She flounced away out into the sunlight, leaving

Joss to breathe a sigh of relief and take a few moments to recover his senses before going back to his neglected duties with the horses.

It was a beautiful spot the MacPhersons had chosen for their picnic, a rolling meadow filled with scarlet poppies and blue cornflowers and graceful trees shading the riverbanks with their gently swaying fronds. Checked linen cloths were laid on the grass on which the food and drink was set out; everybody was quiet as they ate and drank while the horses browsed in the lush grasses and the bees droned in the clover.

Replete, they lay back and listened to the sounds of the countryside. For a time contentment reigned but it didn't last. Angus and Helga Rose were soon up on their feet, relieving one another of their boots, divesting themselves of unnecessary garments, hollering at the tops of their voices as they joined hands and went plunging down the bank straight into the river. 'Come on in you lot!' Angus called when he had recovered from the shock of the cold water.

'Move yourselves!' Helga Rose cried as she danced around splashing her brother in her enthusiastic way.

But George had no intention of joining his brother and sister. Throwing himself down beside Vaila he put a blade of grass between his teeth and gazed up at the sky. They lay like that for a few minutes, not speaking, then his hand crept into hers, he cradled her head in the crook of one arm, and leaned over to kiss her. 'Stop that, George,' she hissed. 'Mark will see and I'm not having you two at each other's throats again.'

'Oh, I shouldn't think he's interested in us,' George replied with a wicked chuckle. 'He's far too busy for that.'

Vaila raised herself up to see Mark flirting with dainty giggly Sophie Marie, tickling her nose with a poppy, sliding his hand up her arm, whispering into her ear, touching her cheek with his lips. Glancing up he saw Vaila watching and throwing her a look of defiance he took Sophie's fingers between his teeth and began gently to nibble them, all the while keeping his gaze fixed on Vaila.

'Don't mind him.' George pulled her down towards him and began kissing her in earnest, his hands caressing her hair, travelling further down to the tender swell of her breasts.

A dark shadow loomed over them and Mark was there, glowering down on George with all his might. 'Don't go too far, MacPherson,' came the quietly ominous tones. 'She isn't yours to do as you like with.'

'She isn't yours either,' George returned, the whites of his knuckles showing in his tensing hands. Scrambling to his feet he put his face close to Mark's and ground out, 'You mind your business and I'll mind mine. I owe you one from that last time and if you don't stop interfering in my life you might get more than you bargained for!'

'Oh, I've had enough o' this! You two fight it out if you like. I'm off!' Vaila got up and went running away to catch hold of her horse's reins. In a flash she had mounted and was galloping away, her hat falling from her head, her hair streaming out as she urged her horse to go faster and faster over the fields.

A thunder of hooves came from behind. She glanced round, her hold on the reins tightening. It was her undoing; the horse reared up, she hit the ground and lay there with her senses spinning, pain searing through her ankle, only vaguely aware that the two boys had dismounted a short distance away. But they didn't come immediately to her aid. They were facing one another with murderous looks, fists balled, jaws jutting, chests heaving, till a cry of distress from Vaila brought them to their senses. Simultaneously they went to help her, pushing one another aside in their anxiety to be first.

'I don't want either of you!' Vaila sobbed. 'You're hopeless, the pair o' you! Oh, help me up. I'll sit here on the fence and wait for Helga Rose. I'm not hurt, just winded, which is just as well, I could have died just now for all you two care.'

Mark looked terribly shamefaced, George looked crestfallen. He apologised in a contrite voice. Mark did the same. Vaila however was having none of them and was relieved when Helga Rose came to the rescue. George helped Vaila onto the back of his sister's horse. Both boys watched as it trotted away.

'You'll never stand a chance with Vaila,' Mark said with conviction.

'And I suppose you think you will.'

'No, I don't, not any more. Vaila's a romantic, she's waiting for some great love to come along and sweep her off her feet – and I don't think either of us will fit the bill.'

'Speak for yourself, Lockhart. We all have our limitations. If you think you're beaten that's your lookout, but I've still got plenty of fight left in me and may the best man win.' With that he was off, riding back to the riverbank to round up the others, leaving Mark fuming but putting a face on it for Sophie's sake when he at last returned to her.

Vaila's fall had caused more harm than she had at first believed. She had badly twisted her ankle, there were cuts and bruises on her cheek, several pins from her hastily tacked up jacket had pierced her flesh and had to be removed by Dr MacAlistair when he came to look her over. Effie bound her ankle and bathed her bruises; she was ordered to stay in bed and rest for a day or two. She obeyed unwillingly, loath to be indoors when the summer sun was beckoning outside and all the world was green and blue and inviting.

George and Mark came to see her in turn, bearing fruit and flowers, each of them fully repentant by now and begging her forgiveness. She turned them both away with a few sharp words but hugged herself with glee at the very idea of them coming to her so humbly. She had power over them, there was no doubt about that, and it was rather nice after all to just lie here in her sunny little room and go over in her mind all the things that had been said at the picnic, the flirtations and the little jealousies that had taken place.

But she wasn't left in peace for long or allowed to become bored. Her family and friends saw to that. Rebecca visited twice; the Henderson Hens arrived with eggs and grapes; Dolly Law entered and left the room in a haze of pipe smoke but cheered Vaila up with her gossip and talk; Essie dumped her dolls on the bed and proceeded to play 'wee houses'; Andy read poems and stories; Aidan chatted to her in his knowledgeable fashion; Euan came armed with a jigsaw and stayed to help her make it.

'Ach, it is terrible just,' Kangaroo Kathy began when she and Janet arrived to commiserate with Hannah over her stepdaughter's accident. 'What a nasty thing to happen to the lass. She should never have gotten herself tangled wi' that young rascal George but there you go, we all have our weaknesses. The gentry have aye been fascinated wi' the working classes and us wi' them. Take that Edward, for instance, it was a well-known fact he hobnobbed wi' showgirls and enjoyed the sleazy side o' life. Lillie Langtry was more in his league but even there he should have known better.'

She paused only long enough to take her knitting from her lapbag before going on, 'Thank goodness I never had to worry about that. My Norrie never married me for my looks or my money, neither of which I've got. We're happy as we are and I wouldn't have it any other way – except for the hair in his lugs and that funny wee habit he has o' clicking his teeth together when he's upset. But och, it wouldny be Norrie if he didn't have hairs and he feels the same about me, I know this for a fact because he told me so himself.'

She looked from one agog face to the other. 'Promise me you'll never tell if I tell you something very very personal.'

'We promise,' came two united voices and Kathy went on in a deep breathy voice. 'We were in bed when it happened. He was lying there all thoughtful like when suddenly he said, "You are just like a pair o' your own knitted socks, Kathy, you have no seams on your body and . . ."' Here she jabbed a meaningful forefinger at the nether regions beneath her lapbag. '"The fiddly bits are the best bits of all."'

With a satisfied nod she took up her knitting once more. 'Oh, ay, my Norrie knows which side his bread is buttered. It was the nicest thing anybody ever said to me and the reason I wouldny change him for anybody – no' even the King o' England himself.'

Neither Hannah nor Janet could imagine the stolid Norrie coming out with anything so fanciful and Hannah, bamboozled as always by Kathy's nonsensical speech, opened her mouth to say something to this effect. That lady, however, gave her no chance. Getting up she put her knitting back into her lapbag and withdrew a greaseproof-wrapped package. 'I'll just go up and give Vaila this tablet. It will cheer her up and get her back on her feets in no time. Sugar is a great way o' giving folks energy and I for one have always enjoyed a nice bit o' creamy tablet.'

'But, Kathy,' Hannah began carefully, knowing how fatal it was to enter into a conversation with Janet's cousin yet unable to resist doing so. 'You are never done telling us about the dangers o' sugar, now here you are, singing its praises. I thought you said it was bad for the health as well as the teeth.'

'Oh, ay, it is,' Kathy returned chirpily. 'But I had to have a wee taste to make sure I had put in all the right ingredients then another wee taste to see if it had set right.' She gazed at Hannah in puzzlement. 'But surely you should know all about that, helping out as you do in The Bread Oven. As for teeth, I lost them years ago and only have the ones the dentist mannie made me. Nothing on earth is going to ruin them – except a good bash wi' a mallet which I don't think will ever happen to mine.'

She went out, then could be heard clumping up the stairs. 'How do you ever understand her?' Hannah said dazedly to Janet.

'I don't, but it's not understanding that makes her so much fun,' Janet giggled. 'It's a bit like a crossword, you can spend hours analysing her after she's gone and might even occasionally come up with an answer. I find it a good way o' keeping myself amused when I have nothing better to do wi' my time.'

'A crossword.' Hannah looked thoughtful. 'Ay, that is an idea, Janet, but there's only one drawback. You could never look Kathy up in a dictionary, she doesn't even fit into an anagram and there are plenty of those in a crossword – if you see what I mean.'

It was Janet's turn to look puzzled and she was really rather glad when Hannah went to put on the kettle and the subject of crosswords was forgotten.

The tea made and Kathy safely back in the kitchen, Hannah took a cup up to Vaila. Essie and Euan were in the room, romping about on the rocking horse, lost in their own little world of make-believe and wonder, Vaila tolerating them as best she could though her stepmother sensed her restlessness and her desire to be up and about and away into the great outdoors with its romance, its excitement, and its young men. Hannah gave a sigh. At least she wouldn't have any worries about Essie on that score for a long time to come. She was only eleven and young for her age, still playing with dolls, still viewing the world through the eyes of an innocent child. Hannah felt good about this. Essie was her baby and she very much wanted her to stay that way for as long as ever she could.

KINVARA

Winter 1938/39

Chapter Twenty-four

Winter was never a season to be relished by the countryfolk of Kinvara. The farmers cursed the shortening daylight and dreaded the terrible rigours of rising on freezing cold mornings to milk and feed the animals and somehow scrape a living from the land. Fishermen struggled on the high seas and spent enforced stays ashore when the weather became too dangerous for them to venture out. People moaned and groaned to each other about the wind and the rain; the readings on barometers became a favourite topic of conversation if there was nothing else to gossip about. Others welcomed the enforced rest the shorter days brought, relishing the opportunity to catch up on all the things they hadn't been able to do in summer when outdoor activities were uppermost on the agenda, including cutting peats and stockpiling wood in readiness for the wintry times ahead.

If the drear dark days came alone it was enough for anyone to bear, if the miseries of colds and chills arrived to dampen spirits already low it became a test of endurance for even the most optimistic of beings. It was difficult to keep warm in houses full of chinks that let in the icy draughts whistling up from the sea. People went to bed early and put coats as well as blankets on top of them to keep warm. Thatched cottages and crofthouses weren't so bad, since their thick walls had been built to withstand the extremes of Scottish west coast winters.

But bricks and mortar, no matter how sturdy, couldn't keep away the outbreak of flu that swept like a tide through the communities of Kinvara just before Christmas 1938. Young and old alike succumbed to the illness as hardly a household escaped the ravages the virus wrought in them. People crawled about 'like washed-out rags' to quote Big Bette who, in common with many others, had to force herself out of bed in order to attend to the wants of her family.

Dr MacAlistair and Effie had been kept busy coping with everyone's needs till they too fell ill and had to call in a locum and a temporary nurse to take over till they were better. The majority of people however could not afford a doctor of any sort and just suffered though certainly not in silence, one and all feeling themselves justified in airing their grievances to anyone who would listen.

The Bowman family had all been laid low by the scourge. Joshua had been first to recover, then Caleb and Rebecca, Miriam taking longer with her poor constitution and low level of staying power. 'Mind over matter, Miriam,' Joshua said loftily. 'Think yourself well and you will be well. And don't forget the strength of prayer. That is what has sustained me throughout all this and why I am the first to be up on my feet. You have no faith, that's your trouble, no wonder you look as sickly as you do. The Lord helps those who help themselves. I don't know how many times I've tried to din that into you but there you go, dragging yourself about like a snail, no go in you, looking a hundred instead of a woman still in her prime with everything to live for.'

Miriam didn't share this view. Her small bare room, despite its lack of human comforts, had been like a sanctuary to her in the last few days. She hadn't wanted to get better, she had scant desire to face a life that had no meaning any more. All she wanted was to bury her head under the blankets and never come out again. Her husband did not allow for such 'malingering'. The minute he was up and about he expected everyone else to do the same and was soon roaring his head off for her to make breakfast, Caleb to bring in wood for the fire, Rebecca to see to the laundry, Nathan to get outside and start business rolling again.

Nathan however was unable to move from his bed. He was a delicate boy of sixteen who had never thrived and looked more like an eleven-year-old as he lay there in his narrow iron cot, racked with coughing, burning with fever, tossing and turning, hearing nothing, never mind his name as his father bellowed for him to get up.

'Go and fetch him, Caleb,' Joshua ordered. 'The boy has never done an honest day's work in his life. Born lazy, that's him. This has been a great excuse for him to lie up there and rot. I'm not having any of that in this house and the sooner he realises that the better.'

Unwillingly, Caleb went to do his father's bidding and had to practically carry his brother downstairs to sit him on a wooden settle by a smoky, newly lit fire. The boy sat shivering in his thin nightshirt, bent double with coughing, looking so drawn and ill Mirian gave Joshua a defiant glance and went to get a blanket from the kist in the lobby. It was damp and settled about the boy's shoulders like a shroud, making him tremble all the more.

Rebecca came in and was shocked to see her brother up, knowing how fevered he'd been when she had looked in on him earlier. Going over she put a protective arm round his shoulders and cooried into him to allow the heat from her own body to seep into his, much to the astonishment of her father who stared at her as if she had taken leave of her senses.

'How dare you lay hands on your own brother in such a fashion?' he ground out. 'Furthermore, how dare you encourage his snivelling? There's nothing wrong with him that a good day's work won't cure.'

Rebecca lifted her chin in a gesture that Joshua knew well. 'I dare because he's my brother and I care about him,' she said contemptuously. 'Which is more than you've ever done or are ever likely to do.'

Turning away from the blazing anger in her father's eyes she addressed herself to Nathan. 'Don't worry, I'm sending for the doctor and you're going back to your bed this minute.'

'Who gave you permission to do any of those things?' Joshua cried, beside himself with rage at this wilful behaviour from a daughter who had always made him feel uneasy with her stubbornness and her keen sense of fairness.

'I don't need permission, I'm a big girl now in case you haven't noticed.' Rebecca spoke loudly and clearly and was further emboldened when Caleb came to stand beside her in a silent gesture of support.

'You can well afford a doctor, a nurse too if need be,' she imparted coolly before turning to her older brother. 'Caleb, run for Dr MacAlistair, he's back on his feet now and doing his rounds again.'

'Over my dead body!' Joshua roared, raising his fist above his head as if to strike out.

Rebecca did not flinch. 'You had better not do that, Father, or I shall be forced to call the village policeman as well as the doctor. I don't really believe you would enjoy that kind of slight on the name you have tried so hard to build up since you got here.' She glanced at Miriam standing by the door wringing her hands and looking as if she were about to faint. 'Go and find some hot bottles, Mother, while I help Nathan upstairs. You go too, Caleb, the sooner the doctor comes the better.'

'Miriam!' Joshua stayed his wife with a sharp command. 'No pampering, no hot bottles!'

'There are no hot bottles,' Miriam said in a flat voice. 'You never allowed any in the house. I'll have to go and borrow some from a neighbour.'

'No!' The protest was torn from Joshua's throat, ragged and high. 'Thou shalt not borrow! You will not do this, woman, think how it will look!'

'You should have thought of that before, Joshua,' she said as she followed Caleb out into the bitter day, feeling strange and shaky but a small triumph growing in her as she went along. At last, she had answered her husband back, and all because of Rebecca with her fearlessness and her sense of justice for those less strong than herself.

Miriam pulled the folds of her shawl closer round her sparse bosom. She felt weak; her legs were trembling from the aftermath of the flu, mingling with the reaction she was feeling from the scene in the kitchen. Yet inside herself she felt better and she hoped Rebecca would always be here to give her the purpose she needed to continue with her life at the Mill O' Cladach.

She couldn't leave. There was nowhere for her to go, no one she could turn to. Besides, she still had the children to look after, especially Nathan. She hadn't been much of a mother to any of them but she was better than nothing and she felt this very strongly as her footsteps took her down the track to the home of her nearest neighbour in a quest for the hot bottles.

When Dr MacAlistair came and saw the state Nathan was in he ordered that he be kept in bed and a fire lit in his room at once. 'The boy must not be allowed to get up,' he told Rebecca who had escorted him into the house. 'He has congestion of the lungs and must have medicine right away.'

This he also imparted to the elder Bowmans when he went down to the kitchen. 'A fire?' Joshua said with a frown. 'We never have fires in the bedrooms. They're bad for the health as well as being hard on the pocket. The boy would be better off with the window open and a good dose of fresh air to clear his chest.'

'A fire, Bowman.' The doctor, still pale and shaky himself after his bout of flu, was in no mood to argue with the miller. 'And see to it at once or I won't answer for the consequences. Your son is very ill, he's got pneumonia and needs all the care and nourishment he can get.' He turned to Miriam. 'Beef tea, broth, plenty o' liquids. Try and see that he takes something, he looks as if he hasn't eaten for a month and could be doing with some meat on his bones. Put more blankets on his bed and a steaming kettle in his room once the fire's lit. It might help to relieve his congestion. I'll come back later to see how he's faring. Meantime, I want Caleb to come with me to collect the medicine.'

With a glower at Joshua he whirled Caleb away in his little black Austin Seven, a fairly recent acquisition and one that had greatly pleased Jeannie who was 'sick to the teeth of gazing up a horse's backside' and never mind if the dung was good for the roses. Big Bette had plenty to spare from the copious amounts her own horse produced and which she sold in good big bags from her shop for just a few coppers. Jeannie had not been sorry to say goodbye to the frisky pony that had been named Pumpkin by the laird's children while under their ownership. Jeannie had always maintained it was a silly name for a horse anyway, one it had seldom answered to, running off, snickering loudly, kicking its heels in defiance whenever it was called. The doctor had been more sentimental at the parting, feeling that an old way of life was dying, one that he had understood and known all his days, forgetting in his sorrow the many cold and wet journeys he had made astride his horse or in the little red jaunting cart with Pumpkin at the helm.

He wouldn't admit to Jeannie the advantages of having a motor car but secretly enjoyed his new-found freedom, the comforts of a roof over his head, the speed at which he could travel on his rounds, dry and safe from the elements. He was glad of it now as he fairly bowled along the road with Caleb to get the medicine, lending the boy his old bike to get back on as he was urgently needed on another call.

'See and give the bottle to your sister,' he told Caleb. 'I know she'll make sure your brother gets it. Tell me if there's any trouble and I'll be along at the toot, I can assure you o' that.'

Nathan had several visitors while he was ill, one of them being Johnny Lonely whom Joshua didn't dare turn away, scared as he was of the hold the teacher had on him. He felt mad at himself for having to eat humble pie in this way, especially to a being who was little better than a tramp in his opinion but who had somehow wormed his way into the laird's affections with his conniving and scheming to make something of himself.

Johnny sat with Nathan for a whole afternoon, reading to him and bathing his brow, talking quietly to Rebecca when she came in to stoke up the fire and bring her brother a bowl of steaming broth. She and Johnny in turn held the spoon to the boy's mouth but he refused to take it, making Rebecca shake her head worriedly, Johnny to signal that there was no use forcing him to take food and tiptoeing away out of the room when it became apparent that Nathan had fallen into a restless slumber.

Vaila felt extremely out of her depth when she entered the mill house and went up to Nathan's room. She hadn't been inside the place before, Joshua never having encouraged visitors of any kind over his threshold, far less the friends of his children. She was determined however to see Nathan, to let him know that everyone was thinking of him, and marched bravely past Joshua in the lobby, ignoring his disapproving scowl when he came out of the kitchen to see who was there.

Captain Rory also arrived, bearing gifts of a suitable nature, making Joshua uneasy in the process, particularly when he went to look over Jacob in his stable. A horse like that was worth keeping an eye on if only to make sure his master wasn't ill-treating him as he had done in the past. Joshua breathed a sigh of relief when Captain Rory took his leave. All that prying and poking, interfering in his life, never letting him forget for one moment that his tenancy of the mill was a tenuous one.

As if he cared! If he could have his way he would be up and running by now. Only his family stopped him, and that slothful wife of his, the proverbial millstone round his neck if ever there was one. Yet he needed her, if only to fill his belly and clean the house. And, if truth be told, he was tired of running; of all the places he'd been he liked Kinvara the best. Rebecca was right, in spite of everything he had built up a name for himself, the widows and the spinsters looked up to him and were grateful for his spiritual guidance, making his efforts on their behalf very worthwhile indeed. The mill had seen brisk trade over the last few years and he was damned if he was going to let anyone spoil it now.

Bugger Nathan for being ill! Opening up a can of worms. Bringing people that he'd rather not see to the house, forcing him into a show of hospitality when he least wanted it, looking at him as if he were the devil personified and all because he wanted his son to behave like a man instead of a simpleton. The runt of the litter, that was how he saw Nathan, only good for day-dreaming and lazing about, reading books, gazing at clouds, hiding when there was work to be done and pleading tiredness when he was taken to task for his idleness.

Joshua wasn't in a very good frame of mind the day Gabby Cochrane called to visit his son, bringing with him some of Jessie's home-made pancakes and a pot of bramble jelly he had made himself.

'Leave them on the table,' Joshua directed sullenly. 'I'll see he gets them when he's better.'

'I've got something I want to give him personally.' Gabby stood his ground, all six feet two inches of him, his long beard flowing down over his sark in silvery splendour. His deerstalker hat was amply decorated with fishing flies of every description though he'd never done a day's fishing in his life, claiming he just wore them because they looked nice and were a great help when it came to dealing with fiddly bits of his clocks. He was also wearing his kilt that day, despite the cold. He was fond of saying to Jessie it was like his own personal heater the way it wafted hot air over his knees and 'kept his arse as warm as a pie'.

All in all Gabby was a very distinctive-looking person and not the sort of man to be trifled with, withering the miller with such a bold stare he sourly stood aside to let the clockmaker past and directed him up to the sickroom.

Nathan's tired young face lit up at sight of Gabby.

He had lost count of the many happy hours he had spent in Clockwork Cottage, somehow managing to visit that wondrous abode in spite of his father, aided and abetted by Rebecca who was always ready to cover up for him and be glad that he found satisfaction in such simple pleasures. Gabby sat himself down by the bed; from an inner pocket he withdrew his precious working model of a steam engine and placed it gently in Nathan's hands.

'For you, lad.' Gabby swallowed a lump in his throat at the shock of seeing how exhausted the boy looked. His eyes were sunk deep in their sockets, feverish and too bright, a dew of sweat gleamed on his forehead, his lips were dry. His open nightshirt showed his bony shoulders and skinny ribcage.

'For me?' Nathan just stared and stared at the object he had so admired every time he visited Gabby in his cottage, 'Oh, but I can't take it, it's much too good to be here in this house. Father would see it and take it away from me.'

'It's yours, son, an early Christmas present,' Gabby said firmly. 'And your father will have me to reckon with if he comes any o' his nonsense. You rest now and I'll come back to see you soon.'

'I didn't think anybody liked me,' Nathan told Gabby with a catch in his voice. 'Now you've all been here and I know I'm going to get better, I can feel it happening already. I'll keep the engine till then – it will be nice – just to lie here and look at it.'

His low self-esteem brought a tear to Gabby's eye. He put his hand on the boy's shoulder and gave it a squeeze. At the door he looked back. Nathan was already asleep, the engine clutched to his chest, looking like a small boy who had plundered a Christmas stocking and had found exactly what he had been looking for all his life.

Chapter Twenty-five

Nathan died as he had lived, quietly and without protest, attended faithfully to the very end by Dr MacAlistair and Effie, Rebecca holding him as he drew his last breath, Miriam by his bedside, her face grey in the cold light of dawn filtering through the window, everything about her still and quiet and as lifeless as the dead body of her youngest son.

The icy breath of winter blew against the panes, wailing like a lost soul in the wilderness, keening round the house, rattling the cowlings on the chimney pots, whipping the marram grasses into frenzied wave-like motion in the dunes. Spicules of powdery snow were whirling over the landscape, blotting out the grey-bellied sea, sucking everyday objects into obscurity, torturing the grove of sycamores that stood sentinel at the east gable of the house.

The bare branches of a rowan tree outside Nathan's room were scrabbling against the window like long black eerie fingers, tap-tapping, tap-tapping, as if trying to gain entry while the witches of hell went riding by on the dark wings of winter, mournful, screeching, ghoulish, neither of the dead nor of the living but trapped somewhere in between. Rebecca shivered. It was warm in the room but she felt cold, as if death had touched her own soul, paralysing her senses, making her feel afraid, for herself, for the transient nature of human existence.

Nathan's head was now a dead weight in her arms. The dark curls that tumbled over his brow made him seem like a small boy who would waken at any moment and be glad that she was there to look after him.

'He never got his wish,' she said huskily. 'Poor Nathan, he asked so little from life and that's exactly what he got.' Gently she took Gabby's steam engine from her brother's limp hands and laid it on the bedside table. Bending down she kissed one of his pale cheeks before leaving the room to go downstairs where she threw her shawl around her shoulders and went out into the hostile day. The wind caught and bullied her, hail bombarded her face like icy pinpricks, she slid and fell, tripped and stumbled, but she picked herself up and went on, straight to No. 5 of Keeper's Row and into the arms of Joss who had seen her coming from the window.

Not a single question was asked. They all knew why she had come and gave her their tactful sympathies. Janet made her sit down and went to make a cup of tea, Big Jock Morgan put his big strong hand over hers and squeezed it reassuringly. Joss sat by her side and said nothing, for what was there to say to a girl who had just lost a brother she had so cherished? All he could do in those bleak moments was to hold her close and show her by his actions how much she meant to him.

Rebecca didn't want him to speak; enough that he was there when she most needed him, enough that the Morgan family as a whole reached out to gather her to their warm and generous hearts. She very badly needed the comfort that only a united family could give her in the terrible aftermath of her younger brother's death. His love for those around him had been gentle and undemanding, all through his life she had tried her best to protect him but in the end it hadn't been enough and he had paid a terrible price for the harshness of his life under the commanding rule of Joshua Bowman, a father who had never given him any encouragement, one who had laughed at his so-called weaknesses and had bullied him unmercifully because of them.

Dr MacAlistair went home with a heavy heart. Jeannie, whose hands were never idle even when she was ill, was sitting up in bed 'mending the arse' of yet another pair of her husband's winter combinations. When he came into the room and she saw the droop of his shoulders she knew his fight to save Nathan had been in vain and she put her mending aside. 'Come on, sit by me, Alistair, and tell me all about it,' she said kindly, knowing from long experience how upset he could be when he lost a patient, especially one so young as Nathan.

Alistair sat, he poured his heart into Jeannie's ears, she listened and sympathised. When he was finished she tossed the bedcovers aside and put her legs over the bed. 'I'm getting up,' she declared determinedly. 'I'm much better, my cold has gone, my head no longer feels as if it's floating into space. I'm going to make you a good breakfast o' ham and eggs and then we're going for a run in that motor car o' yours. Oh, I know the de'il is out there making merry wi' the elements but a wee jaunt along by the cliffs o' Niven's Bay will help to blow away the cobwebs for us both.'

The doctor gripped her hand and felt glad to be married to a woman like Jeannie, matter-of-fact, brisk, a great comfort to him when he needed a shoulder to cry on. The thought of ham and eggs cheered him up considerably. Neither he nor she had felt like eating for the best part of a week, but now his stomach was rumbling in the good old-fashioned way and his step was lighter as he followed his wife downstairs to help her raid the larder. The pair of them were like ravening bears as they staggered through to the kitchen with laden arms, giggling like children as they did so, the doctor's worries temporarily forgotten in the merriment of the moment.

Nathan's funeral over, Caleb went to his father and stood staring at him for long, long considering moments. 'What are you gawping at?' Joshua said uncomfortably. 'Have you no respect? Your brother lies cold in his grave and here you are, looking as if you would like to be in there with him.'

Caleb bunched his fists. His eyes were glittering strangely; there was whisky on his breath; he seemed not to care what he was saying as he stood there facing his father, a brawny lad of eighteen with youth and vigour on his side. 'It's because of you my brother is dead. He never did any harm to anyone and was too gentle for his own good. You were never kind to him.

You treated him like dirt and hounded him at every turn. In the end he had no will to live, you killed him as surely as if you had put a gun to his head and pulled the trigger. I just thought it was time I told you how much I've always hated you and even more for what you did to Nathan. If you were six feet under right now I'd come along and spit on your grave and hope you rot in hell for ever.'

Joshua turned purple and an artery in his neck bulged out like a piece of rope as wild-eyed he stared at his son in total disbelief before springing across the floor with a snarl of rage. But Caleb was ready for him. With a swift movement of one hefty arm he thwarted the downward swing of his father's fist and walloped him squarely on the jaw. It was an easy enough matter after that to twist his arms behind his back, run him over to a chair and throw him into it. He lay sprawled, too frozen with shock to make a movement of any kind while Caleb towered over him, a mean young man with fire in his gut and hatred in his heart. Bending down he leered into his father's red face and said mockingly, 'There you are, old man, time for you to pray for the salvation of your black soul – and while you're about it you can have a little think to yourself about your future. Things are going to change around here and from now on you aren't going to get so much of your own way. You killed Nathan, but you won't kill me or Rebecca, we're strong, we'll fight back, you see if we don't.'

'You're drunk!' Joshua's lip curled. 'False courage, it's about all you're good for. The cold light of day will see you back to your usual useless self, all brawn and no brains, only good for eating and sleeping and chasing after cheap women whenever you think my back is turned.'

For answer, Caleb took the flask out of his pocket, uncorked it and slugged some of the contents down before holding it under his father's nose. 'Like some? Smells good, eh? It wouldn't be your first taste. Empty prayers and alcohol, that's what keeps you going, I've seen you, dipping into the bottle when you think no one's watching. But I suppose we must make allowances. There's nothing but ice in your veins, a drop of the hard stuff might put the fire back for a time but in the end the cold will get you – if the devil doesn't get there first.'

With that he took himself off, heart beating fast, expecting to hear the dread footsteps coming along behind him. But there was only the echo of his own steps on the wooden floorboards as he made his way to his room to throw himself down on his bed. In minutes he was asleep, induced into a dreamless slumber by the raw spirits flowing inside him, his heavy breathing drowned out by the shriek of the wind outside his window while the snow cascaded over a land that was still and white and empty.

Sobriety came all too soon to Caleb. When he awoke the following morning he found himself growing afraid as he remembered snatches of the scene with his father. A cold sweat broke out on him. He had hit Joshua. After all these years of mental torture and torment he had actually fought back, physically hurting the man who had so often hurt him with his evil words and cruel sarcasm. The sight of Nathan's coffin being lowered into the cold hard ground had set something off in his head, an urge to punish his father for all the wrongdoing he had ever committed, a desire to get back at him for his harsh treatment of Nathan who had been too afraid and helpless to fight back. Somebody at the graveside, he had been too choked with grief to see who, had given him a flask of whisky to 'warm his bones'. He had drunk some of it down, had liked the lift it had given him. A catalysis had taken place, making him want to strike out at the instigator of all the pain and hurt . . . Now it was the next day and he didn't feel nearly so sure of himself.

His hand slid under the pillow to see if there was anything left in the flask just as the door opened to admit Rebecca who came immediately over to the bed and sat down. 'I heard what happened last night,' she began. 'I couldn't believe it at first but I'm glad you did it. I always knew you would one day, only thing is . . .' She made a rueful face. 'Things will be worse than ever now, he'll sulk and be silent or else give us lectures about the duties of offspring to their elders and betters.'

'Not if we stick together.' Caleb sat up in bed and grabbed her hand. 'Let's run away, Rebecca, we can do it, we're young, we can find work anywhere.'

She shook her head. 'I can't leave Joss, besides, there's Mother to consider.'

'Mother! She's never considered any of us! If she had, Nathan might still be alive and we wouldn't be as unhappy as we are now.'

'I know all of these things, Caleb. I don't think much of her either but she's our mother and she needs us, she's a lonely frightened woman and if we went she would have nobody.' She ran a hand through her glossy dark hair and gave a sigh. 'When I was younger I would never have said any of this because I loathed her so. Now I can see things clearer and hope I am more tolerant. She loved Nathan in her own way and must be suffering terribly in that private little hell of hers. The time will come for us, Caleb, but for now we must stay and give her our support.'

'I wonder why she ever married him in the first place,' Caleb said scornfully. 'She can't have been a very good judge of character to give up her life for someone like him.'

Rebecca said nothing for a moment. She had never told her brothers that their mother wasn't legally married to their father but was in fact still bound to Johnny Armstrong, her lawful wedded husband. 'I suppose he was all right when they met, he can be charming when it suits him, especially to lone women with money in their purses. Otherwise he's a terrifying man. If I ever let myself slip I know I would go under, just as Mother has done. She's got no strength to fight; maybe she had at one time but now everything in her is dead.'

'He's just flesh and blood like the rest of us,' Caleb said with more bravado than he felt, 'I proved that last night. I could have killed him if I had wanted and might do yet if he ever tries to get back at me.'

'You would be the one to suffer if you did, he's not worth it. One day something nasty will happen to him and he'll get what he deserves. Meantime he needs us at the mill and might think twice about trying to drive us away. He may be frightening but he's also a coward and knows you can fight back if need be.'

Caleb looked miserable. 'That was last night. I don't know how I'm going to face him this morning.'

She got up. 'Just act your normal self – if anyone can ever be normal in a house of hate such as this. But we will stick together, you and me, we'll prop one another up and be ready for anything, so get up now and come and have your breakfast. He's gone out to check the weather and won't come in again for at least another hour.'

Caleb waited till the door closed. Only then did he retrieve the whisky flask and hold it to his lips. There was only a drop or two left, but it was sufficient to fire his taste for more. He vowed he would get in his own little supply at the first available opportunity. Bolstered by the thought he dressed himself with some alacrity and went to get his breakfast in a much better frame of mind than before.

Rebecca was right about one thing: matters at the mill were worse than ever, not for Caleb but for her, Joshua having left the boy strictly to his own devices since the night of Nathan's funeral. Joshua had a new bone to pick, as she very soon discovered when he confronted her one morning after breakfast. It was about her relationship with Joss, and he wasted no time relaying his views to her on the subject. 'Don't think I'm blind, madam,' he began with ill-concealed chagrin. 'I've been hearing things and seeing them for myself. You might think you're clever but you're not clever enough. I have a suspicion you went sneaking up to Keeper's Row the day your brother died. Shamelessly and openly, hardly able to wait till Nathan drew his last breath before going on with your sinful pursuits. I was too grief-stricken at the time to say anything about it, hoping I was mistaken about you, but now I know I'm not. Hints have been dropped, the people here have loose tongues and it's amazing what they let slip in the course of conversation.'

'What of it!' Rebecca fired back. 'I've been seeing Joss for ages and if you weren't so wrapped up in yourself you would have discovered that fact long ago!'

'He's Catholic,' Joshua blazed. 'How can you stand there and tell me you're slutting about with a Catholic? I won't have it, girl, I simply will not stand that sort of rebellion from a daughter of mine!'

'You can't stop me!' Her heart was beating swiftly in her throat, robbing her of breath, taking every ounce of her willpower to stand there and defy him. 'You can't stop me,' she repeated, 'I'm old enough to do as I like and to hell with you and your narrow-minded beliefs.'

'We'll see about that.' His voice was shaking with rage. 'Right this minute, right now in fact . . .'

He hurtled away out of the house, leaving her alone and trembling in the middle of the room, wondering what the future held for her, now that her secret had been discovered by a man who would have no mercy in his soul for young and tender love.

* * *

Jock Morgan, otherwise known as Morgan the Magnificent by his friends, answered the imperative rapping on his door. He was a fine figure of a man was Jock, with his splendid physique and bearing, the little blond ringlet of hair at his nape only serving to emphasise his manliness and strength.

When he saw who was at his door he made no gesture of welcome but just stood there, huge arms folded, blue eyes flashing as he waited for Joshua to speak.

Joshua spoke loudly and longly, accusingly and hotly, but he might as well have been talking to thin air for all the impression it made on Jock. 'Of course my son is seeing your daughter,' Jock stated flatly. 'Have you been going around with your head buried in the sand, Bowman? Too wrapped up in your hell fire and thunder to see what's going on under your nose? Leave the youngsters alone or you'll have me to deal with. I wouldn't kill you, you're no' worth that, but I would make sure you suffered all right . . .'

Pausing, he put his face closer to Joshua's and grinned. 'It's a great place, Kinvara, for talk of all sorts. I've found out certain things about you, Bowman, interesting little snippets they are too – well, you know how these things get about. Your dealings with lonely women, for instance, the way you've wormed yourself into their lives and taken all you could from them. There's more, much more, a wee rumour is going the rounds, some folks are saying Miriam isn't really your wife and is attached in some way to Johnny Armstrong. Fancy that, a law-abiding man like yourself living in sin.'

Joshua's eyes narrowed. 'How dare you make such

wicked insinuations! Any more of it and I'll have you up for slander. What these people don't know they make up! Watch out, Morgan, or I'll, I'll . . .'

'You'll what, Bowman? Hit me? As you did Nathan? I'll take you on if you like, any day, right now if you want.'

Joshua retreated a step or two and Jock gave a short bitter laugh. 'Too scared, eh? Not quite what you had in mind? All you're good for is bullying children and those less able than yourself. You make me sick, Bowman, and if you don't take yourself out o' my sight this minute I'll set the neighbourhood dogs on you to save me getting my hands soiled.'

Joshua laughed mockingly at this. He looked meaningfully at Breck who had taken to sitting outside his door watching the world go by, only rising when he had to answer the calls of nature or investigate a stranger who didn't belong in the Row. 'If you mean that mangy cur you've got more imagination than I thought. By the look of him he's seen better days and probably hasn't got a tooth left in his head.'

He glared at the dog; the dog glared back, a rumbling growl issued from his throat and a perfectly sound set of sharp fangs gleamed menacingly in his contorted face, making him look fiercer than any dog half his age.

Andy, having heard the miller's sarcastic remarks about Breck from his bedroom window, came out to put a restraining hand on his dog's ruff, followed by Essie then Vaila. All three Sutherland youngsters stared silently at Joshua, as if daring him to make more derogatory comments concerning Breck. Rob too came out, then Hannah, drying her hands on her apron as she did so, 'Everything all right, Jock?' she asked, gazing curiously at Joshua as she spoke.

'Ay, as right as rain, Hannah.' He grinned. 'As Mr Bowman here will surely agree.' Lowering his voice he continued, 'On your way, man, I've had enough o' you for one day. Go home and grieve for your son instead of trying to make trouble for your daughter. You're lucky she's stuck by you all this time. If it wasn't for her and Caleb you would have no business to run so be thankful for small mercies. One other thing, if you harm a hair o' Rebecca's head I'll get to hear about it. The nights are dark, you never know who might be lurking round the next corner waiting to pounce.'

Janet joined her husband at the door. She slid her arm through his. Together they stared coldly at Joshua. The Sutherlands did the same, including Breck who was eager to show that he could still make a stand if need be, in spite of having reached the grand old age of sixteen years. Deflated, humiliated and outnumbered, Joshua turned on his heel and went, feeling that his world was crashing about his ears and that Satan himself must surely be snapping at his heels and laughing behind his back for the defeat he had suffered at the mighty hands of Morgan the Magnificent.

Chapter Twenty-six

It was Hogmanay and Effie, still suffering from the aftermath of the flu, wasn't feeling like revelling. Her head was aching, she felt listless and tired, her bones were sore, her nose raw from countless sneezings and blowings. She had gone back to work far too soon, she told herself miserably as she stoked up the fire and stopped to gaze morosely into the flames.

The spare nurse hadn't been a very willing sort of body, being plump and round and not in the least bit agile. She had complained about everything from start to finish and had declared herself 'too damt tired' at the end of each day to do more than get herself to bed for a few hours before the 'whole damt thing' began all over again.

'I'm not very keen on the people here,' she had conveyed tightly to Effie. 'All they ever do is moan and groan and talk to each other as if I wasn't there – mostly about you I may add. Anyone would think you were some sort of goddess the way they go on . . .'

Here she had looked at Effie's homely figure with some disapproval and had sniffed meaningfully. 'Of course, they probably haven't known much else in a place like this, so out of the way and so uncivilised.

They have coarse tongues in their heads too. I tried to give an enema to a dreadful creature calling himself Donald of Balivoe and he practically accused me of indecent assault before throwing the tubes on the floor and stamping on them.'

Effie hadn't heard very much of that last part, so enamoured was she of being described as a goddess even if it had been meant sarcastically. There and then she vowed it was time she went back to 'her people' to give them the kind of loving tender care they were used to. This she conveyed to the doctor and was immediately rewarded by the news that the spare nurse had packed her bags and had departed Kinvara as speedily as she could.

'Alistair and I were glad to see the back o' her,' Long John Jeannie confided to Effie. 'All she ever did at night was sit with her feet up the lum drinking cocoa and eating me out o' house and home as well as expecting table service at every meal. Mind you, she didn't get it. Ina MacNulty was off sick and couldn't come to do the cooking and I was far too ill myself to be bothered with a madam like the spare nurse. In the end she and the locum had to resort to beans on toast for lunch as well as dinner and farted their way up to bed every night like rear gunners wi' too much ammunition. I had to throw the windows wide after they went and even yet the smell o' them lingers like a bad dream.'

Effie had returned to her duties in time to nurse young Nathan Bowman in his last days. The sadness of watching the dying boy growing weaker by the hour in his cheerless little sickroom had taken its toll on her and it was all she could do to drag herself out on her rounds afterwards. Now it was Hogmanay and all she wanted was to put her feet up and listen to the wireless set she had recently acquired, feeling that she deserved some luxuries in her hard-working life.

She paused with the poker held halfway to the flames. Why shouldn't she do just that? Lock and bolt her door, have her supper at the fire, listen to some Scottish dance music on her wireless. She could bring in the bells in peace and quiet and just hop up to bed after midnight. Anybody who came would think she was out and leave her alone to dream her way into the New Year undisturbed.

She enjoyed her evening pottering about and doing what she felt like doing. After the stroke of midnight she went speedily upstairs with a hot toddy and got into bed. The first foots duly arrived. When the door remained unanswered they bawled through the windows but to no avail. Effie simply ignored the ribald yelling and soon drifted off, feeling as if she were floating on a cloud of warmth and pure unadulterated comfort.

She was awakened in the small hours by a frantic ringing of her doorbell, followed by a cacophony of banging, clanging and shouting. Stones were being hurled against her window like showers of hail, the clanging began again. Effie sat up and lit her bedside candle. Her clock showed her it was only two thirty and she gave a loud groan. Wait till she got the buggers who were doing this! New Year or no she would thraw their necks for them. That she would! Oh, was there no peace for nurses on this earth? She was too soft, too lenient, that was her trouble, far too saintly for her own good. Florence Nightingale wouldn't have stuck it for one minute . . .

The ringing and the banging was getting louder, with a sigh Effie rose from her bed, stuck her feet into her slippers, put her arms through the sleeves of her sensible navy-blue dressing gown, and padded her way over to the window. The opening of the sash let in a blast of freezing air. Pulling the folds of her gown closer round her neck she peered down into the brightness of the icy moon-silvered night. A pale blob of a face was craning itself upwards to look at her; a dustbin lid gleamed dully in the moonlight and a voice came, ragged and hoarse. 'Oh, Effie, you must come at once, something dreadful has happened to Wilma, I can't get her to waken and I think – I do believe she's dead!'

'Rona!' Effie tried to gather her wits together as she half-shouted the name, wondering as she did so why the terrible racket hadn't wakened half the neighbourhood. Then she remembered. It was New Year, most of the neighbourhood would still be awake, drinking and making merry and creating far too much of a din to attach anything unusual to a few extra clatterings and bangings. 'Wait there,' she instructed loudly, 'I'll be right down. Just let me get my breeks on and I'll be with you in a jiffy.'

The minute she opened the door Rona fell through it to take Effie's hands and squeeze them urgently. 'Please, oh please, dear lady, you must come with me right away, I don't know what to do, I went in to look at her, she was just lying there still and cold and wouldn't answer when I spoke her name.

She hasn't been very well recently, the cold, you know . . . Oh . . .'

Rona flopped down on the nearest chair, pulled out a large red spotted hanky and began to cry copiously, rocking herself back and forth, saying Wilma's name over and over, crying out for God's mercy in nasal, frightened tones. She was in a dreadful state. Loops of iron-grey hair were hanging about her face, her eyes were red behind her big bottle-glass specs, her face woebegone and streaked with tears. Effie detected the reek of whisky issuing from her breath and couldn't help wondering if Rona was perhaps drunk and incapable and imagining all sorts of dread happenings in her inebriated state.

Yet she seemed sober enough as she once more took the nurse's hands and pleaded with her to do something to help her 'dear, dear Wilma'. Effie, who felt as if her fingers had just been put through a vice, threw an arm round Rona's shaking shoulders and offered words of comfort but Rona jumped to her feet and shook her head. 'No, it isn't me who needs you. Please come with me to Croft Angus at once. I've got the trap, we can be there in no time.'

'Just one thing,' Effie said in puzzlement. 'Why didn't you call the doctor? He lives just over the road from you and he's better qualified than I am when it comes to dealing with such matters.'

Rona averted her face. 'Neither Wilma or I have needed a doctor since we came here, I thought, if you could have a look at her first . . .'

*   *   *

In minutes Effie was dressed and spanking away from Purlieburn Cottage in Rona's trap, feeling as if she was living through some sort of strange dream, one minute lying in her warm bed, the next trotting through the cold snowy countryside where sounds of merriment drifted up from the villages, echoing along the roads as people held one another up on the way to first-foot friends and neighbours.

Croft Angus was warm and tranquil, as if no trouble had touched it, as if everything was as it had always been since the Henderson Hens had come to live in it and endow it with their own particular brand of homeliness. The clocks ticked on the wall, the blue checked curtains were drawn against the chill of the night, the fire glowed cosily in the grate, the table held remnants of black bun and fruit cake, whisky bottles glinted amber in the firelight, two ancient sheepdogs lay sprawled in a corner, a big fluffy white cat was asleep on the hearthrug, oblivious to all but its own enviable state of contentment.

Effie drew her gaze away from the cat and went upstairs guided by Rona. The room was lit only by one lamp and was full of mysterious shadows that cavorted on the ceiling like flapping phantoms of the night, making Effie shiver slightly though she was well used to deathbed attendances.

There was something about the atmosphere of this particular room that wasn't quite right but for the moment she couldn't put her finger on it and concentrated instead on the reason for her visit. Wilma was lying in a huge double feather bed, her head enveloped in big snowy white pillows, glasses perched neatly on top of her nose, abundant grey hair arranged carefully round her large-featured face which was serene and happy-looking despite its obvious pallor, dressed not in a nightgown but in her best black frock with a big cameo brooch at her throat.

'How long has she been like this?' Effie wanted to know.

Rona looked startled. 'What? You mean . . . ? Oh, I told you, I came in and found her this way.'

'Dressed? In her best Sunday frock?'

'No, oh, no, I put that on when I knew I would have to call in help. Wilma has a lot of pride, she and I are casual in the normal way of things but – just occasionally – we like to dress up in all our finery and she would never have wanted anybody to see her in her nightgown.'

Effie went over and felt for Wilma's pulse. She pulled back the quilt, unbuttoned her frock and was about to make an examination when Rona stopped her. 'Oh, please, do you really have to? I mean, can't you tell if she's dead just by looking at her?'

'Of course I can't.' Effie's brow furrowed. 'Why on earth are you so frightened, Rona? I'm only going to look at her chest.'

The expression on Rona's face was one of pure embarrassment; her eyes were fixed on the area of Wilma's bare flesh that Effie had just exposed. Effie was impelled to look down also and what she saw there made her hastily straighten and put her stethoscope back into her bag with careful deliberation. Her heart had begun to beat swiftly in her breast, a condition that did not entirely owe itself to post-flu weakness. A sense of unreality seized her and she felt as if everything was happening in slow motion.

An odd premonition came to her and she knew that something strange and eerie would be revealed in this house before the night was over. Rona was sobbing into her apron in the background, praying for the deliverance of Wilma's soul in a keening wailing voice that sent shivers down Effie's spine.

'I'm sorry, we'll have to call the doctor,' she stated shakily. 'But first, get me a large glass o' whisky, better still, bring the bottle for I'm sure the doctor will also want some when he comes.'

Rona was however in no fit state to go anywhere. Wringing her hands she said pleadingly, 'Oh, please, do we really have to bring him into this?'

'What on earth have you got against Doctor MacAlistair?' Effie demanded with a touch of belligerence.

'I've got nothing against him – except he's a man and might not understand any of this.'

'Of course he's a man!' Effie snapped as she began to lose patience. 'I thought you liked men! Oh, what's the use, you're getting me as mixed up as yourself. Alistair may be a man but he's first and foremost a doctor and a damt good one at that. We do have to call him, Rona, I'm not qualified to deal with anything that is happening here and he'll give Wilma a more thorough examination than I can.' Effie's tone had become kinder when she saw the state Rona was in. 'It won't take a minute for you to fetch him, he's just over the road. I'll wait with Wilma – at least – I'll bide downstairs wi' the cat till you come back,' she added quickly.

After Rona departed Effie settled herself in a rocking chair by the fire with the cat cosily ensconced on her lap and was almost asleep when Dr MacAlistair arrived, his white hair spilling untidily out from under his tweed hat, the tail of his goonie showing under his hastily donned jacket, his feet jammed into a pair of Jeannie's furry slippers, the first he could find in his blind searchings in the dark. He had arisen from his bed in a hurry, he and Jeannie having just got there after the last of the revellers had departed.

Yawning and scratching his stomach he demanded to know what all the fuss was about and Effie rose achingly to her feet. 'Alistair, could I have a word?' she said quickly and took him aside to murmur something into one hairy red lug. He was a good doctor was Alistair MacAlistair. He seldom flapped, took life as it came, was down to earth and blunt and all too used to the vagaries that life had thrown at him over his years as medic to an arbitrary population.

His expression did not change as Effie's disclosures seeped into his weary head. Without a word he went upstairs to go straight to the bed and give Wilma a very thorough examination. When he finally straightened his face still did not give anything away, but his eyes roved round the room, finally coming to rest on an array of pill bottles and cough mixtures on the bedside table. Picking one up he read the label. 'I prescribed these for Wilma, I hope she hasn't been taking too much of them – or . . .' he swung round on Rona, 'mixing them with whisky.'

'We did have a drop earlier, Doctor,' she admitted. 'The New Year and all that.'

'How much?' he barked. 'The truth now, Rona.'

'Well, several large glasses each, she was feeling miserable, all stuffed up and headachy . . .'

'Lethal,' he pronounced heavily. 'Pills and booze, no' to mention cough mixture by the pint.'

'Is she dead, Doctor?' Rona hazarded fearfully. 'I couldn't bear it if she was.'

'Ay, dead all right,' he returned grimly. 'Dead drunk! Tea. Right away, Effie. Strong and black, gallons o' the stuff.' As he was speaking he was swinging Wilma out of bed, jamming her feet into a pair of large checked bootees, ordering Rona to put a shoulder under one oxter while he applied himself to the other. Wilma was like a very large limp rag doll as they pulled her upright. Her wig came adrift and fell to the floor but no one paid any attention, intent as they were on the task in hand. 'We must keep her moving,' Alistair said imperatively. 'No let up till she shows signs o' wakening.'

Together they dragged Wilma round the room, their feet padding on the carpet, the doctor stopping occasionally to slap her face, shake her and call her name, drastic actions that brought little gasping sounds from Rona's throat but none at all from Wilma's. The tea came, the doctor lowered her back onto the bed, opened her mouth and eased the beverage in. Silence invaded the room for several heart-stopping minutes while he worked with Wilma, alternately slapping her, shouting her name, feeding her tea. At last there came a gasp and a splutter. Wilma's eyes opened, she looked dazedly round.

'Wilma!' Rona was over by the bed, sobbing, holding on as if she would never let go, hardly giving Wilma the air she needed in those bewildered disorientated moments of her return from the very brink of death itself. When the doctor

had ascertained that she was out of danger he and
Effie slipped respectfully away down to the kitchen
to give themselves a breathing space and to afford
Rona the chance to be alone for a few minutes with
her beloved Wilma.

Chapter Twenty-seven

Once downstairs, Effie and the doctor eyed one another and Effie, still reeling from the shock of the night's revelations, took a deep breath.

'If you don't mind me saying so, Alistair, I'm buggered.' She sank into a chair and shook her head. 'First having to rise out my nice cosy bed in the wee sma' hours, the fright I got when Rona began battering bin lids outside my house and throwing stones at my window. Now this. Oh, I'll never forget the shock o' seeing Wilma's hairy chest when I was expecting a set o' bosoms in the normal way o' things. It fair makes you realise nothing is as it seems on this earth. I aye knew there was something no' quite right about the Henderson sisters but never in all my born days did I expect this.'

The doctor was slumped in the opposite chair, eyes closed, hands folded peacefully over his stomach, breathing rhythmically and evenly, looking to all intents and purposes to be asleep.

'Oh, Alistair,' Effie said as she emitted a great dramatic sigh, 'how can you sleep when all this is going on? I want to tell you about the room. I didn't think anything of it at first, I was so busy wi' Wilma, but it was masculine that room, a mixture o' both really, some o' it fluffy and coy, the rest definitely not, the shaving stuff on the dresser, the hairy brush and comb, the wig stand. Mind you, it was very very tidy, I'll say that for the pair, they aye did keep a nice home, no' like some o' the bachelor hovels I've seen in my time. They also have a carpet on the floor,' she went on enviously, 'when I think o' my own bare boards wi' just a clickit rug at the bedside to put my feet on . . .'

The doctor opened his eyes. Still retaining the same relaxed pose he said in a deep somnolent voice, 'Now, Effie, this must never leak out to another living soul. These two ladies – in our minds they have to remain just that – must be allowed to go on living exactly as they have always done. A more harmless pair would be hard to find, they lead peaceful and honest lives, they are hard-working and kind-hearted, they give freely to charity and are, in their own way, a great benefit to the community. Will you promise me, Effie, that your tongue shall remain sealed on the matter now and for evermore?'

'But, Doctor . . .'

'No buts, Effie, you are the district nurse and your duty is first and foremost to the health and wellbeing of your patients, both mental and physical. These people must not be mocked. Rona and Wilma need to be allowed to live their lives with dignity and respect. If one word o' this leaks out I will know you to be the perpetrator. For the sake o' your own conscience you must swear your allegiance to the pair, otherwise I shall have no option but to report you to the authorities for professional misconduct.'

They were harsh measures but he knew his colleague only too well. Her tongue was forever running away with her and the only way to deal with her was to shock her into silence.

Effie gasped at his words. She opened her mouth to argue, thought better of it and said sulkily, 'All right, Doctor, I promise, though I don't know how . . .'

'It's quite easy, Effie, put a zip on it – if you don't . . .' He smiled and looked benign again. 'I'll turn you into a horrible warty old toad whose fate will be to end up in the slobbering jaws of your very own pigs.'

'Well, I would rather be turned into a toad than be changed into a man,' Effie blurted in an undignified last stand.

'Effie!'

'All right, all right, it is a lot you ask o' me, Alistair, but I know it's the only way. The Henderson Hens they are and will always remain and I promise on my honour never to divulge a word o' their secret to another living soul.'

But it wasn't enough for the doctor. He made Effie swear on a large bible he found on a shelf, proof enough that the sisters believed in their Maker despite never having been strict churchgoers. With eyes tightly closed Effie solemnly swore, all the while praying inwardly to be strong, strong . . . She opened her eyes. 'Alistair, what would you do if one o' them really did die? What could you put on the death certificate, I'd like to know?'

'We'll cross that bridge together, Effie, if we ever come to it. Till then we must go on exactly as before. I can't even tell Jeannie, only you and I are the keepers o' the key of silence and must go to our graves with our lips sealed.'

Effie liked the sound of that. She puffed out her chest importantly and was able to turn a cheery face to Rona when she at last came into the room, saying that Wilma was resting 'very very peacefully' and she had thought it best to leave her alone for a while.

The doctor cocked an eye at her. 'I could be doing with a wee nip, indeed a big one would be better. I'm sure a taste might help to buck Effie up too, it's been quite a night for all of us.'

Rona nodded. Meek as a lamb she laid out the glasses and the black bun, the shortbread and the whisky, stoked up the fire with coal and logs and sat down to pour the drinks, not forgetting her own glass which she topped up generously before throwing half of it back in two large noisy gulps. She looked at her guests. 'I needed that,' she stated on a deep intake of breath. 'By God I needed it and if you'll allow me, Doctor, I'd like to make a toast to you and Effie for everything you have done for me and my poor dear Wilma this first day of January 1939.'

New Year began all over again for Effie and the doctor, one of the most unusual they had ever known as they drank and ate and listened to Rona as she poured her heart out under the warming influence of the devil's brew.

'We had to do it,' she stated baldly, as if sensing all the unanswered questions piling inside Effie's head. 'You know what people are like? Two men living together, being talked about. Sisters, that's different, sisters living in the same house are acceptable.'

'But surely two brothers wouldn't have raised many

brows.' Effie sounded puzzled and Rona turned away.

'We both like – dressing up – it might seem odd to you but it was a way of life for us.' She gazed at them pleadingly. 'Oh, please say you'll never tell. If Wilma and I are to go on living here we have to do it with dignity.'

The doctor placed a comforting hand on her shoulder. 'In our profession we never tell, and, as you know, Effie here is the soul o' discretion. That fact might not always seem apparent to the casual observer but when it comes down to it not even a navvy could prise her lips apart, I can assure you o' that.'

Rona was profuse in her thanks, after which she relaxed and had a great time. When finally she staggered away upstairs to check on Wilma it was almost six o'clock in the morning according to the wag-at-the-wa' on the shelf. The doctor arose and crooked his arm to Effie. 'May I see you home, sweet maid?'

'More like us propping one another up,' she giggled as she took his arm and went with him to the door. The pair of them reeled into the cold glimmerings of a starry dawn, singing 'Auld Lang Syne' at the tops of their voices, parting company at the road end in the best of spirits.

The doctor only had a short distance to go to Butterbank House. Jeannie was in bed but sat up when she heard him coming in. 'What was all that about?' she demanded the minute he appeared in the bedroom. 'Rona coming here? You staying away for hours on end? What were you doing? Who were you doing it with?'

The doctor hiccuped and tossed his hat onto a non-existent hat stand in a gesture of complete abandonment. 'See no evil, hear no evil,' he intoned drunkenly. 'My lips are sealed, Jeannie, I can only tell you I have been on an errand o' mercy for which I shall be remembered for all time to come.'

'I know what I'll seal in a minute!' she said grimly. 'Coming in here, drunk and disorderly . . .'

The rest of her discourse would never be known. Alistair MacAlistair had simply dived into bed, fully clothed, sodden furry slippers and all, making her screech with indignation when he snuggled into her and plonked a hearty kiss on her cheek.

'Alistair! What have you got on your feet?' she gasped. 'Something wet and horrible and not at all decent . . . and what on earth is that in your pocket? All soggy and crumbly and sticky.'

He rolled on his back, withdrew a crushed piece of Rona's rich fruit cake from the depths of his jacket, gave a beatific smile and was asleep in seconds, while Jeannie snorted her disapproval beside him and vowed she would get to the bottom of the matter if it was the last thing she did.

It took Effie longer to get to Purlieburn Cottage. The snow was cold and crisp beneath her feet, the air was needle-fresh and tangy with the scent of peat smoke rising up from the chimneys of some hidden farm. By the time she reached her gate she was wide awake. Her steps took her to the little paddock behind the house and the pen where Romeo and Juliet were still fast asleep on their bundles of straw. Their much revered predecessors, Queen Victoria and Ruby, had gone the way of all good porkers and Effie had thought it would be a good idea to start breeding pigs of her own.

With this in mind she had acquired Romeo and Juliet with much optimism for a piglet-filled future. Now she gazed consideringly at the two slumbering animals who so far had produced nothing more than large quantities of rich pig manure and very little else.

How did she know if they were what they seemed? Romeo had shown no inclination to do anything more than rub his snout all over Juliet's broad back and talk pig talk into her flapping pink lugs. The breeder might have been wrong about them; they might be two girls for all she knew, or even two boys though that didn't seem likely as they would have fought all the time the way good boars were inclined to do when penned up together. And she of all people ought to know what a sow's private parts looked like and Romeo certainly seemed to be as well equipped as any boar could be in the luggage department . . .

Effie sighed. She was too tired to think straight. Her judgement would be clearer after a good night's sleep. Her brow furrowed. There wasn't much of the night left and she would have to rise in a few hours to start her working day. But how could she rise when she wasn't even in bed yet? Effie gave herself a shake. All that whisky, she wasn't used to it. She went inside, filled a hot-water bottle, made a cup of tea and went up to bed for a blissful hour or two before her clock shrilled her once more into stark and rude awakening.

Chapter Twenty-eight

'Aha! Just the lady we want to see and no' a moment too soon!'

The words fell like a battle cry on Effie's ears as she pushed open the door of the tiny draper's shop in Balivoe on a quest for undergarments of a somewhat personal nature.

Big Bette was at the counter, fingering a display of woollen vests, clicking her tongue at the prices, humming and hawing about their quality, making Tottie Murchison glower long and hard at her for daring to critiscise any of the stock in *her* shop. With her Bette had dragged Mungo so that he could give her a lift back to her grocer's store in Calvost when she was finished at the draper's. He was wandering aimlessly about, stopping every so often to stare rather leeringly at a display of shop-soiled cheap knickers on a revolving stand, turning it round so that it squeaked and made Tillie, the other half of the Knicker Elastic Dears, gaze at him in some disapproval.

Effie did not appreciate Mungo's presence either, knowing that she would have to wait till he was gone before she could start looking for the things she wanted. Not that she would have got the chance to do that anyway. The bell above the door had no sooner stopped jangling than Bette pounced on her like an enormous warrior ready to do battle. 'Just where were you yesterday morning, Effie Maxwell?' she demanded, double chins jutting, eyes gleaming with chagrin. 'Mungo and I and one or two other folk came to your door after the bells and tried to knock you up without any success.'

Effie gave her a sour look and went over to gaze idly at a pile of socks reposing on a shelf. 'To tell the truth, I was in my bed,' she admitted in some defiance, the only sort of stance to take when the mighty Bette MacGill was on the warpath, 'I wasn't feeling well enough to be bothered wi' New Year and thought I would do what I wanted for a change.'

'Oh-ho, is that so?' Bette drew herself up to her full height, threw out her magnificent bosom and positively glared at Effie. 'In bed were you? Why was it then that Mungo and I saw you driving away from your house wi' Rona Henderson when we were coming out o' Garden Cottage after visiting Mattie and Dokie Joe? Explain that if you will, forsaking old friends in favour o' that queer two who never want anybody in to see them, far less a nurse wi' a tongue in her head that could run circles round a ferret when it comes to idle chit-chat.'

'Well, they wanted me,' Effie stuck her nose in the air. 'And what business is it of yours who I visit at any time o' the year? You're just jealous because you weren't asked.'

The shop was agog now. Kangaroo Kathy had come in to look for buttons but stopped in her searchings to listen to the exchanges with lively interest, Tillie and Tottie fought one another for the ear trumpet that always lay on the counter in case it was needed, Mungo rubbed his hands together gleefully and decided this was better than hanging around watching his wife dithering over woollen vests and drawers.

'Jealous!' Bette tightened her lips and folded her hands over her great pudding of a belly. 'Jealous o' the Henderson Hens! Fine you know that isn't true, my girl. You're only saying that to put us off because there was something very fishy going on at Croft Angus the night before last. Not only did we see you going there in Rona's trap but Charlie Campbell saw you and the doctor coming out at six o'clock in the morning, the pair o' you drunk and singing at the tops o' your voices. And don't tell me the Hens were ill, they've never known a day's sickness in their lives as anybody here could tell you.'

'What was Charlie Campbell doing out at that hour?' Effie blurted in a desperate play for time.

'It is New Year in case you don't know. An occasion when most normal folks go and visit their neighbours instead o' lying in their beds like some I could mention.'

Effie shook her head and said almost to herself, 'There are stranger things on earth than there are in heaven, ay, me, the world is a very mixed up place as I myself have witnessed . . .' She stopped dead and Bette immediately pounced. 'Ay, go on, why were you there? What is wrong with the Croft Angus pair?'

'Oh, there's nothing wrong with them, they're both perfectly healthy only . . .' She stopped again, remembering her promises to the doctor, 'Wilma took a wee bad turn on Hogmanay. She is still recovering from the flu so Rona fetched myself and the doctor just to be on the safe side. While we were there we stayed to have a dram or two and were quite touched by their hospitality. Nobody ever goes near them at this time o' the year and I think they were really glad to have us.'

'Och, the souls,' Kathy said sympathetically as her fingers hovered over the buttons. 'They must get lonely betimes and I myself have often wondered what they do wi' themselves when they are all alone together in their crofthouse.'

Effie's face turned red, but she said nothing, Bette looked at her strangely. 'Oh, well, now that you've broken the ice maybe we should go along there ourselves for a wee festive dram.'

'No! I wouldn't do that!' Effie cried explosively. 'Wilma's cold is really bad, she would just reinfect you all and I didn't like the look o' the festering boils she has all over her body.'

'Festering boils?' Mungo moved perceptively away from Effie as if afraid she might be the carrier of some dread illness. 'Come on, Bette, we'll get the vests another day. It's time we both opened shop . . .' Ignoring his wife's protests he hustled her away, Kangaroo Kathy departed also, leaving Effie to lean over the counter and whisper to Tottie, 'Knickers, long ones, over the knees if you have any, my legs are frozen in this damt weather.'

'Eh? Speak up!' Tillie had moved the ear trumpet out of reach and Tottie couldn't be bothered searching for it. 'My hearing isn't what it was and I can't be doing with people who whisper.'

'KNICKERS!' Effie bawled. 'LONG ONES! NAVY BLUE SIZE SIXTEEN!'

The door opened, a current of cold air came blasting in, Mungo popped his head round grinning from ear to ear. 'Bette left her bag,' he pronounced, coming forward to retrieve it. He looked at Effie, rubbed his hands and winked, a habit of his when he was excited and one that totally unnerved the nurse. 'Navy blue, eh, I often wondered what your colours were. Maybe you'll wear them at the dance on Saturday and let us all have a peek.'

He took himself off. 'That man gets worse,' Effie fumed. 'He's coarse and uncouth. He used to have some sort o' manners, now he speaks like a back-street ruffian and I'm thinking he's turned into a heathen altogether since he went and opened that buggering barber shop o' his. I wouldn't like to be a fly on the wall when that lot get going.'

Tottie, who would have loved to be a fly on the wall, shook her head and said smoothly, 'And him a kirk elder too, I'm sure if the minister heard some of the things Mungo comes away with he would think twice about letting him keep his position.'

Tillie hovered. 'Knickers,' she said sweetly.

'How about a couple of pairs from the stand?' Tottie suggested. 'Very good value, navy blue and over the knee as you wanted.'

'You can keep your damt knickers and wrap them round your neck!' Effie blazed. 'I wouldn't give you twopence for the lot! I've seen better on Dolly Law's washing line. And if you can't hear that then get your silly ear trumpet out and I'll repeat it all over again, only next time I might no' be so lenient!'

With that she flounced away out of the shop, leaving the Knicker Elastics to look at one another with tight lips. 'No doubt suffering from a bad head,' Tottie said righteously. 'Fancy, spending all night with the Henderson sisters.'

'The doctor too,' Tillie sniffed.

'Kinvara used to be a nice place.' Tottie was scooping up vests and knickers as she spoke, stuffing them into a drawer marked MISCELLANEOUS. NAVY BLUE & CREAM. ASSTD SIZES, INCLUDING LARGE, X-LARGE AND OUTSIZE. 'Now even the professionals in our midst are at it, doing and saying things that would have their predecessors turning in their graves.'

'It *is* New Year, dear,' Tillie reminded her sister gently.

They looked at one another. Tottie went to the door and turned the sign to Closed for Lunch. She and Tillie repaired to the back shop and didn't come out for at least two hours, immersed as they were in much enjoyable talk about the wrongdoings of the neighbourhood in general – imbibing in 'a wee tiny tot' of the amber nectar while they were at it, just to take away the sting of having sold nothing that morning, in spite of having risen at the crack of dawn to prepare their racks for the January sales.

Once outside the draper's, Effie turned her pony's head in the direction of Croft Angus. She had promised the doctor she would look in on Wilma though hadn't mentioned this fact to Big Bette in case that formidable lady might have decided to drop everything and come along with her.

Rona was in the yard chopping wood when Effie's cart came rumbling in. Rona threw down the axe, wiped her hands on her apron and went forward to greet the nurse, quite returned to her normal boisterous self, a beaming smile splitting her face as she said, 'My dear lady, how nice to see you. Wilma is much better today but I've kept her in bed until she is fully recovered.'

Keeping hold of Effie's hand she began to lead her towards the hen runs. 'Come along, dear, I want to give you and the doctor a little present for all you've done for Wilma, something nice for the pot and the best there is even though I do say it myself.'

Expertly she caught two plump chickens and beheaded them with the axe right there and then in front of Effie's nose. The headless birds ran round in circles for what seemed an eternity before they dropped and lay twitching.

'We'll just let them hang over a cup of tea,' Rona said heartily and Effie's mind went into orbit as she pictured a pair of suspended birds dripping bodily fluids into a row of steaming teacups.

Rona led the way into the house to make tea while Effie went upstairs to see Wilma who was sitting up in bed wearing a fluffy pink shoulder cape and reading a dog-eared copy of Robert Burns' poems.

'My dear,' she extended the same effusive welcome to Effie as had her sister. 'I'm afraid you've caught me with my favourite man. Oh, when I think of the romance and tragedy of his life! So Scottish! So charming! Such a lust for living! So very, very handsome – those little sideburns . . .' She gushed on for another minute before stopping dead and gazing at the nurse with tear-filled eyes. 'What can I say? How can I say it?' She gathered Effie's hands into hers and painfully squeezed them. 'You and the doctor, what a wonderful team. I can't thank you enough. It's been so very very embarrassing but it's over now and never never shall I take so much to drink again. The terrible things it does to people, the illusions, I really did believe I was dead and floating far far away over the great divide. Now it all seems like a bad dream and thanks to you and Doctor MacAlistair I can put it behind me.'

Effie blinked. For one wild moment she wondered if she had dreamed the whole thing also, as Wilma was making no reference to anything other than being drunk. Perhaps Rona hadn't told her any more than that and Effie made good her escape from the room, feeling that she too might resort to drink if she stayed another second in Wilma's company.

Rona had the tea ready. Effie gulped it down and made to go but Rona held up her hand. 'The chickens, mustn't go without them, they'll need to drip for a little while longer but you can do that yourself when you get home.' She fetched two lumpy bags and handed them to the nurse. Effie took off as quickly as she could. 'Will you be at the dance on Saturday?' Rona shouted but there was no answer. Effie was gone, making her way straight to Butterbank House to give the doctor his chicken.

Long John Jeannie came to the door. At sight of Effie she was all for taking her inside to interrogate her about the happenings at Croft Angus on New Year's morning. The nurse was having none of that, however, she'd had enough of the Henderson sisters for one day. Because of them she had been accosted by Big Bette and had lied and cheated to protect their good name at risk of lowering her own. She had done her bit at Croft Angus where murder had been committed right under her very nose and never would she eat that poor chicken though she liked chicken as a rule and often killed her own, but not with a blunt axe. She was sick and tired of New Year and the trouble it had brought without even so much as a good pair of warm knickers to show for her efforts. With all that in mind she fairly flew back to Purlieburn Cottage to feed her pigs, listen to her wireless, and give thanks to the Lord for the sane and orderly life she led whenever she had the chance to enjoy it – which wasn't often in a busy community like Kinvara with all its ails and wants and oddities that seemed never-ending.

Chapter Twenty-nine

The New Year dance was a very important event in the Kinvara social calendar. This year it was being held later than usual but was no less well attended for all that. Everybody who was anybody was there that night. The village hall committee had worked hard to get everything ready on time and now the normally drab interior was hung with streamers and balloons while a large banner strung across the platform wished everybody the compliments of the season. The Kinvara Ceilidh Band was tuning up in a corner, every so often reaching under their seats for a furtive swig of Knobby Sinclair's best ale. 'No' too much, lads,' warned Dokie Joe whose red nose showed that he himself had partaken freely of the brew. 'It's bad for the reflexes and nothing sounds worse than a fiddle wi' the skitters.'

The hall soon filled up. The young people came in, shiny and slick, eager for a night out; Rebecca was on the arm of Joss, quite openly being seen with him now as more and more she defied her father in a bid to gain the freedom she so craved. But if it hadn't been for her mother she wouldn't have been there that evening. Her garb was of the everyday variety, drab frocks and pinafores, shapeless jerseys and skirts.

Miriam however had taken her aside one day and had shown her a case full of beautiful garments made of the finest materials.

'I keep it under my bed,' she had confided to her daughter. 'Your father would have burned the things if he had found out but somehow I managed to hide them. I can't wear them of course but you can. I'll make them fit, I used to be quite a good seamstress and made these myself a long time ago when I was young.'

After that, whenever Joshua was out of the house, mother and daughter got to work, pinning, tucking, sewing, Rebecca feeling an affinity with her mother such as she had never known before, growing closer to her in just a few days than she had ever done in the whole of her life.

The result had been a dress, a simple black creation that looked stunning against the creamy pallor of the girl's smooth skin, offset by a pearl necklace and earrings that had been in the case too and which would most certainly have been commandeered by Joshua if he had ever clapped eyes on them.

On the night of the dance, aided and abetted by her mother, Rebecca had managed to dress and slip out of the house without Joshua knowing and now she was here, radiant and glowing, watched enviously by several pairs of female eyes but most of all by Maida who was like a fairy doll in her dress of pink frills and white lace. But her fluffy prettiness couldn't outshine Rebecca's striking stark beauty and Maida turned away with a dark look on her face. Not that she was short of admirers. Tom MacGill could hardly keep his eyes off her, neither could Caleb

Bowman, who did what he liked nowadays and to hell with what anybody thought. The tension in the Mill O' Cladach had become unbearable of late. He was rebellious and impudent; he and his father were continually at loggerheads but Caleb seemed not to care about anything since the death of his brother – except for Maida. He was aggressive in his attempts to win her over, Tom equally so, both boys vying with one another for her affections.

Maida made full use of this situation. In her efforts to gain Joss's attention she had begun a dangerous game, not only with Caleb and Tom but with several local lads, playing one off against the other, encouraging their interest, always in the hope that Joss would notice and start to do something about it.

'You're wasting your time,' Mark had told her. 'Don't cheapen yourself, Maida, Joss likes you but only as a friend, surely you ought to know that by now.'

Maida hadn't listened. Joss had become an obsession with her, the more he evaded her the more she went after him and that night in the hall was no exception when she made him dance with her and pressed herself close to him while Tom and Caleb watched, one almost resignedly, jealousy mounting in the other till it became a tight throbbing knot inside his belly.

Mark and Vaila had come in together, relaxed and at ease with one another. George wasn't around, so there was no competition for Mark to get upset about. She was wearing a pale green dress that was a perfect foil for her black curling hair and sparkling green eyes. Her figure had burgeoned in all the right places and was graceful yet provocative at the same time. But the biggest surprise of all came in the shape of Johnny Armstrong with Miss Dorothy Hosie on his arm, she flushed and excited-looking and proudly holding up her head, he extremely handsome with his beard and hair trimmed and wearing a new suit that sat well on his lean frame.

The womenfolk had a field day. 'Would you look at that now,' Effie raged as Jessie and Gabby, Harriet and Charlie, Johnny and Miss Hosie, waltzed past her vision. 'Kinvara is full o' brazen women who would do anything to get a man – and most o' them strangers too. Who would have thought it of Johnny, to be taken in by a woman wi' nothing but ice in her veins.'

'You never said that when he was no better than a tink living rough on the shore,' Kangaroo Kathy pointed out. 'I myself think it's a fair treat to see him as happy as he is now and she is quite a nice-looking wee body when you see her without her grey frock and thon funny wee glasses she wears perched on the end o' her nose.'

She jumped to her feet at that juncture as 'her Norrie' came over, slick and polished and red about the ears for he was not at all keen on social gatherings but put up with them for Kathy's sake.

The wallflowers sat, Effie among them, feeling abandoned and ridiculous. Even Wee Fay and Little John had each other. Mungo jigged by in Bette's ample arms and gave Effie a broad knowing wink; then a large shape loomed in front of her and she looked up to see Wilma gazing down at her, big teeth flashing, looking really quite attractive in her best black frock with a large cameo at her throat.

'Shall we dance?' Wilma invited beamingly. 'We women must stick together, don't you agree?'

With that she hauled Effie to her feet and steered her away. She stumbled and almost fell but the next minute she was floating, for in spite of her large feet Wilma was a wonderful dancer and no one paid them the slightest attention as they whirled round in time to the music.

Effie never sat down after that. Rona took over where Wilma left off, followed by the doctor and several really quite decent-looking bachelors smelling of toilet soap and Brylcreem.

'She'll get a man yet,' Mattie MacPhee sniggered wickedly. 'Effie aye said she has no need of any member o' the opposite sex but from the way she's snuggling up to them I don't doubt she's changed her mind.'

'Och, well, she deserves one,' said Kangaroo Kathy, looking quite lost without her needles and her lapbag now that Norrie had deserted her in favour of the bar, 'It aye worried me the way she dotes on these pigs o' hers when she should have had some o' her own by now.'

Mattie looked startled. 'Pigs?'

'Och, no.' Kathy looked wonderingly at Mattie. 'People don't have pigs, I thought you would have known that having had so many o' your own. Didn't your mother ever teach you anything?'

The Henderson Hens were causing quite a stir by this time. Having consumed a fair number of drams they had thrown all caution to the winds and were doing a tango in the middle of the floor while everybody stood round in a circle clapping their hands, spurring the pair to even wilder and more abandoned behaviour as they switched from the tango to a Spanish dance, whirling around, snapping their fingers above their heads, shouting 'Olé!' showing layers of red stockings and just a hint of long white frilly knickers.

'Phew.' One of the bachelors ran his finger round the inside of his collar. 'I never thought o' that two as being sex kittens before but anyone can see they're man-hungry and just asking for it! Look at those red stockings and those white drawers. I'm going in there, it's no' often anybody gets a chance to see what the Hens are made of but tonight just might be the night.'

'No! I wouldn't do that if I were you.' Effie clamped her fingers round his arm, her fascinated gaze on the sisters, terrified that a wig might slip, an errant manly appendage might show. But everything was well and truly in its proper place, the sisters had made sure of that and were revelling in the chance to show off their finery, delighting at being the centre of attraction. The hall was in an uproar by now; the merrymakers were ready for anything and eagerly joined in when the sisters took the lead in a Conga, kicking their legs high as they jigged round the hall with a long snake of sweating bodies behind.

Dr MacAlistair came over to Effie and gave her a conspiratorial look. 'Don't worry about them,' he advised quietly. 'They're having a ball. Tomorrow they'll go back to being the Hens we know, sober, serious, reticent, tonight they're letting their hair down and everybody's loving it.'

'That's what's worrying me,' Effie said with a gulp.
'If they let it down too much it might come off
altogether and where would their dignity be then?'

'You worry too much,' the doctor told her soothingly. 'No one would notice even if it did. Just look
at them, they're blind to all but the excitement o' the
moment so just you relax and enjoy yourself. When
I made you swear on that bible I didn't mean you to
become their guardian angel looking out for them at
every turn. They've come through years together with
every hair in place and aren't about to let anything
slip now.'

Effie released her breath, she smiled at the doctor
and taking hold of her partner's arm she led him into
the fray and soon they were mingling with the crowd
and letting themselves go with everyone else.

Tom had managed to attract Maida into the tiny
empty cloakroom off the porch and was trying to
sweet-talk her into kissing him. When that didn't
work he began fumbling with her clothes, his rough
hands rasping uncaringly over the ruffles and the lace,
coming to rest on her breasts which he began to knead
as if they were lumps of dough. 'Stop that, Tom,' she
scolded. 'Don't manhandle me like that, you'll ruin
my dress with those horrible calluses you have on
your fingers.'

'Aw, come on, Maida,' he breathed into her ear.
'Let me see them, just this once. I know they're big,
I've felt them under your frock once or twice and
just about burst my buttons wanting more. I'd like
to go with you properly, we could have a great time

together. I know you're waiting for Joss but he doesn't want you, he'll never come to you as long as he's got Rebecca . . .'

She pushed him away then and slapped his face as hard as she could. Her knuckle caught his mouth, he drew the back of one hand over it and his face twisted when he saw the blood. 'Bitch!' he oathed. 'Stupid bitch! You'll never get anybody the way you carry on. Asking for it one minute, shying away from it whenever you're cornered. Your arse is as frozen as your heart, Maida Lockhart, it's all show wi' you, just buggering show.'

He lumbered away to join a stream of people leaving the hall. The night was almost over and only the stragglers remained, hanging on till the last minute, enjoying the music from the band who were loath to leave also.

The beer wasn't finished yet, the bodhran beat a tattoo, the fiddles went wild, Dolly Law and Shug played the combs, Willie Whiskers, ignoring Maisie's pleas for him to come home, took up his pipes and began blasting away, stomping up and down the hall, kilt swinging rhythmically over his sturdy hairy knees.

'I'm away.' Maisie Whiskers folded her lips and marched off, throwing over her shoulder, 'See you and be home before I'm asleep, Willie MacPhee, if no' I'll lock you outside and you can sleep it off under the stars wi' nothing to keep you warm but your bottle and your shirt-tails.'

Willie went on playing. As the skirl of the pipes rent the air, Knobby Sinclair produced a couple of bottles filled with whisky, the party began all over

again, music and merriment reeled through the air
and no one minded that the hands of the clock were
now at two after midnight. The night was young yet
and the drink was still flowing. Dokie Joe took over
from Willie and gave of his best as he marched round
and round the room blowing into the chanter for all
he was worth.

Chapter Thirty

Maida was wrapping herself in the furry cape that had been her pride and joy since her mother had presented it to her on her eighteenth birthday. The cloakroom was empty now and she began to hurry. Her father had wanted to come for her after the dance but she had rejected his offer, knowing the restrictions it would place upon her. Mark had gone off with Vaila some time ago, Rebecca with Joss. Maida had been mad at that; she had tried to annoy him by egging Tom on, making sure Joss had seen them going into the cloakroom, but it hadn't worked. He had just ignored her and now she would have to walk home if she couldn't get someone to give her a lift. She could still smell Tom on her clothes; he had reeked of beer and cigarette smoke and she had hated the feel of those big clumsy hands of his pawing her body.

'Like some company on the road home?' Her heart accelerated and she swung round. Caleb Bowman was leaning against the doorpost, his eyes glazed, a leering grin playing on his mouth, his voice slurred by drink, an almost depleted whisky bottle loosely held in one careless hand. Very deliberately Maida finished tying the collar of her cape round her neck, her fingers fumbling as she did so. A warning voice was beating inside her head. She told herself to keep calm even while every fibre in her wanted to escape that tiny room and the cloying disturbing presence of Caleb Bowman.

He launched himself away from the door and swayed towards her, his face twisted and red with drink, his voice growing thicker as he drew close to her. 'Not frightened of me, Maida, are you? Why should you be afraid to be alone with someone as nice as I am? I want you, Maida, I've wanted you for a long time now and I know you want me too. It's what you've been asking for. You were just play-acting with the others. I saw you with poor old lily-livered Tom. No wonder you sent him packing. It's a real man you need and I've got the very thing you've been waiting for, all yours to have and to hold.'

Maida shrank away from him. 'No, Caleb, someone will come in, Dolly Law's coat is still here.'

'What coat?' he sneered. 'The old hag has never worn a coat in all the time I've known her, more like a couple of sacks tied together with bits of string.' Her words however had set alarm bells ringing in his head, and his hand shot out to grab her by the wrist and yank her to the door. She gave a little half scream and held on to the doorpost but he was too strong for her. With a snarl he grabbed her by the waist and dragged her outside, round to the side of the building where all was quiet and only the lights from the hall windows infiltrated the darkness. The moon was hidden by great banks of yellow-black cloud, snowflakes were whispering down, rasping softly in her ears, catching on her eyelashes, making her shiver and hold her clasped hands to her lips.

'Please, Caleb,' she begged. 'Let me go, I'm sorry if you thought I was leading you on, it was just a game, only a game . . .'

'Ay, and one in which I'm about to be the winner.' His voice was hard, mocking. With a sudden gesture he held the bottle to his lips, drained the remaining contents and threw it scornfully away. She heard the dull thud of it hitting against the fence and then he was looming above her, a dark terrifying bulk without mercy in his drink-inflamed mind. With one swift movement he threw her down and dropped on top of her, pinning her to the ground with his knees, holding her shoulders against the hard icy earth with his hands. Terror stark and black invaded her being; she opened her mouth to scream, his hand thudded into her face, her senses whirled away but summoning every shred of her willpower she held on, she couldn't let this happen, she couldn't . . .

But it did. With one swift movement he ripped her dress from neck to navel and laughed coarsely when her big firm breasts leapt out at him. Savagely he bit her nipples, crushed her mouth with his and leered into her face. 'Good, eh? Just the way you've always wanted it. Rough and uncivilised, like you are under all the veneer of frills and lace. I know your type, you want to be overpowered, you need the thrill of it.'

With the last vestiges of her strength she fought him, but he just laughed again and held her harder. Raising her head she bit his ear, at which he gave a yell of surprise which immediately turned into a growl of rage. Anger spurred him on; unable to contain himself any longer he forced her legs apart, unbuttoned his trousers and drove himself into her, and all the time the pipes inside the hall played stirring tunes that beat mockingly inside her head along with the pain and the terror of her ordeal which seemed to go on and on but which in fact was over in minutes.

The brutal weight of him left her body and he was standing up, his heavy breathing sawing into her brain as cold, raw and merciless, swept over her. Then the darkness came, drowning out her senses as it rushed through her and engulfed her in looming inescapable blackness. He stood staring down at her. She was lying there on the freezing ground, looking for all the world like a broken fairy doll with her long fair tresses streaming round her shoulders, her arms outflung, her face white and seemingly lifeless. He was appalled suddenly by what he had done. He swayed away from her, his eyes transfixed by her pitiful body. Desperately he glanced round. He would have to get away, he could never stay here now, his father would kill him, Rebecca would hate him, the community would never forgive him, the law would be after him when it was realised what had happened . . .

He spied Maida's purse lying on the snowy ground. Snatching it up he tore it open and helped himself to the silver within. More, he had to have more. A wave of giddiness made him stagger but he knew he had to hold on, had to keep his wits about him. Fear gave him the strength he needed and he lurched back inside the hall, going to the tiny cubby hole serving as the men's cloakroom. There he began rifling through the coats and jackets, taking the money he found in the pockets. He exchanged his jacket for a warm herringbone tweed coat, threw a scarf round his neck, jammed a hat on his head. The remains of the buffet supper were lying on a table, so he snatched up sandwiches, biscuits, cakes and stuffed them into the commodious pockets of the coat. He would be all right. He had money, he had clothes, he was young and he would make it. There were horses a-plenty in this part of the countryside. He thought of taking one from the shed at the back of the hall where several of them awaited their masters, but no, the smiddy would be better, he could easily lead one away and it would go undiscovered till the morning.

Maisie was fast asleep in her bed and only stirred slightly when the muffled sound of hooves passed by in the lane. That Willie! Home at last! It was as well for him that she hadn't carried out her threat of locking the doors. Turning on her other side she fell into a deep sleep, lulled there by the thought that her husband would soon be in – though wait till she got him in the morning when she would give him a sound piece of her mind for having stayed out so late!

Caleb led the horse onto the road, newly reshod, saddled, frisky and fresh after a whole day spent in the smiddy stables. He filled his lungs with air. His head was clearer now, he would easily get to the station in time to catch an early train that would connect him with one heading south. If all went according to plan he would be well away before the police were alerted. He mounted the horse and rode off into the bitterly cold morning, a lone traveller on the empty road, one who was quickly swallowed up in the flurrying snow and the darkness and who was never seen again in Kinvara after that night.

*　　*　　*

Shug Law came out to relieve himself against the side wall of the building. He was doing up his buttons when he heard a low groan coming from nearby. His blood froze as he swung round, expecting perhaps to see an inebriated party-goer sleeping it off under the hedge. Instead he saw Maida, lying inert and half obliterated by the falling snow, able only to raise her head and hold one trembling hand out towards him in a mute plea for help. At first Shug didn't recognise the girl, so well did she merge with the white landscape in her pale clothes. He went closer and rubbed the snowflakes away from her face. 'Merciful God!' he cried before he was off, rushing back inside to alert his cronies. They stampeded out to where Maida lay, Dolly dropping down on her knees to administer a few drops of whisky from her flask before wrapping the half-frozen young woman in her own woollen plaid, one that had seen much service but was still cosy and warm.

Many pairs of willing hands helped get the girl into Dolly's cart in among the bundles of washing waiting to be delivered to the gentry. Dancer stepped out briskly, glad of the exercise after a night of miserable inactivity in the shed when all she'd had to console her had been a near-empty nosebag.

The big grey house known as The Paddocks was in darkness when the cart came rumbling into the yard at four thirty in the morning. The occupants of the house were however soon knocked up as Dolly and Shug between them battered at the door while Dokie Joe and Willie threw stones at the upper windows. Sandy came to the door, hair on end, struggling into his trousers and demanding to know what the hell was going on. His mouth fell open in shock when Shug quickly explained what had happened. Maida was taken inside and carried upstairs; Grace appeared, then Mark, crowding into the girl's bedroom, Grace going at once to attend to her daughter while Mark ran to the stables and galloped away as fast as he could to fetch the doctor.

For Dr MacAlistair it was almost a re-enactment of New Year's morning when he'd been called out to Croft Angus to see to Wilma. 'Don't be late back!' Jeannie yelled after him. 'You know what happened before – and make sure you put on your shoes! My slippers are in ruins wi' slush and dung and I still don't know how you managed to get them that way!'

If Maida hadn't been wearing her cape, if Shug hadn't found her when he did, she would surely have perished out there in the wintry wilderness. As it was she was in a state of shock but wouldn't name her attacker, saying over and over it was all her fault and she was sorry for all the trouble she had caused. The doctor gave her a sedative and ordered that she have peace and quiet for the rest of the night. When Stottin' Geordie, the village policeman, arrived he was dissuaded by Grace and Sandy from seeing their daughter. By the time he did manage to interview her it was well past ten in the morning and she wouldn't tell him much except to repeat what she had told the doctor earlier.

The finger of suspicion soon began pointing at Tom

MacGill. He had been seen going with Maida into the ladies' cloakroom and his liking for the girl was a well-known fact, but when Geordie went along to see Tom he was indignant in his protests of innocence. 'I never touched her, Ma, honest,' he cried, directing his pleas to the woman he respected more than any law in the land. 'She wouldn't let me! I went away and left her there and came back here to my bed.'

'I believe you, son.' Bette glared at the policeman as if daring him to refute any of the boy's words. 'The de'il makes work for idle hands and that Lockhart lass has done naught else but fritter her days away since she was born, ogling the lads, getting them into trouble.'

Knowing he was wasting his time, Stottin' Geordie went off. After the door closed behind him, Big Bette clouted her son on the ear just to let him know she was still boss and he gazed at her gratefully, relieved to be getting off so lightly and vowing never again to go near the likes of Maida Lockhart, even if she was the prettiest girl for miles around with good big breasts to match.

Tom was further vindicated when Willie Whiskers went to the smiddy stables after a good long lie-in and discovered the theft of the horse. It was even later when he and the other men went back to the hall to collect their belongings and realised that some of them were missing. 'My coat!' Willie yelped. 'Some bugger's taken it and left a horrible old jacket in its place! Maisie will kill me when she finds out!'

'My hat!' Dokie Joe yelled. 'It's gone too! And my scarf!'

The loss of the money from the various pockets was

also noted. The thefts were reported. Stottin' Geordie began making enquiries at various houses throughout the district, leaving the Mill O' Cladach to the end since he didn't like Joshua and never confronted him unless it was strictly necessary.

Caleb of course was not at home and hadn't been since the previous day. It soon became obvious he was the one under suspicion. The news spread. Rape and robbery. They were dirty words. The Inverness police were alerted. A search party was organised by the locals in and around Kinvara while police scoured the countryside. But by then it was too late. Caleb was already over the border and seeking a new life. He had covered his tracks well. In time everyone gave up searching and the incident, a nine-day wonder, gradually lost momentum as the days went by.

Joshua felt as if a ton weight had been lifted from his shoulders. He was glad that Caleb was gone. The boy had been nothing but trouble lately and it was good riddance to bad rubbish as far as he was concerned. He gave no thought to Maida or the terrible ordeal she had undergone at the hands of his son.

She never recovered from the trauma and eventually fell prey to a disabling nervous illness, becoming martyr to a host of ailments including nightmares and other phantoms of the mind. Dr MacAlistair was as baffled as anyone by her condition. But time was a great healer, as he himself had often said, and he could only hope this would be the case for Maida and the Lockhart family as a whole.

KINVARA/SHETLAND/
KINVARA

Summer/Autumn/
Christmas 1939

Chapter Thirty-one

A strange sense of waiting hung over Kinvara that summer. August brought days of flat calm when nothing stirred or moved, ships glided on a mirror-like sea, puff-ball clouds hung suspended over the hills, the birds fell silent, worn out after frantic months of feeding and rearing young.

In among all the usual seasonal activities the talk was of war. It had been there all through that year but now it was stronger, more menacing. A lot of the Kinvara lads had joined the Territorial Army. Captain Rory, with the help of his eldest son, George, had formed a thriving unit within the community. Training sessions were held in village halls, The MacKernon ran camps in the grounds of Cragdu Castle which sometimes included rifle-shooting league matches that attracted competition between the local rifle club and the Territorials, often resulting in Highland dancing and ceilidhs afterwards. Both The MacKernon and Captain Rory, burying their past differences, joined forces and organised transport to field-firing exercises. A pipe band was formed and regularly marched through the streets of Kinvara with the local people coming to their doors to cheer, saying it was 'a fair treat' to see their lads looking so proud and handsome in their uniforms.

The boys thought it to be a grand adventure and talked eagerly among themselves about war and real fighting while the older men who had experienced the horrors of the first war scanned the newspapers with dread in their hearts and grew more tense with each passing day.

But the threat of war seemed as nothing compared with the worries and tensions gathering within the Lockhart household. Maida's condition had worsened over the past months. Gradually she had deteriorated to the point of being almost bedridden, only ever getting up when her father or Mark persuaded her to go out into the sunshine for a while to sit in the big wickerwork chair that Sandy had acquired for her.

'I feel so ashamed all the time,' she confided once to Vaila, who came to visit as often as she could. 'I don't want to face Joss ever again after what happened. It was dirty, dirty, and it was all my fault, I was so stupid and childish and now I'm too tired to care what becomes of me.'

Towards the middle of August she changed her mind about seeing Joss. 'I want us all to go on a picnic to Stac Gorm,' she told Vaila. 'I know it can't be as it was that wonderful day we went there as children but I'd love to see it again – just once more – and I'd like Joss to be there too.'

'Let me come,' George said to Vaila when he heard about the girl's request. 'I promise no funny business, I just want to be there to help. We should go when the tide is in. It will be easier to take Maida over to the island in a boat rather than carry her over the wet sands.'

'Of course you can come,' Vaila told him, smiling at the eager expression on his handsome face. 'I know you and Mark will behave yourselves on a day which must belong to Maida with nothing in the world to spoil it.'

'You go,' Rebecca told Joss when he came to tell her about the proposed outing. 'Maida doesn't want me, I would only remind her of Caleb and the awful thing he did to her.'

'Do you ever hear from him?' Joss asked, looking at her keenly, knowing that she missed her brother dreadfully and was finding life very strange without him, especially now that Nathan was dead and she had no one within the family to whom she could really turn. She and Miriam were closer, certainly, but she had known a real bond with her brothers and nothing could replace their loss in her heart.

'No,' she said quickly in answer to Joss's question. 'He could be dead and buried for all I know and it's better that he never gets in touch with any of us again.' She had to lie, even to Joss. In a most secret drawer in her room she had hidden a letter she had received from Caleb some weeks ago and which she had managed to keep from her father's prying eyes. In the letter Caleb had told her he was safe and well and that she mustn't worry about him. He had been full of remorse about the dreadful events that had led to him running away and had promised to be in touch again. She had told her mother about the letter, if only to alleviate the suffering she had endured since the night of the dance. A great sigh had shuddered out of Miriam at the news. 'Thank God,' was all she had said before reaching up to kiss her daughter's cheek and wipe away her tears of thankfulness.

'Are you sure you don't want to come with us?' Joss persisted. 'It won't be the same without you, Rebecca, everything's empty and dull and incomplete somehow when you're not there.'

'Dear Joss.' Reaching out she touched his fair head with a reverence born of the brimming love in her heart for him. 'I feel the same about you but this is one time I think we ought to be apart. Let Maida have her moment, they are few and far between for her nowadays and it's only fair to let her have something good to hold onto while she has the strength to do it.'

So it was that Maida and Mark, Vaila, George and Joss, paid a pilgrimage to the little tidal island of Stac Gorm on a day of calm seas and azure skies, travelling to Niven's Bay in the MacPherson family trap, leaving the horses under the shade of the sycamore trees surrounding the chapel. The laird had offered his Humber for the day but Maida had declined, saying she wanted to feel the sun on her face, the wind in her hair. Between them the boys carried her down to the bay and the waiting boat but in the end it only needed two of them, so light was she, so fragile her bones. It took only minutes to row over to lumpy little Stac Gorm where the pink rocks caught the rays of the sun and seals lazed on the reefs, calling to one another in haunting voices that were almost half human.

The first of the memories came piling in on Maida when they stopped to picnic on the dazzling white sands of a tiny sheltered cove. George had brought a small padded chair in which she sat, her big hat shading her small delicate face, casting shadows over eyes that were an even deeper blue here by the edge of the sky-reflecting ocean. Her hair was a cascade of golden curls and waves falling down over her shoulders, her hands lay on her lap, unmoving and peaceful, as she just gazed over the water to the tumble of white houses marching along the silvery shoreline opposite. Joss looked at her and swallowed hard. She was so frail, little, somehow. He should have been kinder to her; she was so quiet now, so different from the Maida of old with her blithe talk and chatter and he wondered how anybody so young could be so still and silent.

George too was watching her, puzzlement and sadness in his glance, and both he and Joss were glad when it was time to move up to the highermost point, the one which gave the island its name, the green knoll, a windblown clifftop where the gulls wheeled and wild thyme grew in profusion on the turf and harebells bloomed in every nook and cranny.

'Take me to the edge,' Maida requested. The boys did as she asked and from her little seat she peered over the sheer cliffs and watched gannets launching themselves hundreds of feet down into the waves while the gulls wheeled all around and the guillemots called from their nesting ledges.

'Oh, Vaila,' she sighed, 'do you remember that day we came here? All of us with our hopes and dreams and visions for the future. It must be eight years now yet I can still see and hear it all, every last detail, saying what we wanted to be when we grew up, Rebecca and Caleb throwing their hats into the sea, Nathan following suit.'

Vaila bit her lip as her breath caught on a tear. She knew what Maida meant, yet how everything had changed. The wonderful wild place that was Stac Gorm was the same but fate had woven very different paths for all of them: Nathan was dead, Caleb was gone, Rebecca and Joss were lovers, Maida was dying, Vaila's own simplistic ideas about finding a great love like her father's hadn't yet come to fruition. Her affections were divided between two young men – dear, darling Mark who was watching her now with such feeling in his eyes, and handsome wonderful George who laughed at life and made her laugh too with his fun and nonsense.

She put her arms round Maida and hugged her close. Joss came to throw himself down on the grass beside Maida and Vaila made her way over to a spur of rock where George and Mark were sitting, not fighting or arguing but talking seriously and quietly about war and what it would mean to them if it really did come.

'I'll ask her to wait for me if it comes to the bit.' George changed the subject with a mischievous grin.

'For the umpteenth time, that makes two o' us.' Mark held out his hand, George took it and gripped it, Vaila saw the exchanges and smiled as she sat down beside them. 'My two bonny warriors, don't tell me you've called truce and have suddenly become the greatest o' friends.'

'Oh, I wouldn't place any bets on that,' Mark said quickly.

'Nor me.' George's teeth flashed, 'But for today we'll lay down our arms and surrender to the beauties of this marvellous place – and I don't just mean the attractions of rock and sea.'

All three looked at one another and burst out laughing while over by the edge of the cliffs Maida and Joss seemed to have come to some sort of pact also. 'It was always just you, Joss,' she was saying. 'The others meant nothing and I'm so ashamed of what happened between Caleb and me. I know you love Rebecca and have done from the start. It's a bit late to say all this but I hope you'll forgive me and know how much I want for you to be happy, now and for always.'

His hand came out to take hers and he felt a catch in his throat at the feel of her long delicate fingers in his rough ones. 'Oh, Maida, I'm sorry too. I could have been nicer to you, I could have been more understanding but I was afraid of losing Rebecca. Things happen in life that none o' us can explain . . .'

Bending over he kissed her gently on the lips, a warm sweet kiss that seemed to reach right down and touch her heart with its beauty. Her hand went to his head to briefly caress the fair strands, then a tear glimmered on her lashes as she whispered huskily, 'Oh, if only . . . if only . . .'

She shivered. A cold little breeze was frisking up from below, and taking off his jersey Joss tied it round her shoulders. They all went away after that, leaving behind the dreaming idyll that was Stac Gorm, saying goodbye to memories and laughter and longings, wondering if they would ever come back together like this in days and years and summers yet to come.

Maida died soon afterwards, silently and peacefully in her own bed, oddly content to let go of her life, too frail to care any more about the vageries of an existence that had become such a burden to her in the last few weary months.

'I'm so sorry, Mark.' Vaila came to him to wind her arms round him and hold him near to her heart. 'I know how close you and she were, how much it means for you to lose her like this.'

'We were twins.' His quiet even voice told nothing of the heartache that throbbed and ached within him. 'She and I understood one another, we were born together and when I was young I used to think we would die together. But she couldn't wait. She lost the will to live, she seemed to lose everything after – after what happened to her.'

Vaila pressed his head to her breast and soothed him with words of comfort. He lay against her passively and when he at last glanced up she saw pain stark and raw in the black pools of his eyes. 'I feel numb, in here.' He pressed his fist to his heart. 'The world is a dark place to be in just now, Vaila, and I need to be alone – to think . . .'

He went stumbling away and helplessly she watched, knowing he was going to those wild and empty places of solitude he always sought when he needed to be alone with his thoughts and his heartaches.

She didn't follow. He didn't want or need her just

then. Later she would come to him, later – before it was too late to comfort young men like Mark who had become soldiers too soon yet not soon enough in a world of unrest and imminent war.

Chapter Thirty-two

A few days before the end of August a letter came to No. 6 Keeper's Row. Hannah was in the back green hanging out her washing when it arrived and didn't hear Dougie the Post knocking at the front door. The other members of the family were also out pursuing their various activities and only Breck was there in the kitchen, hiding in a cool corner to escape the heat of the day, his head on his paws as he slept the deep sleep of a very old and tired dog. Almost totally deaf, he didn't hear Dougie at the door and could hardly see him either when he came inside to lay the letter on the table. But he sensed the presence of someone new in his domain and raised an enquiring face in the postman's direction.

'Good old dog.' Dougie fondled the spotted ears as Breck got stiffly up to push his white muzzle between the postman's knees. 'You're getting past most of it now, lad, but you still know when someone comes in even though you canny see or hear them.'

Dougie had known Breck from away back. In the old days the dog had snapped playfully at his heels coming up the path but was far too intelligent to carry the game any further, wisely saving his energies for the neighbourhood cats and his duties as a watchdog which he had taken very seriously indeed.

He no longer chased cats or anything else for that matter. He wasn't interested in going out with Andy any more, and Dougie felt an odd pang of regret for the passing of time as he rubbed the collie's nose and spoke to him as if he could read lips among all his other attributes. Dougie then helped himself to a ginger snap from the table, broke one up for Breck, took a sip of water from a jug on the sink and went whistling on his way, leaving Breck to go back to his corner and while away the morning hours in sleep and dreams.

A few minutes later Rob came in through the front door as Hannah was coming in the back. Both saw the letter at the same time and laughingly pounced but Rob got there first and tearing it open he said, 'It's from Shetland, from Mirren, she wants us to go there for a few days' holiday . . .' He read on for a little longer before going on slowly, 'She's having trouble gathering in her harvest this year, some o' the men are off sick with a summer bug.'

He paused. 'We could go there and help out, Hannah, my own crops can wait for a while and I'll get plenty o' hands to help out when the time comes.'

Hannah took the letter and scanned the pages. It had been a long time since any of them had seen Mirren, since the wedding in fact. They had exchanged letters and cards but that was all and Hannah gave a sigh as she put the epistle back in the envelope. 'You go, Rob. I'd love to see Mirren but I'm really busy at The Bread Oven just now. The MacKernon's having guests next week and we're going all out to get his order ready on time.'

She put her hand on her husband's arm. 'The break will do you good, Rob. I know how much you love Shetland and you can give Mirren a hand while you're about it. Somehow I doubt if the rest o' the family will make it either, Andy has his job at Cragdu, Vaila won't want to leave Mark with this war business looming, Essie has just gone back to school after the holidays and I wouldn't like to keep her off again.'

'Are you sure you wouldn't mind?' Even as Rob asked the question a sense of elation was rising within him. Hannah was right. He did love Shetland. It would be good to wander those wide open spaces again and to help Mirren out in the fields.

'Of course I don't mind.' Hannah was already turning away to set the lunch table. 'You go and enjoy it. I'll be fine here wi' the bairns, my work will keep me busy and the days will just fly by.'

She was right about the family. They would have loved to go but it was too short notice. Essie grumbled about school; she would much rather have gone with her father, but in the end she gave in with good grace and he went upstairs to pack his case. Next morning he was ready. Hannah gave him a chocolate cake to give to Mirren, they said their goodbyes and then he was off to wait for the bus that would take him to Achnasheen station and the second leg of his journey.

Mirren had grown bonnier in the last few years. There was about her a serenity, a fullness of womanhood that had been missing when she was Mirren alone. Her fair hair shone, her figure was more rounded and curvaceous, her blue eyes were shining when she came to the door of Burravoe House and saw Rob standing on the step.

'Rob!' Impulsively she threw her arms round his neck and kissed him. 'Oh, it's so good to see you after all this time. It's been so long, more than three years. But come in, come in, don't just stand there as if you were a stranger . . .' She glanced behind him. 'Where are the others? I thought at least Hannah would have come with you.'

He laughed. 'She couldn't. Pressures o' work you might say. The bairns couldn't manage either so I'm afraid you'll have to put up with me on my own.'

'How did you get here?' she asked in some confusion. 'If I'd known exactly when you were coming I would have been at the harbour to meet you.'

'It was all too quick for that,' he explained. 'Your letter came yesterday, I packed right away and here I am. I got a lift from a farmer in his haycart and will no doubt be scratching for days.'

She gazed up at him, a flush spreading over her fair skin. 'Erik also isn't here, he went off this morning with the herring fleet and after that he's stopping off to see a sick aunt in Lerwick and won't be back for at least five days.'

They looked at one another rather awkwardly till she shrugged her shoulders and smiled. 'Och, well, it won't be the first time we've been alone with each other in Burravoe House and what the neighbours don't know they'll make up anyway. I'll drag you out to the fields every morning and won't bring you back till late at night – that's if you feel you can lend a helping hand?'

His handsome dark face smiled at her. 'That's one o' the reasons for me being here, but first, do you think there might be a cuppy in the pot? It's been a long journey and I could be doing with putting my feet up for half an hour.'

They went inside to the quiet homely peace of Burravoe House. Mirren made tea and cut the mouthwatering chocolate cake sent by Hannah but made by Maudie, a speciality of hers which tempted Rob and Mirren to have two slices each along with large mugs of piping hot tea. They giggled together as they licked their fingers and wiped the chocolate from their mouths, then she glanced up and caught his eye.

'Ah, Mirren,' he sighed, 'I've missed you these last years, all of us too busy to visit one another, allowing time to pass, other pursuits to get in the way.'

'I know,' she said quietly. 'It's just flown in. I've had my fortieth birthday since I last saw you. Imagine, forty past! Yet I don't feel it, I'm just as wiry as ever I was, throwing a tractor about, lifting sheep as big as myself, humping bales of hay.'

'You don't look it.' He eyed her flushed face. 'If anything you look younger than you did before. Marriage has been good for you, Mirren.'

'Ay, ay, it has,' she admitted, keeping her head down to avoid the admiring look in his eyes.

'Are you happy, Mirren?' he went on. 'Are you glad you did what you did?'

'Yes, I am, Rob. Erik's a good man, he's kind to me and we get on well together. He's great around the farm when he isn't at the fishing and when he's away I get my private times to myself. I grew used to my own company during my years alone without Morna . . .' She looked up then. 'And you, Rob? Are you happy? Have you learned to live without the memory of my sister clouding your day to day living?'

'Ay, Mirren, I have. I'll always remember Morna, I know I always will. The years go by, the memories of her are still strong and deep and will be for all time. But I have a good life, Hannah's a good wife, my children have been a joy to me and I can't imagine what life would have been like without them.'

'Ay.' She looked down at her hands. Something secret and still seemed to come over her for a few moments then suddenly she jumped up and became the Mirren he knew best, brisk, businesslike, bossy, ordering him to lie down for an hour as she had work to do and couldn't be doing with him under her feet all day 'blethering like an old woman'.

The next few days went by in a whirl for Rob. Every morning he was up with the lark and out in the fields with Mirren, the great tumble of the Shetland skies above them, the blinding light spilling from the clouds to spread gold on the fields of ripened corn while the lapwings soared and dived and screaming gulls settled in the wake of the reapers to gorge themselves on worms and other creatures left behind in the stubble.

He wanted to hold on to these wonderful days of freedom and never let go. The lighthouse, the sea, the lonely hours he spent on duty were looming too near for him; he didn't want to face any of it just now but inevitably the time arrived for him to leave Burravoe and all it had come to mean to him.

On the night before he left he and Mirren sat and reminisced as they had done every night since his arrival. But somehow tonight was special: cosier, more intimate and meaningful, tinged with sadness that soon it would end with neither of them knowing when, if ever, they would meet like this again.

The fire crackled, the dogs snored, a large grey half-Persian kitten purred in the ingle, sparks flew up the lum, all was peace and quietness and serenity.

'It's been good, Rob.' Mirren was first to break the silence that had sprung up between them. 'I'll never forget it.'

'Nor me.' He had to swallow to relieve the huskiness in his throat. 'I'll think of my days spent here with you when I'm back once more in the lighthouse. I'm getting tired o' it, Mirren. I've devoted half my life to it and feel I need a change.'

'What would you do, Rob? It's all you've known for so many years.'

'Too many, but I've been saving. Me and Charlie Campbell have talked about starting up a little boat-builders within the yard at Balivoe, small craft, nothing fancy. There is a need for it, more holidaymakers than ever are coming to Kinvara and looking for ways to pass the time. I've always enjoyed anything to do with boats. Vale O' Dreip will go to Finlay when the time comes; he's got farming in his blood while I'm a man o' the sea and can't imagine leaving it for good when I say goodbye to the lighthouse.'

'There's a war coming, Rob,' she pointed out pensively, 'God knows what's going to happen within the next few weeks.'

'I know. There's talk o' little else and I've a feeling my days at the light aren't over yet. If war does come there will be convoys, and they'll need guiding so all hands will be needed at the helm.'

They were silent for a few more minutes, each with their individual thoughts, then Mirren leaned over and took his hand. 'Let's talk of brighter things. It's your last night and we should savour every second.'

When the time at last came to go up to bed Mirren extinguished the lamps and lingered for a while by the fire her face shadowed, half hidden by the fair tresses of her hair as she gazed into the glowing cinders. She imagined him to be gone from the room but when she stood up he was there behind her. She gasped and drew back but he captured her in his embrace and it seemed the most natural thing in the world for her to be held like this, tingling with warmth and wanting, his heart thudding against hers, uncaring about tomorrow and what it might bring . . .

And then they were kissing, kissing, carried away on the tide of passion and longing that had been building up in them for the last few breathless days.

War was announced on the day of Rob's arrival home. All the family were gathered round the wireless set when he came in and dumped down his bags. Neville Chamberlain's voice came sombrely over the wires, informing the nation that Britain and France had declared war on Germany. The Second World War had begun but there, in the homely kitchen of No. 6 of the Row, it somehow didn't seem real. The clocks ticked as usual, Breck snored on his rug, a big pan of soup was simmering on the stove, books and jigsaws littered the table, a questing stray cat put its nose round the door and sniffed when it smelled stew as well as soup scenting the air.

Breck didn't stir at the intrusion. At first nobody did, then Hannah came to sudden and indignant life, seizing her broom, chasing the cat with it, helped by Breck who didn't know what all the fuss was about until his nose told him *CAT* which was enough to set his tail quivering even if no other part of him did. After that everyone emerged from the trance-like state the news had wrought in them. As if expecting bombs to drop at any moment Andy went out to the byre to check that his new pony, Beauty, was still hale and hearty in her stall: Essie went upstairs to climb on Prince Charming and rock herself thoughtfully; Vaila backed away from the wireless and turned a tragic face to her father; Hannah put her broom away and went to welcome her husband home while Breck retired once more to his corner to wait for dinnertime.

Rob put out his arms to his wife and his daughter to soothe away their fears, his face dark and solemn as he did so. Shetland was a million miles away now. Mirren belonged to another world. This was his reality: his family, his wife, his home, the precious things and people he had worked for and lived with for most of his life and who needed him more than ever now that war was here with all its unknown terrors and heartaches.

Chapter Thirty-three

The September days were mellow and warm. Scents of newly cut hay hung heavy and sweet in the air, carts rumbled home in the gloaming, lads and lassies snuggled up to one another to whisper and kiss and hold hands as they had done for generations past when all the world seemed made for them alone and it felt right and good to plan for the future. But now they didn't talk of tomorrow. Everything was too uncertain for that; the lads were going away to fight in the war and the time had come to say goodbye, to husbands, brothers, sweethearts.

The Territorial Army unit of Kinvara was heading for the training camp at Fort George, Mark and Joss among them, excitement and apprehension building in them as the day drew nearer and all that was left were those precious last hours with the people they loved.

On the eve of Joss's departure he and Rebecca met for the last time at Oir na Cuan, a house that had known many loves and heartaches in the years of its existence and now wrapped itself quietly and warmly around the young couple as they stood together in the tiny living room, gazing at one another with hearts that were overflowing.

Reaching out he touched her hair, reverently and wordlessly. What was there to say in those moments of bitter-sweet awareness and deep emotion that flowed like burning rivers of fire within them, all mingling and merging with the sadness and the uncertainty of an unknown future?

'Rebecca.' He spoke her name at last; she murmured his and they moved into one another's arms, unhurried at first, then with an urgency born of the love and desire they had shared so eagerly in the last few wonderful years. Tears filled her eyes as helplessly they kissed, over and over, rapture flooding her being at the feel of his beautiful strong mouth on hers, her Joss, her sweetheart, the young man who had brought so much meaning into her life, soon to be leaving her, no more to fill her with his strength and delight and his joy of living. This night was all that was left now . . . when he was gone she would look back and remember, remember how it had been in the arms of Joss Morgan.

'Oh, Joss,' she whispered, 'I never thought it would come to this, I never thought we would ever have to say goodbye.'

'I'll come back.' He crushed her to his heart, his mouth nuzzled hers. 'When I do we'll be married and have our children, it won't be for long, I promise you I'll come back – and I'll write, care of the Post Office.'

His fingers whispered over her skin, the flames of their passion smouldered and caught fire. They were beginners no longer; they knew every plane of one another's bodies, every warm hollow. Reality whirled away. Caution was thrown to the winds.

It didn't matter any more. Nothing mattered except this night, this now, these moments of heartrending love and joyous fulfilment. The house was calm and still around them, an owl hooted from the barn slates, the ocean murmured to the shore, a lone bird cried overhead. Nothing else stirred or moved or intruded. Oir na Cuan slept snug under the stars, providing shelter for those who would ever need a safe and private haven in which to rest.

George came to Vaila in the butler's pantry at Crathmor, oh so exciting and virile in his regalia of The Argyll and Sutherland Highlanders, his bright face glowing and smiling, his fair hair sleek and shining under his bonnet. She had come down to the kitchens to search for an item of crockery in the pantry and caught out like this in the small enclosure she found herself at a great disadvantage when she swung round to see him standing there surveying her with silent appraisal.

'George!' she gasped, 'I didn't hear you coming in. Oh, I wish you wouldn't sneak up on me like this! You're always doing it and it's not fair.'

For answer he came immediately forward and gathered her into his arms. 'Surely I have a right to say goodbye to you before I go off to join my regiment? After all, who knows when I'll be home again? I just wanted to give you the chance to appreciate me in all my splendour and to leave you something to remember me by.'

'You big-headed oaf!' she laughed while her heart played an odd little tattoo in her breast and she could hardly tear her eyes away from his mouth, so near to hers, so very very tempting.

Without turning round he shut the door with his foot and she made no move to stop him when his mouth came down on hers, warm and hard and persistent. A flame of desire leapt between them. As his hand brushed her breast she felt the tingle of it flowing down to her belly where it seemed to swell and grow in volume until the beat of it filled her senses. It would be easy, so easy, just to give in to him, to give him what he had wanted for a long time now. He was going away, far away where she couldn't follow, and months could pass before she saw him again – perhaps even years.

'You will wait for me, Vaila, won't you?' he whispered urgently.

'Ay, George, I'll wait,' she promised, hardly aware of what she was saying in the heat of the moment.

'You mean it, you really mean it?' He was growing hungrier for her body, speaking in rather a delirious fashion as he kissed her eyes, face and neck, his hands travelling further down to the warm mounds of her enticing breasts.

'Oh, George.' A great sigh was torn from her. 'This isn't fair, you know it isn't fair, to ask this of me when – when . . .'

'All's fair in love and war, Vaila . . .' He pulled away to look at her. 'But I think I know what you mean. You've got Mark on your mind, haven't you? You play with us both and lead us on when all the time you really don't know which of us you want.'

She turned her face away but he caught her chin in his hand and made her look at him. 'Ay, George, you're right,' she said on a half-sob. 'I don't know if it's you or Mark. You're both going away and I won't see either o' you for a long time. Perhaps then I can stand back and know what it is I'm looking for.'

She shook her head so that her black curls fell over her sun-flushed face. His breath caught. 'You're so lovely, Vaila. I want you as I've never wanted any girl before but I don't want you like this – undecided and afraid of your feelings, for me, for anybody . . .'

He kissed the tip of her freckled nose, stood back, saluted and said, 'May I be dismissed now, ma'am? My kilt is on fire and needs must that I put it out before it scorches a backside already too hot for its own good.'

'George, oh, George,' she said with a catch in her voice, 'you always could make me laugh. I'll never forget you, and I'll write, I promise I'll write.'

He saluted again, grinned at her, opened the door and went out, leaving her to gather her wits together for several long pensive minutes.

Vaila knew where Mark would be, down at the stables with the horses, only this time he wouldn't be working, he would be saying goodbye, goodbye to a way of life he had loved since he was a small boy, following his father around in the fields, watching him breaking in the raw and frisky ponies, helping with the feeding and the grooming, learning more and more as the years went by.

It was warm and steamy inside the cobwebby building where the good earthy smells of hay and dung hung heavy in the air. The dusty rays of the sun slanted in through the roof, lighting on brasses and bridles, saddles and harness.

'I knew I'd find you here.' Vaila went to him. She took his hand and led him to the loft ladder. Together they climbed it and fell down in the fragrant straw, not touching but close together, lying back to stare at the roof as the thoughts and sadnesses of parting crowded their minds.

His fingers came out to entwine in hers. 'Do you know what I'm remembering most? That day in Shetland when we danced together over the machair. The old man's face when he saw us waltzing about and we nearly died laughing. I'll think about it when I'm far away – so much has happened since then, Maida gone, me going also but to a place far removed from hers. Mum and Dad are finding it hard. Perhaps you would go and see them now and then.'

'Of course I will.' She caught her lip between her teeth. It was difficult saying goodbye to the young men who were such a part of her life. What would she do without them, she wondered, where would she go when she needed a hard shoulder to lean on?

'I want to touch you, Vaila,' he went on quietly, 'but I'm not going to. It will just make me want more and now I know better than anybody that you're not ready to give yourself to any man yet.'

They were profound words coming from a boy as passionate as Mark. Her hand tightened over his. 'Mark,' she whispered tearfully, 'I wish you weren't going away, I wish everything could go on as before.'

'Nothing stays the same, Vaila. Things change, people change, time passes, only the land remains and the hills sleep on forever.'

'Oh, Mark, please stop.' The tears were pouring unheeded from her eyes. 'I never knew you had it in you to be so romantic, I can't bear it, I can't.'

'You don't know a lot o' things about me, Vaila, you've never stopped long enough to find out.'

He sat up and from his pocket he produced a spray of dew-fresh harebells, wrapped in cellophane to keep them from wilting. 'For you, to remember me by, the bonny true bluebells of Scotland, picked with love for my beautiful Highland lass.'

It was too much. She too sat up and buried her face between her knees to weep and weep as if she would never stop, her hair falling sweet and bonny about the young planes of her face, her small shoulders shuddering with her sobs. Gently he touched her and helped her to her feet, then together they climbed back down the ladder. He put his hand under her chin and lifted her face up to his; his thumb caressed the soft bloom of her cheek, his mouth touched her lips, soft and warm and fleeting. 'I'll keep you in my heart, Vaila, wherever I go, whatever I do.' And then he was gone from her, striding off into the unknown, tall and straight and proud in his Black Watch kilt and khaki jacket, the ribbons of his Glengarry bonnet fluttering in the breeze.

She raised her hand but he didn't look back. 'Take care, precious, darling, Mark,' she whispered. Her eyes ached and she felt bereft: first George, now Mark, her two fine lads, so much a part of her life, gone, gone, like a puff of gentle wind in the night. When would she see them again, she wondered. Would they come back to her as whole and as beautiful and as eager for life as they both were now?

Her footsteps were heavy as she returned to the hayloft to retrieve her little posy of harebells. When she went home that night she pressed them into her diary and her eyes were wet when she kissed them and prayed for Mark and George and all the other young men who were leaving their homelands far behind to go marching into strange and unfamiliar worlds that had no place in their hearts.

When October came the voices of young men no longer rang in the glens and in the hills. When the blackout blinds were drawn down it was as if the very heartbeat of the Kinvara peninsula had faded away and only echoes and memories were left to console those who remained behind.

Christmas wasn't very far off when Hannah came down one morning to them kitchen. Rob had cut a little fir tree which now stood in a corner, the fresh balmy scent of it pervading every space, the baubles and the glitter dancing in the dawn light filtering in through the window. Nothing breathed in the room; it was quiet and warm and peaceful. Breck was in his usual place on the rug in front of the fire, a concession she had made in the past year or two when his limbs had grown stiff and he had begun to feel the cold more.

This morning he made no movement. Hannah thought how strange that was as he always greeted her with a wag of his feathery tail when he opened his blind old eyes to another day dawning. A terrible sense of foreboding touched Hannah's heart. Going over she bent and touched him and found that the rug was warm but Breck was cold. She backed away, her hand going to her mouth. How could she tell Andy that his beloved dog was dead? The companion he had known from babyhood was gone – gone from his life and from hers too for she had come to love and respect the loyal creature who had filled all their lives with his wit and humour and endless undying love.

Breck Sutherland – it was silly – it was ridiculous, a dog with a surname . . . Hannah sat down suddenly at the table. She put her head in her hands and cried, feeling that she would never stop. For a dog, only a dog! But one who had been part of the home and the family for seventeen years, almost to the day.

Andy found her there, sitting at the table, staring into space, a crumpled wet ball of a hanky in her hand, her eyes red and sore with crying. Awareness darkened his eyes as he glanced from his mother to the rug by the fire. Without a word he went over to lie down beside his dog and gather him into his arms as he had done when they were both babies together long, long ago. Hannah got up, put her hand on her son's dark head, and left them like that, Breck and the boy, there on the rug by the fire with the silence of the lonely kitchen all around them and the little fir tree spreading its message of Christmas in the cold light shining through the window.

They buried Breck in a sheltered little spot in the garden with his bone and his ball and his collar beside him and on the grave they placed a simple white cross that Rob had made, bearing the words; *My faithful friend, Breck, 1922–1939, from Andy who will never forget you.*

Essie sobbed, Vaila's heart was heavy, Hannah held her apron up to her eyes, Rob remembered a tiny pup given to him by Morna for Andy's Christmas many moons ago. Andy himself turned and walked away. For him it was the end of an era and he had to be alone, to cry, to remember, to think of his life without a big spotted cross collie who had given him mobility and freedom in his growing years but who most of all had given him love.

The Christmas mail went out that year to the boys at war far away and over the sea. As people compared family reunions of yesteryear to the much-diminished gatherings of the present day, a sense of depression fell over everyone. Nineteen thirty-nine was a year no one would ever forget in a hurry. The war had begun, no one knew when it would end, and all that was left was to soldier on and hope for brighter and more peaceful times ahead.

KINVARA

Summer 1940/41

Chapter Thirty-four

'You're with child, girl!' The accusation shot from Joshua like a bullet as he stared at his daughter when she arose one evening from the supper table. She froze as her hand went automatically to her stomach. This was the moment she had dreaded, even while she had known it would come. Loose smocks and pinafores had done their job well; she was tall and slim and carried herself proudly, and it was only in the past month that her condition had really become difficult to hide. She had grown heavier, more awkward, had dragged herself through each day, pining for Joss, haunting the Post Office for his letters which had been few and far between since his departure.

With both his sons gone Joshua had been forced to take on help at the mill and now there was Jacky, a gangly gawky lad with vacant eyes who wasn't quite the full shilling but was as strong as a horse and glad enough to earn a bob or two. Rebecca had let him do all the heavy lifting and laying and had somehow carried on in the hope that her sweetheart would soon be coming back to her.

But the war had worsened, there had been no letters for weeks. She had worried and wondered and had gone through agonies of apprehension. Now her worst fears had been confirmed. Two days ago she had learned that Joss had been killed in the retreat to Dunkirk and would never be coming back to her again. Janet and Jock were devastated. Their only beloved child was dead, taken from them in the flower of his youth. They had cried aloud in their grief and pain but Rebecca had been unable to comfort them, so petrified was she with her own terrible burden of disbelieving horror. It didn't seem real to her. There had been a mistake; any day now she would get a letter from Joss telling her he was alive and well and would be coming home. So she had deluded herself, her heart like a stone in her breast, too numb to weep, too shocked to care about anything.

Now as she faced the wild-eyed beast that was her father her head went up, and she looked at him with hatred in her eyes, 'If you mean I'm pregnant then you're exactly right, and I can only hope you're going to give me all the loving care and support that an only daughter might expect from a devoted father.'

There was a short electrifying silence, then he was up, his chair clattering to the floor, red-hot rage pouring from every taut muscle, fists bunching, eyes glaring their wrath upon her.

'So, you admit to it!' he roared. 'You've whored and lusted like any common back street hussy and now you carry a Catholic bastard! The Morgan boy, no doubt, sniffing and drooling at your skirts like a dog in heat and you allowing him to do it, without shame or thought for anyone else.'

'Like father like daughter!' Rebecca blazed back. 'We're both good at spawning bastards! God knows how many you've got scattered throughout the land!

Oh, I know all about you, Father, your trail of bigamous marriages, how you broke Johnny Armstrong's heart when you stole his wife away from him and how his daughter died trying to find him again!'

With a snarl of rage Joshua sprang, his hand flashing out to hit her just as a horrified Miriam came into the room.

'No!' she screamed. 'Leave her! Leave her! Leave her!' She leapt on him to tear at him with furious hands but scornfully he tossed her aside and spun round to face his daughter once more, chest heaving, face livid.

'I could have you sent to an asylum for this,' he imparted in a dangerously level voice. 'Wilful daughters have been commited for less. Go to your room and don't come out till I have decided what to do with you. You will take your meals alone and if I were you I would pray for your soul before it is condemned to eternal damnation.'

White-faced, all the fire gone from her, Rebecca did as she was told. The small bare cell-like room was uncomfortably warm after the heat of the day. Sitting on the edge of her bed she gave a little whimper and fear stark and raw stared out of her eyes. 'Oh, Joss,' she whispered. 'What am I to do? Please, tell me, what am I to do?'

The floodgates opened. Burying her face in her hands she wept as if her heart would break. She was afraid, terribly, horribly afraid. Nathan and Caleb were gone; Joss was never coming back to her; there was no one she could turn to in her hopelessness. The future looked bleak. Where could she go? Who could she go to? She couldn't face Joss's parents, not now, oh, certainly not now when all she wanted was to curl up in a corner and die herself.

The long night passed in fitful sleep and dark dreamings. Her child stirred within her but not even that was real. It was gone, all gone, all she wanted was Joss but he was dead in some distant land where the only dreams were nightmares and love was only half remembered in the struggle to survive.

It was almost dinnertime next day when Miriam brought Rebecca a tray sparsely laid with bread and milk. Setting it down on the dresser she went over to sit by the bed. Stroking the dark hair from her daughter's troubled brow she said quietly, 'Don't worry, Rebecca, I know the world must seem a grey place to you just now but it will come all right in the end. You have Joss's child to think about, you have that at least to remember him by. It will be hard but you must go on.'

Rebecca looked at her mother's weary face, the lifeless eyes, the brown hair scraped back and tied in a knot at the nape of her neck. Yet there was something refined and gentle about her, a pale ghost of the attractive woman she must once have been before she had taken the wrong path and had lived to rue her mistakes a million times over. Rebecca reached out and took her mother's hand in hers. The knuckles were swollen, the wedding ring embedded in the flesh for all time to come, as if in mockery of a marriage that had been a sham from the beginning. A shaft of pity went through the girl; a tear pricked her lids. None of it mattered any more, the bitterness she had felt for this woman was gone, along with the resentment that had once lived in her breast. They shared a common bond now, both existing rather than living, nothing to look forward to from one day to the next . . .

'You have your child to think about, Rebecca.' Miriam interpreted her daughter's thoughts. 'You're very young, you will go on.' She got up, put her hand on Rebecca's shoulder and squeezed it as a glimmer of a smile touched her mouth. 'The beginning of June, I always loved the month of June, the bursting buds, the life . . .'

She seemed to come back from a long distance and gave herself a little shake. 'Eat your food and take your milk, Rebecca. Don't worry about anything. I have to see to your father now – he'll be waiting – steak and kidney pie – his favourite.'

A short while later Rebecca looked from her window and saw her mother wandering among the flowers in the meadow, humming a little tune as she went, so immersed in what she was doing she seemed oblivious to everything that was going on around her. Rebecca drew back, a new fear seizing her as she began to wonder if Miriam's mind had at last snapped. Her two sons were gone from her life, her daughter was in dire distress, yet she sang as if she didn't have a care in the world as she wandered dreamily in the meadow among the bursting buds of June.

Rebecca began to wonder about the silence in the

house. Dinnertime had come and gone long ago, the sun was sinking lower, yet nothing stirred or moved. Jacky was in the mill building, she could hear him whistling as he went about his work, but the house itself was as silent and as dead as a tomb. Eventually, driven by curiosity and hunger, she crept out of her room and went into the kitchen. Slumped across the table was her mother. On the floor on the other side lay Joshua, arms outflung, his black beard jutting up out of his deathly white face, dead, dead, if his open staring eyes were anything to go by. His plate on the table had been scraped clean, his jug of ale emptied. Miriam had also eaten but hadn't completely cleared her plate.

Rebecca recoiled in horror. For endless moments she remained rooted to the spot before she went running for Jacky to throw her bike at him and yell at him to go for the doctor. There was something she herself had to do, had to see . . . forcing her shaking legs forward she went back into the kitchen to retrieve a piece of paper lying by her mother's hand. *Dear Rebecca*, it read, *you're free now to do as you want. I'm sorry I wasn't a better mother to you and hope some day you might find it in your heart to forgive me. Find Caleb if you can and look after one another. Your loving mother, Miriam.*

When Dr MacAlistair came he found Rebecca sitting on a straight-backed chair in the kitchen, staring at the note, hardly seeing it. Gently he took her hand and tried to help her to her feet but she refused. 'No, Doctor, I'm not leaving the room. I want to know what happened, I don't mind being here when you examine them.'

'Both dead,' he pronounced grimly a few minutes later, going on to ask Rebecca if she had noticed either of them acting strangely of late. She told him about seeing her mother wandering about outside picking something. 'I took it to be flowers, though she seldom does that and I thought it a bit odd, especially when I saw her coming back empty-handed. But she might have put something into her apron. She carried a lot of little personal things about in her pocket to keep my father from seeing them.'

The doctor raked in the large pocket and withdrew the remnants of some leaves and a few spotted pink foxglove bells. 'Digitalis,' he said with a shake of his head. 'Beneficial in the correct doses but fatal if overdone. She most likely made a strong brew of it and put it into the food. But why didn't he taste it? It must have been bitter and she must have heaped it in to kill them both like this.'

'Ale,' Rebecca told him with a grimace. 'He swilled it down like a pig and ate his food like a horse. Mother said something about steak and kidney pie and he would just gulp it down along with the ale without even chewing it properly. He was like that, no manners, no refinement, for all his preaching to us about the self-same things.' She looked beseechingly at the doctor. 'But why did she go with him? We could have coped between us, we would have managed somehow.'

'Your mother was done, Rebecca,' he stated heavily. 'She had a tumour. She came to see me some time ago but by then it was too late to do anything about it.'

'Oh, poor Mother,' Rebecca said tremulously. 'I know she got thinner but I took it to be grief for Nathan, worry over Caleb. Oh, I wish I'd known how ill she was. I liked her, in the end I really liked her. It must have taken courage to do what she did. With him she was frightened all the time but in the end she was strong and brave for my sake.'

'Ay, lass, it took courage, Miriam was a good woman wasted.' With a sigh he put his stethoscope away and laid his hand on Rebecca's arm. 'Come along, young lady, there's nothing you can do here. You're the one who needs taking care of now and Jeannie will see to you. How far on, eight, eight and a half months?'

'More than that, and I will take you up on your offer, Doctor, but only for a night or two till I can find somewhere else. I think the world of you and Jeannie but I have to be by myself for a while. I need space to think.'

'As you like.' His kindly face was sympathetic; he had heard about Joss, of course. The village had been stunned by the news, the boy's parents were beyond consoling, the neighbours in Keeper's Row were shocked and saddened, The Henderson Hens were in a dreadful state and he'd had to give each of them a sedative to calm them down. He knew the girl must be suffering agonies despite her cool demeanour but she was Rebecca and she was brave. The stuffing had been knocked out of her but one day she would bounce back, in time she would get over all this and be free to live her life without the stifling black shadow of her father hanging over her, repressing everything that was natural and good in a young soul who had cried out for understanding and love but who had got neither till Joss had come to her with his youth and his vigour and his boundless joy for living each day to the full. Rebecca had loved deeply and she had loved well and Dr MacAlistair knew it would be a long time before she gave her heart to anyone again – if she ever did.

Janet and Jock pleaded with Rebecca to stay with them till the baby was born but she refused, knowing their grief would crush her in her present vulnerable state. 'If it's Joss's child you're carrying we have a right to look after you as he would have wanted!' Janet cried desperately.

'It is Joss's baby,' Rebecca returned steadily. 'I haven't been with anyone else but I've had to answer to other people all my life and need to be alone for a while.'

'Then you'd better have this.' Janet put a small package into the girl's hand. 'Joss asked me to give it to you if he was away any longer than a year . . .' Her face crumpled. 'No need to wait for that now, it's over, all over, go away now, Rebecca, but please don't shut us out when – when your baby is born.'

'I won't, I promise.' Rebecca laid her hand on Janet's arm then took herself off to a quiet corner to open her little parcel in peace. Inside was a gold ring on a chain and a note which she unfolded with bated breath.

Dearest Rebecca, I miss you already and I'm not even away yet. I've never been very good at

*writing letters so this is just a short note to tell
you how much you mean to me. In case I might
be away too long I'm giving you this ring. With
it I thee wed, with my body I thee worship, with
my heart I love and adore you. We were always
married in spirit anyway and never more so than
now. Always remember that and never forget
what we were to one another. Try to think of it
that way. Take care, my beautiful strong brave
Rebecca. Goodnight from Joss.*

She crushed the letter to her breast and a great sob
tore out of her throat as she kissed the gold ring and
with trembling fingers fastened it round her neck.
The words in the note were imprinted on her mind.
In case I might be away too long. He had known that
he might never come back to her and this was his way
of saying goodbye.

Johnny came to see Rebecca as soon as he heard of
her troubles. 'Come with me, lass,' he told her without
preliminary. 'I think I know the very place for you.
We'll have to ask Captain Rory but he's aware of
what's happened to your family and I'm sure he won't
say no.'

'Oir na Cuan, eh?' The laird shook his head doubt-
fully when the request was put to him. 'It's not exactly
habitable, lass. The roof leaks, it will need repairs
done to the gutters, it isn't the sort of place for a
young girl to be alone in – especially in your – em
– condition.'

'It isn't as bad as you think,' Rebecca hastily told

him. 'I can soon get the fires going and make it cosy.'

'And I'll see to the roof,' Johnny said firmly. 'A few nails here and there will soon set it to rights and the guttering isn't all that bad.'

'As you like.' The laird shook Rebecca's hand and looked at her keenly. 'But you take care, lass, get someone in to stay with you till after the bairnie is born. It's a lonesome place down there on the shore and you'll need taking care of.'

'Thank you, Johnny,' Rebecca said as they made their way down to Oir na Cuan. 'I don't know what I'd do without you.'

'I know you like the place,' Johnny said with a sly little grin. 'I used to see you and Joss, shutting yourselves away in there, and I kept an eye open for you in case any nosy parkers came snooping about.'

The next few days were strange ones for Rebecca. Her parents' burial had been postponed pending an inquiry into their deaths and the neighbours' tongues were red-hot with the scandal. Murder at the Mill. Suicide at the Dinner Table. Poison on a Platter. All sorts of themes and theories were put forward and gone over with a fine-toothed comb while Rebecca's 'condition' was a little bonus for the womenfolk to get their teeth into.

'Of course, she aye was a strange lass,' Effie remarked to Vaila. 'Haughty would be a good word to describe the way she has o' putting her nose in the air.'

'She isn't strange, just different,' Vaila defended

her friend. 'It's a good job we aren't all alike in this world.'

Effie looked at her rather coldly. She had never fully forgiven Rob's daughter for the remark she had made about her nose, even though Vaila had apologised and it was a long time ago. 'I just hope she hasn't got any daft notions in her head about delivering the bairn herself,' she told Vaila huffily. 'It's my job to see to such matters and I hope you remember that too when the time comes.'

'As if I would do anything else,' Vaila said placatingly.

'Ay, as if you would,' Effie returned dourly and went away home to gaze fondly at Juliet who was expecting piglets any day now and was needing all the tender loving care she could get.

Chapter Thirty-five

Rebecca wasn't very welcoming when Vaila appeared at her door one morning and announced her intention of staying for a few days. She had come complete with bags and a basket of food and made no bones about carrying them inside and dumping them on the floor. 'Just till you get settled in,' she said breezily. 'Everyone is worried in case you aren't feeding yourself right. Hannah made the ginger snaps, Maudie the cakes, Granma Harriet roasted the beef and put some gravy in a jar so that we can have it with potatoes for dinner. Maudie also sent some baby clothes because she thought you wouldn't have any and Kangaroo Kathy insisted on giving you a beautiful shawl she made herself and kept in a drawer when her own bairns were past using it.'

'I *am* settled in,' Rebecca said coolly. 'I'm no stranger to this house, Joss and I used to come here whenever we could.'

'You came here? To Oir na Cuan? I never knew. You never said anything.'

'I was hardly going to tell the world, was I? No one knew, except perhaps Johnny, and he could always keep a secret.'

'So, you were the ghost?' Vaila stated with an intake of breath.

'Yes, I suppose you could say that. A few nosy parkers came snooping, especially Effie Maxwell and that Mattie MacPhee but as soon as they saw my shadow at the window they couldn't get away from the place fast enough.' Rebecca still sounded rather distant but relented when she saw the determination on her friend's face. 'Oh, all right, I suppose it won't do any harm you being here. It's fine during the day when Johnny's around banging away at the slates but it's different at night with only ghosts and memories for company.'

They looked at one another. Rebecca's cool front fell away and she was all at once a lost bewildered girl instead of the assured young woman she was trying so hard to be. 'Oh, Vaila,' she sobbed. 'Thank you for caring. I don't know what I'm saying half the time far less what I'm doing. Of all the people in Kinvara you're the one I most want to have near me just now and I'm glad you came, really glad.'

They held one another and cried, for days gone, for the loneliness they were both feeling for young men who had once been part of their lives but who were with them no more.

'I'm so sorry about Joss,' Vaila wept into her friend's glossy black hair, 'so very very sorry. I know he was the world to you and I want you to speak about him while I'm here instead of bottling it up and breaking your heart in the process. You've been through so much, I don't know how you can bear to be so brave.'

'And you, Vaila? What about you? Do you pine for Mark or George or both?'

'I think about them all the time,' Vaila admitted pensively. 'My heart aches for them. I want only to see them and talk to them, and it seems such a long time since last September.'

'We'll talk about them together, our boys, our sweethearts,' Rebecca said as she softly closed the door and led Vaila inside.

That very night Rebecca's waters broke and she went into violent labour. 'I'll get Effie right away,' Vaila cried in some confusion. 'I'm glad I brought my bike, it's a fair distance to Purlieburn Cottage but it will be all right, Effie will give me a lift back in her trap – oh – I'd better hurry, you – you look terrible, give me your arm and I'll help you up to bed.'

'No!' Rebecca stayed her friend with a sharp command. 'I don't want Effie here poking her long nose in where it isn't wanted. I want you to deliver the baby, Vaila.'

'Och no, I can't!' Vaila cried aghast.

'Why not? You did it for Maudie.'

'No, I didn't, I just watched. Mirren and Granma Rita did it between them.'

'You can do it.' Rebecca was pacing about, holding her back, sweat breaking on her brow as she moaned aloud in pain.

'I can't, I can't!' Vaila sounded terrified. 'You might die, the baby might die! I've got no experience of delivering babies.'

'You've helped your father deliver calves and lambs. Human babies are much the same. I'll be doing all the work, all you have to do is be there and bathe my brow when I'm starting to push.'

Rebecca had obviously been reading romantic books for when the reality of giving birth came all she did was sob over and over, 'I can't do it! I never thought it would be this difficult. Oh, God! Help me! Help me! Help me!'

It was possibly the most sincere prayer she had ever uttered in her life and was born only out of the sheer agony and distress she was experiencing as she walked the floor, refusing to go upstairs to bed, saying she wanted Joss's child to be born in the same room they had made love in, on the same couch, using the same cushions they had used when they had lain back in one another's arms to kiss and laugh and dream their little dreams.

'I'm going for Effie!' Vaila shouted.

'No, don't do that!' Rebecca gasped. 'It's too late now! It's coming! I can feel it, pushing down, tearing me apart.'

'It can't be!' Vaila glanced desperately at the clock on the mantelshelf. 'It's only been two hours. No one has babies that quick! I can go for Effie and be back in plenty o' time . . .'

She stopped dead. Rebecca had sunk onto the couch, her face almost purple with the effort of pushing her child into the world. In five minutes it had arrived, bawling and lusty, slithering out like a little fish while Vaila watched, open-mouthed and wide-eyed, hardly able to believe that a real live human baby could have come so quickly.

'I'll get some towels.' She made a dive for the bag she had brought, remembering as she did so the frantic search she and George had made for the self-same items in Maudie's house and the look of pure delight on his face when they had finally unearthed one bearing the words *I Belong to Glasgow* in large purple lettering.

Vaila's hands were shaking as carefully she cut the birth cord and tied it in as neat a knot as she could in the circumstances.

'It's a boy.' Rebecca's voice was husky with exhaustion as she stared at the baby lying on her breast, 'When it was inside me I only ever thought of it as a baby, never as a girl or a boy.'

'Well, I suppose it had to be one or the other, they usually do come out in a certain category.' Vaila felt weak as she made her little joke and she had to force herself to get up to make tea for herself and Rebecca.

It was only when they were drinking it that the full import of what she had just done seized her. She had delivered Rebecca of a baby, a beautiful little boy with dark eyes and flaxen hair and tiny arms and legs that vigorously flayed the air. 'I did it, I really did it,' she whispered in awe.

Rebeca's hand came out to grasp that of her friend. 'Earth sisters,' she said with tears in her eyes. 'Really and truly earth sisters now, Vaila.'

'Ay, earth sisters.' Vaila bent and kissed Rebecca on one warm cheek. 'I'll never forget this night when a son was born to you and Joss. It's been the most wonderful experience o' my life even if I am shaking like a leaf.'

'Joss's son.' Rebecca gazed tearfully down on the child's tiny face. 'He doesn't look like his father, he's too small and wrinkly for that, but he will – one day he will . . .'

Vaila stood up. 'And now I will have to go and face Effie in her den. She'll kill me for this. Last time I saw her she as much as told me not to go interfering in matters that didn't concern me. Now I've done worse than that, I've done her job for her and this time I don't think she'll ever forgive me.'

She was right. Effie didn't forgive her, certainly not that night when she arrived at Oir na Cuan to find mother and baby doing well and only needing her to clear up the messy bits. Later, however, when she got Vaila by herself she said rather grudgingly, 'You did well, lass, I have to give you that, but next time, if there is a next time, don't tie the cord in a slip knot. I had to do it all over again wi' a penny and a binder to stop it from protruding. There is nothing worse in this world than a belly button that sticks out instead o' one you can sail boats in. You will remember that, won't you, lass?'

'Ay, Effie, I'll remember,' Vaila said meekly and managed to keep her laughter in till the nurse was out of earshot and was unable to hear the shrieks of merriment that echoed from behind the wall of Oir na Cuan's tiny garden.

A few days later a letter came to No. 6 Keeper's Row. It was from Mirren and relayed the news that she had given birth to a son. She and Erik were ecstatically happy. They'd called the child Bruce because he was so big and strong and to them he was just like a little king. Erik was intending to join the Merchant Navy sometime in the future but was glad he had been with his wife during her confinement. Mirren had gone on to say how much she would love to see the Sutherlands again and she would get the rooms ready as soon as she heard from them.

Rob made some excuse not to go; too many memories existed there for him and anyway, someone should stay behind to look after the house and see to the day to day running of things. But Hannah went with Vaila, Essie, and Andy, all of them eagerly looking forward to being back at Burravoe House amidst the wild and beautiful scenery of Shetland.

It was round about this time too that Aidan went to his Grampa Ramsay and calmly informed him that he was going off to Aberdeen to take his training for the priesthood. Ramsay stared, hardly able to credit the boy's words.

'The priesthood? Why on earth should you want to do that? Your place is here at Vale O' Dreip, beside your grandma and me.'

'No, it isn't,' Aidan returned steadily. 'I'll never be a farmer, you know that. I've been turned down for the army because o' my health, and there's nothing to keep me here. I've always loved the Catholic Church and have attended St Niven's chapel for years without you knowing. I've been baptised a Catholic by Father MacNeil whom I've always admired and wanted to be like. There's nothing you can do, Grampa. I'm old enough to make up my own mind. I've been saving for years and I've got enough to start me off.'

'It's that name your mother put upon you!' Ramsay blazed. 'I never liked it and now it seems she's reaching out from beyond the grave – getting the last laugh.'

'It isn't my name, it's what I want to do with my life. I'll never cease to be grateful to you and Granma Rita for all you've done for me but I'm ready to begin a new journey, Grampa, and I hope you'll give me your blessing.'

'You'll get no blessing from me, boy!' Ramsay raged, sick to the heart at the idea of his beloved grandson going out of his life, of losing him to the Catholic Church of all things! It was too much, he couldn't take it, he couldn't!

'If that's how you feel, Grampa.' Aidan turned on his heel and went out of the room to go upstairs. He threw himself down on his bed and wept. The death of Joss Morgan had been the deciding factor for Aidan. Joss had been his hero from as far back as he could remember; he had wanted to go into the army with Joss but had been deemed unfit to do so. Now he felt at a crossroads and knew he had to get away. But he wasn't running away, he was setting out to pursue an ambition that had known its beginnings in childhood and which had gone on growing in him till he was certain of the path he now had to take. There was no turning back, whatever his Grampa Ramsay might say and do.

Rebecca took up Jacob's reins and urged him into a trot. Her son lay in a little nest of cushions at her side, wrapped loosely in the soft cocoon of Kangaroo Kathy's shawl. It was a blue blue day in late June; the skylarks were soaring and birling in the sky while the peesies tumbled and dived and uttered their evocative haunting cries. Rebecca felt a strange tight sadness rising into her throat. She loved this place, which had captured her and held her with its caprices and its wiles, its rhythms and its seasons. Beauty lived here among the glens and in the hills, danger crept darkly when winter winds blew and storms lashed the seas. But always the awe and the wonder were there, admiring and sad, ebullient and glad. Love had been born here, strong and young and uncaring, beautiful in its bounteous passions and joyous stirrings. Love would go on here, that which was yet to come, that which was lost but would never die . . .

She had reached Keeper's Row and brought Jacob to a halt outside No. 5. Carefully she lifted the baby down and bore him to the Morgans' front door, going in without knocking, finding both Janet and Jock in the kitchen talking quietly as they drank a cup of tea. 'Rebecca!' Janet's face was a study of emotions as she beheld the girl standing there with the baby in her arms.

'I'm going away.' Rebecca imparted the news quickly. 'And I want you to look after Joseph for me. I can't give him a life till I find one of my own and I know you'll take good care of him. His father was someone I loved deeply and sincerely and if I could I would take his son with me but I can't, because I have nothing to give him but love and that won't be enough for a tiny baby like him.'

She laid the little boy down and took each of them by the hand. 'I know he'll get all the love he'll ever need from you two. When he's older tell him about me and his father, how we met, how we had to part, I hope he'll understand and won't hate me too much.'

'Rebecca,' Janet gasped, 'you can't mean this! You can't just leave your child here and walk away from him!'

Pain raw and deep touched the girl's beautiful proud face and she bit her lip as tears flooded her eyes. 'Oh, please, don't make this any harder for me! I've spent agonising hours reaching this decision but it's the only way. There's nothing here for me now. I have to start afresh and I can't do that with a small baby to look after. My mother left me some money and I've sold Jacob to Captain Rory. Someone will be along shortly to collect him, I've heard from my brother and he's given me a few contacts – I'll be fine, I'll get a job and somewhere to live. I – I must go now . . .' Bending, she took her baby's tiny hand and dropped a kiss on his brow.

'At least let me give you a lift to the station,' Jock cried but she shook her head.

'No, I'm getting the bus and I'll walk to the stop. I want to look at everything and remember how it was on a beautiful summer's day such as this. I've said my goodbyes to Johnny and Vaila, there's nothing left to do now . . .'

A sob caught in her throat; blindly she walked to the door. It opened and shut, leaving Janet and Jock to gaze at one another in wordless poignancy and wonder before they turned to look at the baby, Joss's son, their grandchild, the most precious gift anyone could have bestowed on them at a time when their hearts were sore and heavy with grief.

'Joseph.' Janet whispered the name then she lifted up the child to kiss his satin-smooth cheek and bury her face into the warm folds of his neck. 'Joseph!' she repeated as if she couldn't quite believe it and when Jock came to put his arms round both her and the child they cried together for the miracle that had taken place that day in No. 5 Keeper's Row.

Rebecca left Kinvara without a backward glance at the old mill lying so peacefully in its setting amidst the poppy-strewn cornfields. In days to come it became known as the Mill O' Misery and was never tenanted again. In time it fell into disrepair, a gaunt reminder of the unhappy family who had once lived there. The seasons came and went, the sun shone, the wind blew, ghosts flitted in and out of the crumbling ruins, sad grey shadows that dwelt forever in a place where no laughter lived and only the sound of weeping echoed eternally in the empty rooms.

Chapter Thirty-six

It was a brisk March day in 1941. Out on the indigo sea white horses rode the waves and leapt to the shore in dancing flurries of foam. The sun was streaming into No. 5 Keeper's Row as Janet fed her little grandson and listened to the news of the Clydebank raids on her wireless. On a glorious day such as this it was hard to imagine the carnage the Luftwaffe had wrought in that area and Janet was so lost in thought she almost jumped out of her skin when a sudden knock sounded on her door. With Joseph in her arms she went out to the lobby to stare rather dazedly at the young girl who stood on her step, her hair a tumble of golden ringlets around her pointed little face, her big blue eyes sparkling with anticipation as she gazed delightedly at Janet as if waiting for her to say something.

Recognition dawned in Janet's eyes but when she spoke the words came out, slowly and carefully. 'Bonny? Bonny Barr? It is you, isn't it? I can't be mistaken, those eyes, that hair.'

'Ay, Janet, it's me.' The girl could hardly contain herself. 'After all these years it's me. I was living and working in Clydebank when the raids started a few nights ago. Somehow I got away and all I could think about was coming here to you and Jock. My family are all gone, the boys were killed in the war, my mother died not so long ago. Oh, I know I should have written but at first I was too young then as time passed I was so busy looking after my mother I had no chance to think about anything else. She was never well, never strong . . .'

'Don't mind all that now, come in, oh, come in.' Janet was taking the girl's arm, pulling her inside, making her sit down. 'I can't believe it,' Janet went on, still sounding dazed. 'I've thought about you so much over the years, and I always hoped you would come back, back to Kinvara and us.'

Jock came in at that point, his big laugh ringing out when he saw Bonny, his arms going round her to enclose her in a bear hug that nearly squeezed the breath from her lungs. 'I don't believe it!' he boomed. 'Wee Bonny Barr! Janet almost broke her heart when you left and now here you are, as large as life and twice as bonny.'

Janet made tea, then she and Jock and Bonny talked as if they would never stop, catching up on all the lost years. During a lull the girl looked at Joseph with a question in her eyes and Janet told her about Joss, how he'd been killed at Dunkirk, about Rebecca having his son, her flight away from Kinvara leaving Joseph to be brought up by his grandparents. When she was finished the young woman had tears in her eyes and declared it to be the most beautiful and saddest story she had ever heard. She lifted up the fair-haired little boy whose features were so like those of the young father who had never lived to see him. He would surely have been immensely proud of his sturdy son who gazed thoughtfully at the world from huge dark eyes that were Rebecca's all over again.

The child chuckled as he put out a chubby hand to pull wonderingly at Bonny's ringlets. She laughed, and knew that she had done the right thing coming here to a family and a place she had never forgotten in all her long years of absence.

The Sutherland youngsters only half remembered Bonny but were pleased to make her acquaintance all over again.

'I had a pony called Bonny,' Andy said, sounding gruff, shy as he was of girls in general and never quite at ease in their company. 'But she got too small for me and now I've got another one called Beauty.'

'I've got a pony too,' Essie said eagerly. 'Grampa Ramsay gave him to me, he's white with a flowing mane and tail and he's called Prince Charming. Why don't you come up to Vale O' Dreip and ride him some time? He's very gentle and always comes when he's called, especially if you take him an apple.'

'Ay, I'd like that, only thing is,' Bonny glanced down at her legs, deformed since childhood with rickets but holding her up better than they had once done. 'I might not be able to manage a horse with these and even if I did he might run away when he sees such a funny wee thing climbing onto his back.'

'You're not funny.' Andy reddened but went on doggedly. 'In fact, you're quite pretty really. I've got bad legs too but the horses never bothered. Animals don't mind about such things, only humans do that and even they don't notice after a while.'

'I never forgot Breck.' Bonny spoke reminiscently. 'I was very young but I remember him pulling us about in the cart and how good he was being tugged this way and that yet somehow knowing which way to go without hardly being told.'

Andy turned away. He still missed his companion of many years' standing and knew he would never get another dog to take Breck's place. Bonny put her hand on his arm; a surge of empathy rose up between them and they both reddened when Essie impishly began to tease them and tell them to kiss one another and get it over with.

'Aw, you!' Andy gave his sister a little push and grew redder still when he saw Bonny's bright eyes smiling at him as if daring him to do as Essie had suggested and never mind what anybody thought.

Andy soon lost his shyness of Bonny. She was easy to get along with, easy to like. In a very short space of time he and she bonded with one another and became inseparable. It was the most wonderful summer of Andy's life. Bonny's blitheness of spirit instilled in him a confidence that grew stronger as the days went on. She persuaded him to go places and to do things that he'd never thought of doing before. Together they attended ceilidhs and dances in the village hall, giggling as they held one another up on the dance floor. As the days lengthened and brightened they went riding through the country lanes with Beauty at the helm, talking and singing, revelling in the freedom, in the summer sights and sounds, and in their deepening feelings for each other.

'I think they're falling in love,' Janet told Jock as she watched the two young people walking along hand in hand.

He nodded. 'Ay, it certainly looks that way, Andy Sutherland and our little Bonny Barr. Fate has a way of playing odd little tricks on folks when they're least expecting it.'

Hannah and Rob thought so too. 'How strange it seems,' Hannah said with a catch in her throat. 'Our Andy, walking out with a lass. I thought he'd always be with us, now I'm not so sure.'

Rob put his arm round her and said softly, 'Time changes everything, Hannah. Children grow up, they need to lead lives of their own. Andy's no exception.'

Hannah looked shamefaced. 'I used to think he was, I imagined he'd never be fit to manage on his own; I feel very guilty about that. He's a son to be proud of and I've come to rely on him for the little man that he is. I'll hate it if he decides to marry and leave home. The house would be empty without him.'

'He'll never completely leave us,' Rob said with conviction. 'Andy will always love his home and his family and will never stray too far from either.'

There were two weddings that year in Kinvara, the first being that of Johnny Armstrong and Miss Dorothy Hosie. Johnny was exuberant these days. He had travelled far from his broken-down hut on the shores of Mary's Bay. He had passed several happy years in his cottage on the Crathmor Estate and was soon to fill the vacancy in Balivoe Village School, the

previous teacher having left to do his bit in the war.
The local youngsters were delighted by this since they
all loved Johnny. They loved his stories, they enjoyed
his unconventional way of doing things and actually
looked forward to sitting in the classroom listening
to his teachings and his words of wisdom.

On the day of his wedding he was sunburned and
handsome in his dark suit with a pink carnation in
his buttonhole, a confidence in him now that he was
a man who could hold up his head and be counted.
Effie had gotten over her infatuation with him some
time ago and threw a portion of rice and confetti with
enthusiasm as he and his new bride came proudly out
of kirk, the cheers and the cries of good luck splitting
their eardrums. The new Mrs Armstrong winced just
a little as an extra handful of rice stung her cheeks.
She looked up quickly and saw Effie's eyes upon her,
Effie's grin splitting her face. 'For luck!' Effie shouted.
'Just for luck!'

The new Mrs Armstrong tightened her lips. For a
moment she looked like the dragon of old who had
driven the MacPhersons daft with her complaints and
her disapproval. But she had emerged triumphant
from the rigours and restrictions of her spinsterish
existence and had good reason to feel that she was
a person of some standing among her fellow human
beings. The laird and his family had been present in
kirk to witness the wedding, Emily had kissed her
and cried, Captain Rory had put his arms round her
and had wished her well, Ross Wallace had actually
thanked her for putting up with him when he'd been
younger. Oh, she'd done well all right. She and Johnny
had a great deal in common. She had never known

what happiness was like till she had met him; his past life was over and done with and a bright future loomed for them both. He and she would live in the Schoolhouse, no more lonely days and frustrated nights, a nice little garden to tend, children nearby but not too near . . .

She straightened, she smiled, she drew her arm back and tossed her bouquet into the gathering. It sailed straight into Effie's hands and she gaped at it in astonishment. She had given up bachelors and widowers for good. Pigs and nursing were her life, not necessarily in that order but at least with pigs you knew where you stood and they always gave something back in return – even if it was just prodigious helpings of dung for the garden to get the tatties going.

She looked up and grinned once more at Johnny's new bride before they were off, trotting away to Crathmor where the reception was taking place, the old boots and the tin cans jangling at their rear together with a notice which wished them well in the days and years to come.

The marriage of Andrew Sutherland to little Bonny Barr was an occasion to be remembered in Kinvara for many a long day to come. Andy was bursting with pride in his clan kilt and Prince Charlie jacket, Bonny radiant in her dress of white satin with flowers braided into her golden hair. Her two bridesmaids, Vaila and Essie, looked solemn and shining in blue silk and ruffles of white lace, the latter blushing when she tripped on her hem on the way up the aisle but next minute stifling her giggles as she was wont to do on any occasion that merited too much concentration.

Mirren had arrived from Shetland the day before, leaving her son in the care of a neighbour. She found herself crying a little as she sat beside Hannah in kirk and listened to the young couple taking their marriage vows.

'Weesht.' Hannah prodded her in the ribs. 'You'll have me off in a minute. It's so strange to see Andy like this, all grown up and ready to face a new life as a married man.'

The Sutherland family as a whole took up most of the front pew. Ramsay sat beside Rita, who was weeping unashamedly into her hanky; Finlay and Maudie were with their three children who looked like cherubs while surreptitiously kicking one another under their seats; Euan, his red head gleaming along with his eyes, watched Essie in all her finery; auburn-haired Aidan's serious expression belied the relief he was feeling because his Grampa Ramsay had somehow come round to his way of thinking and had wished him well in the new life he had chosen, even if it was grudgingly.

As guests of honour Janet and Jock were also at the front along with Johnny and his new wife, Andy knowing that the day wouldn't have been complete without the presence of the man who had unstintingly given of his time and his patience to a young boy searching for his way in the world. The newly wed couple walked arm in arm out of the kirk into a world of sunshine and flowers. The fields and meadows were ablaze with them, the air fragrant with rose petals as they left the clutches of the waiting crowd to rain down on the bright heads of Bonny and Andy.

'Ach, my,' Dolly Law said as she held a grey tattered square to her nose and blew it loudly. 'I never thought I'd see the day, wee Andy Sutherland married, all it needs now is old Breck to be here to complete everything. Oh, it's sad! Sad! I could just greet and greet and still have enough tears left to drown myself in!'

'Why do women aye think weddings are sad?' Shug said with a grin, his thoughts on the ale and the drams waiting in the beer tent in The MacKernon's sumptuous gardens. 'I myself think it's men who should be feeling like that wi' all the troubles and woes a wedding ring brings them.'

'What wedding ring!' Dolly belted him over the head with her hefty handbag and in the process knocked the grouse feather out of her nearly-new straw hat. 'That damt ring was no sooner on my finger than you pawned it for beer and baccy and nary a sight have I seen o' it since! If you were in any way a decent mannie you would have redeemed it by now to make up for everything I've suffered since I was foolish enough to wed myself to you.'

'Aw, come on now, Dolly, that ticket was lost long ago as fine you know and anyway, you helped me drink the beer and smoke the baccy and you aye did say yourself you had no time for jewellery except for the sort smothered in diamonds and you know we could never afford anything like that.'

The argument might have proceeded to more unruly levels had not a shiny-eyed Maudie begun to sing a song in her sweet melodious voice.

Oh little Bonny Barr went flying far.
Yes, little Bonny Barr went flying far.
Well she landed on a star
Because she had travelled far
Yes, Bonny Barr had landed on a star.

The crowd took up the song, which in minutes was swelling and beating through the air till very soon it wasn't just Dolly who could have drowned herself in buckets of tears. The young couple climbed into a ribbon-bedecked coach sent down specially from Cragdu; everyone else followed along in whatever mode of transport was available for not only was the reception being held at Cragdu but an open day for the villagers had also been arranged with Lord and Lady MacKernon acting as hosts. It was their way of showing their affection and appreciation for Andy who had worked for them faithfully and well over the last few years and had straightened out not only the library but also the offices, cataloguing and filing everything in sight and making life easier for John Taylor-Young, the secretary.

Uniformed men were working in the fields all along the way to Cragdu and Babs MacGill, sitting beside Big Bette and Mungo in the family trap, almost burst a blood vessel as she tried to attract the attention of one dark-skinned young man who was labouring away with a scythe. 'It's Mario, Ma,' she cried excitedly.

'Mario?' Bette made the name sound like an oath.

'Ay, you know, I told you about him, he's an Italian I met at one o' the film shows in the hall. He says he's coming back here when the war's over so that he can marry me.'

'Ay, that'll be right,' Mungo said grimly. 'We don't want an Eyetie in the family, it's Tom and Joe we'll be looking out for if they're ever lucky enough to get out o' it alive.'

Babs said nothing but hugged herself with glee. Ever since the POW camp had been set up in Kinvara many unmarried maidens had found a sudden and pressing need to seek work in the labour-depleted farms throughout the district. Young German and Italian prisoners were brought daily to these places and many a romance had sprung up between them and the local lasses, much to the annoyance of the up and coming local Romeos who, though not yet of an age for enlisting, were nevertheless old enough to argue over what they felt was rightly theirs. Babs had left her job at Bougan Villa and had found work as a kitchen maid at one of the farms just to be near Mario. Her plumpness delighted him. He had told her in his country they liked their women well padded and so Babs came into her own at last, impatient for the war to end, living for the day when her handsome dark Italian would be hers for good – and see what Tom and Joe thought about that if they lived long enough to find out!

Chapter Thirty-seven

The atmosphere at Cragdu was festive and happy. Lord and Lady MacKernon, as they mingled with the guests, were only now beginning to accept the loss of their eldest son, Max Gilbert, who had flown Spitfires during the early part of the war and had been shot down in the German bombing attacks over the Firth of Forth and the Rosyth Docks. Roley's big gushy smiles were hiding a lot of her heartache but Max had left a precious legacy behind, a little daughter called Maxine, born to him and Catherine Dunbar who had once taught at the Balivoe Village School.

Catherine had once carried a torch for Rob and was overwhelmingly pleased to see him again. Her glorious red hair shone in the sun, her green eyes flashed as she greeted him rapturously. They caught up on all the news and might have attracted some cryptic comments if the crowd had been thinner, the beer and buffet tents less popular. As it was everyone was too preoccupied with enjoying themselves to bother very much with anything else as laughter and banter filled the air. The MacKernon and Captain Rory, having swallowed a lot of their old differences, sat in the shade of big yellow umbrellas with jugs of ale and discussed the latest happenings in the war while everyone else had a great time eating and drinking or just soaking up the sunshine.

Maudie had begged and borrowed sugar to make the cake for the event, a great four-tiered work of art in white icing and pink sugar roses with a perfect little bride and groom at the top standing beside an enormous horseshoe. More tears were shed as the young couple wielded the knife; the children crowded round to be first in line for the favours, plates rattled, cutlery jangled.

The time came for Andy and Bonny to say their goodbyes. They were starting off married life in a rented flat on the outskirts of Inverness where Andy had secured a job as a journalist with the paper that had been printing his articles and columns since he was a young lad. Bonny had got a job as a typist in the offices of the same newspaper, so the future looked good for them both, particularly as Andy was also getting poems and stories published in anthologies and magazines and had been commissioned to write a book on his experiences as a handicapped child living and growing up in a close-knit lighthouse community.

The goodbyes were said. Johnny encased the boy in a bear-like hug and hoarsely murmured his words of farewell while Janet, crying copiously, took Bonny to her bosom and ruffled the girl's golden curls.

'I'll be back, I'll be back,' Bonny promised, her big blue eyes drowning in tears, 'and you'll come to visit us, you and Jock and wee Joseph, your beds will always be waiting.'

It took Rob all his time not to break down in front of the son he had always said would be as good as or better than anyone else. For a precious few minutes Andy savoured the feel of his father's strong brown hand in his, the vibrations of the big loving heart beating against his own, the warmth and assurance of the powerful arms that had held him and loved him throughout the difficult years of his childhood.

'Thank you, Father, for everything,' he said huskily and then it was Hannah's turn, kissing him, telling him how proud she was of him, how empty the house would be without him.

'I love you, Mother,' he said simply. 'And I always understood you. I got to know your soft spots and after a while I knew you were all soft and just a little bit afraid of life as I was in the beginning.'

She ruffled his dark curls. 'Och, you. You think you know everything but you won't learn it all till you are older and wiser like me.'

It was the turn of Vaila and Essie, then Mirren and everyone else coming at once to overwhelm and shout out their congratulations. Beauty was all ready and waiting in her finest livery, mane and tail bound up with ribbons and bows, sprays of carnations and sweet peas tied into her harness. She was taking the young couple on their honeymoon, a leisurely journey to Inverness, stopping at post inns along the way and anywhere else that took their fancy.

Andy gazed around him, at the sea glistening below and the tall column of the Kinvara Light out there on the reefs, at the coastline way down yonder, the tracks and the roads he had travelled with Breck in harness. He could picture the big cross collie in his mind, bounding to meet him, eager to be hitched up and on his way, taking his young master on trails of wondrous freedom that would never have been his without his dog and his cart to make it all possible. Breck and the boy. Such a long way off now but never forgotten. Now there was Beauty and a fine strong jaunting cart to take him where he would yet nothing could ever compare with those magical days of wind and rain and sun and Breck stepping happily out in front . . .

Andy bit his lip; his throat tightened. Then Bonny's hand touched his and he took up the reins, off, off, to a new life, a new beginning, the faces of his family and friends blurring into the distance as Beauty got into her stride and fairly bowled along.

'It's going to be strange without Andy in the house,' Essie sighed when the family were gathered in the kitchen that night, her big blue eyes dreamy and faraway as she went on. 'I'll never forget Vaila and me going into his room when we were younger to play bouncy on his bed and Breck groaning and moaning and getting down on the floor to cry and sigh.'

'Ay, you thought I didn't know about that,' Hannah said drily. 'But I used to hear you cavorting about and the bed springs creaking. It's a wonder to me it never collapsed with the strain.'

'Oh, but it was a lovely wedding,' Essie went on romantically, 'and Bonny was the most beautiful bride ever. I want to get married and look like that some day only my dress will be red velvet with a big plume o' feathers on my head and silver shoes on my feet. I'll have a golden coach to whisk me away and I'll ride on and on with my groom beside me all dressed up in a suit o' black silk with buckles on his shoes.'

She made a dramatic sweep with her hands and gazed round at everyone with tragic eyes. 'Only thing is, I'll be grown up then and I never ever want to grow up, I want to be like Peter Pan and be a child forever. I'm getting older all the time and sometimes when I look back I feel as if my days as a little girl are all so long ago and far away.'

Hannah laughed. 'You sound like a hundred instead o' just fourteen. You'll be young for a long time yet, Essie, and won't be bothering your head about marriage for a good whily to come.'

Vaila noticed how quiet Mirren and her father were. They hadn't had much to say to one another since Mirren's arrival the day before and Vaila found herself remembering how he had made excuses not to go to Shetland when little Bruce was born and wondered if he and she had argued that time he had gone to Burravoe to help out with the harvest.

It was her turn to sigh now. He was returning to lighthouse duty tomorrow, Mirren was going back to Shetland the day after and the house would be quieter than ever. With a heavy heart she went upstairs to gaze from her window and remember the summer days of her early girlhood. They had been good those days, the picnics, the outings, the adventures she had shared with Mark and George, Rebecca and Joss, all of them laughing and arguing and thinking the carefree times would never end. How golden these days, how sweet the laughter, how trite the little huffs and disagreements. Mark was in a POW camp in Germany, George was fighting in Libya, Joss had fallen at Dunkirk, Rebecca had joined the WAAFs and had written to say she was enjoying it but missing Kinvara, signing herself *Rebecca, your earth sister, now and always*.

No end of the war was in sight. Clothes rationing had just been introduced in Britain; years could go by before things settled down and went back to normal. Normal! Vaila gazed at the vista before her through a glimmer of tears. The sky was a palette of soft pink and gold in the afterglow, the sea a shimmer of turquoise and silver, the curlews were calling from the shore, vying with the plaintive cries of the oyster catchers as they gathered to feed among the rocks. All that was nature was normal, all that was human was in a state of unrest. Vaila got into her nightdress and reached for the diary under her pillow. From it she extracted the little posy of harebells given to her by Mark in the Crathmor stables. She kissed it, then wrote in her diary: *I miss you, Mark, I love you*. His voice came to her. *Nothing stays the same, Vaila, only the land remains and the hills sleep on forever*. She remembered George's laughing handsome face. She loved him, she loved Mark, she didn't know which of them truly held her heart and now, in the loneliness and uncertainty of night, bereft and afraid, she could bear to be alone no longer.

Essie was sound asleep in the next bed, tired out after such an exciting day. Vaila slipped out of bed and made her way to the little boxroom at the top of the landing. Mirren was only half awake but made no protest when Vaila snuggled in beside her and cooried into the pillows. 'I was lonely, Aunt Mirren,' was all she said by way of explanation.

'Me too,' Mirren murmured. In minutes they were breathing gently and evenly while the night slept all around them and everything seemed safe and secure.

KINVARA

1944/45

Chapter Thirty-eight

Ramsay felt uneasy as he watched Essie and Euan walking hand in hand in the misty sunshine of the autumn day, heads close together as they whispered and giggled into one another's ears, seemingly unaware of anybody else but themselves. Ramsay had always thought of the two as children, play-acting and fooling around, never taking anything very seriously, doing and saying immature things, living in their own small world of make-believe and fantasy. Now it came forcibly to Ramsay that they were no longer children. Essie must be seventeen, Euan a year older, both of them growing up fast and ready for adventures that weren't of the fairy-tale variety. He rocked on his heels and frowned, the unease in his belly becoming tighter as the two young people paused to kiss and nuzzle in a very adult manner indeed.

Ramsay cleared his throat. 'Rita, you'll have to do something about that pair. I don't like the way they're behaving, you know they can't be allowed to enter into any sort o' intimate relationship as matters stand.'

'You do something.' Rita raised her head from the sock she was mending and eyed her husband over her specs. 'It's your problem and aye has been since

Catrina left the lad here to be cared for. He's your son, your responsibility, ever since you raped his mother and thought you could get away with it by practically ignoring the part you played in the affair.'

Ramsay stared at her aghast, furious at her for bringing such a sore subject out into the open, stark and unadorned, 'Be careful, Rita,' he said warningly. 'You can't start casting all that up now, it was a long time ago and I've paid for what I did a thousand times over.'

Rita bent her head to her darning once more. 'As I've always said, the chickens come home to roost, Ramsay, and Euan is one very big chicken with a mind and spirit o' his own. He and Essie have grown up together and nothing will keep them apart now, I can't stop them seeing one another any more than you can.'

'No, but I can have a damned good try!' He spoke grimly, his pulses racing at the implications of her words, his palms sweating when in the next minute she said calmly, 'Only the truth will suffice now, my man, you'll have to tell them what they are to one another before they are very much older and things between them get out o' hand.'

Ramsay looked at her with dislike. She was enjoying seeing him squirm, she had always enjoyed it, those accusing eyes watching his every move, never letting him forget. She and Hannah between them were a fine pair with their spiteful innuendoes and veiled insinuations.

He said nothing more on the subject but as soon as he got Essie on her own he sat her down and told her quite bluntly that she had to stop seeing so much of Euan. 'You spend far too much time with each other,' he said with brutal frankness. 'I will not have it, Essie, shamelessly flirting under my nose and generally getting yourself talked about. The boy is far too idle for his own good and I've been meaning to talk to him anyway. He's old enough to enlist and I'm going to make certain that he does. Meantime you must stay away from Vale O' Dreip, you're upsetting everyone with your behaviour and I simply won't stand for it any longer.'

'Stop seeing Euan?' Essie's voice was incredulous. 'But we love each other, Grampa. Some day quite soon we want to be married and go somewhere we can get work in a theatre. We've always loved play-acting and hope to end up on the stage after we've trained a bit and gained some experience.'

'The stage! Pah!' Ramsay spat the words out scornfully. 'Childish dreams, nothing more! There's a war on, girl, and it's high time the pair o' you realised that! Now run along like a good lass and do something useful with yourself. It's a proper job you need and I don't mean the sort you have in mind. Helping your mother out in a baker's shop is hardly my idea o' hard labour. The devil makes work for idle hands, remember that, Essie, and start behaving like a young lady instead o' some farmyard harlot with only frivolous pursuits on your mind.'

Essie backed away from him, shaking her head in horror, then she turned and went fleeing away home to hurl herself into her mother's arms and sob her heart out. When Hannah finally managed to get her daughter to speak she silently shared some of her father-in-law's opinions regarding the relationship between the two young people. Essie wasn't ready to be married to anyone yet, far less Euan with his braggish ways and aimless way of life. Even so, she was annoyed at Ramsay for hurting Essie's feelings as he had. She felt there was more to this than met the eye and wondered afresh just what sort of secrets lay behind Vale O' Dreip's closed doors. That business about Catrina, for instance, running off and leaving Rita to bring up her son, the strange covert expression Rita sometimes wore whenever Catrina's name cropped up. Ay, she was hiding something there all right, covering up for her husband yet unable to keep the bitterness out of her voice when she spoke to him or the resentment from her face whenever she looked at him.

Hannah vowed she would one day get to the bottom of it. Meantime she consoled Essie as best she could and tucked her up in bed that night as if she was still the little fairy doll child she had worshipped since the day of her birth.

Euan and Essie soon sought one another out and between them concocted a daring plan. Excitement seized them as the idea took shape, part of it being to run away and get married in the registrar's office in Inverness. Carried away with enthusiasm they gave no thought to real practicalities. Let tomorrow take care of itself; today was what mattered, the romance and derring-do of going off on Prince Charming to another life was enough to keep them going for the moment. Between them they had some money, they would survive, they had each other and that was all that mattered. They were level-headed enough however to each seek out their birth documents and surreptitiously pack their bags in readiness for the big day.

Vaila looked rather suspicious when she saw her normally untidy little sister searching through items of clothing and placing them in neat bundles in a separate drawer but she accepted Essie's plausible explanation for her actions and thought no more about it.

As for Hannah, she was only too pleased to see the colour back in Essie's cheeks and the sparkle returned to her eyes, thinking that the child had got over her disappointments already and was back to her usual happy self.

Two days later Euan and Essie met at the foot of the Vale O' Dreip farm track. The time was one o'clock in the morning. Euan had brought Prince Charming, all ready attached to the family trap. 'It was easy,' he assured Essie. 'I harnessed him earlier in the shed and only had to hitch him up. The wheels rumbled a bit when I led him out but they were all in bed and didn't hear a thing.'

They looked at one another and excitement bubbled out of them. Reaching across he took her hand. 'Your carriage awaits, my lady,' he said with a perfectly straight face. She giggled, they kissed, he climbed up beside her and took the reins, and in no time at all they had disappeared into the autumnal mists of morning with only a faint set of wheel tracks imprinted in the dust to show that they had ever been there at all.

* * *

Their disappearance wasn't noticed till late the next morning. Essie often had a lie in; Euan too was a sleepy head, so it wasn't unusual for both to be absent from breakfast when everyone else was having theirs. Even when their empty rooms were discovered no alarm bells were raised. It was assumed they had simply gone out walking or visiting as both were inclined sometimes to do in the wanderlust of their youth.

By eleven o'clock, however, the respective households began to grow uneasy.

'It isn't like Euan to miss breakfast altogether,' Rita said to her husband. 'He has a healthy appetite as a rule and though he's often late he's never *this* late.'

'Oh, he'll be in when it suits him,' Ramsay stated bluntly. 'He's never around when there's work to be done. I told him last night I wanted his help this morning so maybe that's why he's making himself scarce.'

Hannah was also growing worried. 'Essie's never stayed away as long as this before,' she told Vaila. 'I hope nothing's happened to her. Did she say anything to you about going off this morning?'

'No, not really. She was in good spirits last night and was sound asleep when I went upstairs to bed. She's been a bit restless since Grampa forbade her to see Euan but she made no mention of that yesterday.'

For the umpteenth time Hannah went to the door to look up and down the road, her brow furrowing with puzzlement and worry when still there was no sign of her beloved Essie. Oh, where was the child? What was she doing? Surely she would come home any minute now and put all their minds at rest. Hannah went back inside. She sat down on a chair, growing more and more uneasy as the clock ticked the minutes away in a house that had become silent and watchful and waiting.

Yet despite the fears and anxieties of the respective households, no one was prepared for the arrival of the police bearing the devastating news that the two youngsters had been involved in a serious collision with an army lorry on a narrow country road. Euan had been killed outright, Essie was critically injured. Prince Charming had survived and was being looked after by the farmer who had rushed from his house to the scene of the accident.

The next few days were horrific ones for both families. Rob was brought back from lighthouse duty; he and Hannah, Vaila, Andy and Bonny spent long hours at the hospital in Inverness where the young girl lay, hovering between life and death, her head encased in bandages, her limbs broken and twisted. During this time Euan was buried, bringing to an end a young life that had always been caught between dreams and reality, a boy who had died in the pursuit of his most romantic ambition of all.

Rita was in a state of shock after the funeral, so quickly had everything happened, so final was the outcome of an impulsive youthful adventure. 'I keep feeling he'll walk through the door at any minute,' she told Ramsay. 'I grew so used to having him around, talking and laughing and keeping us all amused. He was a good lad in spite of everything and became like a son to me. It seems so sad that his own mother isn't here at such a time but she'll have to be told, she'll have to be found.'

'Chance would be a fine thing,' Ramsay said drily. 'Her own grandmother doesn't know where she is, her sisters haven't heard from her for years. What would be the point anyway? She wasn't here for him when he was alive so what good would she be to him now that he's dead?'

Rita glowered at him. 'Do you feel anything at all for the boy, Ramsay? He lived here in this house beside you. He ate and drank at your table. He worked beside you in the fields yet not once have I heard a word o' regret from you about his passing. Surely you must feel something for him. Like it or no he was your son, your flesh and blood, he looked up to you in his own way and considered himself to be part o' this family.'

Ramsay looked uncomfortable. 'Of course I feel sorrow, Rita, I'm not as hard as you might think. Over the years I came to have a great affection for the lad and can't rightly believe that he's gone. But you know the circumstances. I can't allow myself to become too involved with my feelings and must keep a level head if I am to come through all this unscathed.'

'Your feelings!' Rita threw at him scornfully. 'That's all you've ever cared about. Euan lies cold in the ground, a young lad who should have had all his life before him, and all you care about is your reputation. I sometimes wonder how I can go on with it – the lies, the deceit, the pretence. It's a miracle you've managed to get away with it for so long. It wouldn't surprise me in the least if someone started asking questions as to why you forbade Essie and Euan to see one another. They were just innocent children, never dreaming they were doing wrong, simply because you didn't have the courage to tell them the truth about their blood ties.'

Ramsay turned away, unease tightening his belly, his conscience heavy with the guilt that had beset him since hearing about the injuries his perfect little granddaughter had suffered; the death of the son he had never acknowledged as his but who seemed to be reaching out from beyond the grave to torture and torment him. At last Essie was taken off the critical list and was allowed home, never to walk or talk again the doctors said. But those who loved her best refused to believe such a drastic diagnosis.

'She *will* be my Essie again!' Hannah cried, gazing at her daughter's sweet and bonny face in its frame of flaxen tresses, the trembling rosebud of a mouth silent and without laughter. 'She must or I don't think I can bear it.'

Chapter Thirty-nine

In the weeks that followed Hannah tended her daughter devotedly but from one day to the next there was never any response as Essie sat in the kitchen, huddled into blankets, her hands still and lifeless in her lap, blue eyes looking inwards as if at terrible dark phantoms flitting through her mind.

'It was *him*,' Hannah muttered one day while Vaila was in the house, speaking as if her step-daughter wasn't there. 'He did this to Essie. I've thought and thought about it and will surely go mad altogether if I don't find out the truth. Why did he forbid her to see Euan? What terrible secret lies hidden in that black heart o' his?' She got to her feet. 'I'm going up there to see him and ask him outright what Euan was to him, right now, this very minute.'

'Hannah, please wait!' cried Vaila. 'It won't do anyone any good bringing all of this up now. Wait till Robbie comes home and we can tackle Grampa together. Don't do it on your own! Please, don't.'

Hannah, however, was already running away from the house, never stopping in her demented flight along the road and up the farm track that led to Vale O' Dreip. After a few moments of indecision Vaila followed, calling first on Janet to ask her to keep an eye on Essie for half an hour.

Rita was peeling potatoes at the sink when her daughter-in-law came bursting in, a white-faced Vaila bringing up the rear. Without pausing for breath the enquiries and accusations came pouring out of Hannah in a torrent, eyes wild and staring as she spoke, as if she had taken leave of her senses and wasn't fully aware of what she was saying.

Rita wiped her hands on her apron and sat down heavily. 'I can't keep this to myself any longer,' she said in a tormented voice. 'Ever since Euan died it's being going round and round in my mind and I've got to tell someone before it drives me crazy.' She looked straight into Hannah's eyes and went on in a frighteningly breathless voice. 'Euan was Ramsay's son, born to Catrina after he defiled her one night when I was ill upstairs after my stroke. The boy was Essie's uncle, he was also the brother of Rob and Finlay. Oh, dear God, I never wanted them to be hurt by all this and that was why I never said anything. Now it's too late – Euan's gone, Essie's body is broken beyond repair . . .'

Hannah stood up, her mouth twisting in contempt as she spat out, 'I always knew something was far wrong in this house but never, never did I think it could be anything as evil as this. Where is the hypocrite? Just tell me where he is, Rita. I've got a few things I'd like to say to my dear God-fearing father-in-law!'

'He's over at the quarry, the sheep have been falling in and he's thinking of putting up a fence – but please, please, mind how you go, Hannah, mind how you go!'

Rita's face was deathly pale and she was lying back in her seat, gasping for breath. Alarmed, Vaila rushed for the brandy bottle and administered a tot to her Granma while Hannah flew out of the house like a creature demented. A few minutes passed, Rita's breathing became easier, she hoisted herself up in her seat and gripped Vaila's hand. 'Go after her, lass, please go after her! The Lord alone knows what's going to happen between those two. Oh, my lassie, it's been terrible for you to have to bear witness to all this but I couldn't keep it to myself any longer, I just couldn't.' Vaila bent to kiss her grandmother's cheek before she too was off, running, running, over the fields to the old disused quarry lying in a hollow some considerable distance away.

Ramsay and Hannah faced one another at the edge of the quarry, she a truly fearsome sight to behold with her livid expression, the tears pouring unheeded down her face, her hair in disarray around her shoulders, her eyes mad and staring, words of scorn and hatred pouring from her mouth.

'Stop that, Hannah!' he ground out when at last he could get a word in. 'I'm just as upset by all this as you are. Essie means the world to me, it hurts me to see her as she is now and I'd do anything to have her whole and well again. As for Euan, he became part of my life, in time I grew to have a deep affection for him and eventually even to love him. I can't believe he's dead, I can't believe Essie's so ill. I pray for her return to health every minute of every day. As part of the family you ought to know better than anyone how I feel and as my daughter-in-law you should be showing some consideration for my feelings instead of trying to make trouble for me.'

Hannah gave a shout of derision. 'Part o' the family! That's priceless coming from you. I was never counted good enough to be a Sutherland and you know it! From day one you rejected me. I could never do anything right in your eyes. I know you blamed me for Andy being born the way he was and it wasn't till Essie came along that I felt I had done something good at last. You're nothing but a sanctimonius hypocrite, Ramsay Sutherland, you look for perfection in others when all the time you're about the most imperfect specimen of human nature that could be found anywhere. You are also a coward! If it wasn't for you being so afraid to own up to your ungodly lusts Euan would still be here and Essie would be as perfect as she once was.'

He heard her out, his lip curled, his cool blue eyes regarding her with disdain and dislike. 'Who are you to accuse me of anything?' he said vindictively. 'A nobody who thinks she's a somebody only because marriage to my son gave you the Sutherland name. Oh, ay, you're right about that. I never thought you were good enough for my family. You're nothing, Hannah Houston, and nothing is how you'll stay as long as I'm around to see you don't get above yourself. No one will believe what you say about me, I'm too well thought of in these parts. Euan's gone, he can't speak, his mother slunk off like some thief in the night and will never show her face here again. Rita's past it and beginning to ramble like an old woman, you're about as mad as anybody can be and will no doubt end up in an asylum before you're very much older . . .'

He said no more. She sprung at him like a wildcat, tearing at his throat with her nails, kicking him with her feet, pulling at his hair, biting him on the hands, the face, the neck. His yells of pain rent the air. They tussled and fought, the rage-filled world spun round for her, the earth quite literally moved for him because suddenly it crumbled and gave way under his desperately scrabbling feet.

He staggered and fell backwards, taking her with him, but while he gained a foothold on a tiny ledge she went down, down into those waiting watery black depths, hardly a sound to be heard from her throat as she hit the surface and went under. A moment later her upturned face bobbed, white and petrified, her hands came up, she cried out once, and she disappeared from view as if she had never been.

When Vaila came panting up she absorbed the scene in one glance: the ripples on the oily stagnant water far below, her grandfather hanging onto the edge of the pit for dear life, gurgling sounds coming from his gaping mouth as he fought to draw air into his lungs.

'Help me, child, for pity's sake, help me!' The plea came out, ragged and fear-filled. Vaila hesitated. She gazed at him without mercy. Her foot moved closer to his raw-knuckled hands. He let out another tortured cry and deliberately, without any hurry, she got down on her belly and held out an unwilling hand for him to hold onto.

The farmhands came running. All was confusion and noise. The sheepdogs barked, the men shouted;

Vaila turned away and with sagging shoulders made her way back to Vale O' Dreip and the grandmother who was waiting to know the outcome of that dreadful meeting between Hannah and the man whose guilty secrets she had taken to her watery grave.

Many questions were asked about Hannah's death. The police interviewed everyone connected with her but most of all they interviewed Ramsay who, pale and shaken, could only repeat over and over that it had been an accident, that he still didn't know himself how it had happened and was too upset to discuss the matter any further.

A stunned neighbourhood discussed these latest dreadful events in hushed voices. 'The poor, poor soul,' Big Bette said sadly. 'What a terrible way to go. I would never have wished the like on anyone, far less Hannah who became such a likeable body over the years.'

'Ay, she was just like one o' us.' Mattie shook her head and sighed. 'At first she was a square peg in a round hole but as time went on she fitted in and could have been born and bred here, so well did she come to know our ways.'

'She was a good neighbour to me,' Janet said with tears in her eyes. 'And she was also one o' the best friends I ever had. I don't know what I'm going to do without her, she was always there for me when I needed a shoulder to cry on.'

'Och, it's terrible, terrible just.' Kangaroo Kathy, her knitting forgotten for once, took out her hanky and gave her nose a good blow. 'I know she was aye a wee bit scared o' me and my stories but in many ways it was all part o' the fun. I think she secretly enjoyed these tales o' Uncle Tam and my cousin Morag and now there's no one else in the place who will listen to me the way Hannah did.'

'Rob is taking it bad,' Jessie put in. 'First Essie's accident, now this. Oh, Hannah will surely turn in her grave wi' worry knowing her man and her lassies will have to cope without her. It's just as well Harriet Houston from Ayr is the strong body that she is. I know I never always saw eye to eye wi' the madam but I have to admit she's good in times o' trouble and will no doubt help in any way she can.'

'Oh, ay, she's a good soul is Harriet,' Dolly said as she sucked thoughtfully on her clay pipe. 'Mind you, I wouldny like to be on the receiving end o' her administrations. I'll never forget how she nearly broke my wrist when I asked her once to tie a bandage on my finger. By the time she was finished I had to wear my arm in a sling for days and her hooting wi' laughter as if the whole thing was a joke. She's hard hearted is Harriet as well as being built like a navy but will no doubt be as gentle as a lamb where Essie is concerned.'

The villagers dispersed to go about their business, quiet and sad and sorry and hoping that things must surely get better in Kinvara after all the troubles and woes of the last few years.

'You mustn't tell anybody about the things you know, Vaila. For God's sake, don't ever tell. It would break me if a thing like this ever leaked out.' The funeral was over, the mourners had dispersed, only Harriet and Charlie remained behind at No. 6 of the Row to do what they could to comfort the family that was left. Ramsay could hardly wait to get Vaila on her own and now there was a quiet moment, out in the byre where she had gone to be by herself in her favourite peaceful place. But there was no peace to be had yet. The master of Vale O' Dreip was pale and weary looking as he pleaded with his granddaughter for her tact and compassion.

'Not for God's sake, for yours, for your own hide,' Vaila said coldly. 'You can't go on hiding behind religion forever, Grampa. You never really cared for anybody but yourself, far less God. Euan is gone, Hannah too, my darling little sister is maimed for life and all you can think about is how it will affect you and your ego.'

Something that might have been a sob broke from him. A shaft of pity went through her. He was suffering all right, and with so much on his conscience he would go on suffering for the rest of his days, that would be his punishment, now and for evermore.

'Of course I won't tell,' she went on in a kinder voice. 'And I know Granma has got it out o' her system and won't ever mention it again either. What would be the use? What's done is done and none o' us can ever go back. Hannah's death was an accident but it need never have been if you had been more honest with Essie and Euan. You're not such a bad man really, Grampa. There's a lot o' good in you and you could atone for all this by thinking less o' yourself and more of other people, especially Granma, who is going through a terrible time just now.'

His head was downbent as he stared unseeingly at the floor; when he looked up she saw tears in his eyes and knew that he had learned a lesson he would never forget. 'You're a good lass, Vaila.' His hand came out to grip hers tightly. 'Wise and strong like your mother. Oh, ay, I remember her all right, fearless and spirited, brave and good.' He looked her straight in the eye. 'Leave me now, child. I have a lot to think about and need to be by myself for a while.'

She turned and went out, leaving him there in the quietness, humble and dispirited and not at all like the arrogant man who had bulldozed his way through life with a show of righteousness and religion to prop him up.

Chapter Forty

The winter passed slowly and sadly for Vaila. She had given up her job at Crathmor so that she could devote herself to Essie. Every minute of every day was taken up in looking after the young girl who had once shone with the joy of living but who now sat lifeless and still, a spark of interest only ever showing in her eyes when Janet brought little Joseph in to see her. He was now a lively imp of four, dumping his toys on Essie's lap, chattering away to her in his uninhibited way and never seeming to care that she couldn't answer or make any sort of move to show him that she understood. Essie also loved it when her father came home. Her face would brighten, she watched every move he made and Vaila often felt that some words were bound to come out to show that she was aware of what was going on. But they never did and Vaila was glad of the neighbours who came and went from the house, their cheerful presence bringing normality to an abnormal situation.

Maudie came and drank tea and talked non-stop. She and Vaila made merry with flour and between them produced tiny iced fairy cakes and little brown-bread sandwiches warmed in the oven and filled with home-made bramble jam to tempt Essie's appetite.

Harriet came almost every day, her strong attractive face showing the concern she was feeling as the days and weeks went on and there was still no sign of improvement in the granddaughter she so loved.

Ramsay was also a regular visitor. He wasn't praying nearly so much these days and wasn't so eager to attend the Free Kirk. More and more he was leaving the running of the farm to Finlay and finding time for his family. He took Rita out and about, was frequently to be seen at River House with his grandchildren, he read patiently to Essie and talked to her and was altogether a much nicer and less arrogant person than the Ramsay of old.

But the night and the silence inevitably came for Vaila. Then it was just herself and Essie, the firelight flickering over Essie's delicate doll-like face as Vaila bathed her in the zinc tub in front of the fire and sang to her as she brushed her long golden hair, the swishing of the brush keeping time with the rhythm of the melody. When Rob was home he carried Essie up to her bed in Vaila's room; when he was away Janet came faithfully in to help with the task and would later sit in the kitchen for a cup of cocoa and a blether before taking herself off to her own bed.

And then it really was just Vaila alone, curled up in front of the fire, remembering how it had been when the house had rung with voices and with laughter: Essie and Andy squabbling over a jigsaw at the table, Hannah scolding and fussing as she got them ready for bed, Breck in his corner waiting for a chance to slip upstairs with Andy, Rob sitting with his feet on the hearth peacefully smoking his pipe. He wasn't enjoying it now at the lighthouse but couldn't leave because of the war and the constant need for vigilance on coastal waters.

Vaila often wondered about Aunt Mirren, who hadn't attended Hannah's funeral but had sent flowers and cards of condolence. She wrote every other week, Vaila wrote back, unable to report anything hopeful about Essie but trying her best to keep everything on a cheerful level.

Her thoughts would then wander to Mark and George and she would sigh with the pain and the hurt of her memories of those wonderful yesteryears they had shared. It was like a dream, a beautiful dream, one that lingered yet was so transient she sometimes wondered if it had all really happened. Would they ever come home, she asked herself? And if they did what would they be like after the terrible experiences they had endured? God alone knew what it must be like for Mark counting away the minutes, the days, the years, in a prison camp, for George in central Burma fighting the Japanese. She couldn't begin to imagine the sort of conditions in which they existed and drove herself to distraction worrying, waiting, hoping.

She wasn't the only one to feel that the world had crashed about her ears. Her father was lonely too. Every time he came home she could see it in his dark eyes, could feel the weight of the burdens he carried on his shoulders. There was about him a terrible emptiness and one night after he had carried Essie up to bed she saw him in his chair by the fire, his head in his hands, racked with dry harsh sobs.

'Robbie.' She went to him and put her arm round his shoulder. 'What is it? What ails you?'

'I can't go on, Vaila,' he said brokenly. 'Seeing Essie like this, never showing any improvement, unable even to say our names and know that we are here! And you, my lassie, what about you? Frittering your young life away, never any fun, nothing to lighten your days, Hannah gone, Andy married and living away from home, your lads at war, me never here for you. It's too much, much too much!'

'You *can* go on, Robbie, and you will,' she said firmly. 'You did it for Andy, now you must do it for Essie. She'll get better, I know she will, but she needs our help to do it. We're all she has left now and I'll never leave as long as you both need me.'

She fell on her knees beside him and buried her head in his lap and they stayed like that for long tender moments, father and daughter, drawing comfort from one another, silent and caring, there in the firelit room with the shadows dancing on the ceiling and the whisper of the wind blowing against the window panes.

It was a soft little tap that sounded on the door of No. 6 of the Row on an April day in 1945. Winter had thrown off its traces, daffodils were dancing in the woods and in the verges, the world was altogether lighter and brighter, with a promise of better and more happy days to come.

Rob got up from the table and went out to the lobby. He was totally unprepared for the sight of Mirren on the step holding onto the hand of a little boy with bouncy black curls and big dark eyes that gazed up enquiringly at the big man gazing down at him.

'Mirren!' Rob cried. 'It's you! It's really you!'

She laughed at the expression of surprise on his face. 'Ay, Rob, it's me, though it's a wonder you remember after all this time.'

His eyes went from her to the boy. 'And this must be Bruce. He's certainly got his father's colouring.'

'He's also got your eyes, Rob.' She studied his face; her breath caught in her throat as she waited for his reaction.

'My eyes? You don't mean . . . ?'

'Yes, Rob, I do mean. Bruce is your son, I couldn't tell you when Hannah was alive, nor Erik. He was killed last year in the Russian convoys in the North Atlantic at the time of Essie's accident and Euan's death. You had so much to cope with I couldn't burden you with more. When Hannah died I was ill myself after a spell of poor health and couldn't make it to the funeral.'

He was lost for words. All he could do was look and look at her and after a while she gave a little laugh and said, 'Could I come in, Rob? It's been a long journey and a cup of tea would be nice.'

Rob moved aside as if in a dream but before he could do anything about tea Vaila came in to stop short at sight of Mirren. 'I don't believe it!' she cried. 'At last! At long long last!'

'Vaila.' Mirren took the girl into her arms and held her close. 'Oh, Vaila, it's so good to see you again, I've been neglectful I know but things happened that changed my circumstances.' She told Vaila about Erik then with a faintly apologetic glance at Rob she took her son by the hand and pulled him forward. 'This is your little brother, Vaila, it's no use trying to hide it.

There have been enough secrets in this family without adding more. Your father and I—'

Vaila held up her hand. 'I know, I guessed, he was so strange that time he came back from Shetland and again when he wouldn't go there with us when your baby was born.'

'But I didn't know he was mine.' Rob dumped himself down on a chair and simply stared at the boy, 'I just didn't want to go there after – after . . .'

'Och, don't be so shy, Robbie, these things happen.' Vaila was blithe suddenly. Life had come back to the house and everything seemed all at once wonderful. It was sad about Erik, who had been a fine man, thoughtful and kind. She had only met him a few times and had come to like and respect him. Now he was gone, another casualty of war, but he had died bravely and had fought for his country to the last.

She looked at Mirren, who was watching her rather anxiously. 'Erik wouldn't want you to be lonely, Aunt Mirren,' she said softly, 'stuck there in Shetland on the farm, all by yourself. Robbie here, all on his own . . .'

'As a matter of fact . . .' Mirren had lost her usual composure as she went on breathlessly, 'I've sold off some of the land and the steadings but kept the house. It will be nice for us all to go back there for holidays and I could never completely cut myself off from Shetland.'

'Hey, what is this?' Rob looked from one dimpled face to the other. 'You two, planning and plotting, don't I have a say in all this?'

With a laugh Vaila pushed him back into his seat and went to make the tea, throwing over her shoulder,

'Take off your coat, Aunt Mirren, and make yourself at home. No doubt you'll be staying for a while and will want to put your feet up.'

Mirren went over to Essie and gently kissed her, then beckoning to her son she placed him next to the girl's chair and said softly, 'This is your brother, Essie, his name is Bruce and I know you and he are going to be good friends.'

Bruce put his little hand over Essie's and held onto it in a quaintly old fashioned manner. Nothing happened. Bruce began to fidget, then out of the blue a voice came, hesitantly but plainly. 'Brother – my brother.' They were the first words Essie had spoken since her accident. Rob and Vaila looked at one another, unable to speak themselves in those joyous moments but soon crowding round Essie to hug and kiss her with tears in their eyes.

'We'll get a dog,' Rob said huskily, 'a pup the same as Breck. We'll start all over again. Essie *will* get better and when the war is over I'm leaving the lighthouse for good to start up that little boatbuilder's business with Charlie.'

Later, when it was just Rob and Mirren by the fire, she put her hand over his and said quietly, 'It's been a long time, Rob. So much has happened since we last met, so many heartaches that can never be fully assuaged. Erik was a good man, Hannah a good woman. We'll never forget them. But you and I must go on. It's lonely for me now at the farm, it's lonely for you here, Vaila must be allowed to live her own life, because God willing our lads will soon be home and she can be free to make her choices.' Her hand tightened on his and she went on urgently, 'You are glad to see me, aren't you, Rob? I couldn't bear knowing I've come here to be with you only to find that you don't want me. Before I left Shetland I drove myself nearly crazy with indecision. I kept thinking of Morna, how much you loved her and how you said you could never forget her.'

'Mirren,' Her name was just a sigh on his lips. 'If you only knew what this means to me you wouldn't say the things you're saying now. Of course I'll never forget Morna, a part o' my heart will always be for her. I can't forget Hannah either. When she died I felt crushed with despair and realised how much she had come to mean to me. I'll remember both Morna and Hannah forever but I can't ignore this thing that is life in me. When I saw you today I felt good and happy again. Over the years I grew to admire you; when you came here that time for Andy's fourteenth birthday it became something more. What happened to us in Shetland wouldn't have happened without love and now that you're here I never want you to leave me again . . .' He couldn't go on.

She reached out for him and held him close. His mouth was warm and firm on hers and they cried in one another's arms for love and for hope, for sorrow and for joy. 'Rob,' she whispered in his ear, 'you don't know this but I was thinking of you when I gave Bruce his name. I thought of Robert – that led to Robert the Bruce, so our little boy is named after the spider king and also after you because Robert is his middle name.'

He had to laugh at this. 'I never thought o' you as a romantic, Mirren.'

'Then you don't know me at all, do you, Rob?'

'It's going to be fun finding out,' he murmured as he gathered her once more into his arms leaving her with no more breath for further words.

No one ever forgot VE Day in Kinvara. Everyone was out on the streets, dancing and singing, waving anything they could get their hands on, including a pair of Shug's drawers from Dolly's washing line along with a vest that had been hanging on one peg for weeks. The Bread Oven baked batch after batch of savoury sausage rolls and opened its doors to all comers; Wee Fay used the sugar ration she had been saving and made batches of tablet to hand out to the children; the Knicker Elastic Dears pranced along the street waving victory banners in a most unladylike manner; the Henderson Hens rode ribbon bedecked bicycles through the village, displaying long red bloomers in the process while Effie tied a big pink bow round the neck of her latest sow Souffle and paraded her proudly through Calvost.

George came home first, a much-changed young man from the one who had gone off with his regiment five years before, pale and racked with pain from a leg wound he had recently received in battle but for which he had refused hospital treatment, so anxious was he to get back to his family. Dr MacAlistair and Effie soon saw him to rights; he regained some of his sparkle and spent his days recuperating in the sun, doting little Fiona Joy in attendance, living up more to her middle name now and hardly able to believe that George was her big brother but loving him anyway because he was so handsome and funny.

Angus too came home, whole and unharmed. Family picnics were held on the lawns, Captain Rory and Emily overwhelmed with happiness to have their sons back home again. Vaila spent as much time as she could with young Crathmor. They laughed and reminisced, he teased and tormented her but one day he put his hand under her chin and said seriously, 'I imagined you would have been married by now with six children at your skirts.'

'Oh, no.' She shook her head and turned her eyes away from him. 'I haven't found the right one yet. I'm still waiting . . .'

'For me? Or for that great love of yours to come along?'

'I know who he is now, now that I've seen you again.'

'So, the best man won after all and I've kept myself alive all this time for nothing.'

'Not nothing, George, you're here, surrounded by love, who could help but love someone like you with so much to give?'

'But not to you, Vaila, that's what you're telling me.' He let go of her and gave a great sigh. 'Oh, well, I suppose I'll have to marry one of those dreadfully dull rich girls – if they remember me, that is.'

'Of course they'll remember you, George MacPherson. Who could ever forget you?'

He was looking past her, back towards the house. Slowly she turned her head to follow his gaze, and her heart leapt. The figure had stopped; she couldn't see his expression but she knew how it would be, wary and watchful, thinking the worst at seeing her and George together . . .

'Mark!' She was on her feet, running, running, her black hair streaming out behind her, never stopping till she reached him to throw herself into his arms and say, 'It was you! All along it was you but it took the war to make me realise how precious you are to me and how much I love you.'

'Of course it's me, who else did you think it would be?' He was smiling now, a smile that took away the weariness from a face full of hollows but to her the dearest, most handome face on earth.

'Come on, I've got something to show you. Captain Rory didn't let it fall down after all, it's been papered and painted, the roof's been done, the chimneys fixed.' She took his arm and began to pull him away but he held back and turned to gaze at George lying on his sunbed watching the reunion with a wistful little smile on his face. 'What about him? What will he do?'

'Marry a rich young lady who will keep him in the manner he deserves. It would never have worked between George and me. It was great fun, it was unforgettable, but I was a child then and didn't know my own mind about anything. He knows that, I think he always knew it, so stop worrying and come along with me.'

She urged him forward. Hand in hand they walked away from Crathmor and down over the shimmering sands of Mary's Bay to Oir na Cuan, that little white house on the edge of the ocean where it had all begun, where it had ended, and where it would start all over again.